NUCLEAR SUMMER

EVERGREEN BOOK 4

MATTHEW S. COX

DIVISION ZERO PRESS

ISBN (ebook): 978-1-950738-12-0

ISBN (paperback): 978-1-950738-13-7

CONTENTS

SUMMER VACATION

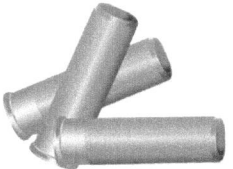

Acceptance that the world irrevocably changed hadn't come easy, but it also made the weight on Harper's shoulders feel a bit more manageable. She occasionally daydreamed about waking up from an apocalyptic bad dream and finding her life back to normal, but only as idle fantasy rather than sincere hope. The people who had been in power really had lost their minds; her parents—and an uncountable number of others—really had lost their lives.

And everyone lost their futures, or more accurately, had their futures drastically altered. Only the dead *really* lost their future. Harper still had her life, such as it was. She also had a little sister and two more siblings to look after. None of them would ever go to high school or college. Lorelei would probably never truly understand what college even was. On the other hand, they wouldn't end up in a nine-to-five job either, slaving away to make someone else rich. Despite the condition of the world, the notion of falling in love and having a family hadn't been destroyed, only changed. Gone was any dream of finding a nice quiet house in a neighborhood that had good schools and nice lawns. Having access to any sort of organized school would be rare enough. No one would care how *good* they were. What little medical care existed would largely be gone in only a few years.

Evergreen had two doctors and a former military corpsman, but they could do only so much in the absence of real medicine and supplies. Future generations would have to make do with people learning how to be doctors the way tradesmen learned, working alongside a real doctor. By the time Madison had a grandchild—if she lived long enough—no one who attended a genuine medical school would remain alive. At least, not in the US. If any trace of the modern world remained intact, Harper figured it would be in a country that none of the superpowers believed significant enough to nuke. Of course, the vast amounts of dust kicked up into the atmosphere by the bombardment could easily spread ruin over the entire globe.

The handful of actual farmers who helped get the crops going in Evergreen noted that the weather had cooled a little, but not as much as everyone feared possible. It seemed, at least for the time being, the Earth had avoided a full nuclear winter.

Harper wandered along a row of squat, broad-leafed plants, as best she could remember, turnips. Every so often, she tried to pick out Madison, Jonathan, or Lorelei's voices from the din of people all over the farm. School had been out for a few weeks, but the kids didn't end up having all day every day to themselves. It bothered her somewhat that children as young as eleven had been put to work. Of course, it wasn't as if some shifty company exploited them—they worked on the farm, learning how to survive and feed themselves. Cliff said something about summer break originating due to kids needing to help out on their family farms a long time ago. He'd been kinda fuzzy on exactly when it evolved from school closing down for agriculture to the summer break she'd grown up looking forward to every year.

"Guess we've gone in a circle…" Harper idly kicked at a turnip leaf, then sighed at the shotgun in her hands.

Lorelei, or anyone under age eleven, didn't *need* to be on the farm. In her case, she tagged along to be near her siblings, and spent much of her time zooming around exploring, saying hello to chickens and the handful of cows. At first, Harper wondered how a kid could be so content without television, video games, or tablets… but then she remembered the dismal life that the girl had before the bombardment. Her mother had little money and less desire to spend it on fancy toys. The woman barely bought the child clothes, wasting most of her income on drugs.

A few other smaller children roamed the farm as well, some finding it fun to feed the chickens. One little boy was morbidly terrified of the birds and kept running away screaming as though a velociraptor chased him. Teens and adults did the heavy work while the tweens tended to pick vegetables, hunt down weeds, or learn from the farmers.

While Harper had also come to the farm to work, her job didn't involve vegetables or animals. Well, it might involve animals, but not the good kind. As part of the militia, she had to keep an eye out for anyone who might be a danger to Evergreen or its citizens. Outsiders had already attacked the farm once, a raid that ended with Logan hospitalized after taking a bullet to the lung. That attack ended the notion of this farm being a nice trip to the countryside like when her parents had taken them to pick pumpkins for Halloween.

People could show up at any minute to attack.

Harper turned in place, staring out over the swath of land to the left of Route 74 at the northern end of Evergreen. A warm July sun thickened the air, a light breeze making the taller plants waver like ripples in an ocean of green. Here and there, bugs zipped back and forth, and she even spotted the occasional sparrow or whatever gliding overhead. Water spritzing from a leaky irrigation pipe near the potatoes sprayed a rainbow into the air.

If not for it being beside the highway on formerly empty land, the farm would've felt normal, no different than if she'd gone out into the sticks. Another glaring difference: not one tiny bit of machinery operated here. No tractors, tillers, or whatever they called those huge things. All the work here had to be done by hand.

Does that make it a giant garden instead of a farm? Eh, maybe not. They had farms before machines.

She hoped the majority of outsiders inclined to raid the farm would be there to steal food rather than hurt or abduct anyone. Thus far, the Lawless—or the 'blue gang' as she initially knew them—hadn't ventured far enough away from Denver to make an appearance in Evergreen. At least, not that anyone noticed. Perhaps they had come close enough to observe and decided against challenging the militia. More likely, they'd contented themselves with controlling Denver and didn't want to risk being too far from their territory.

Despite having no desire to go back there, the thought that her childhood home had become a playground for murderous thugs got under her skin like a small splinter she couldn't get to. For seventeen years, that house had been her sanctuary. Until the war, she never could have imagined it becoming dangerous or a place she wouldn't want to be.

Unfortunately, even if the Lawless died out, she couldn't return. Not only did the backyard contain the graves of her parents—thanks to Cliff and some other militia people—the house itself held far too many memories that she wanted to preserve as happy. Seeing her former home broken and ruined would turn it into too much of a metaphor for what happened to her future.

Someday, she would go visit her parents' graves, but not until after Madison had grown up. Harper caught herself sliding into worry that her sister's future adulthood wasn't guaranteed. Granted, even before society collapsed, no child really enjoyed a 100% survival rate, but few people in the US gave much thought to all the various ways life could go wrong—until it did. Without real hospitals and modern medicine, disease and infection became deadly. No kid would be hit by a moving car again for a long damn time, but the civilized world didn't usually have roving bands of armed people willing to kill each other for food.

Raiders most likely wouldn't *try* to kill the young or unarmed, but crossfire didn't care who got in its way.

Amid the din of people calling out to each other or the occasional laugh of a child, the sun crept across a sky still hazed from the aftereffects of war. The impenetrable dust clouds everyone feared hadn't shown up to block off all daylight, but the war did have a noticeable effect on the temperature. Despite it being late July, the heat hadn't yet become too punishing.

"Could be cooler up here. Maybe the Lawless down there in the city are too hot to move."

She frowned at herself for wanting to shoot more of them, but like visiting home, a quest for revenge would be a needless risk of her life. Besides, being forced to shoot someone in self-defense didn't cause the same level of guilt as actively hunting a person down with the intent to kill them. Barring one exception, she'd killed only to protect herself, Madison, or others from an imminent attack. The outlier, a man who'd suffered a fatal dose of radiation poisoning, had been an act of mercy.

The memory of that barely alive, swollen man made her shiver. He would have died in hours, anyway. Whatever substance he'd exposed himself to already killed him, Harper merely spared him a few hours of misery. That thought sent her careening down another morbid mental debate. If anyone here got cancer, they would die. Dr. Tegan Hale or Dr. Arjan Khan might try to use their x-ray machine against tumors, but this place had nothing even close to chemo or real cancer-fighting drugs. And the way the solar panels had been lately, they could go days without power... so the x-ray machine might not even work.

If someone became terminally ill with no hope to save them, at what point would it become humane to end their suffering? *People in the 1800s didn't euthanize the sick. They put them in sanatoriums to suffer in company. Ugh, I hope TB doesn't come back.* Harper paused in her patrol, closed her eyes, and mentally wrapped her siblings up in metaphorical bubble packing to keep them safe.

"So many things could go wrong in so many different ways, thinking about it is going to drive me crazy." She sighed out her nose. "People back then didn't constantly worry about it. I shouldn't either. 'Course, they probably thought cancer to be a witch's curse or something. They wouldn't have known it hopeless. It's kinda hard to worry about stuff you don't know about or understand."

A trio of twentysomething men went by, carrying digging tools. All nodded at her in greeting as they went by, heading out to the northwest end of the planted area to expand the field. She waved back at them, no longer feeling strange when adults treated her like an equal. That had been one of the strangest parts of acclimating to life here. Even before she turned eighteen, as soon as she'd joined the militia, most everyone gave her the same respect as any other grown-up. Could be because she'd killed people or maybe due to her earning Walter Holman's trust. The people likely assumed if he considered her good enough for the militia, they would, too.

In another world, I'd be hanging out with my friends at the pool on a day like this. We would've graduated high school a couple weeks ago and been worrying ourselves nuts over college. Harper looked down, again kicking a random turnip leaf on the way by. One by one, she thought of her friends who she hadn't seen since before the bombardment: Christina, Andrea, and Veronica. Harper tried to guess which school they'd have gone to. Andrea, definitely, would have remained close to home. The others probably would've attended out-of-state colleges and stayed wherever they went after graduation. Most likely, she wouldn't have seen them much after graduation, anyway. Her mother always used to talk about all the friends she rarely got to see.

Her friends Renee and Darci had—miraculously—turned up. Renee, she'd stumbled across by chance, finding her among a group of Lawless who had essentially abducted her and forced her to join. Darci, she'd found a few hours' ride north in a survivors' camp run by the Army at Eldorado Springs. There, she'd also chanced upon Madison's friend Eva and the girl's mother. Few things depressed Harper as much as that squalid, overcrowded camp. Hopefully, the Army would figure out a better way to feed and house everyone soon.

Despite the gloom that hung in the background of every idle thought, two things kept her spirits reasonably high considering the state of everything. One, Logan had mostly recovered from being shot. The doctors still hadn't let him go back to work on the farm or do anything stressful, so he'd been staffing one of the food-distribution tables at the quartermaster's building, putting bundles together, and so on. Maybe if he did well, they'd let him stay there.

The second thing that kept Harper's spirits high was Madison.

For the better part of the last month, her little sister had been back to her old self. Mostly. She no longer stressed out about school or dance class or gymnastics or whatever other activity ate up her time. This new existence with no homework, no adults telling her she had to be at X place at five on the dot for a class, or practice so many hours at home each night, allowed her to relax. The slower pace of life eliminated the bratty streak that often surfaced when Madison found herself having no free time, racing to wolf down some quick microwave meal between scheduled activities. That Madison had not once yelled at or even scowled at Harper in the ten months since the war stood out as the biggest difference from before.

Though, Harper would happily go back to that life if at all possible. Having screaming arguments with her kid sister a couple times a week would be a small price to pay for their parents—and the other millions of people—not to be dead.

Still, Madison's personality now came close enough to how she'd been before her extracurricular activities stacked up into unmanageable territory that Harper felt hopeful. Her sister hadn't been permanently damaged mentally by what happened—or at least not permanently crippled. She couldn't claim anyone hadn't suffered *some* degree of mental damage, especially herself. Nightmares of blasting a guy's face into a spray of gore inside a Walmart never plagued her before the bombs dropped.

She reached the end of the turnips and hooked a left, walking down a large dirt 'road'. Dozens of crop rows stretched out on either side of the maybe ten-foot-wide passage. Perhaps since the guys in charge of the farm had been actual farmers before the war, they'd planned things out to make room for tractors and farm equipment. Mechanized farm tools had long since stopped working due to a lack of gasoline. Rafael worked on biodiesel, but engines designed for gasoline wouldn't handle it, and he'd said something about it putting greater wear on engine gaskets or something like that. Also, using crops for fuel instead of food hadn't gone over too well with some people. At least not until they had an ample surplus and no one worried about one bad cold snap making everyone starve.

Basically, no one yet knew if the biodiesel project would ever work.

Harper didn't worry too much about that. Not like she wanted to travel long distances. In fact, the city having no usable vehicles put a definitive end to far-reaching scavenging trips. This, she considered a good thing for entirely selfish reasons. It meant she wouldn't need to go out of town away from her family. Granted, the down side to that would be that *if* they decided to go scavenging, it would turn into a multiple day extended camping trip rather than a few hours' on the road.

A tall man in a yellow ball cap went by in the other direction carrying feed buckets. He nodded, muttered, "Hey," and kept on going. She vaguely recalled his name as Steve. He hadn't been in Evergreen long, but she remembered him because he'd been checking her out. Though he looked a little older than her, early twenties maybe. Surprisingly, once he noticed Logan with her, he stopped trying to catch her eye. The first she'd seen the guy had been the July Fourth event the city council put together. It hadn't been much of a celebration per se, but Anne-Marie and Walter wanted to do *something* at least, so they'd had another giant communal meal.

The Fourth passed almost three weeks ago, having only slightly more fanfare than an ordinary day. Some people didn't want to call attention to the day because the 'country was gone.' Others got fired up at that, screamed about America being a concept more than physical space. A few fights broke out, but no one had been seriously injured. Walter strongly encouraged people *not* to fire handguns in lieu of fireworks to save ammunition for life-and-death situations. Naturally, a few idiots still tried to kill clouds, but it hadn't been widespread. Harper couldn't figure out what bothered her more — that 'don't waste ammo because you might need it to protect yourself' was a true statement, or that such a statement had more success than telling people not to shoot into the sky because falling bullets could kill people.

Of course, as soon as Earl's beer made the rounds, more arguments started. People wanted to get angry at whichever country nuked the US, though not one person had a clue where the strike came from. Russia made for the most obvious choice since they possessed the most nuclear weapons. China came in at second place, North Korea a distant third. When the anti-China shouting started, Jonathan hid under a table and didn't come out until Cliff found him.

For her part, Harper spent most of the 'cookout' running around helping break up fights. She still had a dull ache in her cheek from where an accidental elbow caught her. After that, she stopped trying to run up behind people fighting. When guys in the midst of a brawl saw her, they mostly calmed down. A few picked her up and threw her aside like an annoying kid getting in the way, but no one actively tried to hit her.

She wandered something akin to a patrol route around the farm for a while, thinking mostly about her siblings having found a place of relative contentment. Madison and Jonathan sometimes still did dance class type stuff together, though nowhere near as often as before the war. Also, lacking actual instructors, they mostly performed random moves they remembered. As much as her sister used to love dancing, it probably reminded her too much of the civilized world. That might explain why she'd started losing interest.

Beth went by following a group of other teen farm workers, carrying baskets of picked veggies. She looked up at Harper, her face blushing red in seconds. Ever since she'd caught that girl and her boyfriend Jaden in a house that should've been empty not quite a year ago, the girl couldn't look at her without a reaction. Beth turned seventeen last January. By some miracle, she hadn't gotten pregnant yet despite rumor claiming she and Jaden still frequently had sex. As in, almost daily. Then again, Evergreen didn't have much in the way of entertainment.

People in the 1800s got married at that age. Harper half-shrugged. The modern world would freak out at the idea of a seventeen-year-old and a boy one year older having kids together as part of a loving relationship. This shifted her thinking to Logan. His getting shot had put something of a damper on physical love up until recently. Despite his seeming up for it, she'd been afraid to do more than kiss him or hold hands and cuddle.

There's no more birth control. She lightly scratched her fingertips over her stomach. *Getting knocked up could kill me.* This worry occupied her mind for a while as she wandered the veggie rows, observing people as well as the distant edges of the farm for signs of danger. At times, she felt awkwardly lazy, as though she merely roamed about with a gun rather than did actual work. But, if anything bad happened, she'd be running *at* the problem while everyone else ran the other way. No one gave her any attitude about 'not working' because they all expected her to do whatever it took to protect them.

And, for the most part, she would. However, a suicidal charge at a large pack of bad guys wouldn't happen unless they had grabbed Madison, Jonathan, or Lorelei.

Her thoughts eventually returned to Logan. Of the friends she had before the war, she and Renee had been the only two not to have lost their virginity yet. Renee came *damn* close when the Lawless abducted her, but she faked them out by pretending to be younger. Darci went through several boyfriends already and willingly traded sex for extra food during her time at the Army survivors' camp.

Harper shuddered at that idea, thankful that whatever forces of the universe aligned to lead her and Madison here safely. The idea of an Army-run camp to protect survivors sounded good in theory. If she'd heard about that before rumors of Evergreen, she'd likely have gone there. Only, rumors and reality often didn't align.

She distracted herself from those bad thoughts by picturing Logan shirtless. *Not like getting pregnant will ruin my future anymore… unless it kills me. Not gonna be going to college, finding a career.* She huffed, blowing hair up off her face. *At least I got out of having to decide on a major.* She resumed daydreaming about him, her cheeks warming at the thought of letting Logan see her body. On a dare freshman year, she'd flashed her boobs at a boy during a house party. Alas, at fourteen, she hadn't developed much, and he laughed at her. After that, she'd been too embarrassed to do anything of the sort again, even with boys she'd dated for a few months.

Okay, so I'm a bit self-conscious. She daydreamed about her and Logan somewhere private, if she'd have the nerve to let him see her naked. Her feelings for him had started off under a cloud of pain and doubt from Tyler. With him, she'd practically thrown herself at the only boy in town near in age to her. That had been a panic situation, the only two teens around. Maybe even the only two teens left alive —or so she'd thought back then. Additional people her age had arrived since then, the hockey team plus cheerleaders, as well as others trickling in month to month. She didn't trust herself to have real feelings, suspicious she merely wanted to attach herself to the first boy who smiled at her out of some weird obligation not to 'let humanity die out.'

What she felt for Logan finally shed the discoloration of Tyler and grown into a thing she had no real way to describe. She couldn't quite bring herself to say she *loved* him yet. At least not out loud. Her emotions toward him still held quite a bit of fear, nervousness, and shame. But the society of before had become ashes. She could die tomorrow, as could he.

I mean, people back in the day still had babies, right? If they didn't, none of us would exist. Maybe it's not as deadly as I'm thinking… but still. Not in a hurry. Least we still have two real doctors. But they won't last forever. Do places like El Salvador still have modernity? Who'd nuke Central America? Humanity probably isn't screwed… just us. Or major countries anyway.

If some places still had civilization, it might be possible for modern life to recover over several generations. With that hope in mind, she smiled and resumed walking. A few minutes later, a giggling Lorelei raced out from tall green stalks on the right, darted across the dirt path in front of her, and disappeared into slightly shorter plants still tall enough to engulf the almost seven-year-old on the left side of the path. Her birthday came August second, roughly two weeks away.

That poor kid almost didn't make it to seven… we're going to give her a huge party.

Smiling, she again resumed daydreaming about Logan for a little while… until the shrill scream of a child somewhere off to her right broke the relative silence of the farm.

Oh, shit!

Harper tightened her grip on Dad's Mossberg and ran as fast as she could in the direction of the screaming child.

2

CRIMES OF THE OLD WEST

H arper rushed into rows of tall tomato plants lashed to thin sticks, running flat out until she spotted a slender brown-haired girl in a plain dress.

She recognized Emmy right away. The now-nine-year-old still woke up shrieking sometimes due to nightmares about the 'sky fire.' That girl had probably seen people burned to ashes by a nuclear blast, or at least witnessed the post-flash fireball. Upon realizing *who* screamed, Harper calmed down and jogged the rest of the way. Sometimes, Emmy would scream at stuff in her head.

"Emmy? What's wrong?"

The child backed away from something on the ground and pointed.

Harper walked up to stand beside her.

There, in the dirt between rows of climbing tomato plants, lay the remains of a dead man in a plain white T-shirt marked by multiple stab wounds and blood. His jeans and work boots appeared undamaged, though dirt caked both knees as if he'd been kneeling on the ground. Flies gathered on his pallid face, crawling around his lips and into his nostrils. He didn't yet stink.

Despite having shot people, the sight of a corpse startled a gasp out of Harper.

Emmy looked up, shaking and crying. "I almost stepped on him. Was just running down the tomatoes and there's a dead man here."

Harper moved to stand between the girl and the dead guy, waving a hand at her face to shoo a curious fly away. "Are you okay, Emmy?"

"I'm scared."

"He can't hurt anyone. Yes, he looks really scary, but he can't hurt you. Okay?"

Emmy sniffled, nodding once.

"Can you be brave and do something really important?"

"I don't wanna touch a dead man."

Harper chuckled at the unexpected statement. "No, Em. Wasn't going to ask you to. I need you to do one of two things, and you do whichever one you want to do more, okay?"

"What are they?" Emmy wiped tears from her face on the back of her arm.

"If you're scared, go to your mother. If you're not too scared, please head down the road into town and tell Walter what happened here, what you found."

"Therese isn't my mother." Emmy looked at the ground.

"She's taking care of you, right?"

Emmy nodded.

"Then it's okay to think of her as a mother. Your actual mother will always be special, but it's okay to let someone else take over until she finds her way here."

"She isn't coming. She's dead. The Sky Fire ate her."

Harper grimaced inside. *Dammit.* "I'm so sorry."

"I think she's still watching me." Emmy dug her toes into the dirt. "I think she doesn't mind Therese likes to take care of me now."

"I'm sure she's happy that you're okay."

"Yeah." Emmy managed a weak smile. "Do I have'ta leave the farm?"

"No. Just thought you might want to. If I found a dead guy at your age, I'd have crawled under my bed."

Emmy laughed. "No way! Not you. You're brave."

"I just play brave on television." She winked.

"Be back. Gonna tell Walter." Emmy ran off.

Harper watched her go until she disappeared behind corn, then turned to look at the dead guy. She teased a finger at the air horn on her belt. Finding a corpse didn't really qualify as a 911 emergency. If she sounded an alarm, Dennis, Lennie, and Josh—the three other militia defending the farm during the day—would come running, leaving the perimeter open. The body might have been planted to cause all the militia to converge on the same spot so raiders could run in. However, that didn't make a lot of sense, as raiders would have needed to sneak in to plant the body. If they could do that, they'd have already started shooting.

The dead guy appeared slightly familiar. She'd seen him around Evergreen once or twice before, but hadn't developed enough familiarity to remember a name. He'd definitely been at the July Fourth meal, since she remembered his curly strawberry-blond hair and thick mustache. She remembered that yellow-hat guy trying to pull him away from one of the fights, but it hadn't been a particularly violent one.

Dirt on his knees made her think he'd been forced to kneel, but his arms lay loose at his sides, no evidence that he'd been tied. His knuckles didn't have any damage either, not even red spots. So he didn't appear to have been involved in a fistfight any time recently. Three wounds on the chest indicated where a knife-sized blade pierced, all relatively close together, somewhat left of center.

At the approach of footsteps behind her, Harper stood and whirled.

Two dusty workers walked up to her. She recognized them both, Dean and Maitland.

Dean Gibson looked at her, large eyes in his narrow face widening in concern. Short for a guy, he only stood about her height, but had a thick, muscular physique. Dust trailed out of his afro in the breeze, almost like smoke from a fire. Maitland had the widest, squarest jaw she'd ever seen on a person outside a comic book. His short, wild brown hair looked like he cut it himself with a dull table knife… while drunk.

"What's the screaming about?" asked Maitland. "Some kid get hurt?"

"You okay, Harper?" Dean started to say something else, paused to peer past her, then whistled. "Oh. Damn, is that Weldon?"

She backed against the tomato plant behind her so they could see the body. "Not sure what his name was. Emmy almost stepped on him."

"Poor kid." Maitland approached the body, shaking his head. "Yeah, that's Weldon, all right."

"Do you know anyone who might have wanted to kill him?" Harper tilted her head. "And I've watched way too many cop shows."

The men chuckled.

"Not rightly sure." Dean scratched his head. "Far as I know, he rolled into town like a month or so back with a couple other people. Five of 'em I think. Just a bunch of wandering survivors like most of us. Seemed like a decent guy. Chose to work on the farm."

"Yeah." Maitland nodded. "Damn shame."

"If he's on the farm crew, that explains what he's doing out here." Harper stepped over Weldon's body, examining the ground. Cliff had started teaching her how to track, but the lessons had been few and short so far. Some marks in the dirt kinda looked like heels being dragged, but she didn't trust herself to consider that certain truth.

"Yeah, it would." Dean shook his head. "Poor bastard."

"Guess that also explains why he didn't show up at breakfast." Maitland nudged the body with his boot.

Harper tapped her foot, thinking. If the dead man missed breakfast, that probably meant he'd been killed last night sometime.

Thinking about TV cop shows, Harper crouched and studied the corpse's hands and fingers—while simultaneously cringing. *Gah! What is wrong with me? This is a dead guy. Shouldn't I be throwing up and running away?* She swallowed bile and kept looking. *No marks on his hands. Defensive wounds? Either he let someone stab him or didn't see it coming.*

"Do you guys know the other people he arrived with?" She peered up at them. *At least I sound like a cop even if I have no damn idea what I'm doing.*

"Not really. Just that they all work on the farm. Three other guys and a lady," said Maitland. "Seemed pretty normal, though the woman's on the quiet side."

"Probably saw some bad shit." Dean sighed. "Ain't that uncommon anymore."

Harper leaned over the body to examine the stab wounds. The size and shape of the injuries suggested a knife made them. These looked about the same as the holes left in bodies when Cliff stabbed the Lawless. *Someone kill him over the woman? Or do we have a random psycho?*

"Harper?" called Roy Ellis.

"Here!" she shouted, while standing. Hearing his voice increased her confidence. He'd been an actual police officer prior to the war. Up on her toes, she peered over the tops of the plants at Roy, Annapurna, and Sadie walking generally toward her.

Emmy, too short for her to see past the tomatoes, seemed to appear out of nowhere at the entrance to the row where Harper stood a few seconds later. The child pointed to indicate which row contained the corpse, then ran off to the south. Soon after, the militia approached, squeezing past Dean and Maitland. Harper remained on the opposite side of the body not to crowd them. Roy, sporting a shaved head and blue police vest, looked like the cop he used to be prior to the strike — only dustier. Even though no true infrastructure remained, he still carried himself the same as she imagined he did while officially a cop. Granted, the militia were as official as it got in terms of law enforcement in this world.

"What'cha got, Harp?" asked Roy.

She explained finding the body, what the two guys shared regarding the group of four new arrivals, and her non-professional assessment of finding no defensive wounds. Last, she pointed at what she believed to be drag marks. "I think he died somewhere else and whoever killed him moved the body here. Most likely died at some time last night. These guys say he missed breakfast."

Roy crouched next to Weldon and examined the stab wounds. "I can hear my old captain complaining already about contaminating the crime scene."

He's joking, right? Harper shifted her weight from leg to leg, unsure how to react.

Neither Annapurna nor Sadie appeared to have much interest in examining the body up close, but they also didn't seem squeamish. More people gathered around, no doubt word spreading across the farm about the discovery. Even a few of the kids tried to get a look at the remains, though nearby adults held them back.

"Gonna be damn near impossible to prove anything," said Roy.

"Someone killed this guy." Harper gestured at the body. "There could be a killer around and they might go after someone else. We should at least try to figure out who did it. Not like it's going to end up in court where a bunch of lawyers would attack the forensics evidence."

"Heh." Roy chuckled. "No kidding."

Walter Holman made his way past the crowd, whistling upon seeing the dead man. "Damn. That's not good. Any ideas what happened here?"

Roy stood. "Little Emmy stumbled across the body. Guessing he's been here since last night. Harp thinks the killer did the deed elsewhere last night and dumped the body here. Reasonable enough idea. None of the tomato plants have any damage. Doesn't look like any sort of altercation happened here. Also, the guy doesn't seem to have put up a fight at all. Only marks on him are the three stab wounds. Might've been in bed when he got it."

Great. I didn't even think of that. As if I needed more trouble falling asleep.

"Hmm. That it?" Walter glanced around at the crowd. Sunlight filtering past the tomato plants danced in tiny spots on his lemon-yellow polo shirt. "Weldon Moss if memory serves. Came in a little over a month ago in a group of five. If any problems followed this guy here, that group might know about it."

"Right. Any idea how long they ran together?" asked Roy.

Walter smiled. "Recall them saying since soon after the blast.

Don't think any reasons from pre-nuke would matter or they'd have offed him before they got here."

"You think his friends killed him?" Harper blinked.

"Not saying that specifically. If someone did this for a personal reason, it is most likely one of them since they have history. Unless he ended up in bed with someone's wife in the month or so they'd been here. Roy, you mind heading up this investigation?"

Roy bowed his head, sweat beads on his scalp shimmering in the sun. "You know I'm not a detective. Asking me to lead an investigation might get the police union mad at me."

Walter chuckled, as did some of the farm workers. "I'm sure they'll make an exception, considering the circumstances."

"Right." Roy laughed. "If they file a grievance, I expect you to testify on my behalf."

"You got it." Walter patted him on the shoulder.

Harper let a silent sigh of relief out her nose at not being thrown into a metaphorical frying pan. She hadn't gotten stuck with the 'case' of investigating who killed Weldon. A case that, given the 'Wild West' state of the world—or at least the USA—could easily be impossible to solve. Annoyingly, she also felt somewhat slighted. After all, she'd been the first militia person to discover the remains, and he hadn't even thought to give her the job.

Walter putting Roy in charge of the investigation made sense, considering the guy had been a cop for something like fifteen years before the war. Even though Walter had also worked with the Sheriff's department, he mostly sat behind a desk. She had no idea if sheriff's deputies had experience investigating murders or not. Either way, Walter *still* mostly sat behind a desk. He probably couldn't manage the militia and investigate a case himself simultaneously.

"Well, first step. Let's get him over to the medical center and see if the doctors can tell us anything useful." Roy looked at Harper. "Would you mind grabbing the cart?"

"Sure." She slung the Mossberg over her shoulder on its strap. "How did detectives do stuff before computers? I mean, we don't even have cameras."

"Lots of legwork," said Walter.

Roy chuckled. "Yeah. Talking to people, reading their responses, mostly. And they did have old time cameras. People got so used to using phones for pictures, actual cameras kinda died off. At least ones that used film. Unless you're talking about professional photographers."

"They found a bunch of camera stuff in one of the houses when we gathered up everything useful, but no one bothered to take any of it." Walter shook his head. "Don't really need to worry about that, anyway. It'll be a couple decades before jury trials are a thing again… if ever."

"Want me to do a sketch?" Harper pulled her little notepad out of her back pocket.

Roy made a 'be my guest' gesture. "Knock yourself out."

She took a few steps back, surveyed the layout of the dead man, and sketched out a basic drawing that captured the overall position of the remains in relation to the surroundings. On the next page, she drew a close up of the three stab wounds to show their relative size and arrangement. That done, she tore both papers from the notepad and gave them to Roy.

"Not bad." He held the drawings up. "You must've gotten an A in art class."

"Doodled a lot. Mostly dumb stuff." She exhaled and stuffed the notebook in her pocket. "Be right back with the body cart."

3

OPTIMISM

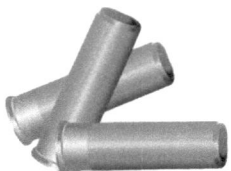

E xcept for finding a dead man, the day ended up being fairly
routine.

Free of worry about solving a murder, Harper spent the
rest of the afternoon walking patrol, returning home to watch her
siblings at around the time they would normally have been out of
school. The kids got to leave the farm at noon, or as close to noon as
anyone could guess. It bothered her somewhat not to rush right
home with them, but Carrie Rangel from next door happily looked
after them whenever needed. The woman had fallen into a sort of
mom role to all of them, even Harper. Lorelei, however, still
considered Harper to be more of a mother than an older sister,
always running to her on the occasion something scared her.

The kids liked Carrie, and so did Cliff.

Since Madison had more or less put the pieces of her shattered
emotional state back together, the driving need to stay by her side
constantly had diminished to a strong want. While Harper would
have preferred to be with her kid sister all the time, she could handle
'growing up' and having a job to do without being a huge bundle of
nerves the entire time they remained separated. Madison still had

bad dreams every so often and needed comforting, but that only happened at night when they'd all be home.

Patrolling the residential area south of the school had become an ingrained habit after most of a year. Hours every day going in circles around the neighborhood allowed her to pick up on anything that appeared out of place as well as get to know—and be known by—everyone living there. A few older people regarded her as a kid, though didn't act too patronizing. Every time Mr. MacPherson told her she ought to settle down and just be a kid, she'd end up having a somber daydream about her old life. Once or twice, she even considered stepping down from the militia, but didn't know what she'd do 'job' wise other than that. Things had been relatively stable for a while, but she couldn't give up Dad's shotgun and she would never forgive herself if anything happened to her expanded family. As opposite to her old personality as being a 'cop' was, it had come to feel normal, even comforting.

Harper arrived home a little after two in the afternoon to an empty house.

Assuming the kids would be at Carrie's, she went there and knocked.

"Come in," said Carrie. "Harper, you don't have to knock here."

"Sorry. Old habit." She poked her head in, spotted the woman on the couch, and no sign of the kids. "Umm, where is everyone?"

"Out exploring. They're roaming around the unassigned houses in the northeast."

"What?" Harper stared. The world to her still felt like it consisted of Evergreen, surrounded by the Lawless gang—or people just like them—waiting to attack any defenseless children. "They're running around on their own?"

"Things aren't like they used to be." Carrie patted the sofa next to her. "None of them are *that* little. When my parents were kids in the seventies, they didn't need to have a parent up their noses constantly. Used to go outside in the afternoon and come home by dark. Soon as the street lights came on, that was time to get your ass home. We've gone back to a world like that—except the street lights don't work. Tight-knit community. Everyone here more or less knows everyone.

Not like we have nut jobs from out of state driving into town willy nilly."

Harper leaned the shotgun on the sofa arm and flopped down to sit. "I guess. Still going to worry until they're back."

"It's been quiet a bit. Don't rightly figure another missile's going to hit us. And if any outsiders show up wanting to stir up a mess, they'll go for the farm."

"What if someone wanders into town and sees a group of defenseless children?" Harper raked her hands through her hair, pulling it down over her face. "Argh. Am I being paranoid?"

"I made sure they know they're expected to run away from anyone they don't recognize."

"They could get into all sorts of trouble in random houses. What if they find knives or start a fire or—"

Carrie squeezed her hand. "This isn't the same world you grew up in, hon. A person doesn't build up resistance to getting sick by living in a germ-free bubble. Better they learn how to cope with what's happened, this new world, gradually, on their own terms than something catches them off guard down the line and they don't know how to react."

"Like me…" whispered Harper.

"Hmm?"

"I hesitated when Dad died. Maybe you're right. I wasn't ready for the world to change so much in only two months." Harper let her head sink back against the sofa. "Maddie's already shot someone and she's not even eleven yet."

"Another one?" Carrie blinked. "You didn't tell me she killed a man."

Harper smiled, shaking her head. "No. She hasn't killed anyone. Just winged the one guy I already told you about. But, seriously… she went from being all about dance class, dolls, and Starbucks to needing a gun to avoid being kidnapped by a gang of thugs. Guess letting them explore the town on their own probably isn't *too* horrible. Probably not too safe either."

"I'm sorry. I didn't think it would bother you that much." Carrie let go of her hand. "I'll keep them in sight from now on."

While that would make her feel better, she wondered if being too clingy and controlling might cause Madison, Jonathan, and Lorelei to either grow to resent her, rebel and do something far more dangerous, or end up unprepared to handle a situation the same way she'd been when the Lawless invaded her former home. Her parents had—by any normal person's estimation—kinda coddled her. Being thrown into a broken world almost overwhelmed her ability to handle it. If not for Madison to look after, she probably wouldn't have survived those first few days before meeting Cliff and Jonathan.

"As long as they stay relatively close, avoid people they don't know, and get back here before dark, it's okay. Guess they have to do something more mentally stimulating than throwing a ball around." Harper scratched at her leg. "Where's Renee?"

"Meeting with Anne-Marie. They're working hard learning how to make fabric and clothing from scratch. Starting to get some usable flax from the farm to make linen from, and the seeds are nutritious. Can't say I fancy the flavor, but they taste better than starvation."

Harper nodded. "Neat. That sounds useful. Better than standing around holding a howitzer."

"Heh. Don't go feeling all useless now. What you do is important, too."

"I know. Just wish it could be something less violent. The universe has such a lame sense of irony."

Carrie stood. "That it does. Tea?"

"Sure."

After talking with Carrie over tea for a while, Harper returned home to do a little cleaning.

Even nuclear war didn't bring an end to housework. While scrubbing the toilet, she got the bright idea to have Jonathan and Madison start helping out on some easier tasks like sweeping. Enough modern cleaning supplies remained to see them well into next year, but eventually, they'd be full 1800s. Then again, what purpose did it serve to keep the place immaculate?

We're clinging to life after nukes. Who cares if I scrub the floor? She frowned. *Everything's going to fall apart, eventually. If I have grandchildren, they'll be living in shacks made of rusting cars or tents. Ugh. No they won't. I've watched too many damn movies. People had normal houses in the 1800s, right?* She argued with herself about how far back things went. In the Old West, everyone had been used to building things using the tools and techniques available at the time. Modern people, even those trained as carpenters or engineers, had become reliant on technology that no longer worked.

"Meh. It can't be *that* hard to build a house. Just feels hard to me because I don't understand it."

She resumed cleaning the bathroom, more than a little annoyed that the end of civilization hadn't gotten her out of doing chores.

ONCE SHE'D DONE ENOUGH CLEANING TO FEEL JUSTIFIED IN relaxing, Harper flopped on the sofa and pulled out *The Secret Garden*. She stared defiantly at the book that refused to let her finish it. Before she could even open the cover, the voices of kids arose outside, among them Jonathan, Madison, and Lorelei. She also picked out Mila, Eva, and Becca.

She set the book down and ran over to Carrie's backyard to make sure none of the kids had lost any limbs. All appeared intact, though Lorelei looked like a clown, having gotten into someone's cosmetics stash.

Soon after the kids returned, Carrie collected enough food to make up for her and Renee joining them for dinner, and brought it over to the cinder block grill in the yard behind Harper's home. Renee arrived while dinner cooked. She gave off an air of exhaustion, reminding her of the expression on Mom's face almost all the time when she came home from work.

The kids ran around the yard playing while Carrie did most of the cooking. Harper and Renee relaxed on the tiny back porch, trying to remember how to be teenagers. Of course, neither of them talked about music, movies, boys, school, or any of the things they'd once been interested in. Renee had gotten wind of the dead man, so Harper told her about it before they migrated into a conversation about flax, weaving, and frustration.

Cliff showed up a few minutes after the sun weakened and turned orange. Everyone filed inside for dinner, which consisted of canned beans, box spaghetti, and various grilled fresh vegetables. Carrie had made 'steaks' out of thick turnip slices as well as potatoes. Despite the food being nowhere near close to anything she'd have eaten before idiots turned the world on its head, Harper felt eerily normal.

Having dinner at home with two 'parents,' Madison, two additional siblings, and her best friend struck her as simultaneously wrong and perfect. It felt as though she'd gone back in time, a spirit inhabiting the body of some other girl who belonged to some other family who lived before electricity had been discovered. She still missed her real parents to a painful degree, but Cliff made for an excellent adopted father. Carrie, too, had become more like a mother than 'the woman next door.' Except for Lorelei, the siblings knew exactly what happened when Cliff went over to visit her sometimes at night. Madison always made icky faces at the thought. Harper had almost teased her by asking what she thought Mom and Dad used to do when alone together, but kept quiet. Nothing could ruin a moment of levity as fast as reminding her of their dead parents.

Too soon, as it were.

However, in the moment sitting there having dinner with her new family like something out of the frontier days, she felt lucky for the first time since Dad hauled her out of bed minutes before the sky burned. Ending up here in Evergreen with her sister alive, having people she considered family around her, food, and a roof over their heads had to be way better off than most survivors. Sure, a serious problem at the farm could still result in food shortages, but it still beat living in a place like the Army camp.

Harper nearly choked on a mouthful of potato at the thought of her friend Darci in that place, sleeping with random men in exchange for food. She wondered if the three who tried to rape her had taken her friend up on that offer. That thought made her skin crawl more than watching the soldiers execute them. If she and Madison had been collected by the Army and brought there, not only would they have confiscated Dad's Mossberg, Harper more than likely would have done the exact same thing to make sure Madison got enough to eat. Also, she'd never have met Cliff and had the benefit of some instruction in hand-to-hand combat.

She sat still for a moment, fighting the urge to cry or look emotional. Her first time *couldn't* be something as horrible as trading herself for survival. Even though the world had crumbled, she still wanted her first time to matter, to be wonderful. That being here in Evergreen, having this life, spared her from the need to do something like that, stole her voice. Cliff noticed her unusually grateful stare, but no one else appeared to pick up on the brief surge of emotion radiating from her.

Once the expected talk of the dead man discovered that morning got out of the way, dinner conversation mostly consisted of the kids talking about their exploration and what they did on the farm.

After dinner, Harper returned to the sofa, determined to make some progress in *The Secret Garden*. Renee followed, also deciding to read something. The kids went outside to play in the yard, soon joined by Eva, Becca, and Mila once they finished having dinner at their homes.

Harper managed a chapter and a half before the kids distracted her with a conversation about ghosts. They debated if spirits really existed and if all the cities that got nuked would contain 'millions' of angry ghosts. This, of course, sent Harper's mind wandering in that direction. She daydreamed a movie of people stuck in a bombed-out city populated mostly by angry ghosts.

"'Nee?"

"Hmm?" asked Renee.

"You think society's going to pull itself back together or are we three generations away from people going tribal?"

Renee closed her book over one finger to hold her place. "Hmm. I don't think it's going to be 'spears and loincloths' tribal. The tech that survived isn't going to evaporate. Like, there's bicycles and people know how to make clothes. People didn't lose all knowledge of what we used to have. I think it's gonna turn into some kind of weird steampunk Old West sorta thing where a guy in a cowboy hat rides up on a mountain bike with saddle bags and like pulls out a beat up laptop."

Harper laughed. "Where's he going to find a laptop a century from now? And how'd he charge it?"

"Steam generator, naturally." Renee held her nose up, but only kept a serious face for a moment before cracking up.

"Right. Not solar panels?"

"Seriously? The way they go down?" Renee sighed. "It was nice for a little while, but the power is off more than on now. I heard someone talking at the quartermaster's this afternoon. Jeanette and her people are trying to make windmills for electricity."

Harper perked up. "Oh, cool. That sounds like a better idea than solar. Never run out of wind."

"The sun's not gonna dry up either." Renee poked her.

"No, dork." Harper poked her back. "I mean, the solar panels don't last forever and they're fickle. Wind generators are much simpler, right? Just coils of wire and some stuff that rotates. No funny chemicals."

Renee shrugged. "Yeah, I guess. But it's not the panels that are fickle. It's the wiring they've Frankensteined together. True, the skies are kinda hazy, so the panels aren't putting out as much as they could. Wind doesn't have that problem. Someone was even talking about trying to take fan blades from jet engines at Denver airport, but I don't think they're going to even try that until they have a working truck."

"No kidding. There's no way they'd be able to even move one of those things without a truck… and the blue gang is all over that place."

"I hope they all die." Renee looked down, shivering.

Harper took her friend's hand. "You know how I am about killing bugs. I don't have any problem shooting those bastards. They're lower than bugs."

"Thanks for finding me."

"Totally by chance."

Renee shrugged. "Still. Thanks."

"Are you okay?"

"Yeah." Renee exhaled. "Just bad memories. I'd never been so damn scared for so long in my life."

"'Nee?"

"Hmm?" She looked over.

"If anything happened to you that you need to talk about, it's okay."

Renee's cheeks reddened. "Thanks. It didn't. Well, nothing worse than being groped a lot. I wasn't trying to avoid talking about stuff when I told you they fell for me lying about my age. You're like the only person left alive who I'd tell if anyone... you know."

They hugged for a few minutes. Renee cried a little, though Harper only grew angrier at the Lawless gang. She focused as much energy as she could projecting her desire into the universe that her other friends got far away from Denver before the Lawless appeared.

"Even if it happened without a war... maybe you're the only one I could have told, too." Renee sat back out of the hug, and sighed at her book. "Drat. Lost my page."

"Happened without a war?"

"You know. If some guy attacked me. The end of the world really didn't change the odds of that happening too much." Renee gestured around at random. "Actually, I think it might have lowered them... now that I'm here. When everyone in town knows everyone, isn't it less likely they'll, umm, you know."

Harper pondered. "I dunno about that. The last time people in this country lived in places like this with conditions like this, girls weren't allowed to vote or hold jobs. Pretty sure women still got attacked back then, but they couldn't really talk about it or had no police to go to. Hell, remember that time we went to the mall on your twelfth birthday?" She scowled at the memory of three guys catcalling them, not even high-schoolers—grown ass men. They even started walking closer. And no one could've accused either Harper or Renee of looking older than their ages.

"Yeah… that was *so* creepy." Renee whistled. "Your dad wanted to hunt them down."

Harper gave a sad little laugh. "Yeah… I'm glad he didn't find them."

"He could get away with it now. There's no real law left. It's frontier justice if any."

"I would totally blow the head off anyone who laid a hand on you." Harper grinned.

"That's both reassuring and psycho at once." Renee gave her side eye. "Because I don't think you're kidding."

Harper shook her head. "I'm not. Unless you begged me not to, I would."

"Thanks." Renee picked up her book and proceeded to hunt for her page. "If it happens to you, I'm not sure I could hunt down and kill the bastard, but I'd tell Cliff. That's as good as killing the guy myself."

"Yeah." Harper fidgeted at *The Secret Garden*. If someone here in Evergreen raped her, she'd go shoot the son of a bitch herself, provided she hadn't been too injured trying to fight the guy off to do so. If anyone was going to do that to her, they'd *really* have to work for it. She couldn't decide if she'd be able to tell Cliff, but leaned toward probably. "We need to talk about something happier. I'm getting myself into a mood like I want to hop on a bike, go to Denver, and hunt Lawless for sport like some kind of *Call of Duty* level."

"Umm… so we're figuring out how to turn flax into linen." Renee flashed a cheesy smile. "This is super boring, but it's kinda cool. Couple months, we'll be making actual clothes."

"Nice."

Cliff, having finished the dishes, walked into the living room and leaned over the sofa back, his head between the girls. "If anyone lays a hand on either one of you, that hand's going straight up their—"

"Cliff?" called Carrie.

He tapped his arm. "Right up to the elbow."

Harper smiled at him, blushing hard since he'd clearly overheard the entire conversation. Renee couldn't quite look him in the eye.

"Yes?" Cliff stood and twisted to peer back at Carrie.

"Got a couple mini logs in need of splitting. Would you mind giving me a hand? Then there's a pretty serious problem with the bathtub."

Cliff patted Harper and Renee on the head, then walked over to Carrie in the kitchen archway. "What's wrong with the bathtub?"

Carrie wrapped her arms around his neck. "There's no one in it."

Harper bit her lip. Renee shot her a 'did I just hear what I think I just heard?' stare.

"You two behave yourselves," said Cliff. "No wild parties. And be in bed by… whatever time a kid your age is supposed to be in bed by."

Harper laughed. "Okay. No parties. Promise."

Cliff and Carrie headed out to the backyard.

"They're totally into each other." Harper sighed wistfully. "It's kinda cute."

"Yeah. Does that mean we're technically sisters? I mean, if Carrie's adopted me and Cliff's adopted you…"

"If we want it to. We're both—okay, I'm eighteen and you will be in September, close enough. So we're not like kids who really need parents. We can stay best friends, consider ourselves sisters; whatever you want."

"Cool. Being best friends for our entire lives in the old world is a link that like not many people have anymore. We should be more than just friends. Sisters works."

Harper fist-bumped her. "Done deal."

A few minutes of random talking petered out to another attempt to dive into their books while the not-too-distant repetitive *thwunk* of two axes splitting firewood came from outside. The shouts, cheers, and laughter of the kids migrated back and forth as they ran around playing soccer or a game similar to it.

Harper read for a while before realizing she'd been looking at weird marks on the paper without comprehending them, mechanically turning pages—so she backtracked. Staring at the same paragraph for ten minutes without processing its meaning morphed into daydreaming about where she'd be if the war hadn't happened. This would have been the summer break after her senior year in high school. Most likely, she'd have picked a college by now and no longer needed to worry about where to go, only what to major in. She and her friends would have been working summer jobs, hanging out when they could, going to movies or whatever, all looking forward to the adventure of college. Except maybe Darci. That girl didn't want to go to school again. She'd constantly joked about dropping out of high school even, because she thought it 'bogus.' Only Harper and Renee insisting she'd regret it kept her from doing so. If anything, Darci might've gone to art or trade school. In Harper's case, she would've been eager to put some distance between herself and the drama of a stressed-out Madison and her mother... and her kid sister wouldn't have minded.

While she'd more or less gone back to her old self, post-nuclear Madison remained far clingier than her pre-war version. Of course, she'd relaxed that about a thousand percent compared to how she'd been in the months right after they had to flee home.

Being militia, Madison's brittle emotional state, finding a dead guy, worry that Lawless would invade Evergreen at any minute, having killed people, anxiety over her feelings for Logan, and deep sorrow over her parents all jammed together in Harper's head at once. She wanted to scream in frustration, wanted to hit a big red button and reset the world back to normal so she didn't have to deal with all of this responsibility, guilt, and anxiety.

Eventually, she caught herself staring at *The Secret Garden* without reading it.

Dammit. I'm never going to finish this book. Eyes closed, she let a sigh out her nose. *I am strong. This is my world now and I'm grabbing it by the balls.*

Her emotions sorted, Harper resumed reading.

Grace breezed in the door only a few minutes—one page—later. "Hey, guys."

"Argh!" Harper raised the book in a mocking gesture as if to throw it at her.

"Eep!" Grace playfully ducked. "Sorry!"

"Hey." Renee waved. "How's it going at the clinic?"

"Fine. So far so good. Found some books at the library. We're reading up on old-world medicines, trying to find things we can make for ourselves and not run out of. I never knew how many plants had medicinal purposes." Grace held up a small dress. "Where's Lore?"

"Kids are out back." Harper pointed over her shoulder with the book.

"Wow, not on the video game?" Grace glanced at the TV.

"Power's down again." Harper frowned. "Been out for two days now. Seriously hoping it's back up before bath day."

Renee shivered. "No kidding. It's still weird thinking of a specific 'bath day.' I used to shower every morning and almost every night before bed."

"We should go scavenge up some candles." Grace raised an eyebrow. "Head up the road to the next town. A road trip could be fun."

"Not a bad idea, but we don't have working vehicles anymore. The gas is all gone. Not worth the risk to take a two- or three-day trek for candles." Resigned, Harper stuck the bookmark in and closed the novel. "Easier to just go inside after dark."

"Yeah," said Renee. "And we'll eventually make our own candles here."

"From what petroleum? Paraffin is made from oil." Grace sat on Cliff's recliner. "There's no such thing as an oil industry anymore."

"They had candles long before they had oil." Renee scrunched up her nose. "What did they make them out of?"

"Wax?" Harper shrugged. "Bees, right?"

"Come on, Grace. You got the huge brain." Renee stuck out her tongue.

"Umm. History was never my favorite subject. But it's gotta be in a book somewhere." Grace fell dramatically back over the recliner, the back of her hand to her forehead. "Oh, I miss Google."

Harper and Renee chuckled.

"And pumpkin spice coffee," said Renee in a voice like she mentioned a dear departed relative.

"Eww." Harper scrunched up her nose. "Mocha all the way."

"So basic." Grace rolled her eyes.

Again, they laughed, but Harper's ended on a somber sigh. Maybe someday, she'd be able to think of the normal world and not feel sad. *I'm making progress. No way should I be missing freakin' Starbucks when I'm happy to have food at all.*

"At least the farm's doing well." Grace smiled.

Whoa. Is she psychic? "For now. Still kinda worried. One bad season and we're still going to be in trouble."

"Try to stay positive." Renee bonked her with the book. "Positive thoughts attract positive reality."

"Thank you, motivational office poster girl," said Grace.

"If only." Harper rolled her eyes. "And I'm trying to stay positive, but I don't want to be caught off guard."

"I hate how the war changed you." Renee looked down. "You used to be such an optimist."

"I used to be a kid who had parents," muttered Harper.

Renee snapped her head up, staring at her. "I'm sorry. I didn't mean that."

"It's okay. I'm just whining." Harper took a deep breath, letting it leak out of her nostrils. "None of us are who we used to be. And it's okay. We can't change what happened."

"Umm…" Renee drummed her fingers on the book in her lap. "So what did people our age in the 1800s do for fun?"

"Heh." Harper shrugged. "No idea. But they probably spent a lot more time trying not to die than modern people."

Grace stretched back on the recliner. "Sometimes, they just relaxed. This chair is really comfy."

"Relaxed? That's kinda boring." Renee yawned.

"Not when you've been doing housework all day. We'd all probably have been married by now back then, maybe even with an infant to look after." Grace patted her stomach. "But they had books, going to the theater—live plays and such—drinking, gambling, I guess. But, I don't think girls were allowed to do the drinking and gambling thing. At least, not without being considered a 'loose woman' or something ridiculous like that. Girls probably weren't even allowed to have fun in public."

"Ugh. That's infuriating." Harper folded her arms. "We can't let that happen again. We're not maids and baby factories."

Renee raised a fist in the air. "Preach."

"Doubtful it will." Grace smiled at her. "There's too much modern society ingrained in everyone's psyches. Our technology went backward, not our brains."

"Yeah, for now. What's it going to be like when we're old?" asked Renee.

Harper eyed the .45 handgun on her hip. "Are we going to get old?"

"Oh, *stahhhp!*" Renee fell into a hug and squeezed her. "Please, cheer up."

Yeah, because 'cheer up' will let me forget freakin' having to kill people to stay alive. A dozen random memories of her and Renee hanging out played a slideshow in her head. Not even a full year ago, they'd both been innocent kids with no worries scarier than the SATs and college, and didn't have to kill anything other than boredom. The worst thing imaginable for Harper had been not getting the perfect new laptop for school. Now, she'd lost count of the number of people she'd had to kill, not so much due to there being a ton, but that she hadn't wanted to keep tally. It bothered her even more that she'd kill them all over again if put back in the same situation. As long as she had the means to defend herself and others, she would.

Yeah. I belong on the militia.

"Okay." Harper focused on being happy to have gotten Renee away from the Lawless so she could smile. "Trying to cheer up."

Grace tossed a small pillow at her. "Try harder. Bad stuff happened, but we're doing okay."

Harper caught the pillow after it bounced off her face. "Yeah. I guess we are." She smirked, then walloped Grace over the head with it.

4

IN THE MOMENT

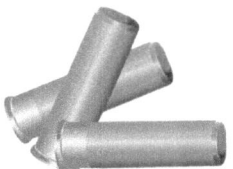

Weekends made Harper feel strange.

Before the world went to hell, she had worked a part-time job or two after school and over the summer break. Not one of those jobs had ever let her have weekends off routinely. Even requesting the occasional Saturday off because her parents wanted to take the family somewhere caused static, and even once got her fired—for merely requesting.

She hated that job anyway. The manager of that burger place basically thought himself Napoleon.

Having the entire weekend to herself with no obligation other than keeping an ear out for an emergency air horn call gave her a sense as though she'd grown up and gotten a 'real job,' like Mom or Dad pulling the old nine-to-five Monday through Friday. After that Brad guy fired her for requesting a Saturday, someone—maybe even her—had joked that the world would end if teenagers got weekends off.

This particular Saturday, Harper decided to finally attempt being happy and enjoying the day.

In not quite two months, the world would have been dead for a year. In not quite four months, her parents would have been gone for a year. That had to be enough time mourning. They wouldn't want her to spend the rest of her life in a constant state of crippling sorrow. She'd managed to get herself and Madison to a place of reasonable safety. What was the point of doing so if she kept dwelling on the past?

Harper hadn't exactly planned on trying to have fun, but Logan showed up at the house and invited her out on a date of sorts. Given the state of the country, they couldn't exactly go catch a movie, hit the mall, go out to eat, or attend a concert. They ended up roaming around Evergreen, checking out new areas. In homage to her 'day off,' she'd left the Mossberg at home in her closet, mostly because she had a .45 on her hip. The only other time in her life she'd worn a holstered pistol had been at the firing range when competing in mixed-discipline shooting that combined both rifle and handgun targets. Before the war, the only time she'd worn a pistol on her hip *with bullets in it* had been during the competition runs. The rest of the time she and her father were on the range, it remained unloaded.

Being on the militia required her to keep a weapon nearby at all times, but she still half expected her father or the range people to yell at her for carrying a loaded weapon out of the designated zone. Walking around town holding hands with Logan and not having anyone try to grab, rob, or shoot her in a while worsened the sense that carrying a weapon would get her in trouble. Evergreen had slid into a bizarre state of being simultaneously normal and post-apocalyptic. One direction she looked in, everything appeared so ordinary she could almost pretend the war never happened. Turn the other way, corn stalks grew up from a golf course and people used candles or torches for light while armed militia stood watch.

They spent a while wandering the streets, looking at—but not going into—apparently empty homes while attempting to guess what the people who used to live there might've done for a living based on the look of the property or whatever car remained abandoned there. In between talk of executives, artists, lawyers, and so on, Logan slipped in questions about how she was holding up. Every time she claimed to be okay, she believed herself a little bit more.

Okay didn't have to be perfection, it just had to be okay.

Random wandering eventually brought them to the southwest part of the upper half of Evergreen. On a lark, they went into the high school building. In a way, she still felt as though she belonged there. The almost-year that passed since the nuclear strike went by in such a blur that the destruction of civilization could've happened a week ago. Entering the building triggered a flood of memories along with a mild spike of dread at not having finished some assignments the teachers gave her the day before everything stopped.

"What?" asked Logan.

"Hmm?" She glanced at him.

"You tensed up and kinda gasped a little."

"Oh… just being stupid." She tossed her head to get hair out of her face. "For a sec, I kinda freaked out over not finishing some papers I had to write."

He chuckled.

"Hard to process it's been as long as it has. One day I went to school, the next we hid in our basement while everything went crazy." Harper traced her fingers over the lockers as they walked. "I could totally just resume going back to school like it had only been a week or two."

"Dunno about going back, but yeah… doesn't feel that long."

"Sorry about your sister."

Logan let out a long sigh. "Thanks. I guess I've accepted it as much as anyone can. Not sure where my head would be if I hadn't met you."

She squeezed his hand. Having Madison to protect kept her focused on something beyond grief, but no matter how much she loved her little sister, she would never be able to confide in her the same way she could to a parent or an equal. While sitting beside his hospital bed, she'd told Logan things she hadn't even been able to say to Cliff. They'd spent hours together talking. He'd helped her process the loss of her parents and friends enough that she could even talk about her mother and father without wanting to cry anymore. Not knowing what happened to her friends Andrea, Veronica, and Christina made it worse, but also let her hope they survived.

"This place is creepy." Harper looked up at the ceiling. "So quiet."

"No different than being here after hours."

She grinned. "You got detention a lot?"

"Nah. Hockey practice. I think schools always seem unnaturally quiet when they're empty because they're so loud normally. Like the cafeteria at my school, I had to shout to talk to Jason sitting right next to me."

"Mine wasn't quite that bad." Harper leaned closer to him, figuring talking about his friends from school would ruin his mood. "We used to sit way in the back corner though, so maybe it didn't get so loud there."

Their sneakers squeaked, echoing down the vast empty corridor. With the exception of a layer of dust, the school hadn't changed all that much in the aftermath. Here and there, signs of catastrophe appeared in the form of a drink bottle, blanket, or random personal item left on the floor. But, for the most part, the place looked as though classes might resume at the end of summer.

She expected to find a refugee camp in the gym, but upon reaching it, blinked in shock at the surprising normality. The room didn't contain rows of sleeping bags or cots, abandoned by survivors when the Army whisked them away. Because Evergreen avoided the worst effects of a nearby blast, all its buildings remaining intact and uncontaminated, people didn't need to abandon their homes here like they would have in Lakewood. A six-foot hole in the roof tended to ruin a place. By now, her old home had to be a moldy disaster.

"Wow…" Harper's voice echoed in the gym. She gazed up at a ceiling crisscrossed by exposed metal beams bedecked with lights, extra basketball hoops retracted up, and a bunch of team pennants. "It's so damn normal here. Like all the kids and teachers and janitors and whatever could just show up in the morning and keep going like none of this ever happened."

Logan raked his hair off his face—it had gotten kind of long—and gazed around. "Yeah. It's sad in a way, but also kind of hopeful."

"Hopeful?" She wandered across the dusty, polished floor to a stack of blue padded mats. "Think the town will get big enough again to need two schools?"

He sat on the pads, tugging at her arm until she joined him. "Maybe, but even if they never use this as a school again, it's like a museum of what we used to have. This place survived, so others had to. People have this stuff to remember. We'll eventually get back to the way it used to be."

"Think so?" Harper gripped the edge of the pad on either side of her legs.

Logan put an arm around her shoulders. "Yeah. I do. It might not come out exactly the same as the world we grew up in, but there's a much better chance the future's going to be civilized than we go full Mad Max."

"How can you be so sure?" She smiled at him, liking the thought the world might not be completely ruined forever, but wanting to tease him a little.

"Simple. There's no gasoline." He laughed. "Can't drive around the desert attacking people when all the gas is rotten. Maybe they'll use skateboards."

Harper laughed. "All those post-nuke movies, everything's so blasted-out and broken. It's weird seeing this school look like this."

"Those movies are usually set like fifty or a hundred years after the bombs. I guess stuff might fall apart if it's abandoned long enough, but you gotta think the directors making those movies want to make it look as unlike real life as possible for the story."

"Yeah. That makes sense."

"You know, since the oil industry is pretty much gone, the new society might be all about wind power. I'm not sure how many scientists are still around, but if you think about it... humanity got to where it did once. They didn't understand superconductors and stuff in the 1800s. We've got a massive head start."

"I guess." She peered up at motion that caught her eye, a sports jersey hung from the rafters. Number 03 with the name Baker. "How good does a high school kid have to be to get their number retired?"

Logan snickered. "Probably set some kind of record or something. Maybe helped them win a tournament some year."

"This feels like we've stepped into a different world. It's what we knew before, but it's become alien. That's so weird. Guess I've gotten used to having to literally fight for survival."

"Yeah. People freaked out, trying to deal with what happened. I think now that the shock has worn off, mostly they're going to focus on putting things back together."

Harper leaned against him. "Not everyone. Lawless... there's gotta be other gangs out there like that. Criminals."

"Not *everyone* in jail is a psycho. Look at Deacon. Some prisons were full of people who got caught carrying pot. We've always had criminals. They're gonna be a problem until we've got real cops again."

"I'm not a real cop?" She stuck her tongue out at him.

Logan fidgeted. "You know what I mean. Organized cops with computers and radios and stuff, the force of a state government behind them."

"Yeah." She looked down at her stomach, full of butterflies.

For a few minutes, they sat there alone in silence, surrounded by the vastness of an empty high school gymnasium. She thought about her friends Darci and Veronica. Both of them claimed to have done it at school. Darci under the bleachers and Veronica in the principal's office—after hours of course. However, Veronica's story sounded too wild to be true. She might have been merely trying to one-up Darci.

Silence eventually gave way to eye contact.

Being in the gym felt far too normal. It didn't take much effort for her to pretend the world hadn't exploded and she'd snuck into school after hours to find a private spot where no one would catch them. Each minute that passed pushed the horror of nuclear war further from her mind, her immediate reality morphing into a fantasy that nothing had really changed. For this brief moment, she'd become giddy with anticipation for what could happen between them at any minute.

Logan's 'you wanna?' expression made her smile. She leaned in to kiss him. The butterflies swarming around in her gut doubled in size and fury. He kissed her back, the touch of his lips on hers firing electrical sparks throughout her body. Caught up in the moment,

Harper made out with him in earnest, pushing him over onto his back and climbing on top.

His hands roamed and caressed her through her clothes. She mostly held onto his shoulders, too inexperienced and hesitant to do much else. The stuff they'd talked about while he lay in the hospital, all the sorrow and loneliness and worry she'd confided in him had left her exposed. He'd been in a similar headspace, having lost his entire family and all his friends. Harper pictured it as them both pulling their chests open to reveal a glowing magical core or something like in the books she read. Logan reached inside her emotionally and gently caressed the most vulnerable part of her being, protecting and embracing it. She'd done the same for him.

At first, she slid down that emotional hill, fighting every step of the way not to let herself end up in a position to be destroyed all over again. She didn't fear Logan deliberately hurting her as much as the world taking him away. Nearly losing him during the farm raid proved she'd already gone well past that point.

No regrets. If I'm going to lose him, I'm going to love the time we have together as much as I can.

Caught in the moment, she came up for air and peeled her T-shirt off. Logan removed his as well. She hadn't thought much of not having a bra in a post-nuclear society until the moment it hit her that Logan saw her topless. His loving smile embarrassed her, but not as much as realizing she didn't mind him seeing her. Worse, she *liked* it.

What would Follows Rules Girl say?

Somewhere, she and Introvert Prime recoiled in horror as Harper lowered herself to kiss Logan again, nothing but a layer of warm sweat between their skin above the waist. Eventually, she propped herself up and stared down through a tunnel of red hair at his dazed smile. He reached up to touch her chest, but hesitated, his fingers an inch away.

"Is this okay?" whispered Logan.

"I've never done anything more than kiss a boy before." She bit her lip. "You're the first guy to see them… who didn't laugh."

"They are perfect, just like you." He looked her in the eye, his expression a mix of love and seriousness. "You are the reason I keep going."

"That's a lot of responsibility." She bowed her head. "I hope I'm worthy of it."

"You are." He brushed a hand over her cheek. "I hope I'm good enough for you."

Happy tears gathered in her eyes. "You are."

She took his hand in both of hers and gently put it over her left breast. A boy touching her there sent tingles into weird places.

"You're nervous."

"A little. Never did this before. But… I like it." She let go of his hand, letting her arms hang limp at her sides.

Logan didn't seem entirely to know what to do, but after holding her breast for a moment, decided to brush his thumb back and forth over her nipple.

Harper shivered at the tingles shooting deep into her body.

"Still okay? Whatever you're comfortable with. Not gonna demand you do anything you don't want to."

For most of her life, Harper had daydreamed about some mythical 'perfect' first time. Sometimes, that meant a fairy tale impossible wedding came first. Others, it would follow meeting a guy who she'd *know* to be the one for her. Meeting Logan hadn't zapped her with the instant lightning bolt of total adoring love like from a fantasy novel, but the feelings she had for him now came pretty darn close… only it had taken months to get there rather than an instant.

Doing it in a high school gym felt kinda sleazy and cheap, something that would turn her into the sort of girl the other kids at school spoke of in whispers or made odd faces at when they thought she couldn't see them. However, this moment didn't feel cheap at all. They hadn't truly 'snuck around' to break any rules. This building didn't even count as a high school anymore. No such thing existed anywhere in the USA—at least as far as she guessed. Either one of them could die tomorrow.

Any chance of meeting the perfect guy and having the perfect wedding where a thousand guests attended a big reception, party, and honeymoon had gone up in smoke as had most of the country.

'Married' now only went as far as two people deciding to consider themselves a couple.

"Yes. It's okay. I'll let you know if it isn't." Shaking from excitement, apprehension, and that wonderful feeling of getting away with something she probably shouldn't do, Harper kicked her sneakers off, then opened her belt.

Logan's eyes widened to saucers as she pushed her jeans down over her hips and sprawled there beside him wearing only panties. "You've got me at a disadvantage…"

"Oh?" She raised an eyebrow.

"I'm not wearing underwear."

Harper blushed, but smiled. "I don't have to be. Up to you."

His astonished, joyful expression sent a wave of warmth over her chest. Nervously, he opened his belt and wriggled out of his jeans and sneakers. Soon, he sat there wearing only socks. Harper stared at his rather obvious sign of excitement. Other than a few pictures her friends sent her as jokes, she'd never seen one for real before. Like a snake mesmerized by a flute, she stared at it while her hands moved as if of their own accord, slipping her panties off.

"You are the most beautiful woman I've ever seen… inside as well as outside." Logan slid closer, grasping her shoulders as if afraid to really touch her while both of them were naked.

Harper leaned into him, pushing him over backward and laying half on top, half beside him. She trembled from nerves and excitement, but couldn't stop smiling. *What am I waiting for? Dammit, I love him…* Getting pregnant could kill her, but that thought barely registered in her mind besides how badly it hurt to see him get shot. If she kept denying her feelings for him, she would feel ten times worse if anything happened.

"Logan, you're the only boy I've ever felt like this about. When you got shot, I…"

He kissed her for a long moment. "I didn't really like that either."

She chuckled into the crook of his neck. Having her everything pressed against his everything, skin on skin, stirred feelings deep inside her she'd never known before—and they excited her. "We're right out here in the open where anyone could see us."

"Yeah. But no one's going to walk in here."

Harper blushed, despite laughing. "I'm not sure I'd care if they did. I want the whole world to know I love you."

"Are you sure this is what you want?"

"I am." She smiled, running a hand over his chest. "Let's see where this goes."

5

SLACKER LIFE

Monday morning saw Harper escorting the kids to the farm, then heading east to the residential neighborhood that had become *her* territory. She'd spent a surprising amount of time with Logan Saturday and Sunday, though they didn't come close to repeating what happened in the gym. He hadn't been prepared for the blood. Harper knew it would happen, but the pain turned out to be worse than she expected. Could be that redhead pain tolerance thing. In the moment, it hadn't been too bad, but the stinging afterward plus bleeding sent her to see Tegan at the medical clinic.

Being given birth control pills had been strange. Not only because—to her astonishment—the clinic actually had some, but simply for the odd normality of it. Tegan said she'd be sore for a couple days, and not to worry about it. Though, Harper couldn't help but worry. The pills helped ease her mind, but if she got pregnant, she feared they'd kick her off the militia.

Still, those hours she and Logan shared would be forever enshrined in her memory as the happiest time of her life after the bombs. Having gotten past her fear of the first time, she expected they'd be making more happy memories often enough.

Considering she'd been wearing a near permanent blush ever since, she figured Cliff, Carrie, and Madison knew what happened. If Jonathan did, he hadn't looked at her or acted in any way that suggested so. Lorelei had no idea what could potentially happen if a boy and girl spent enough time alone together, so she remained oblivious, mistaking Harper's flushed cheeks for sunburn.

Perhaps an hour into her patrol, Darci emerged from a side street and trotted over. Seeing that girl in an ordinary T-shirt and jean shorts seemed about as wrong as the sight of a nun in a bikini. The entire time they'd known each other, Darci always dressed goth. The girl rocked black lipstick as young as fifth grade and always wore black clothing in various degrees of frilly. She also rarely wore shoes outside of school or work where she *had* to, in which case, she put on heavy boots or maybe heels if struck by a 'fancy goth' mood.

Darce probably feels naked without black toenail polish on.

"Sup," said Darci, upon falling in step beside her.

"Not much. Technically working."

"Technically lying." Darci winked. "Not much? Seriously."

Harper gave her side eye. "What?"

"So the princess is no longer a virgin. I'm so happy for you guys." Darci grinned.

"Umm. No idea what you're talking about." Harper stared at the street ahead, trying to make a hole open so she could jump into it and hide.

"Wow, your face is the same color as your hair. Guess it's true. And you are walking a little funny. My first time hurt like a bitch, too."

"Ugh. Rumors? Really? Great..." Harper became acutely aware of soreness affecting her stride and tried to conceal it.

Darci playfully punched her on the shoulder. "Don't freak out. It's not like school. No one's going to tease you. News flash, Harp. We're adults now. Besides, it's not like the whole town is talking about you. Renee suspected, and you just confirmed it."

Harper stared up at the clouds, wishing her face didn't have a direct wire going right to her brain so every thought or emotion she had instantly displayed to the world. "It's not like you're thinking."

"So, what? You guys did butt stuff or something? Trying to keep that technical virginity?"

"No." Harper gasped, squirming. "Seriously? Why would you ask that?"

Darci laughed. "Mostly to get you to make that face. So if it's not 'like that,' what *was* it like?"

"Love." Harper smiled. "It's like all this horrible crap happened to the world, but there's still a little bit of hope left."

"Aww, that's adorable." Darci leaned against her, batting her eyes.

Harper smirked, pushing her friend upright. "I'm serious."

"Yeah, I know. Doing it is *much* better when love's involved."

"Sorry you had to deal with that."

"Forget it." Darci shrugged. "If I didn't want to do it, I wouldn't have. No one forced me to."

"No one except the people responsible for the conditions at that camp."

Darci pulled her T-shirt up to expose her flat stomach. "I don't have much room to lose weight. And despite what those bitches at school said, I'm not—nor have I ever been—anorexic. Trust me, not going hungry was worth it."

Maybe for you. Harper cringed internally. Granted, Darci lost her virginity over a year before the nukes, so she didn't have that hesitation in her way. Purely for herself, Harper would have taken hunger. For Madison… She thought about Eva, who'd been almost as starved-thin as Lorelei was at first despite being at the Army camp. Mrs. Parsons hadn't slept around for extra food either, even with a child to care for. Then again, that woman had given up on life.

"Argh," muttered Harper. "Why do I keep doing that?"

"Randomly screaming?"

"No." Harper sorta chuckled. "I keep thinking depressing things."

"This is hard for you. I can't imagine. You were always so happy, optimistic, and sweet." Darci poked her in the side. "I feel sorrier that you've had to cope with this war than I kinda went prostitute to avoid starvation."

"Gee thanks."

"I mean it, sweetums." Darci made an overly adoring face, then grinned.

Harper stuck her tongue out.

"So here we are. Is it okay for me to hang while you do the cop thing?"

"Yeah. I mean, I guess it is. As long as I'm not like stopping and just sitting there with you."

Darci nodded. "Cool. Yeah, don't mind walking."

"I liked it."

"Huh?"

"What Logan and I did." Harper smiled despite blushing again. "I liked it way more than I expected. Feels like I should be getting in trouble, but I wanna do it again."

"See." Darci patted her on the shoulder. "Told you it's fun."

"It's not just a physical act. It's fun because I'm in love with him."

"Cool."

Harper glanced over at her. "You don't believe in love, do you?"

"Isn't that a song?"

"Maybe."

Darci grinned. "Love is like unicorns or faeries. If I ever see one, I'll believe in them. And stop blushing. There's no reason for you to give a shit what society thinks about girls who've had sex before marriage."

"What's marriage anymore?" Harper shrugged. "There's no society."

"Exactly!" Darci thrust her arms up high, head back. "Society is dead. Live for *you*. Finally! You've seen the light and gone anarchist."

"Hardly." She hefted the Mossberg. "I'm technically 'the man' now."

"No you're not. What you're doing is protecting people. You aren't doing the bidding of corrupt politicians and even more corrupt corporations while claiming to be 'protecting' the people."

Harper chuckled. "You mean I'm not harassing people for drinking or smoking weed a little too young."

"That, too. Damn, those cops were such pricks. Like who cares if a girl wants to toke up? No one on weed ever broke the law. Way too mellow."

"Putting Skittles and gummi bears on pizza is breaking the law." Harper gagged.

"What? That was awesome." Darci sighed. "Damn, I miss pizza. Can't believe that place actually made that pie."

"Blech. Neither can I. There is no way in hell you would've even been able to eat that monstrosity if you weren't higher than hell."

Darci wagged her eyebrows. "Good thing I'm always half baked. Sobriety is overrated. And how messed up is this?"

"Is what?"

"I'm a slacker and proud. Bad grades don't mean a damn thing anymore. All those teachers bitching at me for getting Ds can go to hell. Oops, I didn't get into a good college." Darci clapped her hands to her cheeks and gasped in fake horror.

"Yeah well... some people wanted to go and can't."

"Did you really, though? Or did you only expect to go to college because it's what your parents wanted you to do?" Darci swung an arm around her back in a buddy hug. "It's a whole processing machine they had. Children were like wads of ground beef put in one end of the machine and spat out the other. The education system didn't want to actually teach anything as much as it existed to produce an army of identical worker bees who knew just enough to operate the machinery of the world but not enough to question anything the people in charge did."

Harper patted Darci on the head, ruffling at her hair.

"What are you doing?"

"Looking for the tinfoil hat."

Darci raspberried her. "It's true. Or was. That whole thing is gone now. If so many people didn't die, I'd be happy about it. This is a painful but necessary rebirth for humanity. Kinda like radiation therapy for the Earth."

"Dark."

"Hello? This is me you're talking to." Darci laughed. "Though I do feel weird dressed like a straight."

Harper grinned. "It is so bizarre seeing you not wearing black."

"Liz didn't have any clothes that fit my personality. Renee's going to try to make me some stuff when she can."

"Neat. She's really getting into the making clothes stuff."

"Suits her. She used to make clothes for all her dolls. That girl had even more dolls than you did."

"I was never doll crazy. You're thinking of Madison. My thing was collecting faerie stuff, and stuffed animals."

"Aww, you're so adorable. You know, it's usually women past thirty who keep having twenty-first birthdays, not girls our age repeating their twelfth over and over."

Harper picked her eye with her middle finger, making Darci laugh.

"You're like that meme of the kitten carrying a gun."

"Yeah, yeah. I don't feel harmless anymore." Harper kicked a rock off the road.

"Nah, you're a total badass now." Darci winked. "That's why it sucks the world did what it did to you. You were too innocent to have to face that. I know I'm gloomy all the time, but that doesn't mean I can't appreciate the cuteness of a pink faerie."

"Ugh." Harper rolled her eyes. "I'm not cute."

"Which one of us used to rescue bugs from the house? Little nature pixie."

"Says the hippie."

Darci smiled. "Think I'll get in trouble if I went full hippie?"

"No idea. Lorelei 'forgets' her clothes all the time, and no one seems to care."

"Except you."

"Well, duh. People aren't supposed to do that." Harper looked at her. "And she's a traumatized little kid. You're a… traumatized adult."

Darci raspberried her.

"Okay, traumatized big kid."

They walked for a few blocks in silence, both at the edge of laughing.

"Any idea yet what you're going to do?" asked Harper.

"Smoke pot and try not to die."

Harper raised both eyebrows. "So... pretty much the same as before."

"Yeah." Darci chuckled. "More or less... without worrying about getting a job. I mean, it really sucks that so many people died. Except for all the death it took to get here, I'm not sure we're worse off."

"The end of the day job is hardly worth everything we've lost as a society."

"Is it? Constant remakes of the same movies, derivative video games, fancy food, cars, airplanes we can't afford to go on for vacations we can't afford to take. Endless consumerism, profit at all costs."

"Medicine. People are going to die of cancer and other crap now that could've been cured."

"Maybe in other countries. Here, they'd have died anyway because curing people isn't as profitable as letting them die." Darci frowned off to the side. "Not much different really. We've gone from people dying because insurance companies won't pay or the drugs cost too much to people dying because there *are* no drugs or hospitals. All that's truly changed is that we no longer have people making tons of money off the death. Hate to break it to you, but we were technically a Third World country already for ninety percent of the population."

Harper whistled. "You almost sound happy the nukes fell."

"Nah. I'm just trying to find ways to keep away from the edge, 'cause I don't wanna fall into that endless black pit. I almost did, back in that camp."

"Darce..." Harper stopped walking and faced her friend. "Are you okay?"

Darci stared down at her toes. "I am now. Losing Dad got to me for a while there. And being alone. Like not knowing what happened to you and 'Nee, and the others. I got a real bad case of the screwits and almost jumped into that hole. No, it had nothing to do with sleeping around for food. Just... why the hell did I survive when everyone I knew didn't?"

Harper hugged her.

Darci didn't move. "You're getting squishy and cute again."

"Yeah. That's me, remember? The pink faerie empath."

"Heh." Darci sighed, but returned the hug. "Thanks for existing."

Harper blinked. "No one's ever said that to me before."

"Well, they should have."

"So you're good? Not thinking of hurting yourself anymore?" asked Harper.

"No. I've found a nice little pocket of Zen. Got two of my friends back, things don't seem bad here, and Lucas is into me."

Harper blinked. "You're dating that guy from the pirate show?"

"Yeah. My 'job' is probably going to be helping him grow weed for the town. Everyone needs to loosen up a little, right? People have always wanted to escape reality… and this reality is kinda escape worthy."

"No kidding." More or less convinced her friend didn't seem likely to harm herself, Harper resumed walking. "If you start feeling depressed again, please talk to me. Or Tegan, okay?"

"Yeah. I'm not legit mental. Just got really sad and lonely there for a while. Like I said, I'm good now. Back to not caring what happens."

Harper waved at Eleanor Price, a fairly recent arrival who'd moved into a house here four months ago with her two kids, Max and Julie. She'd stopped to chat with the woman often enough to know her husband, a recruiter for the Army, was in central Denver when the blast hit and hadn't been seen since. She and the kids made a go of hunkering down in their basement much the same way as Harper's dad wanted to, but eventually ran out of food and followed a rumor of safety to Evergreen.

"Not caring isn't exactly healthy either," said Harper.

"No, not like that. I mean more like not getting upset over whatever happens."

Harper grinned to herself. "I imagined you sitting there on your bed in the basement, staring up at the sky after the nuke ripped the house away saying 'well, that sucked.'"

Darci laughed. "I'm not *that* laid back. If my house went flying, I'd probably have freaked the hell out."

"So you and Lucas are going to be Evergreen's weed merchants?"

"Basically. Only, there's no money anymore and food is free, so we just give it away if anyone wants it. Most times, people hang out with us and smoke it there. This is such a better way to live than everyone trying to hoard as much cash as possible."

Harper waved at Mr. Santiago, who sat on a patio chair in front of his little house. He'd lived there for years, which explained how a single elderly man occupied a residence in the area usually given to parents of school-age kids. She considered him the friendliest old man she'd ever met. Alas, the poor guy still hadn't quite been able to comprehend there'd been a nuclear war. He thought the people who brought him his allotment of food worked for social services under some 'wonderful new government program.'

"Which world do you think is better?" asked Darci.

"The one we used to have, no doubt. It had its problems, but you didn't have twelve-year-olds like the boy who lives three houses back, Max Price, needing to shoot people just to stay alive."

"Yeah, it did." Darci hooked her thumbs in the pockets of her shorts. "Just not in the US. Africa and the Middle East had child soldiers. Maybe they still do. Dunno why anyone would nuke those places for any reason other than pure spite. Plenty of horrible stuff happened on this planet before, even if we lived in a nice little bubble and didn't see it."

Harper looked down. "You make it sound like we deserved it."

"Nah. Not at all. Except for the one percent, everyone who died to the bombs had nothing to do with making the world suck. Not saying I'm glad it happened, only that the reason things suck changed from greed to desperation." Darci pulled a joint out of her back pocket. "So, why give up?"

"You're just gonna stay high all the time?"

Darci grinned at her. "Nah. Not all the time. A girl's gotta sleep."

6

THE OLD WORLD

Hanging out with her friends in a bedroom, caught in the cloud of Darci's pot smoke, had been the closest Harper ever came to getting high on purpose. She still didn't have any desire to smoke weed. Even if that feeling did mostly come from her parents constantly talking about how drugs were bad more than any opinion of her own. Whether or not it made her uncool, she decided to avoid any sort of 'illegal drug' since it's what her parents would have wanted her to do.

Darci pulled a joint out of her back pocket and stuck it in her lips. Expecting her to ignite a match or lighter at any second, Harper took a deep breath and held it, looking out among the homes in the area. Everything appeared quiet and peaceful as it should have — except for one house with an open front door. That normally wouldn't have bothered her, except she knew the place had been assigned and shouldn't be empty.

"Crap," muttered Harper.

"Hmm?" Darci peered over, joint sticking out of her mouth, lighter poised but not lit.

"One sec."

Harper adjusted her grip on the shotgun and headed toward Mr.

Beasley's house, nerves on edge. The guy didn't exactly count as 'friendly.' He'd wandered into Evergreen soon after the evacuation, before the militia had truly established itself, and claimed that house. While he had never given *her* too difficult a time, he constantly argued with the militia. He also had an annoying habit of referring to her as 'little missy' and loudly announcing his opinion that he didn't have to listen to the militia since he had a personal garden and didn't touch the town's food supply. Approaching his house had as much chance of setting off a gunfight as a two-hour-long political diatribe.

The guy's first name was Duke, but she often mentally replaced the u with an ic and dropped the e.

She had no idea why he even bothered complaining about politics anymore, but he loved screaming about it as well as freaking out that the militia would show up to confiscate his weapons. For the first few weeks of her walking a patrol, he'd been watching her go by through the scope of a hunting rifle, not that she'd known. That factoid, she didn't discover until he emerged from the house three weeks ago to accuse her of 'scouting him out' for a militia attack. He'd accepted her explanation of 'just being on patrol' a bit too easily to be legitimately insane, but she didn't completely trust him.

Each step closer to the house made the hairs on the back of her neck stand higher. He could have the crosshairs on her face already, though she didn't see anything in the windows. Worried about provoking him, she kept the shotgun aimed to the side in a nonthreatening posture.

"Mr. Beasley?" called Harper. "Are you okay?"

She paused in the street, listening. When no reply came, she moved to the end of the long driveway. From there, she had a view around the overgrown front lawn at the front stoop. Mr. Beasley lay face down on the porch, his legs still inside the house.

"Mr. Beasley!"

Harper slung the shotgun over her shoulder on its strap and ran over to him.

He emitted a faint wheezing gurgle. He'd landed on his chest, right hand clutching at his heart. Sweat poured down his face, which had become red as a tomato. All the veins in his forehead swelled up prominently.

Crap! I think he's having a heart attack.

Darci padded up the driveway, the unlit joint still hanging from her mouth. Upon spotting the gurgling man, she plucked it out and blurted, "Holy shit."

Harper stared at him. No way could she and twig-thin Darci lug a six-foot-two almost 300-pound man anywhere. He had the physique of a long-retired Marine, complete with the brush cut, muscles, and beer belly. She pulled the air horn from its belt clip and sounded one long blast, a 911 tone.

"Gah!" Darci grabbed her ears. "What the hell?"

Harper dropped to crouch beside Mr. Beasley and took his hand. "Help's on the way. I can't carry you."

He shifted his gaze to her, his expression somewhere between pleading and accusatory as if to question why the militia would allow a 'weak little girl' to join.

Most men would struggle to lug this guy around alone. He's still awake, so I don't think I need to do CPR. "Is it your heart?"

He wheeze-grunted in a way that mostly sounded like agreement.

Answering air horn pips came from nearby.

"Where is it?" shouted Darnell.

"Harper?" yelled Marcie. "Was that you?"

She turned her face toward the driveway and shouted, "Over here!"

Darci ran back to the street, also shouting, "Over here! Some dude had a heart attack."

"It's gonna be okay," said Harper. "We'll get you to the med center and Dr. Hale or Khan will fix it."

He groaned, eyes closing.

"Don't go to sleep. C'mon, Mr. Beasley. Stay with me." Harper shook him and touched his neck, checking for a pulse, which he still had, though irregular.

Darnell arrived first, skidding to a stop by the porch and also dropping to one knee. "Oh, shit."

"Yeah. We need to get him to the med center fast. He's too big for me to carry."

"He's big for me to carry." Darnell slung his rifle over his shoulder. "Check the house for aspirin."

Marcie jogged up. "Aww, dammit."

"Maybe the four of us can carry him?" asked Harper.

While Darnell and Marcie got into a rapid debate trying to decide if they should carry him or run for the body cart, an old construction trailer that generally served now for the transportation of corpses, Harper ran inside.

She went straight to the bathroom medicine cabinet. Turned out, he *did* have aspirin. She grabbed the bottle—despite thinking it ridiculous. Aspirin for a heart attack felt like putting a Band-Aid on a blown-off leg, but Darnell sounded like he knew something. She rushed outside, dropped to her knees by Mr. Beasley, and fed him a tablet.

Mr. Beasley lost consciousness.

"No!" shouted Harper. She tried to lift him to roll on his back, but couldn't manage it.

Darnell and Marcie helped. As soon as they got him flipped, Harper pressed her ear to his chest.

"He's still got a heartbeat."

"Still breathing," said Darnell, holding a hand over the man's face.

"Hey!" Darci jogged out from the corner of the house with a big wheelbarrow. "Found this in the yard."

"That works." Darnell jumped up.

All four of them working together hoisted the big guy into the wheelbarrow. Grunting, Darnell managed to lift the handles and get him moving. No way could he manage going over uneven terrain, so they followed the street south to Lewis Ridge Road and took that west to Route 74, which went straight to the medical center.

Once they reached the highway, progress sped up a little.

Ken Zhang rolled up on a mountain bike, also responding to the 911 call, though he'd been farther away. He jumped off the bike, shoved it to Harper, then took one handle of the wheelbarrow, helping Darnell and allowing them to move faster.

Unfortunately, the wheelbarrow wouldn't fit through the door of the medical center. With everyone grabbing hold, they managed to collectively lift Mr. Beasley and carry him inside, going straight to the nearest treatment room while Ruby Dorsey—the woman who staffed the counter out front—darted into the back, shouting for a doctor.

Both Tegan (Dr. Hale) and Dr. Khan rushed in to check on Mr. Beasley. Grace, as well, joined them as an apprentice. Harper and the other militia backed out into the hall to give them room.

"What happened?" asked Ken.

"I was just walking my usual route and saw him lying on the ground."

Ken bowed his head, shaking it. "Poor guy."

Marcie grimaced. "Damn. That sucks."

"Is that dude gonna be okay?" whispered Darci.

Darnell scratched behind his ear. "Dunno. Ain't lookin' too good."

Harper leaned against the wall beside Darci. "I feel bad."

"Don't feel *too* bad. That guy's huge. No way you could have done anything." Darci scratched her left shin with her toes.

"Not that. I mean, the guy was kinda rude and aggressive. I feel guilty for thinking poorly of him."

Darci cupped Harper's chin and pulled her head around so they made eye contact. "We need to have an intervention. Your empathy is in overdrive."

"Hah."

"Seriously. You told me the dude almost shot you." Darci let go of her. "You don't need to feel guilty over a guy like that. But, you wouldn't be you if you didn't."

"Thanks." Harper sighed at the floor.

Everyone stood around in relative silence for a while. Eventually, Dr. Khan emerged from the room. The look on his face said they'd lost him.

"Too late?" asked Darnell.

"Unfortunately, there was nothing we could have done. He didn't respond to blood thinners and we don't have the equipment for cardiac catheterization. CPR and oxygen were ineffective as well. The man's heart just gave up."

Harper un-leaned from the wall and walked over. "Doc? Would he have made it if, you know… we still had real 911 and ambulances and stuff?"

Dr. Khan made a 'who can say' gesture. "Only about five percent of those who suffer sudden cardiac arrest survive. It's impossible to say for certain that he'd have survived otherwise, though proper EMTs arriving with the equipment on an ambulance *might* have made a difference here."

"You did as much as you could." Darnell rested a hand on her shoulder.

"I guess. Wouldn't have even been on patrol here in the real world, right? No one would've found him until way later when people came home from work." She exhaled. "He'd have been long dead by then."

"Good point." Marcie forced a smile she clearly didn't believe in.

"Guess I should go get the cart," muttered Harper.

"Not yet." Ken shook his head. "Wait until they get a grave dug for him. Better he stay in here where it's cooler than lay out on that thing in the sun."

Dr. Khan returned to the treatment room.

Harper, Darci, and the militia went outside under a cloud of grimness.

"You guys hear anything about the Weldon case?" asked Harper after the door shut behind her.

"Doc said he'd been killed probably around one or two in the morning." Ken mimicked stabbing himself in the chest. "Three stab wounds, no other injuries."

"Roy's been interviewing people from the farm," said Marcie. "Hooper and Sanchez were on sentry duty that night. Hooper said he heard a muffled noise, but figured someone staggered out of Earl's bar and fell. Couldn't find anyone in the dark."

Harper fidgeted, shifting her weight from leg to leg. "I'm pretty sure Weldon died somewhere else and got dragged into the tomato plants. Maybe Hooper heard the killer struggling to move the body."

"Could be." Darnell nodded. "Far as I know, Roy hasn't come up with anything yet. No idea why anyone would want to attack the guy. Not like robbery's a motive anymore."

"Not for money. Maybe he had an expensive watch or gun or something." Harper stared up Route 74 toward the farm. "Or we have a killer running around."

"Ugh, don't say that." Marcie closed her eyes. "You'll set off a panic."

"People deserve to know they could be in danger." Harper hooked her thumbs in her jean pockets. "We can't just keep it quiet. What if the person who killed Weldon goes after someone else?"

Ken raised a placating hand. "Give Roy a little more time to get some facts before we let speculation run wild. The killing looked like an assassination. He thinks someone targeted Weldon specifically. Maybe even made him kneel to be executed."

"That doesn't make sense." Harper patted her knee. "He had dirt on his jeans like he'd been kneeling, but who makes their victim kneel so they can stab them in the chest? And, he hadn't been tied up."

"The killer could've removed the rope when they dumped the body," said Marcie.

"He'd have bruises or red marks on his wrists. Unless the guy *wanted* to die and didn't fight at all. I looked at the body and didn't see any—oh what the heck did they call it on *Law & Order*… umm, 'defensive wounds.' I don't think he fought back."

"Yeah. Harper's right," said Darci. "Even like fifteen minutes of struggling against ropes leaves marks on your wrists. And I wasn't even afraid for my life and seriously fighting."

Harper gawked at her. "What happened?"

"Relax. Dylan was into kinky stuff."

Ken, Darnell, and Marcie all coughed and fidgeted uncomfortably.

"I, uhh, didn't think you were into that." Harper blushed.

"I'm not. Just gave it a try because he wanted to." Darci shrugged.

"Okay then," said Darnell in a loud voice. "So, he wasn't

executed. What was he kneeling for?"

"Praying?" asked Ken.

"He's a farm worker." Harper thrust her left arm out in the direction of the fields. "Why are we assuming he got dirt on his jeans at the moment he died? He could've been kneeling by a row of plants all damn day."

"Oh, true. The dirt could be meaningless." Ken chuckled. "Roy's probably already dismissed it for that same reason."

"Yeah." Marcie picked at the AR-15 strap over her chest. "Not like the guy worked inside the quartermaster's building. Dirt on his clothes wouldn't be unusual."

"If he died at around one in the morning, he definitely wouldn't have been working on the farm," said Harper. "But his clothes still had dirt on them. Did he go to Earl's?"

"Pretty sure Roy checked, and no one remembered him being there." Darnell swiped at a fly buzzing by his ear. "The five of them, Weldon and the people he showed up in town with, haven't really been the most social sort of people. Friendly enough if you go up to them, but they keep to themselves."

Harper furrowed her brow while thinking. "Could he have been stabbed in his sleep? That's easier to believe than he didn't try to fight back at all."

"Possible." Ken smiled. "Sounds like you're trying to take over Roy's investigation."

"Nah, not really. Just worrying that there could be someone going around town killing random people." Harper gestured to the door. "I should get back to my zone. Thanks for the backup."

"Hey, that's what we do." Darnell winked. "We're a team."

"I wish there's more we could have done for Mr. Beasley." Harper sighed.

"Can't save everyone. All we can do is try." Ken picked the mountain bike up onto its wheels and got on. "Stay safe, all."

Harper plodded back up Route 74 to her patrol area.

"You sure you don't want a hit or two, take the edge off?" asked Darci, following her.

Harper shook her head, then grinned. "Nah. I'm on duty."

7

EXPLORERS

Mila Cline didn't enjoy working on the farm, mostly because it made wearing black uncomfortable.

The July sun definitely didn't get along with dark dresses. Having turned ten a few days ago on the 19th, she'd ended up in the group of kids 'old enough' to be required to help out doing light farm work. Lugging a bag of chicken feed around definitely beat sitting in a cage, her hands tied behind her back, but she'd much rather just be a kid and try to forget about the Shadow Man entirely.

Even though she'd watched Harper blast the guy right in the face and knew for a fact that the men who kidnapped her and forcibly trained her for several months had died, every sufficiently dark shadow still gave her a prickle of fear that one of *them* might still be out there. Mila didn't blame her new, adoptive mother for what happened to her real mom. The woman also hadn't requested they reassign Mila to someone else for being too weird and creepy. In fact, the stranger she acted, the more protective and nurturing the woman became. As if her new mom thought any mental problems could be fixed by pouring on ever increasing amounts of love.

Not that Mila would ever admit it to anyone but her new mother, but she kinda liked that. Her real mom hadn't been physically affectionate, so it took getting used to being constantly squeezed, kissed, head-patted, and checked in on. At times, it grew annoying, but again... she much preferred that to a crazy assassin cult holding her prisoner.

Yeah, as far as she figured, she'd been messed up in the head by that experience. But, normal was boring. And she could reliably hit a target the size of a human eye at twenty paces with a leaf knife. That had to count for something? Even though no one would crack a wooden paddle across her backside if she missed the target anymore, she still feared not being perfect—so practiced throwing at least an hour every day. That fear didn't come from any threat of punishment, but from knowing that a missed throw could kill her or one of her friends. Since she was *not* an assassin, the only time she'd whip a leaf knife at someone involved self-defense. So... missing would be *bad*.

In between grumbling at schoolwork, grumbling about farm work, honing her skills, and trying not to have too many nightmares, Mila occasionally attempted another challenging task: being a child. That Madison girl had been a total basket case at first, clinging to a dead cell phone expecting her dead parents to call, but she'd gotten better. Mila suspected Madison's brother Jonathan liked her in a 'let's hold hands' kinda way. She didn't really know how to process that. Her new mother had acclimated her to being touched in good ways, hugs, kisses atop the head, and so on. So if the boy ever made a move to grab her hand, she probably wouldn't break his nose. Her real parents had been nice, but emotionally remote. Mother cared more about her work with the symphony than anything else, and her father had been devoted to his job at the chemical place.

As much as it felt wrong, she almost preferred her current adoptive mother to her bio parents.

Since the real threat of the Shadow Man was gone, Mila no longer went out of her way to act like an even more psycho version of Wednesday Addams. Even though it bothered her to be ridiculed and avoided, that bugged her less than having to see the Shadow Man kill—or abduct—any kids who might be near her at the time he showed up to drag her back to the hideout. Mila didn't have any unusual talents or abilities prior to being taken off the street, so that guy would probably have grabbed any kid small enough to train.

The strangest part of living in Evergreen had been having friends. In her old life, she'd rarely gone outside or played with other kids. Most of her time went to reading or video games. She doubted her bio parents would have let her spend time among 'normal' children, thinking them beneath her. Not that they'd been tremendously wealthy, but they definitely didn't count as middle class. Her father was an executive or someone pretty high up.

In a way, Mila smiled at the idea of money being gone. She didn't miss the huge house or all the boring people who'd show up to her parents' social events. The friends she'd made here beat any amount of money.

And they definitely beat a locked cell.

Yeah, she hated the Shadow Man's hideout even more than her father's stuffy parties and friends. She'd never chewed through rope and gone out a window to get away from her parents' awful music. Of course, her parents never tied her up in a locked cell, so perhaps that didn't make for a fair comparison. The childish fear she once had for the Shadow Man, believing him a genuine supernatural being capable of using magic had become a mixture of loathing and contempt. What kind of idiot would *forcibly* train a kid against their will and keep them captive? Wouldn't he expect them to attempt to kill him or eventually escape? Or did he think they'd eventually crack in the head and go along with it? It had probably been his goal to make her crazy. The worst beating she'd ever received from him came after she refused to shoot a captive man to death 'as a test.'

Mila kicked a rock off the side of the street, deciding not to think about the Shadow Man anymore. Harper killed him for real. All Mila had to do was kill his memory.

She'd gone with her friends, Jonathan, Madison, Eva, Becca, Christopher, and little Lorelei, out exploring again. Since the town's attempt at restoring electrical power had been off more than on lately, they'd all kinda given up on the video game system Jonathan found. Today, they'd headed east along Hidden Village Drive. The road didn't have many houses on it, but Christopher insisted a big one sat all the way at the end.

Of their group, only Jonathan had shoes, but they all wore mismatched clothes a little too big for them. Mila didn't mind going barefoot as it let her be quiet and sneak around if she had to. She also didn't mind the old, worn dress her new mother had gotten from the town, but would've preferred it in black. At least blue didn't suck too badly. Not like she got stuck in pink. Or worse, white like Lorelei. No way could anyone hide at night in a white dress. Jeans like Madison's would be best for fighting, but the Shadow Man hadn't taught her much about that since she'd been too small. Black yoga pants or leggings with a black shirt made for the best 'hidey' clothes. Those, she'd left at home since she didn't plan on sneaking anywhere; plus, they made for miserably hot attire on the farm.

The people who'd done the scavenging had evidently not paid much attention to kid-sized shoes. Mila—and most of the tweens in town—ended up in a size void where all the shoes in the quartermaster's were either way too little, or too big for them. Mila still had the sneakers she'd worn the day she'd crawled out of the collapsed ruin of her house. Madison and Eva had their old sneakers, too, but thought it too warm to wear them and so didn't bother. Lorelei sometimes took that idea to the extreme, considering it too warm for clothing at all—though she'd been doing that less and less lately. Mila figured Harper yelled at her for it.

"We should go to the pool. This is kinda boring," said Becca.

"Swimming!" cheered Lorelei. "I like swimming."

Mila looked over her friends while walking at the back of the group.

Jonathan, she both trusted and liked. He had a protective nature toward the other kids, even Christopher who was older than him by a year. Some people had teased and even attacked him for being Chinese because they thought he'd had something to do with the nukes. She guessed his real parents had been killed over that due to the way he freaked out whenever someone complained about Chinese people starting the war.

Christopher Dominguez, the oldest of their group at twelve,

probably also counted as the smartest. Mila regarded him as a bit of a nerd, but not in a bad way. The world needed some nerds if it would ever go back to normal. He possessed a gentleness that didn't seem terribly boy-like, which meant if anything happened, she'd likely have to protect him.

Madison had become something of her best friend. She'd been ruined by the loss of her parents, but had stopped being so weird and moody. Becca and Eva knew her from before, which sometimes left Mila feeling like an outsider whenever they talked about stuff that happened in the past. But, the girls all welcomed her into their circle, more so now that she'd given up the creepy act.

Lorelei, Mila thought of as a spastic kitten that kept trying to bite electrical wires or eat dangerous things. She had a hyperactivity and *loud* cheerfulness to her that routinely caused Mila to daydream about applying a little duct tape to her mouth or stuffing her in a bag, but the 'damaged kitten' part always made her feel too guilty to actually follow through. Like that annoying but lovable stray cat, she tolerated the little one tagging along. Also, despite finding the girl irritatingly loud and extroverted, she had a soft spot for her. If anyone messed with Lorelei, they'd regret it. Only *Mila* could stuff Lorelei in closets to keep her quiet. Or idly daydream about stuffing her in closets. She hadn't actually done that yet. While it would keep the girl safe from trying to pet a bear again, it wasn't nice.

Having actually *been* stuffed in a cell with tape over her mouth, hands and feet tied, Mila didn't want to do it to anyone else. That had sucked, big time.

"We can go swimming after we check this place out." Jonathan pointed ahead. "It's so far away from town, maybe the people who collected all the stuff missed it."

The last few hundred feet of road went up a relatively steep hill to a nice house at the top. They had to be at least a mile away from the center of town, at the *very* limit of Evergreen. Mila stopped at the loop in the road where it curved back on itself into a driveway, standing at the edge of the paving, her toes in dirt. She gazed down a hill dotted with trees at a road running past the bottom. To the right, it headed back toward Evergreen, but the other direction curved eastward past another really small town nestled beside it.

More than the little town, the wreckage of a passenger jet nearly slumped in a creek ditch beside the highway caught her eye, its nose pointing at her. The plane appeared to have mostly survived a crash landing, though most of its right wing had broken away. Two big yellow drapes stuck out of that side like giant hazard yellow curtains, one near the front and one at the back. Blackening covered the road behind it, suggesting a fire had burned big, but somehow, the plane itself had escaped the inferno.

"Whoa," said Jonathan, from her left.

"That's a plane." Christopher pointed. "It didn't explode. The pilot must have been trying to land."

"I think they missed the airport," deadpanned Mila.

"Why is a plane on the road?" asked Lorelei. "Planes aren't s'posed ta fly on roads."

"It crashed." Becca made a 'plane going down' gesture. "Sometimes they land on roads in emergencies."

"Oh." Lorelei twisted side to side, her dress flaring out. "They have a 'mergency?"

Obviously. Mila rolled her eyes, but didn't say anything.

"Yeah." Jonathan folded his arms, tapping his foot. "There might be neat stuff to check out. Better than a house."

"That's going outside town." Madison looked at him. "We're not supposed to leave town. Even this house is kinda far away."

"It's quiet. Nothing's moving down there." Jonathan pointed.

"If anything bad was down there, we'd know about it already. I think that's Kittredge." Christopher scrunched up his nose in thought. "Anyone down there would already have discovered Evergreen and moved in."

Eva squatted at the edge of the road, fussing at a dandelion. "Let's go to the pool instead of planes or houses."

"It's a *plane*," said Jonathan. "How can you not wanna check out a *plane?* We can see all the stuff they'd never let people see before. C'mon."

He darted off the road down the hill.

Madison looked at Mila with a 'we're gonna get in a ton of trouble' expression.

"Don't split up," shouted Christopher. When Jonathan didn't slow down, he emitted a nervous whine, then ran after him.

"Ugh." Becca grumbled and followed.

"Fine, whatever. But this is not gonna be my fault." Madison took Eva's hand and walked with her down the hill.

"Yay!" cheered Lorelei, before running after them.

Mila stood still for a moment, watching the distant wreck until the other kids disappeared into the forest. Reasonably confident that no one else would be down there, she pulled her necklace of leaf knives out from under her dress and let it fall against her chest. Harper either got permission to—or swiped—all the knives the Shadow Man and his friends carried for her. She had like forty of them back home, but carried five on the necklace she made. Hiding them under her clothes prevented adults from getting weird about a kid walking around with a bandolier of knives across their chest. She felt rather proud of herself for making the bunch of tiny sheaths from material she'd taken from old belts.

About a quarter-mile hike downhill through the woods ended at pavement. By the time Mila set foot on blacktop, the other kids had already reached the crashed plane. Up close, it looked in worse shape than it had seemed from up on the hill. The body broke in multiple places, more than half the wings had sheared off. The smashed remains of two engines sat on the road a long distance back, right in the middle of the burned area. It appeared the landing gear collapsed or hadn't come down all the way, causing the aircraft to bottom out and skid on its belly. The pilots had clearly attempted to land on a road far too narrow for a plane. They'd slid to a stop at the start of a curve in the road. The more-intact left wing stretched down into a burbling creek that followed a sunken channel alongside the highway. The right wing, only about a third the length it should have been, rested on a rocky hillside, atop a handful of trees it knocked down during the crash.

Jonathan and Christopher stood near the yellow thing hanging from the door on the nose end. It appeared to be an inflatable escape chute that had lost its air.

"C'mon." Jonathan grabbed the flexible yellow plastic and monkey-climbed it up to the open door.

"Be careful!" yelled Madison. "If you fall, you're going to break your legs."

Christopher went up next, followed by Becca. Eva whined, seeming scared. When Becca reached the door, the boys grabbed her by the arms and pulled her inside. Lorelei struggled for a while until she figured out how to get a grip on the deflated ramp with both arms and legs, then scurried up. As soon as the boys pulled her into the plane, Eva finally found the nerve to attempt the climb. Mila waited for her to go inside before following. The only way to get a grip on the limp chute required koala hugging it and shimmying up as if climbing a tree trunk that kept changing size. Not the most difficult climb Mila had been forced to make, but not the easiest either.

She grabbed the floor at the top and started to haul herself up, but, Jonathan and Christopher grabbed her wrists and pulled her in. Unsurprisingly, Jonathan didn't let go right away. Smiling might send too much encouragement, so Mila responded with a calm 'you may hold my hand' expression.

"Whoa, cool!" whispered Christopher.

The interior smelled funky, likely the combination of spilled jet fuel, mildew, and burned plastic. Jonathan bee-lined for the cockpit, practically dragging Mila along. She didn't much care about the plane or what they'd find as much as wanting everyone to get home unhurt. Exploring the inside of a crashed airplane didn't seem like the safest thing in the world, but she couldn't deny it had a strong sense of cool to it.

Jonathan flopped in the pilot's seat and played with the controls. To her absolute lack of shock, they didn't do anything. Much of the console had blackened, one of the screens even cracked. Maybe EMP had fried the plane in midair? The boy supplied jet engine noises and pretended to radio a control tower. Mila checked a few storage compartments, but they didn't contain anything more interesting than a small fire extinguisher that made her laugh. Considering the huge fire a plane crash would cause, an extinguisher the size of a soda bottle wouldn't be worth much.

The other kids made their way down the aisle, checking overhead bins. Many had already been opened and didn't contain much. Most likely, someone else had already raided the plane. Considering all the blackening on the road behind the aircraft, the original passengers would have been in far too much of a panic to get out before an explosion to care about their luggage.

Eventually, Jonathan grew bored with the cockpit. He got up and walked out into the aisle, hurrying toward where the other kids had collected. Mila trailed behind him, surveying all the empty seats. It relieved her to see that all the passengers made it off the plane alive. That had the added benefit of not having to hear Lorelei or Eva scream in disgust at finding a dead person.

She thought about Emmy finding the man on the farm. It impressed her that the girl who still cried at nightmares over the 'sky fire' brushed off seeing a corpse and more or less went right back to picking vegetables. *Everyone's a little messed up in the head.* Mila smiled at having company in the 'weird room.' No one had asked Mila about it, but she thought the guy on the farm had been attacked from behind. The look of the stab wounds made her picture someone grabbing him, giving him three quick inward jabs, then tossing the body down. Fast, clean, and quiet. The Shadow Man preferred going for the neck since ribs wouldn't get in the way there. But, it took longer for a man to die from a slit throat than a stab to the heart, so tradeoffs.

About midway down the length of the plane, the fuselage had snapped in half, broken into two separate pieces. They lay close enough together that even a child could step across the separation, climb down into the luggage compartment below the cabin, or even slip out a crack in the hull on the side nearer the creek. Going down there did not appear to be the safest thing in the world due to numerous jagged bits of metal sticking out at random spots plus exposed wires that might still have electricity... though Mila doubted that considering this thing crashed about a year ago. None of the other kids even hesitated in curiosity at the hole, stepping over it with barely a downward glance.

She stepped over the gap, cringing as her bare foot squished into wet carpeting. Rain had made it into the cabin due to the crack continuing around the outer wall to the ceiling. That explained the mildew smell. A few steps later on dry carpet, she paused long enough to wipe her foot, then approached the others, who all crowded into a tiny alcove containing a pushcart and micro-refrigerators. Becca and Eva rummaged the cart, picking among long-spoiled food and tiny bottles.

Christopher plucked a can out of one of the fridges and held it up. "Hey, this is beer."

Becca picked up a little bottle of brown liquid that looked like a toy version of real booze. "Tay-quell-something."

"Tequila," said Christopher, laughing. "Don't drink that. It'll knock you straight out. My dad says skinny blonde girls can't hold tequila. You should start off having a rum and coke."

Becca glanced at the bottle in her hand. "He's stupid. I'm holding tequila right now."

Mila face-palmed.

"Duh." Becca prodded her in the arm. "I'm kidding. I'm not *that* blonde. I know what he meant."

"We shouldn't drink any of this stuff." Madison plucked the tequila from Becca's hand and put it back on the cart. "We're too little. It will make us sick."

A low groan of stressed metal came from the entire aircraft along with a faint shudder that vibrated the floor.

"It's breathing," whispered Eva. Giant fearful brown eyes peered out from beneath a curtain of long, straight mouse-brown hair.

"It can't breathe. It's a machine." Jonathan looked up. "Gotta be the wind."

Mila grasped Jonathan's hand. "We should get out of here before it falls down the hill into the creek."

"It's not that far a fall. Like six feet. And there's a wing." Jonathan shrugged. "Don't be scared."

Mila smiled. "I'm not scared. I'm being practical. The wings are on the other piece. If this part rolls down the hill, we're going to get bounced around and hurt. It might even collapse and trap us under broken seats while it fills up with water and we drown."

Madison stared at her. "I thought you stopped saying creepy stuff."

Eva whimpered. "I wanna go back."

"I'm not trying to be creepy. That seriously might happen. I don't want to get hurt. And I don't want any of you guys to get hurt."

"Okay. Okay." Jonathan looked around. "We'll go. Umm. Where's Lore?"

"Crap," muttered Madison before yelling, "Lore!"

"I didn't even see her go anywhere." Becca flailed her arms. "Lorelei!?"

A faint murmur made Mila hold up a hand. "Shh!"

Everyone got quiet.

The murmur, less faint, came from across the aisle in the other pantry alcove. Mila walked in and gazed around at various cabinets and storage compartments. Thumping drew her attention to the lowest one on the left side, a door about the size of a beer fridge, though it didn't look like a fridge, just a storage cubby.

"Lore?"

"Yeah," said Lorelei from behind the door. "I can't get out."

Mila grabbed the latch and pulled, but couldn't budge it. She planted one foot on the wall, took hold of the latch in both hands, and strained, but succeeded only in leaving a footprint on the steel. "Damn. I think it bent during the crash. How did you get in there?"

"It was open before."

"Why did you close it?" Mila huffed.

"I dunno," said Lorelei.

Jonathan also strained at the hatch, but couldn't get it to open.

The frame had a slant that pinned the door in place.

"Look." Mila pointed. "The whole thing bent. Maybe that noise we heard was the plane changing shape, not the wind."

"Please let me out," said Lorelei.

"We're trying." Jonathan kicked the door—which didn't help at all since it opened outward.

Lorelei pounded on the inside, rattling the steel.

Madison paced around in a near panic muttering 'crap' over and over.

Christopher took a shot at opening the door. He, too, failed to pop it. "Everyone, look around for something to pry it with."

The kids spent a few minutes hunting for anything they could use as a crowbar, but came up empty.

"Okay, I don't care if we get in trouble. We gotta go back and get help." Madison patted the door. "Wait here, Lore. We'll come back as fast as we can with Dad or someone who can get you out."

"No!" wailed Lorelei, kicking and pounding on the door. "Please don't leave me alone."

"It's gonna take longer arguing than just going and getting an adult." Jonathan started walking down the aisle. "Just hide there. No one's gonna find you."

Lorelei burst into tears and pounded on the door from inside, cry-begging them not to leave her behind.

"Someone should stay here to keep an eye on her," said Christopher.

"We shouldn't split up." Madison looked back and forth between the departing Jonathan and the cabinet trapping her little sister. "She's got a safe place to hide where no one can get her. It's dangerous for someone to go alone back to town. We have to stay together."

"Maybe one of us could stay with her so she's not lonely and we could hide in a cubby?" Eva pulled open a nearby chamber, but found it too full of boxes of plastic cutlery to get inside.

"I'll stay." Mila patted her knives. "I'm the only one of us who has a chance if bad guys show up."

"Don't go," yelled Lorelei.

"I'm right here." Mila leaned on the door. "Relax."

Madison lingered as well.

"Go on. Harp will freak if you stay here." Mila nudged her.

"I don't wanna leave Lore alone."

"You're not leaving her alone. I'm here."

"Still. I wanna stay. That's my sister. Jonathan, Chris, Becca, and

Eva will be okay without me. Sec. Be right back." Madison followed the others, helping them climb out the door onto the deflated slide.

Mila folded her arms, leaning out of the pantry alcove to watch.

"Well now," said a man outside. "Look at that."

Eva screamed.

Mila's heart raced.

"What have we got here?" asked a different man. "'Mon down from there, sweetie."

Madison started to back up, but stopped abruptly with a gasp as Becca and Eva screamed again.

"You don't listen too well, do ya," yelled the man.

"Please don't shoot me." Madison raised her hands.

"What we gonna do with 'em, Melvin?" asked a third voice. "They're kinda little."

"Big enough to work," replied the man likely named Melvin. "C'mon, sweetie. Get on down here."

Madison turned to back out the door, sending a pleading stare down the aisle.

Mila yanked one of her leaf knives out of its sheath and mouthed, "Stall them."

8

BAD GUYS

Tears in her eyes, Madison lowered herself out the door.

Mila ran down the aisle, keeping her weight on her toes to be as quiet as possible.

"Come on, kid. Let go and drop down," said a man.

"I'm scared," whined Madison. "It's high up."

Grinning at the deception, Mila skidded to a stop at the crack in the floor. She peered back down the aisle at the tail door, but decided against that. The other escape chute also went to the road on the same side as the bad guys. If she went out that way, they would definitely see her before she could get close enough to do anything. Scaling the jagged metal of a broken airplane barefoot in a dress made for a dumb idea, too. But it beat letting her friends be kidnapped.

Mila squatted, braced her hands on the opposite side of the breach, and lowered her feet down to the least sharp place she could find. As careful as she could be while trying to hurry, she descended into the narrow gap. Her dress only snagged once, but came free without too much trouble. Men outside discussed how to keep the kids from running off and debated tying them together, but had no rope.

"Easy. If y'all run, I'm gonna shoot whoever's closest," said Melvin. "You don't want to be responsible for your friend getting killed, right? Behave yourselves and stay together."

Mila glowered at a pointy bit of metal sticking up in front of her face. *He's gonna lose an eye.*

She grabbed the bottom of the hollow compartment under the passenger cabin floor, a void space about twelve inches tall full of wires and cables. Her feet couldn't reach the bottom of the cargo deck, so she let herself hang by her fingertips. Most of the luggage must have all gone sliding toward the front of the plane, leaving the space below her sparsely packed. Dangling put her feet close to the floor, enough that she didn't think it would make too much noise to drop.

"You either climb or I'm gonna rip that damn plastic down," barked a man.

Madison wailed.

Her fear sounded only somewhat fake. She didn't really have that bad a problem with heights as far as Mila knew, though a guy did point a gun at her. *Harper is going to completely freak out.* Mila dropped to land on all fours like a ninja, then crawled to the opening in the side. The plane's fuselage had come to a halt right at the edge of the hill, leaving no pavement for her to step onto. She suffered a slight scratch on her left forearm as she slipped out to the cliff along the side of the creek. Ignoring the ouch, she crept to the right, closer to the voices. The plane sat on its belly, the landing gear broken, so it blocked her view. However, that also kept the men from seeing her. Mila pulled herself up onto the road and ran to the tail end closer to the Kittredge side. There, she crouched low and crawled far enough to peer around.

Four men stood around the cluster of her friends, herding them in like sheep. They looked somewhere between neo-tribal and biker gang that had spent months riding in a dust storm. Two of the guys had 'war paint' on their faces, probably motor oil or grease. One man held a pistol pointed up at Madison who koala-clung to the deflated chute only a little bit down from the airplane door. A shorter, potbellied guy held a katana. The third man, with curly red hair, slapped a wooden baseball bat into his left hand in a threatening manner while glaring up at Madison. The last man, thin and wiry, leaned on a fireman's axe like a cane.

Mila stared at Melvin, the only real threat due to the handgun. At least to her. She could outmaneuver the others enough to stay away from them. Since Madison screaming, crying, and carrying on absorbed the men's attention, Mila crept out from her hiding place and moved to her right, as far across the street as the steep hillside walling in the road allowed. The farther out of their peripheral vision she could get, the better.

The kids spotted her right away, but kept quiet. Jonathan swatted at Eva to get her to stop staring at Mila and possibly causing the men to wonder what had gotten her attention.

"Dammit, kid. Get the hell down now. Gonna give you three more seconds," shouted Melvin.

"Just grab it and shake. She'll fall." The potbellied guy laughed.

"Y'all need to calm down," said the man with the bat. "You ain't gonna be hurt or nothin'. Just workin'. Kids shouldn't be roamin' around out here on their own."

"We have a home," said Christopher. "And we don't want to go with you."

"Well, now, you're gonna have a different home." Melvin aimed at Madison. "Gonna clip you in the leg if you don't slide down right this second."

"Scatter!" yelled Christopher. "He can't shoot all of us."

The instant Melvin twitched to reorient his aim at the kids on the street, Mila whipped her leaf knife at his left eye.

"You ain't that fas—" Melvin screamed as the blade sank into his skull. He staggered back, fumbling the pistol and grabbing at his face, blood pouring between his fingers.

Mila sprinted at him, yanking another leaf knife from her necklace as she leapt, planting her feet on his thighs, grabbing his shoulder in one hand, and slicing him across the throat. She jumped down before he started to fall backward, somersaulted over the abandoned pistol to grab it, and rolled up onto one knee—shooting him almost point-blank in the face.

Brain and blood spattered out onto the pavement.

Mila whipped her arm up, aiming at the katana guy. "You have two seconds to go away or I will kill all three of you."

"You can quit acting creepy now," whispered Becca in a brittle voice.

Madison stopped crying and panicking—clearly an act—and slid down the yellow plastic to street level as fearlessly as a fireman going down a pole in a station.

"That wasn't creepy," said Jonathan. "That was *awesome.*"

"What now, Rhett?" whispered the man holding the bat while eyeing potbelly.

Rhett lunged to the side, grabbing Eva, pulling her up against his chest like a human shield. He started to move the katana toward her throat, but before the edge came close, Mila shot him in the left kneecap. He screamed, lurching over sideways. As soon as his ear hit the street, Mila shot him in the forehead.

Eva scrambled around to hide behind Christopher, refusing to look at the dead man.

Mila stood, walking toward the wiry axe-wielding man, aiming at his face. "You are still standing there and not going away. That must mean you wish for me to kill you. Three... Two..."

"Jesus freakin' Christ. This kid is psycho." He sprinted off down the road, the other guy running in the opposite direction, heading toward Kittredge.

Mila held her head high. "I'm not psycho. I'm just not afraid of idiots."

"Damn," whispered Jonathan. "You are amazing."

"How'd you get so good with a gun?" asked Christopher.

"I had to practice." Mila examined the weapon. The 9mm didn't hurt her hand as much as the .45 the Shadow Man made her use. She flicked the safety on. For now, she would carry it in case those guys came back, but she didn't want to keep it. Also, she doubted the militia would allow her to. At least, not until she got older. She crouched to pick up the knife she'd used to slice the guy's throat, and put it back in her 'necklace.'

Jonathan walked over to her. "You okay?"

"I'm fine." She glared down the road, trying to stay angry at those men so she didn't have to think about what she just did.

"You kinda look like you're upset."

Mila shifted to put her back to the other kids, but didn't hide her face from Jonathan. "The Shadow Man wanted me to shoot a guy in the head for training. He didn't do anything wrong. Just some poor man he kidnapped. I wouldn't do it, even though the Shadow Man beat me for refusing." She looked down, letting the gun hang at her side. "Being good at shooting doesn't mean I *like* killing. I've never killed anyone before. Stabbed, yes. But not killed. These men were gonna shoot Maddie and kidnap us all. They deserved it. I'm sad but not sad. These guys were bad and deserved being shot."

Jonathan hugged her. "You are awesome. That was like straight out of a movie."

"Do you think I'm psycho?" whispered Mila.

"No. Psychos *like* killing. You don't."

Mila smiled, feeling a little less guilty. "Okay."

"Are you still gonna stay here to watch Lorelei?" Jonathan looked toward the road. "Might not be safe. Those guys could come back and bring friends."

"Umm." Mila crouched and yanked her other leaf knife out of Melvin's eye, then wiped it clean on his shirt.

Jonathan picked up the katana. "Mine now."

"That's a Japanese sword. You're Chinese," said Christopher.

"What's your point?" Jonathan smirked.

Christopher laughed. "Just saying. You're the Chinese ninja."

"Ninjas are Japanese," said Becca, her back turned to the dead people. "And that's a samurai sword. Ninja's didn't carry katanas. They had straight swords. Can we please go away from dead people now? I really wanna go home."

"How the heck do you know that?" Christopher stared at her.

"We watched a ton of anime," said Madison, striking an odd pose with Becca—probably something from a cartoon.

"Mila's a ninja." Jonathan grinned.

"Yeah, no kidding." Christopher whistled.

"Hey!" shouted Lorelei from the aircraft door.

Everyone looked up at her.

"You got out?" asked Jonathan.

"The gunshot scared me and I kicked the cubby really, really hard. It opened." Lorelei crouched as if about to jump down.

Christopher, Jonathan, and Madison scrambled to grab the bottom of the chute and pull it away from the plane so it became something of a slide again. Lorelei dropped, slid down the yellow plastic, and crashed into them like a living bowling ball. The kids fell in a heap, but no one got hurt beyond a momentarily painful bump.

"Can we go home now?" asked Eva. "I'm gonna throw up."

"Don't look at the brains on the road," said Christopher.

Eva retched, doubled over, and gagged.

"Stop that!" shouted Becca. "There aren't any brains on the road."

"Yeah. I wanna go home, too." Madison picked Lorelei up.

Mila waved at everyone to get going. "Yeah. We should get outta here fast. The gunshot might make more bad guys come looking."

9

BAD DREAMS

Harper decided to try a taste of extreme normality once her patrol ended.

Upon returning home, she changed from her jeans and T-shirt outfit to a plain white sun dress and went barefoot. The much lighter, airier outfit made the July day almost tolerable without air conditioning and gave her the illusion of being an ordinary young woman in a world where nothing catastrophic had happened.

She daydreamed about her first time with Logan, clinging to the much-needed happiness. Both Renee and Grace had been getting on her case about her constantly navel-gazing over the direction life had gone. They had a point. Of course, having her parents murdered right in front of her left a mark, a shock not easily set aside. She couldn't tell what had been more of a jolt to her system — witnessing that, or a girl like her being put in a situation where she had to kill someone.

Either way, it happened. She wasn't the same kid who started her senior year of high school a week before everything died. Renee said she'd been 'hardened.' Harper didn't fully agree since she couldn't kill anyone or anything and not feel remorse. She *could*, however, defend herself or others and not feel — much — remorse. Considering the overly sweet, timid place she started off, maybe that still counted as hardened.

Regardless, today she decided to be happy and normal. Her parents would not want her wasting her life in a constant state of sorrow. And, after ten months, she had finally reached a point where not being miserable didn't feel like she failed to show sufficient respect to their memory. Mom probably wouldn't have been happy she basically had sex before graduating college, but after that initial shock wore off, she'd most likely have wanted gossip. She and Logan had come pretty close to having sex… what they did probably counted as it, even if she'd been too frightened to let him go all the way, especially without a condom. But… what they *had* done went well beyond making out. Her parents would probably consider it sex. Also, they would likely have approved of Logan. Father and older sibs in the military, respectful, polite, caring.

She sighed wistfully, wanting to be with him, wondering if she'd ever be ready to risk breaking down that one last barrier. Harper didn't distrust him or fear him as much as she dreaded what might happen to her if she got pregnant. She dreaded the effect her death during childbirth would have on Madison… but she also held onto some hope her fears were exaggerated.

Keeping a shotgun in arms' reach did break the sense of normality a little bit, but such was the world she lived in. Like some kind of happy housewife from the 1960s, Harper hummed to herself while collecting vegetables for dinner. Cliff planned to bring home a chicken tonight, which they'd work on for a day or two. Despite the town's food situation—one calamity away from starving—she still didn't want anything to do with killing a chicken or even watching it die. While she wouldn't cry over it like Madison, she couldn't bring herself to kill an innocent animal. Thankfully, Cliff would take care of that part.

She arranged the vegetables and got to slicing them.

A few minutes later, the front door flew open hard.

Expecting the militia to have come looking for her about a problem, Harper dropped the knife and spun, reaching for the Mossberg so she could run out to see what happened—but stopped short at the sight of the kids rushing inside. Jonathan had a katana and Mila carried a handgun. The weapons didn't alarm Harper as much as the sight of blood spritz on Mila's face.

"Crap," rasped Harper. "What happened?"

The kids ran over to her. Madison clamped on, almost but not quite trembling. Eva looked ready to melt into a puddle of anxiety. She eyed the door like she wanted to run home to her mother but didn't want to be alone that long. Also, her mother would likely be working. Becca shivered, but her expression didn't appear too freaked out. Both Jonathan and Christopher had the wide-eyed look of boys who had seen the coolest thing in the world.

Mila had an 'ugh it's Monday' expression.

"What's going on?" asked Harper. "Mila?"

She held up the gun. "You're going to take this away from me anyway, so here."

Harper glanced down at a Beretta 92. "Smells like powder. You shot someone?"

"Yes. Two men."

"We're sorry," whimpered Madison. "We broke the rule."

"Okay." Harper held her hands up. "Slow down. What rule? What happened?"

Jonathan took a deep breath. "We went house exploring, and walked out on Hidden Village Drive to that place all the way at the end. Only, we didn't go inside. Down the hill, we saw a crashed plane. So we wanted to check it out."

"We went outside town." Madison sniffled, exhaled, and appeared to collect her emotions. "Not by that much. Maybe Kittredge is still part of Evergreen? I dunno."

"We went inside the plane to look around. There's some beer and alcohol, and a couple bits of luggage left but we didn't get a chance to look inside them." Mila grasped Lorelei by the collar of her dress and pulled her over.

The little blonde girl grinned, then waved at Harper. "Hi!"

"Lore crawled into a storage cabinet and got stuck." Mila grabbed her in a headlock from behind. "She scared us to death. We couldn't get her out, so they were going to run back here to get help while I stayed with her."

"But, when we got out of the plane, bad guys found us." Jonathan held up the katana. "One of them had this. Another guy had the gun. They threatened to shoot us if we ran and wanted to kidnap us and make us work."

Harper gasped. She grabbed her three siblings—plus Mila since she'd been standing close—into a hug. "Dammit. I don't want you guys going that far outside town again, okay?"

"No way." Eva shook her head rapidly. "I don't even wanna go house exploring anymore. I'm gonna stay right in the yard."

"Yeah." Becca ground her toes into the floor. "Me too."

Mila explained how she snuck out of the plane and ambushed the bad guys while Madison stalled them by pretending to be too scared to climb down. When she described shooting the guy in the head, a little twitch in her lip poked Harper straight in the feels. She'd probably made that same facial twitch the first time she'd pulled the trigger on a Lawless. But at least she'd been seventeen... not ten. Much less ten years old for only a few days. That still counted as being nine.

"That was incredibly brave of you." Harper put a hand on Mila's shoulder. "You okay?"

"Yeah. Mostly."

Harper ran around checking all the kids over for injuries while asking them repeatedly what the men did to them. Fortunately, it sounded as though they'd only been forced to stand in a group waiting for Madison to climb down. Christopher and Eva had been grabbed and shoved around, though neither suffered even a bruise. Harper hated that Mila had to kill two men, but couldn't say she didn't approve of their deaths. Had she been there and seen a guy point a gun at Madison, she'd totally have fed him buckshot.

"Okay. You guys stay in the yard for the rest of the day. Or inside if you want." Harper set her hands on her hips. *I'm going to have to report this. Dammit. There goes normal. Let me tell Cliff first. I don't need to run right out the door. He'll be back soon.*

With slightly shaky hands, Harper resumed preparing dinner

while the kids went out to the backyard. Eva and Becca sat on the porch together, not seeming interested in playing Frisbee or soccer. Lorelei zoomed around, unfazed. Then again, she hadn't seen the violence or even the men. Madison kept her attention and carried her away from the scene so she didn't see or touch the dead guys. Mila, as well, didn't look too enthusiastic about the Frisbee throwing, but still participated. Probably to take her mind off what she'd done.

I should ask Tegan to talk to her. She's not a psychiatrist, but she's as close as we have. Harper chuckled. *This entire town is full of people who need shrinks.*

CLIFF ARRIVED HOME LATER THAT AFTERNOON CARRYING AN already-dead chicken by the legs.

He whistled like some sort of hayseed farmer, swinging the bird idly side to side on the way in the door. Harper laughed at the sight, which got a playful narrow-eyed glower from him. Not long after he returned, Mrs. Parsons came to collect Eva, who leapt into a hug and exploded in tears.

Cliff looked up from plucking the bird with a 'something happened, didn't it' expression.

Harper nodded to him, then pulled the woman aside to give her a quick explanation. Mrs. Parsons also declared that Eva wasn't allowed to go anywhere near the edge of town. The girl tearfully replied she didn't want to and promised not to do it again. Becca, Christopher, and Mila left to go home, walking with Mrs. Parsons as well since they all lived a bit north in the area Harper usually patrolled.

Harper sat on the back porch watching her siblings playing in the yard while Cliff finished cleaning the bird. In a rare moment of convenience, the power decided to be working that day, so the chicken went into the oven. Carrie and Renee came over, bringing a large portion of potato salad.

Cliff leaned out the back door. "There's something you need to tell me."

Here we go. Harper stretched her legs out, toes splayed. "Yeah."

"Want to come inside or should I have a seat?"

"That depends. Is this about why Eva freaked out or about Logan?"

"What about Logan?" asked Cliff, leaning farther out the door.

"Oops. Never mind." Harper patted the porch beside her. "We can talk out here."

Cliff emerged from the doorway and sat on the step. "So what happened to Logan?"

"Not *to* him." Harper gave him side eye. "Come on. You can guess. You've been giving me weird looks ever since Saturday."

"Ahh." He nodded. "Well, as your father, I'm contractually obligated to be completely opposed to you doing anything of a sexual nature until you're past forty."

Harper chuckled.

"However, I am not beyond reasoning that you are eighteen and this is a different world." He put a hand on her shoulder. "Just be careful, okay?"

"I will. It felt right." She smiled.

"You love the kid?"

"Yeah. I do." She hugged her knees to her chest, smiling.

Cliff's mood brightened. "All right. If he breaks your heart, I'll break his legs."

"Thanks, Dad." She laughed.

"So what happened with the rugrats?" He gestured a thumb toward the kids.

She explained the story.

"That explains the '92 on the counter."

"Yeah."

He exhaled. "You really think that girl shot two men?"

"I do. Saw it in her eyes. And she had blood on her. She totally didn't want to do it, but didn't hesitate."

"Gee. That sounds familiar."

She stuck out her tongue. "She's only nine."

"Didn't we have a tenth birthday for her a couple days ago?"

"Pff. She had a birthday on the nineteenth. It's the twenty-third. She's still nine."

"That's not how it works. Midnight on the eighteenth, she's ten."

Harper fake pouted. "I still think of her as nine."

"Slow down there, Mom."

She sighed. "Yeah, yeah. She's too little to kill anyone."

"I agree, but between some jackass putting a bullet into one of the kids or one of the kids putting a bullet into some jackass, I'll take option two."

"Definitely."

"So, plane crash. Where'd you say that was?"

Harper scratched her head. "Umm. Sounded like right outside Kittredge. The plane was halfway into a little river."

"Oh, that's gotta be Bear Creek Road." He patted his knee. "I'll take a couple guys out there after we eat to check it out."

"Okay. Want me to come?"

"If you want, but I think the kids would rather have you around. Besides, we'll just be scraping some roadkill off the highway." He looked up, watching Lorelei run by making a doll fly like Superwoman. "The kid's unflappable. Damn nuclear war could happen and she wouldn't even notice."

"Hah."

OVER DINNER, CLIFF BROUGHT UP THE CRASH SITE AGAIN, MOSTLY to muse aloud how the militia hadn't mentioned it before.

"They probably know," said Jonathan. "Most of the luggage was missing. Someone already looted it, but they left behind a bunch of beer and alcohol."

"Strange." Cliff stabbed his fork into a hunk of chicken. "Figure the booze would be the first thing they take."

"Maybe they thought the plane could explode again, so they didn't go inside except for the cargo area?" Harper shrugged.

"Grownups couldn't get inside too easy," said Jonathan. "We had to climb up this plastic stuff hanging from the doors."

Harper shrugged. "Pretty sure they scavenged the hell out of Kittredge since it's so close."

"Without a doubt. Damn sure that plane didn't fall out of the sky recently." Cliff wagged his eyebrows. "In fact, might even be some people from that flight living here. Maybe in the south part."

She nodded.

Jonathan re-told the story of what happened, but made Mila sound like some kind of anime ninja terminator.

After dinner, Cliff headed out to round up some militia and go check on the site. He'd also pass along word to Walter that a 'tribal' type gang may have moved into the area and could be a problem. The kids' description of being carted off to 'work' somewhere suggested the four men had come from a larger encampment, probably one with a farm. It didn't seem likely anyone ran a factory or mine, so the 'work' in question almost certainly involved agriculture or survival.

Harper and Carrie did the dishes while the kids plus Renee went out to the yard to play in the last of the daylight.

"You were right. I'm sorry," said Carrie.

"No, it's fine. It wouldn't have happened if they listened to the rule and stayed inside town."

Carrie gave a sad chuckle. "Yes, but I should have expected kids would break a rule like that. Never had any little ones of my own. This parenting thing is new to me."

"Well, you should get used to it. They're kind of thinking of you as Mom now and me as big sis."

"That's flattering. You know, I'm not trying to replace your mother."

"I know." Harper smiled at her. "But it is kinda nice having someone around who's kinda like a mother… if you don't mind it."

Carrie grinned. "Not at all, but don't expect perfection. Like I said, no practice."

"That might not be true forever. You're what, thirty-five? The way you and Dad 'spend time together,' I'm pretty sure I'm going to have another sibling sometime soon."

"Oh, dear." Carrie blushed. "I'm not having this conversation with my daughter, am I?"

"We don't have to." Harper offered a blasé shrug. "And yeah, I suppose I shouldn't be making jokes about my technical parents in bed."

"Technically not. That's supposed to make you squirm even thinking about." Carrie whistled innocently.

"I'll get right on that. Squirming I mean." She grinned.

HARPER SAT ON THE BACK PORCH WATCHING THE KIDS CHASE A ball around.

Renee's work at the quartermaster had exhausted her, so she went inside to sleep early. Carrie sat in the living room, waiting for Cliff to return home, probably reading.

"Harper?" asked Mila—right behind her.

"Gah!" Harper jumped. "Where the hell did you come from?"

"Aspen."

"Dork." Harper smirked. "You know what I mean."

"Walked around the house. Can I sit here?"

"Of course."

Mila sat next to her. "Can I ask you a question?"

"Anything. Except stuff you're not old enough to know yet."

An almost smile formed on the girl's lips. "Do you have bad dreams about shooting people?"

"Sometimes, yeah." Harper let a long sigh out her nose. "But I've had worse dreams about the one guy I didn't shoot. Couldn't bring myself to kill a guy even though he was pointing a gun at me. I used to be a bit of a chicken. 'Too squishy' as my friends would say. But, yeah… I do sometimes have nightmares about the people I've had to shoot."

Mila bowed her head. "I'm sorry."

"For?"

"Shooting people. But they were gonna hurt my friends. I didn't wanna do it, but I had to."

Harper put an arm around her, pulling her into a hug. "I know exactly how you feel."

"Am I going to have bad dreams?"

"Maybe. You're too young to be in that situation. I'd be worried if you *didn't* have a nightmare or two about it. Don't freak out if you do, though. Bad dreams are normal. Having a nightmare about something that scary only means your brain is working right."

"So I'm not psycho?"

"Nope." Harper made a face off to the side, thinking of what Renee said. "We're just... hardened."

"What's that mean?"

"It means we saw crap that people our age aren't supposed to see and it changed us so we can survive it. Nothing to be ashamed of."

"Okay. Thanks." Mila looked up at her. "I'm sorry for not making them stop."

"Stop?"

"Going to the plane. I think Jonathan would've listened if I demanded he not go."

Harper chuckled. "Yeah, I think so, too."

"If you want to ground me or punish me for breaking the rule, it's okay."

"You've punished yourself enough already. But... if you think you deserve more... wear pink tomorrow."

"Eep. Couldn't you just like hit me on the ass with a board or something?"

"You're too young to say 'ass,' and no. I don't want to hit you."

"But pink!" Mila thrust her arms out to either side. "That's cruel."

"Didn't say you had to. Just if you thought you deserved to."

Mila fake wiped sweat from her forehead. "Whew. That wasn't a big enough rule break to warrant punishment that severe."

"Wow. You really hate pink."

Mila rolled her eyes. "You have *no* idea."

"Right."

"Harper?"

"Yeah?"

"I shot two guys. I think I can say 'ass' now. Not like it's an f-bomb."

Harper sighed. "Okay, but don't abuse the privilege."

"Promise." Mila held up her hand. "And I'll also keep Jonathan in town."

"There we go. That's the punishment. You guys should stay within eyesight of the house for a week."

"I think they're gonna do that, anyway. Everyone's freaked out." Mila scuffed her feet back and forth. "I am, too. Being kidnapped really sucks. And there are more of those guys. They're gonna come back for revenge, aren't they? Should I have killed all four of them so they didn't know who did it?"

"No. If they ran away or surrendered and you still shot them, it would've been murder, not self-defense."

"But killing them when they come back for revenge is self-defense?"

"Exactly." Harper grumbled. "That makes it their choice, not yours. Let's hope they're not that stupid."

"They painted their faces with motor oil. They *are* that stupid." Mila frowned.

"Right. You guys stay near the house until further notice."

"Okay."

Harper looked over in surprise. "Wow. No protest?"

"I'm precociously adult and brave, but not stupid."

"Hah! You are too much."

Mila smiled. "I know."

10

ABSOLUTION

After what happened at the crash site, Harper expected Madison to have a bit of a breakdown that night. Her sister didn't really freak out, though she did seem more reserved as no trace of goofiness or whimsy showed itself. Lorelei behaved as though nothing whatsoever happened.

Even with the window wide open, the July night made co-sleeping uncomfortably warm even wearing a nearly insubstantial nightgown. Lorelei decided even that was too hot and crawled into bed only wearing underpants. She also crashed face down on top of Harper, arms splayed out like a crime victim who'd fallen off the roof of a tall building. The kid passed out in mere moments. Never before had she been jealous of a six-year-old.

How can such a little girl be so damn heavy?

With Madison attached to her left arm and Lorelei on top of her, Harper felt like a hiker trapped under a boulder after an avalanche. Of course, she made no effort to escape. The little one clearly trusted her and demanded affection to fill the void left behind by her horrible bio mom.

Never thought I'd have kids until I graduated college. She fussed at the girl's pale blonde hair, taken by a sudden sense of inadequacy. Any little screw-up she committed could forever change the person this tiny human grew into. But… she set that fear aside after only seconds. Nothing she could possibly be capable of doing would be as bad as what the girl's real mother did to her.

Aside from snuggling a little closer than usual, Madison appeared to have taken the attack in stride. It could mean that after watching their parents die, pretty much nothing else could be bad enough to leave an emotional wound—short of watching Harper shot to death. Of course, it could also mean that her kid sister had broken deep down inside and the relatively happy-slash-normal version of her that had been running around for the past several months a pretend mask.

In a reversal that came straight out of nowhere, Mila seemed more affected by it than Madison. The creepy, overly mature little goth girl who made sarcastic jokes about death showed more emotional response than a formerly kinda spoiled suburban kid who used to freak out like being late to dance class would kill her.

Maddie didn't shoot two men in the head. Mila's just showing that she's a real person.

Harper stopped staring at her ceiling by closing her eyes. She had no idea if ghosts or any kind of afterlife existed, but she still sent out a mental projection to the universe asking her mother to help her not screw up. The idea that Lorelei could probably watch someone blown to bits by a hand grenade, then merrily charge into the gore to pick up something pretty and shiny almost made her laugh.

Seriously, this kid isn't even afraid of giant bears. She yells 'fuzzy' and tries to pet them… 'course, she did the same to Dennis when he grew a beard.

Worrying what to do with a small army of emotionally disturbed children, Harper drowned in anxiety and sweat until at last, she found herself lying on the floor without the crushing weight of a too-thin six-year-old on top of her. Madison and Lorelei working together in a fitful sleep might have kicked her out of the bed, but that had never happened before.

Harper sat up and stared around at her old bedroom, conspicuously lacking a giant hole ripped in the ceiling from a chunk of debris. She gazed at the spot that had been open to the sky the last time she'd seen it. A piece of concrete the size of a Prius had landed right on her bed, smashing it into the floor, which had nearly given out and fallen into the downstairs.

All her stuff remained as she remembered, though it had a strange blurry quality. She stood, turning in place, staring at old shooting competition trophies, pictures of her parents, the computer desk, stuffed animal army, bookshelves, dresser, the pink faerie music box 'Madison' gave her for her fifteenth birthday. Technically, Mom bought it, but her sister picked it out, being only seven at the time.

"Yeah. This is definitely a dream."

Some of this stuff, she'd gotten back thanks to Cliff, but she hadn't the heart to put it out on display. Partly because she didn't really want to be surrounded by painful memories, but also she didn't have a room to herself. Setting up all her old stuff would feel too much like creating a shrine to a life she could never get back. Or worse, denying anything happened by remaking her old bedroom.

"Wonder where this dream is going."

Harper looked around for a shotgun, but in this world, it never left Dad's gun safe unless they went to the range or a competition. In this world, no one randomly kicked in doors and tried to take your stuff. At least, that sort of thing didn't happen in Lakewood, Colorado.

She went out into the hallway, looking around at the house she remembered. Knowing she dreamed it steeled her emotionally, so she didn't surrender to hope that the apocalypse had been a nightmare. *This* house felt unreal... but she still remembered every stain on the wall, imperfection in the carpet, and all of Mom's little bluebird paintings in silver frames.

Is this my brain gathering up memories for long term storage? Harper went down the hall to the bathroom. *Yeah, I'm not Riley Anderson. If I've got little people operating a control room inside my head, they're all alcoholics by now. Sadness probably died from exhaustion.*

Madison's toothbrush lay out on the sink counter, lazily dropped wherever it fell as she usually did when finished. A crumpled pair of leggings plus underwear sat on the rug where her sister changed.

Harper imagined Mom shouting at her to pick up after herself. *That* finally caused a twinge of sorrow. Even if the woman shouted at them, she'd have given anything to hear her voice one more time.

Curious about her sister, she backed out of the bathroom and poked her head into Madison's room. Not a single spot of rug showed beneath a layer of clothes and dolls. The bed, the neatest thing in the room, remained made and unoccupied. Her sister's room had usually been messy, but this looked extreme. A distortion of her memory, perhaps?

"Why am I dreaming about the old house? Is this me finally coping or am I afraid I'm forgetting?"

Harper continued to explore the upstairs, surprising herself at the amount of detail. It didn't really feel like she had control of where she went or what she looked at. The dream took her on a tour wherever it cared to. Mostly, her mood remained wistful but in control. Remembering what once was didn't need to make her miserable. Happiness did not dwell exclusively in the past. While she would much rather the world hadn't blown itself apart, the notion that she'd probably come to accept things hit her.

This dream is me dealing with crap.

When she reached the stairs down, anxiety reared up. The calm wandering of her old house would soon turn into a nightmare of blood and violence, or so she feared. Her dream self, fully apart from any conscious control, descended to the living room. Madison's dolls littered the floor in front of the television along with a scattering of PlayStation stuff. Still, no one else appeared to be in the house. Everything looked normal except for the windows, which had become black and impenetrable.

She crept across the living room to the dining room.

As soon as she reached the spot where she'd been standing when the Lawless thug booted in the front door, Dad appeared in front of her, transparent and glowing blue. Harper stared at him, almost wanting to make a Ben Kenobi joke about how he looked. That her first reaction to the sight of her father's ghost was laughter set off a wild tangle of emotions, but she still ended up laughing more than anything else.

"Hey, kiddo."

"Dad?"

Mom appeared beside him, also ghostly. "We're proud of you, dear."

"Very." Dad smiled. "You are doing great. Much better than either of us could have hoped for."

"That little blonde girl is so precious." Mom smiled. "You are her entire world. It's a big responsibility, but it's totally worth it."

"I don't know what I'm doing, Mom." Harper tried to hug her parents, but they had no substance.

Dad chuckled.

"That's normal." Mom made a silly face. "You didn't pop out of me with a user's manual in your hands. I had no damn idea what to do either at first."

"You had Google though." Harper frowned.

"The internet just makes things easier, not possible," said Dad. "There are plenty of people around you with experience. Mrs. Wheatley for example. I understand you're on the shy side, but talk to people. Don't be afraid to call in reinforcements. Parenting can be rough. There's no need to take it all on yourself."

"We're really proud of you." Mom brushed a spectral hand at Harper's hair, creating a faint electrical tingle down her cheek.

"You're not even upset that I've had to kill people?" Harper fidgeted.

Dad shrugged. "We're upset you *had* to, not that you did. Protecting yourself is nothing to be ashamed of. We hate that you've lost that innocence, but it's much, much better than losing you."

Rather than cry, Harper found herself feeling reassured. "Whew."

"You know." Dad put an arm around her shoulders. "Sometimes life throws you off a cliff and there isn't a whole lot you can do about it."

"Except grow wings," said Mom. "Even if they're little and only slow the fall."

"Yeah." Harper closed her eyes, imagining herself as a faerie.

She'd been obsessed with them for most of her life, though not to the point she believed they really existed. *I will fly.*

"It's time." Dad's hand on her shoulder gained solidity, offering a reassuring pat. "The only thing you will accomplish by clinging to the past is feeling bad about the future. Don't compare where you are now to the world that used to exist. You got this, Harp."

She bowed her head. "Thanks, Dad. I'm trying… I really am."

"Harper?"

"Yeah?" She cringed.

"What happened here was *not* your fault. I'm proud to have raised a daughter with such a great respect for life that she couldn't even kill a man pointing a gun at her. You went from a school to a warzone overnight. Don't be ashamed of being normal." Dad took a step back. "I'd take a bullet to protect you again and again and again. It's what Dads do. I forbid you to feel guilty about it."

Harper looked up, but the spirits had disappeared.

The silence in her old house hung on her shoulders like a lead apron.

She knew she basically talked to herself. These ghost parents weren't really the spirits of her murdered mother and father coming back to speak to her. The apparitions had formed out of all the memories she had of them, said what she thought they'd say… and what she needed to hear. Even if the words came from inside her own mind, hearing them said in his voice offered a much-needed sense of absolution. She'd finally forgiven herself.

"Hope you guys are okay."

One last time, Harper looked around at the dream world of her old house. "I really am gonna miss this place, but this isn't where I belong anymore."

11

TRACKS

Tuesday, late morning, Harper took a short break from patrolling her usual area to visit the farm. Mostly, she wanted to check in on her siblings as well as Mila, Becca, and Eva. Over breakfast that morning, Cliff relayed that they'd found the two men dead in the road where they'd fallen, so they decided to burn the remains—much easier than burying them.

While the militia *had* made multiple scavenging runs into Kittredge prior to Harper and company arriving in Evergreen, they'd avoided going into the upper portion of the jet out of concern it would collapse or slide into the water if disturbed. Cliff, Dennis, Ken, and Marcie all came back loaded up with luggage, more clothing for the quartermaster to hand out.

The kids all seemed in good spirits. They resembled country bumpkins in dirty clothes, barefoot, and smiling—except Mila, who had a grim expression. Even Jonathan left his sneakers home today. Despite the haze in the air, the sun decided to work overtime, hot to the point that even Harper considered walking patrol in a skirt so she didn't melt. However, skirts and dresses wouldn't work too well if she got into a gunfight, foot chase, or brawl. They'd either tangle her up, slow her down, or result in her showing off more of herself than she wanted.

So, she suffered the heat of jeans.

Madison seemed normal, though Mila had a look about her like she'd done something really wrong and waited to get in big trouble. Harper pulled her aside from the group feeding chickens, standing at the edge of the crude fence made of scrap metal and wood.

"It gets easier," said Harper in a low voice.

"I know."

"You're not going to get in trouble. You did the right thing. Good people have to do horrible things sometimes now. Don't let it eat you up inside."

"Mom was upset. She cried all night." Mila jabbed her toes at the dirt. "Don't know if she was more freaked out that I almost got kidnapped or that I shot two guys."

Harper put a hand on the back of Mila's head, pulling her into a hug. "You're way behind. I'm at least up to twelve now."

"It's not a video game." Mila squirmed. "And don't hug me when people can see. They'll think I'm girly."

"Heh." Harper let go. "You can tell them I hugged you despite your protest."

Mila smiled, but didn't let go of the hug. "So I'm really not in trouble?"

"No. You're not going to get in trouble for defending yourself. People are just struggling to deal with a world in which a kid your age has to do that in the First World."

"Umm, Harper... we're not in the First World anymore. It kinda burned down."

She exhaled hard. "Yeah. Good point."

"The Shadow Man wanted me to kill someone to show him I could do it. I refused."

"Yes, you told me."

Mila looked up at her, a hint of worry in her eyes. "Am I an assassin now?"

"No. It's completely different to kill someone who doesn't deserve to die than it is to protect yourself and your friends. It's very possible to pull the trigger on someone and still *hate* having to do it."

"Okay. I'll try not to get any more psycho then. I still don't wanna kill anyone."

Harper ruffled her hair. "Good."

Mila ran back to resume tending chickens.

Satisfied that the kids appeared to be okay, Harper made her way east, intending to return to her patrol area… but detoured on a whim to the spot where Eva found Weldon's body. Lacking the chaos of a crowd or the mental pressure of having a dead man right in front of her, she examined the area, trying to recall what Cliff had taught her about tracking.

Marks in the dirt suggested the corpse's heels had been dragged along. She spotted a few broken leaves hanging from the tomato plants. Along with the drag path, they suggested a route someone took to reposition the body after death.

Maybe I watched too many cop shows, but I don't think this happened here.

Harper crept along the trail she believed she'd found, out the end of the row and left. Though she lacked full confidence in her interpretation of the gouges in the dirt, she did follow the trail enough to get the feeling it would lead away from the farm, west into the hills. The farm occupied a swath of formerly empty field on the opposite side of Route 74 from the golf club, quite close to the school and the residential area she usually patrolled.

As she neared the edge of the farm area, the trail mostly disappeared under signs of more recent activity from those working on the farm. The line she'd walked pointed straight, so even without a clear trail, it hinted that the killing occurred off the farm.

"Why would a killer drag the body *into* the farm where it would definitely be found?"

She thought that point over on the walk back to her patrol route. Most killers went out of their way to prevent anyone from finding the victim's body. It could be they had a total nut on their hands who wanted their work discovered to scare people or as a point of pride. Or, maybe Weldon had been killed in a location that would make the killer's guilt obvious. That still didn't explain why they moved the dead man into such an obvious high-traffic place. No one—as far as she knew—lived in the hills right to the west of the farm, so there went the idea that he'd been killed in his sleep.

It also didn't sound plausible that someone would've dragged Weldon all the way up here from the area where farm workers who didn't have kids lived. Perhaps if they had a cart or wheelbarrow, but the body had clearly been dragged, heels on the ground. A hunting accident also didn't make any sense as people generally didn't attack deer with knives at close range. Never mind the idiocy of thinking someone jumped on a guy, mistaking him for venison. Someone killed him on purpose out in the middle of nowhere and didn't want him found near that spot for some reason.

That meant the place of death would either implicate the killer's identity or had some other significance to the murderer that he or she wanted to conceal.

Okay. Not a random act of violence. I don't think we've got a crazy person in town.

She mulled various explanations. Perhaps Weldon had gotten into a fight at Earl's bar or had some other personal conflict with someone. Roy Ellis would no doubt be looking into that angle already, talking to everyone who might have seen Weldon on his last day alive. Considering how recently he'd arrived in Evergreen, the most probable source of bad blood would be the people he arrived with. Or, he might have been caught in the wrong woman's bed, killed by a jealous man.

Harper chuckled to herself. *Yeah, I'm not in a regency romance novel here.*

Trusting that Roy would figure it out, she resumed walking her patrol route. Most of the residents were out at whatever jobs they'd been given or volunteered for, though she did run into a handful of elders. They all asked her about Mr. Beasley, mostly wanting to confirm the rumors that he'd been killed by the same guy who got Weldon on the farm. Apparently, fear had been spreading around Evergreen that they had a serial killer on the loose.

Harper did her best to assure everyone who approached her to talk about Mr. Beasley understood he suffered a heart attack—and had not become a second victim of a killer. As tightly wound as the guy had been, it made sense that he suffered such a fate. Plus, she suggested anyone who didn't believe her could go talk to the doctors. Doreen Mack, the once-overweight former day care owner who now looked after Evergreen's tiniest orphans, quipped that she 'should probably lay off the cheeseburgers' so she didn't have a heart attack.

As if fast food still existed.

Harper laughed. "Yeah... all that grease will kill ya."

12

COPING

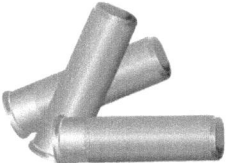

L ater that afternoon once her patrol shift ended, Harper decided to throw an hour at practicing with the compound bow. Her backyard offered limited range, so she set up a target out on Hilltop Drive in front of the houses at about fifty yards. The straight section of road didn't exactly make for the safest or wisest place to fire a bow and arrow. However, if she missed, the shot would skip down the paving and hit either dirt or trees. She had enough visibility into the distance that she felt comfortable being able to avoid accidentally hitting anyone walking on the road.

The kids in the area, mostly just her siblings since school-age children all lived quite a ways north from her house, didn't make a habit of darting randomly across the street. Her siblings and their friends presently ran around in the area behind the house, going back and forth between Carrie's yard and theirs, playing soccer.

Harper still laughed at Lorelei's idea for teams. Christopher suggested the old standby of 'shirts and skins' to tell teams apart despite girls outnumbering boys. Lorelei took that in a predictable direction and flung her dress off. Fortunately, Madison intervened and they didn't start the Evergreen Nudist Soccer League.

Using a compound bow no longer felt utterly alien, though

Harper still preferred the shotgun, considering she'd been training with and using the Mossberg since age twelve. However, she'd started to get a feel for the aiming the bow, albeit at a mere twenty-five yards. According to Cliff, the 'expected' range of a compound bow ended up being between forty and sixty yards, and accuracy at sixty tended to be equal parts luck and skill. That didn't change much as the approximate kill range of twelve-gauge buckshot tended to be around fifty yards as well.

So, when the day came that she ran out of shells, she wouldn't lose engagement distance. Defensive encounters didn't often require firing on targets hundreds of yards away. That, she'd leave to Cliff and the rest of the militia who carried military rifles. Her father used to own an AR-15, Ak-47, an FN-FAL, and an SKS, which she'd all fired before, though not to the same degree of familiarity as the shotgun. His AR likely ended up taken by the Lawless. The rest of his weapons hopefully remained in the gun safe, where they would stay for the rest of time since the combination to open it died with him.

He might have written it down somewhere, but if he had, he'd never told Harper where to look. Nor did she think it worth the danger to risk a trip back to Lakewood to hunt for something that might not exist, merely to collect a few rifles and about a hundred rounds of ammo. They'd spend half that in bullets fighting their way in. Of course, killing Lawless would be worth it... but dying wouldn't be.

Eyes narrowed in anger, Harper drew an arrow, aimed at the target, and pictured the bulls-eye as the face of a moron with a blue bandanna. She loosed, and put the arrow in the yellow ring an inch north of bulls-eye.

"Well, that's pure luck. First shot at fifty yards and I almost hit the center?"

Her second shot had a more expected outcome—going straight over the target and skipping down the street. She methodically fired the rest of her eleven arrows, working on getting a feel for the behavior of the shots at a longer range. It required holding the bow higher and using a different sight post to aim. All but four hit the target, though only the first shot came that close to the center.

After collecting the strays, she loaded up her quiver and jogged back to her firing position to do it all over again.

Three full volleys later, Harper loaded her second arrow of the fourth barrage, but a distant 911 air horn call went off before she let it fly.

In a total moment of 'oh screw it,' Harper released tension on the bowstring and went running toward the call, carrying the bow rather than losing time to ditch it and grab the Mossberg from the house. She still had the .45 on her belt anyway.

The air horn came from the south, but didn't sound too far away. She ran out onto Route 74 heading in that direction as more—and more distant—air horns went off. Ken Zhang rode past her on a mountain bike.

I need to grab one of those.

"What's going on?" shouted Harper.

"No idea," called Ken, pedaling faster.

Gunfire started up ahead, as well as a whole bunch of shouts, both angry and other militia coordinating movement.

Crap! Raid.

She slowed to a jog amid a momentary hesitation that she ought to head back for the Mossberg, but decided to keep going rather than waste time. Her run down the highway came to a stop where Stagecoach Road crossed Route 74. Nine members of the militia had taken up positions behind cars left abandoned in the road ever since the war, trading bullets with a group of men in dusty handmade leather clothes. They kinda resembled a bunch of modern people dressing up like Frontier explorers.

Only three or four of them had rifles, the remaining twenty trying to rush the militia position carrying swords, hatchets, hammers, and other improvised melee weapons. One guy learned the hard way that a wooden shield didn't do much good against an AK-47 bullet. Watching Leigh Preston, the bubbly woman with curly, fluffy hair, cut the guy down in the middle of the street struck Harper nearly as surreal as ten-year-old Mila killing two men.

Harper ran for cover behind a pickup truck on the right side of the intersection, not far from a Coldwell Banker sign on a tiny hill. The sign *looked* like it would make for a better shooting position, but flimsy plastic didn't stop bullets.

She held the bow horizontal, pointed off to the side, and watched down the street as bullets sparked off other old cars where the invaders had hunkered down.

"What's going on?" shouted Harper.

"Good question," yelled Ken.

"They just started attacking," called Leigh. "Ran in from the east. Anna saw them coming and sounded a warning."

Harper looked around at the militia, not seeing Annapurna. "Where is she?"

"Med center. Took a bullet in the shin," shouted Dennis.

Anger welled up. Harper liked Anna. These losers shot her friend.

"Same sons of bitches from the plane crash," yelled Marcie.

They tried to kidnap Maddie.

Harper drew her bowstring back, popped up, zeroed in on the closest head poking up over a car, and fired. A man with long, shaggy black hair took the arrow in the cheek, a little under his right eye. He fell backward out of sight, screaming. She grumbled at putting a target arrow into him, but she'd left the bladed ones at home. No sense damaging or breaking those on practice. Still, the bow gave her more reach than a handgun, so she loaded another.

Besides, these guys tried to kidnap Madison. They deserved to scream.

One advantage of having a bow, she didn't appear to rank as high on the threat level as the other militia who carried rifles; the four invaders armed with guns didn't lob any bullets in her direction. Of course, those bastards also had taken up covered positions too far away for her to reach using an arrow.

Amid the *clank* of a bullet skimming off metal, Marcie fell to the road, gasping in pain and clutching her right shoulder.

"Marce!" shouted Darnell.

"I'm fine. Just winged me." Marcie lifted her hand to look under it. "Yeah. Not too bad."

Six men all jumped out of cover behind dead cars at once and charged.

Harper popped up and fired an arrow at the first man she spotted. It hit lower than she aimed, burrowing into his chest near the base of his ribcage. He slowed from charge to stagger, but kept coming. She pulled another arrow, loading as fast as she could despite her hands shaking from the unfamiliarity of using a compound bow in a life-or-death situation.

Darnell nailed one of the enemy rifleman in the forehead and racked the bolt of his hunting rifle. Leigh leaned around the back end of a sedan, firing her AK rapidly at the charging men, dropping three of them and destroying a fourth man's right knee before her magazine ran out. Harper aimed at a guy running toward them waving a legit medieval claymore over his head. Two invaders got close enough to the militia position for Ken to fire his handgun. A man wielding a fireman's axe took two .45 slugs to the chest and dropped like a sack of topsoil.

Harper narrowed her eyes, furious at these people for the mental torment they'd forced on Mila—not to mention trying to kidnap her sister—and let another arrow fly.

Her shot nearly went up the claymore man's nose. At less than twenty yards, Harper could reliably hit a spot the size of a half-dollar coin. The back end of the arrow jutted out from the front of his face, a few inches poked out the back of his skull. He collapsed to the road in an instant, no sound or fanfare.

Leigh hammered a fresh magazine in, but stayed hidden behind the car's rear wheel as the three remaining invaders using rifles all focused on her position. That gave Darnell a clear shot to take out one more.

"They're freakin' crazy!" shouted Ken. "Who runs *at* people with guns?"

Harper leaned around the back end of her cover, another arrow loaded. The count of dead in the road appeared to be edging past a dozen at this point. The remaining invaders had all ducked down into cover, only a few peeked out at them. Both remaining rifleman also stayed out of sight, hiding behind cars at roughly 180 yards. While she *might* be able to get an arrow to fly that far, she'd be firing upward at such an angle that hitting an individual person would be basically impossible.

The little trees in the dirt strip along the side of the road moved.

Cliff sprang out into a charge, pouncing on the closer rifleman and re-enacting the shower scene from *Psycho*.

"Harp!" shouted Leigh. "Your right!"

She swiveled, locking stares with a 'tribal' trying to sneak up on her. He'd made it to about twenty feet, creeping around behind the opposite side of the Coldwell Banker sign. The man rushed at her the instant she noticed him. Harper hastily aimed and loosed an arrow, hitting him high on the left shoulder. It didn't slow him down; he ran in, swinging a hatchet at her face. She thrust the bow up in a two-handed grip, blocking the tiny axe under the head. The surprisingly powerful impact sent a jolt down the bones of her forearms, but sheer desperation gave her the strength to keep the edge away from her forehead. That, and maybe the arrow sticking out of his shoulder weakened him. Snarling, she rammed her knee into his groin. He faltered, staggering back a step. Harper grabbed the .45 off her belt, pointed it at him, and pulled the trigger.

Nothing happened.

He grinned, and lunged, grabbing her by the throat and shoving her against the pickup truck. "Bad time for a misfire, sweetie." The man raised the hatchet.

She thumbed the safety off, put the gun under his chin, and fired. A geyser of nastiness flew out the top of his head as he collapsed over backward. "Forgot the damn safety." *I shouldn't forget that. I'm freaking out. Stupid.*

"Clear!" shouted Cliff… a second before he shot a guy attempting to run and jump over the guardrail away from him.

The corpse landed out of sight, below the road level.

He shot a guy trying to run… Harper frowned. *Screw it. They tried to kidnap Maddie. Roaches deserve better treatment.*

Harper put the safety back on and holstered the .45 before

walking out from behind the pickup and staring at the guy face down next to the giant sword. *I just shot a dude carrying a big ass sword with a freakin' bow. When did we go* this *far back in time?* For a moment, she felt like a character in a medieval fantasy video game, using arrows and swords. She cringed at the thought of trying to pull the arrow out of a person's head, but decided to do it anyway. Any arrow she could re-use was a good arrow. The Mossberg made for a far more effective defense weapon, but it wouldn't last forever.

Yeah… this will work once I get used to it. She crouched by the dead guy, set the bow on the road, and struggled to pull the aluminum shaft out of the man's skull. Despite bleeding from the shoulder, Marcie joined the other militia in moving forward to clear and check the bodies. Evidently, she hadn't been hit too badly.

"What possessed you to go old school?" asked Cliff, startling her from how quietly he'd approached.

"Uhh. Just had it in my hand when the alarm went off. Didn't really think much about it." She stepped on the guy's head and pulled. "Damn this is stuck pretty good."

"Suction."

"Yeah, it sucks all right." She grabbed the arrow in both hands, pulling on it while stepping on the guy's cheek to hold his head down. "You know what's really bugging me?"

"Killing a dude with an arrow?"

"Sorta, but not really." She stopped pulling to rest a breath. "Killing this guy bothered me less than you killing that chicken for dinner."

Cliff laughed. "Not that silly, really. I mean, you vegans are kinda nuts, but it does make a little bit of sense. That chicken didn't try to kill you. This dude did."

"Grr. I'm not a vegan." Harper yanked the arrow out in one hard pull. "Ooh. Not even bent. Don't have to be vegan not to want to see an animal be killed. Ate it, didn't I?"

"True." He set his hands on his hips, glancing off down the road to watch the search of bodies.

"Same guys from the airplane?" asked Harper.

"No, they were dead."

She frowned. "Really. Who's got the dad jokes?"

Cliff laughed. "I know what you meant. Yeah, looks like the same sort of clothing. Must have been a revenge raid."

She wiped the blood from the arrow on the guy's shirt, then put it back in her belt quiver. "You think Mila should've executed them all instead of letting two guys run away?'

"Nah. That would've been cold-blooded. She's just a kid."

Harper nodded. "Yeah. Not her fault they attacked us."

"You okay?" Cliff lifted her chin with one finger. "Little bruise on your neck there."

She offered a blasé shrug. "I don't think I'll ever be 'okay' again unless someone rewinds time so the war didn't happen. But..." Harper smiled, thinking of Logan. "I'm coping."

"Good." Cliff kicked the dead guy. "You're more than coping, hon. You're surviving."

"I'm being melodramatic, too." She chuckled, heading over to the guy who tried to ambush her and recovering that arrow. "It's not really okay that getting into a gunfight—or whatever you call it when a bow is involved—doesn't faze me anymore. Killing two guys before dinner shouldn't be routine for a girl my age. But, it is. And here I am. And, well, I guess it was bound to happen."

He raised an eyebrow. "What was bound to happen?"

"Another raid. More shooting." She folded her arms. "I dared to be happy the other day."

"You are kidding, right?"

She smiled. "Yeah. Just making a bad joke. Can't let you have all the glory."

"Oh, one quick thing." Cliff picked up the hatchet. "Block this like you did a moment ago."

As he slow-motion chopped at her, Harper raised the compound bow in a two-handed grip almost in the manner of a quarterstaff. The hatchet shaft hit the bow an inch beneath the head.

"See how the blade has hooked over?"

"Yeah."

"That can work for you or against you. The guy could try to take your bow." He pulled on the hatchet, demonstrating how an attacker could rip it right out of her grasp. "But you could have used that against him, especially after introducing your knee to his balls. Pivot to the left and push with both arms, you'll yank the axe right out of his hand."

Harper pretend rammed her knee into Cliff's groin. As he fake doubled over, she wrenched the hatchet from his grip, trapping the head with the bow and shoving it away.

"Good. We can work on that a bit more later if you want."

"Wow, you really are turning into Dad. Even a near death experience becomes a lesson."

Cliff patted her on the back. "Near death experiences *are* lessons. The trick is paying attention to what almost happened."

Darnell jogged up to them. "Looks like twenty-seven. All men. Definitely some kind of organized group. No modern clothes. Most of them have prison tats. Maybe more former inmates or something, wanted to get rid of the orange jumpsuits."

"Could be, someone's rolled into Kittredge." Cliff spat to the side. "We should check that out in case there are any more surprises waiting."

"Yeah. My thinkin' exactly." Darnell shook his head. "Think there's more?"

"Possibly. These guys don't look like geniuses. Maybe they all came after us at once." Cliff glanced at Harper. "You want to come along or sit back here and make sure no more of them get into town?"

She shrugged. "Whatever you think is better."

"Go grab the cannon and head on back. We'll take a walk." Cliff winked.

"'Kay." Harper hurried off up the road, heading home.

Going on a combat patrol with her new father felt entirely way too exciting not to be a little unsettling.

Yeah, I'm no longer normal. Most girls want to go shopping with their dads, not go door kicking.

13

COMBAT PATROL

H arper walked down the road, clutching the Mossberg tight.

Too tight.

She hadn't been that nervous even the first time she competed in front of an audience. No matter how badly she did in the competition, paper targets and clay pigeons didn't shoot back. Sure, she'd been on scavenging missions before, highly aware of the risk that people might attack them at any minute. However, following Cliff, Darnell, Deacon, Sadie, Ken, and Eddie Sanchez toward Kittredge differed from every other 'mission' she'd yet done for the militia in one critical way: this time, combat wasn't a risk—it was a certainty.

The militia went to Kittredge with the intention of clearing out whatever remained of the gang that attacked Evergreen. Based on what the kids said about being put to work, they also expected to find prisoners. Searching for people held against their will, more than retaliation, motivated them to go.

Anxiety churned in Harper's stomach. Going on this raid—she could think of no other word for it—felt too much like revenge. Those sons of bitches tried to kidnap Madison, Jonathan, Lorelei, and the other kids. Why did she even cling to Dad's Mossberg if not to use it to protect her family? Running headlong into certain danger isn't what an eighteen-year-old voted sweetest in her class should be doing, but dammit... she wanted to.

Being on the aggressor side of a gunfight felt wrong even if the people they intended to attack deserved it. She had no idea what it would look or feel like. Where to go, what to do... all of it blurred around in her head in a nauseating, fatal what-if scenario.

Maybe if I think of this like a video game or a range. Target pops up, shoot it. They're not people. They're monsters.

She swallowed on a dry throat.

Cliff walked at her side in a strange sort of posture, legs slightly bent. He didn't make much noise, his eyes shifting side to side in a constant search for threats. It honestly scared her a little since no trace of 'dad' remained in his expression. He'd switched on some sort of *Terminator* mode. Deacon, the giant ex-convict bank robber, carried a pump shotgun that looked like a toy in his meaty hands. The fire axe he had when they first saw him in the Walmart hung over his shoulder in a handmade sheath. Even that looked like a 'small stick' compared to him.

Sanchez carried an AK-47, Sadie had a legit M-16, Darnell brought a scoped rifle with a handgun for backup, and the others all carried AR-15s. Except for their lack of uniforms, Harper kinda felt like part of a military patrol walking in formation down a highway into enemy territory.

"If it hits the fan," said Cliff in a low voice, "stay down and watch our flank."

She swallowed dry again. "I'm scared, but I can do this. They tried to hurt the kids."

Cliff nodded once. "Scared is normal. I'd be worried if you weren't. Only the real psychos wouldn't be scared going into a kill zone."

"Right."

He glanced at her, a little of his normal personality showing under the soldier veneer. "Didn't mean to imply you were overly scared or a kid. You've got a short range weapon. No point in you exposing yourself to fire when the engagement's going on past forty or fifty yards. Keep an eye out for idiots coming up behind us."

"Okay." She half turned to the right, scanning the pine trees and grass on the side of the road.

As they approached a curve in the road, where it went around an enormous rock the size of a small hill, Harper stared down a long driveway on the right at a blue house that looked abandoned, no signs of activity. Still, she kept the shotgun trained in that direction until the huge boulder got in the way. A small creek ran around the rock in a stone-lined ditch that paralleled the road.

The wreckage of the crashed jetliner came into view past the end of the curve. Harper blinked in awe. She'd expected an airplane crash to be... different, more like a scattering of tiny pieces. Other than broken wings and collapsed landing gear, this plane didn't look *too* badly damaged. The fuselage, for the most part, appeared whole. Two deflated yellow escape chutes hung from doors on the side to her left. The plane had come to a halt at the edge of the road, crumpling the metal guardrail and nearly sliding into the creek.

The militia filed around it on the left, everyone falling extra silent.

Char blackening covered the road behind the plane, all the way to a side street appropriately called 'Troublesome Gulch Road' by a surviving street sign. They continued ahead past several houses, cutting south and fanning out to go past a little playground, fallen telephone poles, and loose wires. Despite knowing that none would have any power in them, Harper still held her breath, frightened of touching downed wires.

They reached a road heading south, and followed it into the heart of Kittredge's residential neighborhood. Many of the houses here had bullet holes and broken windows. Over the eerie silence, the distant angry shouts of a man floated from farther south.

When they reached what appeared to be the southernmost row of houses, Cliff held up a hand indicating stop. Men in the distance berated someone for going too slow. Other men laughed. Cliff patted Darnell on the arm and pointed at a stepped hill beyond the houses. He nodded, ducked low, and climbed a series of stone retaining walls separated by short swaths of gravel before scurrying into a cluster of pine trees at the top.

The others waited in silence, listening to the distant men verbally abuse someone and laugh about it.

Darnell came back a few minutes later, his expression grim. Everyone gathered around him.

"The farm's just over this hill. Split in two areas. Bunch of goats in a valley on the right. Planting area's kinda small… to the left. They got a couple contractor trailers set up that look like holding cells, chains and padlocks on the doors. But they open now." Darnell took a knee and sketched in the dirt. "Three guys armed with bats and stuff near the goats, plus two men who look like forced laborers. Another six armed men by the farm area. One's got an AR-15, the other a pump shottie. The rest all got knives, swords, or shit like that."

Cliff nodded. "Okay. Civilians?"

"Yeah. Bunch of them. Six or seven, plus two little girls."

Harper bit her lip. The other militia stifled grumbles.

"How bad is it?" whispered Sadie.

"Them kids is sittin' by the trailers. Don't look hurt or nothin', just sad and frightened. The laborers all got leg irons like a prison chain gang. Two of 'em are wearing uniforms, maybe cops or correction officers."

Cliff spat to the side. "Harper was right. Ex cons."

"What did they do to the kids?" whispered Harper.

"Can't tell from here." Darnell shrugged. "They're just sittin' there by the trailer. Don't look like they're hurt."

"They tried to kidnap Maddie and the others, and put them to work," said Harper. "They're keeping slaves. We need to help those people."

Everyone nodded.

"Do you think the bad guys will surrender?" Harper fidgeted. "Do we really have to run in there and mow them all down?"

Cliff sighed. "They ran at us with axes and crowbars and shit while we had rifles. Pretty sure they don't give a damn about survival. And, what would we do? Drag them back to Evergreen and put 'em in jail? Send them on their way so they attack us a couple days from now?"

"Nah, man." Darnell shook his head. "I see what she's saying. I don't really get off on killing people either, but these motherf—" He glanced at Harper. "These dudes ain't worth the food they'd take, keepin' slaves. There's kids in there, too."

"Please tell me they didn't put the little ones in cuffs." Sadie stared at him.

"Nah. Don't look like it." Darnell cracked his neck side to side. "Ain't even making them work. 'Course they're really little, like five."

Harper exhaled in relief.

"Can you take out that AR?" Cliff glanced at Darnell.

Darnell leaned back, making a face that said 'shit, man, who you think you're talking to'. "Straight up."

"All right." Cliff looked around at everyone else. "Here's the plan. We got a scoped rifle, might as well use it. Darnell's going to get into position at the top of the hill and give us sniper cover. The rest of us will get as close as we can before they see us. Sanchez, Walker, with me. Owens, Zhang, Harper, you three head toward the goat pen. Neutralize the three hostiles there as fast as you can, then cut across to the vegetable field and pincer the rest from behind if we haven't finished them by then."

Everyone murmured agreement.

"Weird they don't have scouts and sentries out in the town," whispered Sadie.

Cliff grinned. "We already took care of those scouts and sentries back home. These guys had no idea what they were dealing with. Probably expected some little camp they could roll over."

The militia formed into their groups and crept up the hill. Cliff, Sadie Walker, and Edie Sanchez on the left, Darnell in the middle. Harper, Deacon, and Ken moved to the right. She looked up at Ken, hoping he planned on being in command of their little 'platoon' since she neither felt right doing it nor wanted to.

Everyone crouched low, except for Darnell who flattened out on his belly behind his hunting rifle.

From the top of the hill among the pine trees, Harper had a clear view down a hill covered in underbrush and trees. A house stood nearby a little to the left, offering cover from the slope. More or less straight in front of her, the ground angled downward past a pair of dirt roads that led to another more distant house. Beyond that house in a shallow valley, the convicts had constructed a fenced-in area full of goats. From this distance, she made out about six or seven people in the pen among the animals, but couldn't tell gang from prisoner without binoculars or a scope.

The area with vegetables occupied a small field at the bottom of the hill to the left, about half the distance away compared to the goat pen. Two white trailers sat at the rearmost end, most likely where the prisoners were forced to sleep. She figured the convicts helped themselves to houses back in the town proper. Fortunately, more of them attacked Evergreen—and died doing it—than remained in the field. If not for the forced labor, the overwhelmingly brown and green landscape in front of her would have been beautiful.

"We're going to need to hustle," said Ken. "Let's follow that road, head for the house, use it as cover. When the shooting starts, the bad guys from the goat pen might run to the field and we can get them from behind."

Harper nodded. "Okay."

"Right, everyone," said Cliff. "Check your god damned targets. Watch your line of fire. We got civilians down there who don't deserve to be shot."

Crap. She worried how she'd tell the bad guys from the innocent people in a split second. *Anyone pointing a gun at me is a pretty good sign they're hostile.*

Murmurs of acknowledgement came from everyone.

"Guys like this give ex-cons a bad name," muttered Deacon.

Harper smiled at him. "You're not a criminal. What you did hurt big banks, not the little guy."

He chuckled. "Well, would have hurt the banks if I succeeded."

"Get a bead on the AR," said Cliff.

Darnell aimed. "I'm on him."

"Take him down as soon as we're spotted or we open fire."

"You got it."

Cliff looked at Harper and made a hand signal for 'go.'

She nudged Ken and hurried down the hillside, heading for the dirt road that ran in a slight curve to the house in the distance. Ken and Deacon rushed after her, trying to be quiet, but a guy Deacon's size could do only so much insofar as stealth. She focused entirely on the house where she planned to take cover, not looking over to see where Cliff and his squad went.

The idea of running down there and opening fire on people still bothered her, but she didn't slow down. *These guys almost took my family.* A mental image of Madison enslaved on a farm let her push past her unease at being the attacker. She wouldn't shoot anyone in the back, but wouldn't hesitate if they came at her.

Her group made it only about halfway to the house before Darnell's rifle went off with a sharp *bang*. She poured herself into a hard sprint, racing to get behind the rectangular grey building past a dirt lot at the bottom of the hill. Seconds later, a series of rifle cracks came from the left. Men shouted and roared war cries, other men yelled things like 'get down.' A woman shouted, "Kelsey, stay down."

Harper jumped over a small rock, weaved among a cluster of trees, and ran hard until she crashed shoulder-first against the building, gasping for breath. Hopefully, the house blocked her team from view and the bad guys coming from the goat area didn't notice them.

Ken hit the wall next to her, his rifle aimed to the right. Deacon stopped a few steps back, trying to watch both corners. More shouts, screams, and gunfire came from the planting area. A little child shrieked for Daddy.

The tiny voice kicked Harper in the ass, urging her into motion. She ran to the corner on the left, aiming around. Three men ran up the hill less than forty feet away from her, heading for the other site. One had a katana, one a sledgehammer, and the other a monstrosity of a club made out of rebar and concrete.

She had only a few seconds to react before they got out of range. *They take slaves.*

Harper aimed at the big dude carrying the rebar club, imagining his head as a low-flying clay pigeon. She acquired the target and squeezed the trigger with an ease born from thousands of practice hours.

Blam.

The left side of his face turned into a ruin of red tatters. He staggered to the right and collapsed. The other two guys near him spotted her. Sledgehammer man roared like an idiot and came charging at her while the katana guy appeared momentarily torn between rushing at her or fleeing.

Boom.

Deacon's shotgun left a ringing in Harper's left ear. Sledgehammer guy ate dirt, his chest awash in red dots. Harper aimed at the guy holding the katana, but couldn't bring herself to kill him or shout something lame like 'drop it.'

Two shots in rapid succession from the opposite side of the house accompanied a spurt of blood from katana man's chest. Ken's AR-15 ended him where he stood. Watching him die didn't bother Harper anywhere near as much as shooting him would have. She dismissed guilt and ran around the corner, heading toward the goat pen.

A quick visual check found no more bad guys, merely four men lying on the ground.

She ran left, rushing toward the farm. The fighting had migrated away from the field except for one guy. A seriously tall man with a shaved head and an ornate cross tattooed on his face held a blonde woman as a body shield to his chest while taking pot shots from a pistol one-handed. At his size, the woman's feet didn't reach the ground, the chain between her ankles rattled as she struggled to get away from him. The hostage prevented Cliff, Sadie, or Sanchez from shooting him back, but her thrashing—plus extreme range for a handgun—also prevented him from hitting them.

Harper had him dead to rights from behind, sight unseen, but his head and the woman's head came awfully close for comfort, especially using buckshot. If he saw her running toward him, he wouldn't hesitate to shoot. Considering he hadn't yet died from a long-distance bullet, Darnell probably also worried about hitting the woman by accident.

Deacon surged forward, sprinting way faster than she expected a musclebound giant to be able to move. The man heard him coming and glanced back only briefly, probably expecting him to be one of the other gang members from the goat pen. He realized too late the bull charging at him wasn't one of his buddies and spun to aim at Deacon, but the big guy flattened him—and the woman—in a bear hug tackle.

Harper ran up and pointed the Mossberg in the guy's face as he lay on his back.

The tall man froze.

Deacon pinned the guy's wrist to the ground with one hand while pulling the woman away from him and giving her a light shove. She crawled toward Harper, shackles clicking.

"If you're not hostile, stay on the ground," shouted Cliff from a fair distance off to the left.

"Now what?" asked Harper, still aiming at the man's face.

Deacon stood, taking the handgun. "Pretty sure you know what now."

"I can't execute a guy." She fidgeted.

"Umm." Deacon glanced at the handgun, sorta aimed it at the man. "Not really my thing, either."

The woman yanked the .45 from Harper's hip and shot the tall man in the chest three times while shouting, "Die, you son of a bitch."

Harper lowered the shotgun. *Oh, no.* "Guess I won't ask if you're okay."

"I'm not okay. I'm Amy." She handed the gun back to Harper and walked as fast as the leg irons let her move toward the trailers.

Harper holstered her .45 and headed for the farm area, doing the 'soldier walk' Cliff taught her. She kept her vision sighted over the Mossberg, ready to fire on anything threatening while navigating among potato plants barely up to her shins, past one other woman and four men all face down on the ground like citizens in the midst of a bank robbery. Bruises covered their faces and arms, the two men in corrections officer uniforms by far the most battered. All the adults had police style shackles on their ankles and red marks on their wrists.

No hostiles appeared to remain alive.

She hurried over to where the former body-shield woman had taken a seat on the ground by one of the trailers, clinging to a pair of little girls who appeared about six and four, both in Disney shirts and jeans too small for them—likely the same clothes they'd been wearing for a year.

The older girl, also a redhead, spotted Harper and broke out in a huge smile. "She looks like me!"

The younger sister clung to the woman, her face concealed under a thick wall of black hair.

"Hi. My name's Harper. Don't be scared of us. We're here to help."

"I'm Rain," said the little redhead. "My sister's Kelsey, and this is my mommy."

The blonde woman focused a thousand-mile stare off to the side, not looking directly at Harper. "You killed them all, right?"

"Not me, personally. But yeah. They're all dead. I got a few of them."

"Good."

Harper crouched, gently grasped Rain's arm and examined her wrist. No sign of bruising there or on the girl's face. She almost even looked well fed. "Did those men hurt you?"

"Not really. The bad guys weren't mean to me or Kelsey. But they said if we ran away, they'd hurt Mommy and Daddy, so we didn't run away."

"They're not going to hurt anyone now." Harper stood and approached the open trailer door.

A thick tow chain hung from a hole where the knob used to be, an open padlock dangling from the end. Another hole in the wall served as a place to lock the door shut, trapping people. She poked her head inside, peering around at clumps of bedding. A cardboard box containing handcuffs sat against the wall next to the door. Two foul buckets served as bathrooms at the far corner. She imagined the gang put handcuffs on all the workers at night to make it harder for them to escape, then left them locked inside the trailer overnight.

At the thought Madison almost wound up in here, rage tears

gathered in the corners of Harper's eyes. *I should have shot him. Why did I wimp out? They would've done horrible things to the girls and Jonathan.*

"Will you please get my doll?" asked Rain. "I don't wanna go in there 'cause it's scary an' the door never opens. If I go in, the door will shut and I can't get out."

"Sure." Harper stepped up into the trailer, holding her breath at the stink of human waste, urine, and general funk.

She found the doll on a pile of bedding, wearing a dress made from a scrap of cloth. Harper picked it up and hurried back to the door in search of fresh air. She found Ken crouched in front of Amy unlocking the shackles from her ankles. A thirtyish man, also with red hair, a swollen purple left eye, and a strong resemblance to the girls, sat on the ground beside her, both kids clinging to him. Harper handed Rain her doll, nodded at them, and walked off to give the family some privacy. She headed toward Cliff and Sadie who de-shackled the rest of the laborers by the edge of the potato plants.

"Damn good to see you," said a grey-haired man in uniform. "Started to wonder if the world had any decent people left."

"Dunno about decent, but I ain't got no patience for this kind of bullshit." Cliff smiled. "You folks been here long?"

"'Bout six months. Kinda hard to say." The former guard scratched his head. "Them sons of bitches hit me in the head so much I barely remember my own name. Charles St. John, I think."

"Cliff Barton." He nodded left. "Sadie." He nodded right. "Harper."

"Hi." Harper waved.

"Good on you for killing those bastards." The other guard, a black guy with an equal amount of bruises as Charles but no grey hair, spat to the side.

"Guessing they objected to your former job." Cliff offered him a hand up.

"Yeah. Tyreek and I are the only two guards from that bus to make it this long. Used to be five of us. We was takin' a busload of eighteen of the worst to ADX Florence. Used ta be a supermax facility for anyone society wanted to forget existed. Damn nuke punted us straight off the road like a matchbox car. Bus ended up flipped in a culvert upside down. By the time I woke up, they'd gotten loose… game over."

"They dragged us around for amusement at first," said Tyreek. "But when they found this place, decided to put down roots. You can assume the rest."

The only other woman among the laborers also had a far-off look in her eyes. It didn't take a genius to assume what a busload of escaped prisoners in a world without any semblance of law would have done to two women. Deacon and Sanchez escorted the three laborers from the goat pen over, having unlocked their restraints.

Harper kept an eye on the surrounding area while Cliff and Sadie explained about Evergreen, the militia, and apologized multiple times for being so close but never noticing this situation.

"They came through here scavenging stuff before I made it to Evergreen, so I can't really say what happened then. I'm guessing the people who lived here when you and the convicts showed up must have taken up residence after our militia left."

"Most likely." Charles coughed, winced, and coughed again. "You said something about a doctor? Think I oughta see him on the sooner side."

Amy and her husband approached, each one carrying a child. He went around shaking hands with the militia, introducing himself as Michael Ryan and thanking them for 'making sure those bastards all died.' Once the laborers gathered in one area, Cliff started a discussion about what to do.

"We're not going to drag you anywhere you don't want to go." Cliff smiled. "But this place is a bit far afield for us to keep secure. You're welcome to come back with us."

All the former captives readily agreed. None appeared to have any interest in staying here.

They discussed relocating the goats to the main farm at Evergreen, and possibly transplanting the potatoes as well. Apparently, they had carrots as well in there somewhere. Deacon decided to collect all the shackles and handcuffs to bring back, intending to dump them in a militia storeroom so no other gang could use them for sinister purposes. Maybe if someone figured out how to blacksmith, they could even melt them down and put the metal to better use.

Harper kept quiet so no one would hear the emotion in her voice. Her siblings almost wound up as prisoners kept by a gang of convicts—and not merely convicts, supermax convicts who'd probably done the most horrible things. Serial killers, rapists, murderers, arsonists, and so on. Worse, the only reason they *didn't* end up here is that a ten-year-old girl had shot two men in the head. A little girl who herself had been kidnapped and forcibly trained by a complete psycho.

The world is going crazy, isn't it? How much longer can we hold it together?

14

DELIVERY RUN

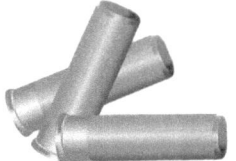

The combat patrol into Kittredge would haunt Harper for a while.

Not for having to shoot a guy, nor for anything she witnessed; rather, it would haunt her for what almost happened to Madison and the other kids. She couldn't stop picturing her siblings locked in that trailer, forced to work like a chain gang. It depressed and infuriated Harper. More so because that brutality called into question her hope that civilized society would return. How could it be possible something like that could go on so close to Evergreen for months and no one here knew?

Having to walk—or bike—everywhere made the world a lot bigger. A matter of a few miles now meant an entirely different world. The people of Evergreen had been so focused inward, they didn't even think to routinely check the nearest town over. Why would they? The militia had already scoured it of everything they considered useful.

She had zero regrets over wiping that gang out to the last man, and even second-guessed her opinion that Mila was right not to finish off the two she let run away. But… she couldn't expect a ten-year-old to execute people, even scum like that.

It hadn't yet been a full year after the war and already, a gang had resorted to slavery. She tried to find comfort in the idea that they hadn't been ordinary citizens who'd descended into feral savagery but a busload of men on their way to a supermax prison. Those men had been anything but normal. Half of them probably counted as clinically psychotic—most likely why they rushed a line of armed militia when they only carried bats, axes, and swords.

What sort of freak had the man who grabbed her by the throat been? The same hand that clamped around her neck might have done unspeakable things to innocent people. Garden variety bank robbers or car thieves didn't often end up in super high security prisons.

She shuddered, not even wanting to roam down that mental road.

Thinking about what nearly happened to her siblings made Harper want to forbid the kids from even going outside again. However, as emotion faded to rational thought, she figured it wouldn't have been *too* long after they disappeared before a search party discovered the convict gang. Kittredge, after all, was fairly close. Also, aside from threatening to kill their parents if they tried to escape, the convicts hadn't been overly mean to the two small girls. Hardened prisoners had a reputation for murdering pedophiles after all. They probably wouldn't have been horrible to Madison and the others either, though kids growing up raised by violent convicts would certainly have developed issues.

On the upside, the freed people eagerly joined Evergreen as citizens, bringing with them all the goats and some knowledge of how to process hide into leather and make clothing from it. That explained why those gang members and most of the laborers wore 'tribal' looking apparel. Both former corrections officers expressed interest in joining the militia, though it would be a while before they could, given their physical condition from frequent punitive beatings.

By the time Harper and Cliff returned home, the kids had already eaten dinner at Carrie's. Harper had no appetite left, and didn't bother scrounging up anything to eat. Instead, she spent the last hour or so of daylight on the couch holding Madison and Lorelei like giant teddy bears. Upon sensing her mood had gone into the pits, Jonathan added himself to the pile.

She told the kids they found the rest of the bad guys who tried to take them and saved some other people who had been kidnapped. When Madison asked why that had upset her so much, she deflected by claiming 'they hit them a lot and I didn't want that happening to you.'

That apparently satisfied them enough that they tolerated her clinginess.

Not that Lorelei ever needed a reason to tolerate being held.

HARPER WOKE THE NEXT DAY, LARGELY HAVING DEALT WITH HER worries.

Bad people did bad stuff. Worse could have happened and didn't. The people she cared about were safe, so she moved on. After breakfast, she walked the kids to the farm, then crossed Route 74 to wander her patrol area. She still felt kinda weird about the kids having to work over the summer on the farm, but asking them to learn how to run a farm plus keeping the town afloat made sense. Not like anyone forced them to toil in the field under threat of violence. They all knew everyone chipped in to keep everyone else alive.

Darci joined her again, having nothing else to do with herself and being 'awake stupid early' as she put it. She still wore a half-tee, but had swapped the denim shorts for a miniskirt. Due to a lack of pockets, she'd also added a hip satchel—probably carrying a pot stash. Not like anyone needed cell phones, wallets, or money anymore. Darci usually wore her jet-black hair short during civilization, but had let it grow past her shoulders either through laziness, apathy, or a deliberate intent to do something different.

"You're letting your hair grow out?" asked Harper.

"Yeah, why not." Darci shrugged. "Figured I'd see what it felt like."

Harper smiled. "Oh. I thought you might've just been too lazy to cut it yourself."

"That, too."

"Heh."

Darci glanced over. "You cut your own hair? Must be since it's not down to your ass by now."

"No. Madison's doing it. I'm trimming hers. Lorelei won't let anyone near her with scissors. It's going to be dragging on the ground eventually."

"She really is a nature child."

Harper laughed. "Yeah. I hope she grows out of her ambivalence to clothing before she gets too old for it to be simply cute."

"That would require she know what embarrassment means."

"Ugh. She's a handful."

"I think she's fierce." Darci smiled.

"Fierce is what you call a child that's a handful when you're not the one responsible for her."

Darci tapped a finger to her chin, pretending to be in deep thought. Harper assumed it an act since deep thoughts weren't usually her thing.

"Harper?" called Marcie.

She stopped and spun around.

Marcie Chapman cruised out of a side street on a mountain bike, riding up to a stop beside the girls. "Walter wanted to talk to you."

"Okay. How's your arm?"

"Burns. Shallow hit, nicked the bone. Nothing too bad." Marcie patted her right shoulder. "Rather this than taking it in the face. Lucky for me, those guys weren't very good shots."

"No kidding." Harper whistled. "Any idea what he wants? I don't think I did anything wrong."

Marcie smiled. "Nah, he's got an errand he wants you to run."

Sigh. Guess the kid gets the errand job. Oh, well. Beats being sent into a gunfight. "Cool. Thanks for letting me know."

"No problem." Marcie waved and rode off.

"Why aren't you on a bike?" asked Darci.

"I thought about it, but I'm supposed to be patrolling this area, observing, and looking for stuff that seems wrong. If I had a bike, I'd probably end up just riding in circles." Harper chuckled. "The bikes are for covering ground fast. Like responding to 911 calls."

"Shouldn't you at least *have* one with you then? Pushing it if you walk? I mean, if there's an emergency far off, you wouldn't be able to get there as fast."

Harper shrugged. "I guess. But pushing a bike around all day would kinda suck. And it would slow me down if a bad guy rushed at me."

"Do you really think someone's going to ambush you here?"

"No, but I also don't trust they won't."

Darci pursed her lips. "Okay. Fair point."

They headed south out of the residential area to Lewis Ridge Road, following it west to Route 74 and down to the militia headquarters. Darci tagged along, making random conversation about Lucas, growing weed, and what she imagined various famous people might be doing at that moment. While laughing at the idea that the Kardashians probably still hadn't figured out why no one they called answered their phones, Harper walked into Walter's office.

"Good morning." He smiled. "It's nice to see you in high spirits."

"Morning."

He looked at Darci. "Who's this?"

"My friend Darci. We knew each other before the war. I hope it's not a problem if she's following me around."

Walter shook his head. "Nah. Not a problem. I don't expect you're the sort of person who'd just sit there all day chatting instead of keeping your eyes open."

"Nope." Harper smiled. "Darce isn't getting in the way at all."

"All right. Then don't worry about it. Anyway, the reason I asked for you is that we got a ping from Janice in the south. One of the residents down there, guy by the name of Henry Rogers, has an ongoing medical situation. Think it's heart-related, but I'm not entirely sure. Anyway, he's on medication and ran out of pills. Just so happened we got some of whatever he needs when you and Dr. Hale visited that hospital couple months back."

"That was more than a couple months ago, but okay. And you need me to run them down there?"

"Yep." Walter smiled, gesturing at a white plastic bottle on his desk.

Harper picked it up. "Prednisone?"

"That's the stuff he needs according to Dr. Hale. He's on Pine Road down near Evergreen High School. I understand you are familiar with the location of the high school?"

Harper's cheeks caught fire—metaphorically. "Umm. Yeah." *Crap! Does everyone know?*

"Something wrong?" Walter tilted his head. "Why are you blushing? Did something happen at the school?"

"You could say that." Darci grinned.

Harper gasped, then stared at her. "Really?"

"Oh well, I'm sure I don't need to know if you're having that sort of reaction." Walter leaned back in his chair. "Near the football field, swing a right off Buffalo Park Road onto Valley View, then that first right is Pine. Henry's going to be in the second house you'll pass on the right. Go on and grab a bike from the pool."

Darci blinked. "Why are there bikes in the pool?"

"I'm going to assume your friend has a dry sense of humor." Walter raised one eyebrow.

"Yeah, she likes to pretend at being blonde." Harper poked her in the side. "Either that or she's smoked herself brain dead."

"You guys are no fun at all." Darci rolled her eyes. "Weed doesn't kill brain cells. That's a lie from big pharma."

"Right." Harper mouthed 'don't get her started' at Walter. "We'll get going right away."

He nodded.

Harper headed outside to the stash of mountain bikes next to the HQ building. Luckily, the bikes had been modified by the addition of small storage boxes, mostly containing first aid supplies. She stuffed the pill bottle in one so she wouldn't drop it on the way. Darci helped herself to a bike as well.

"You wanna grab shoes real quick?" asked Harper.

"Why?"

"I dunno. Seems kinda weird to ride a bike barefoot."

"Maybe to you." Darci hopped on. "Been a while since I rode a bike at all. It would feel weird no matter what. Damn. Maybe I should go put on underwear at least."

Harper gawked. "You are not running around in a mini without panties on."

"Hah. Wow, it's so easy to make your face match your hair." Darci flapped her skirt up to show off a sky blue bikini bottom. "Not exactly Calvin Klein, but it gets the job done."

"You are ridiculous." Harper laughed, swung a leg over her bike, and started riding.

Amid the clicking of a ratchet gear, Darci rolled up alongside her. "This is wild. How do you work these gear thingees?"

"No damn idea. Never rode a bike like this before."

"Oh, right. You had one of those pink ones with the white tires."

Harper gave her the finger for barely a second before trying to steer with one hand nearly caused her to wipe out and dump the bike.

This, of course, made Darci laugh.

"Bite me." Harper couldn't help but laugh, too.

"How do I be non-conformist when there is no society to conform to?" Darci leaned back, savoring the wind in her face. "Can't listen to my music anymore. What's the norm now?"

"Umm, I don't think people care that much about conformity anymore. We're all trying not to die."

Darci hummed to herself for a moment. "Well, I don't want to go around attacking people. Can't get tattoos now. No one bats an eye at weed. My goth clothes are all back in Lakewood. Guess I can buck convention by declaring clothing evil and going full Lorelei."

"Please don't."

"I'll claim I've embraced Gardnerian Wicca and it's my religious freedom if anyone complains." Darci grinned.

"Darce. Honestly. Renee would kill you if you went nudist."

"Aww, you're no fun." Darci raspberried.

"And you're not really being serious." Harper shot her a look.

Darci laughed. "No, I'm just messing with you. Gotta have fun or you're going to turn into an old woman. Like, one of those nasty bitches who watches everyone outside their window and calls the cops on kids selling lemonade."

"Hah. Okay, fine. Let's dance naked around a bonfire tonight and summon elemental spirits or something."

"Okay."

Harper turned her head in a slow *Terminator* fashion. "You weren't supposed to agree so fast."

"You aren't serious."

"That's beside the point."

"I'd totally have done that if you were serious. Don't think we'd have been able to convince Renee or Grace to go along with it though."

Harper laughed. "That's right, you did mess around doing occultist stuff, didn't you?"

"Yeah. Been a while though. Think I've more recently been on a bike than tried to contact The Goddess."

"I haven't seen you on a bike since sixth grade."

"Yeah, that's about right."

"You were into witchcraft at Madison's age?"

"Yeah." Darci shrugged. "Isn't every girl a 'witch' at like ten-through-thirteen?"

Harper sighed. "No. Guess I was too, umm, 'preppie' for that."

"Dear, the word you're looking for is 'basic.'"

Harper raspberried her.

"This would be much cooler if we had horses." Darci pedaled faster.

"Horses?" yelled Harper before working to catch up. "Why horses?"

"If we're gonna be stuck in the Old West, we might as well go all the way."

"Nah. That's not going to happen. No reason for it." Harper eased off, cruising.

Darci slowed a bit as well to keep even with her. "Why not?"

"Umm. Cliff said people are going to use bicycles and other tech stuff before horses, since you don't have to feed a bike. People would be more likely to eat horses than use them for transportation."

"Eww." Darci gagged. "Eating horses? That's horrible and sad. We shouldn't eat horses."

"Yeah. I agree, but we're not really in the Old West. We have modern ideas still in our heads. We know cars are possible and bikes don't take a lot of technology to get working. I'd rather eat a horse than starve to death, but I haven't seen any around here."

"We have cows on the farm. And chickens. No need to eat horses." Darci shook her head. "Not gonna do it."

They rode down Route 74—aka Evergreen Parkway—discussing what factors differentiated 'food animals' from other animals people wouldn't eat. Darci suggested that it had something to do with cuteness until Harper disputed that horses counted as 'cute.' They agreed on 'magnificent' for horses, thus 'magnificent' animals didn't qualify as food. No one ever rode a milk cow or bull into battle in dramatic fashion.

Cruising down the road on a bike with a shotgun across her back, laughing herself silly at the mental image of the Lone Ranger trundling off into the sunset riding Bessie took on a sense of the surreal. Never in the past seventeen years of her life could Harper have ever imagined a scene even half as strange. But as crazy as the world had become, a moment like that of pure goofiness felt as precious as anything.

They rode past Evergreen Lake where Route 74 changed names to Bear Creek Road. A narrow bike path ran along the street, sandwiched between the guardrail at the edge of the road and a rusty metal fence at the lake's edge. The water almost came right up to the highway, only a six-foot incline separating the road from the surface. Several people fished from there, glancing over at them as they cruised by on their bikes. Neither Harper nor Darci bothered taking the bike path since no working cars remained anywhere in the country—unless the remnants of the US Military had some way to produce gasoline or diesel fuel.

Bikes made the trip down to the high school much faster than the other day when she and Logan walked it.

They swung to the right around the loop past a little decorative stonework wall, rode by a building covered in old road signs, Cactus Jack's Saloon, then passed a water filtration plant. She didn't know for sure if it still operated. Evergreen, at least the part of it she lived in, still had functional plumbing. So someone managed to keep that part of it going. The day may come when it failed, and everyone would be forced to take water from the lake and boil it, or collect rainwater… hopefully, it would be a while before the town had to deal with that.

They kept going past dead traffic lights, riding on a road devoid of cars except for the occasional abandoned one, past stores that hadn't seen use in over a year and the ghosts of a recently dead civilization. Riding a bike through the streets of a mountain town would have been relaxing if not for the constant reminders of the world being broken.

A garage on the left still had an army of ATVs arranged in front of it. *Must have been some kind of dealership.* She figured the militia would definitely have already raided it for any usable gasoline. Riding ATVs instead of bikes would've been cool… but those ate fuel no one had anymore.

They took an off ramp to the right near the Evergreen Library, following a looping road around a tree-lined stretch flanked on both sides by numerous houses and a few businesses. The trip from North Evergreen where she lived down here felt like a real undertaking in an era without motor vehicles, though the bikes definitely helped.

Eventually, they came within sight of the high school and, following Walter's directions, veered off to the right down a road opposite the football field. Straight ahead, the street led past homes, but she took the first right turn onto an unpaved dirt road. A few locals working among plants in a garden behind a house on the left paused to watch them ride up to the second home on the other side.

Harper stopped, got off the bike, and took the pill bottle from the storage box before approaching the door and knocking. Darci took the opportunity to stretch and complain that they hadn't brought along water bottles.

A man quite well into his fifties if not past sixty already, answered, regarding the girls with a note of confusion. Only a little black remained in his mostly grey hair. "Yes?"

"Can we interest you in some Thin Mints?" asked Darci, making her voice sound like a twelve-year-old's.

The man blinked.

"Ignore her." Harper sighed. "Are you Mr. Rogers?"

Darci snickered.

Henry Rogers smiled, no doubt having heard that joke for most of his adult life. "Yes."

"I'm Harper Cody, with the militia? They asked me to bring these to you." She handed over the pills.

"Oh, wonderful." He took the bottle, smiling broadly. "Cutting that a bit close." He patted himself on the side. "Damn kidney's going to go into full rebellion if I run out of these."

Harper grimaced.

"Aww… I know." He sighed. "Gonna happen sooner than I'd prefer. I'm well aware that no one's making this stuff anymore. If I can last another year or two, that'll be something."

"Sorry." Darci's smile faded. "I didn't know you were that sick."

"It's not that I'm sick… had a kidney transplant a while back. Probably before you two were born. Gotta keep taking these pills or my body's going to reject it. I'm already on borrowed time as it is." He rattled the pill bottle. "This is what a few more minutes looks like if it turned into a physical object."

"You're going to die in minutes?" Darci blinked.

That time, she didn't sound like she joked.

"Nah, this might see me through about four months. Could roll the dice and under-dose to make them last longer, but that could bite me in the ass." He shrugged. "Not sure if that's worse than running out all at once. I need to get my hide up north and see that doctor, but it's a heck of a walk for a man my age."

"You're not *that* old." Harper smiled.

"Now what was that about Thin Mints? Do you actually have cookies or are you teasing an old man?"

"Sorry. Only kidding." Darci winced. "They just told us you needed pills, not that you were like seriously sick."

"It's all right. We're all gonna die sooner or later. No point losing sleep over the timing of it." Henry held the bottle up. "Thank ya for bringing these all the way down here. Tell that doctor I'll see about going up there sooner or later."

"Okay."

A woman inside the house asked, "Who's at the door?"

Henry waved at them and went back inside, muttering something about the town arming Girl Scouts for defense.

Harper chuckled, despite feeling guilty as hell.

"That sucks that he's gonna die 'cause there's no medicine left," said Darci.

"Yeah."

Darci exhaled. "We're screwed, aren't we?"

"Depends. I mean, no one did kidney transplants back in the 1800s, right? Humanity survived past that part. A lot of people who used to die for medical stuff are going to die again. But that doesn't mean we're going to go extinct."

"I want to find a guitar."

Harper blinked. "Random much?"

"Miss playing. And the world needs music since all the stereos and stuff are broken."

They turned to walk back to their bikes, but stopped short at the sight of a small crowd. Eight men and three women had gathered behind them, blocking them from leaving. Fortunately, none of them appeared hostile, more insistent.

"Umm... can I help you?" asked Harper.

"You militia?" asked a thirtysomething Chinese guy in a flannel shirt.

"Gotta be, Sam." An Indian man next to him pointed at her. "She's got a rifle."

"That don't mean nothin', Sanjay." An annoyed fortyish woman who appeared to have rapidly lost weight from somewhat heavy to quite thin rested a hand on the pistol at her hip. "Could be an outsider. Ain't like them militia nitwits have a uniform."

Sam grasped the woman's shoulder. "Easy, Penny... no need to pull a gun on a kid."

The woman swatted his hand away. "You're gonna end up dead, Yang. You wanna trust everyone."

"Can everyone please calm down?" Harper held her hands up in a placating manner. "Yes, I am with the militia. Just delivering some medicine to Henry."

Penny gestured angrily to the side. "When y'all going to get the power back on down here. Hear you people got it going up north. South Evergreen counts, too."

Others in the group murmured agreement, growing restless. A few made comments that the people up north considered them unimportant.

"I would very much like power to be here," said Sanjay. "It is most difficult to read in the dark."

"I'm sorry. Totally understand what you mean." Harper pulled her hair out of her eyes. "The militia isn't making decisions about who gets power or doesn't. That's between Mayor Ned, Anne-Marie, and Jeanette. We're just trying to keep everyone alive and safe. Even the power up north isn't exactly working well. Lately, it's been off more than on. I know there's been a few fires with the panels. They really don't tell me much since my job's mostly protecting the area around the school and making sure no one hurts the kids. Happy to talk to Ned or Anne and let them know how you feel. You can also take your concerns to Janice at the sheriff's station."

The discontent among the citizens eased off somewhat as they appeared to take in her age.

"Why they hoggin' all the solar panels up north?" asked a scarecrow-thin man in overalls.

Since the crowd no longer radiated a sense of imminent violence, Harper relaxed enough to think. "It doesn't really matter where the panels are. They can fix the wires running down here to supply power once they work out the problems. It's easier to maintain if all the generation stuff is in the same place. But... like I said, the electricity has been down more often than it's been on. Pretty sure they're trying to build windmills instead of solar panels anyway, since those are less complicated. Solar panels don't last forever and we can't make new ones."

The crowd murmured amongst themselves.

"They're trying, but I dunno what's going to happen," said Harper. "It wouldn't surprise me if we're back to candles before I'm forty. If I even live that long."

A somber silence fell over the group. Penny, who still appeared personally angry at Harper as if their lack of electrical power had been her fault, finally looked at her with pity rather than resentment.

"C'mon, she's just a kid," muttered a guy in the back. "She wouldn't know nothin' about why they do a damn thing."

Sam Yang set his hands on his hips and sighed at the ground. "Sorry. We're frustrated being stuck living medieval."

"It's not just you. We're cooking on wood fires all the time, too. It's like every six hours some new fuse somewhere explodes or a stray dog pees on the machinery and starts a fire in the panel farm." Harper smile-shrugged in a 'what can ya do?' way. "They're working on it."

The people nodded and dispersed, still grumbling. She stood there watching them trudge back across the street to the garden, unsure if she should be relieved or feel defeated.

"What's wrong?" asked Darci. "I think you handled them pretty well."

"Really?"

"Yeah, they didn't beat the hell out of us."

Harper chuckled. "Kinda looked like that was coming, didn't it?"

"It did. Nice with that 'I dunno if I'm gonna live to see forty' line."

"Not a line. I'm really worried I won't make it. Either for getting shot or who knows how much radiation I was exposed to? Might run out of food. What if I get sick? There's no medicine. Logan could knock me up and I die in childbirth."

"He's cute, but I wouldn't say he's to die for."

The moment he'd been shot during the farm raid replayed in her mind. She'd definitely risk her life to protect his. Darci's joke didn't even make her smile. Harper let out a long, soft sigh. "I'd totally run into a gunfight to protect him."

"Wow, you got it that bad for him, huh?"

"Yeah."

"If he breaks your heart, I'll cut his balls off for you."

Harper fist-bumped her. "Thanks. If that happens, it should be easy to catch him. Cliff's already going to break his legs."

Darci laughed.

"Logan won't do that to me though. We talked so much when he was recovering. Can't fake that connection." She smiled. "Besides, if he was going to cheat, he would've already gone after Grace."

"That girl's so hot, *I'm* tempted to ask her out." Darci made a *rawr* noise.

"Since when are you bi?"

Darci sighed. "I'm not. That's the joke, Harp. Just not fair."

"What isn't?" Harper got back on her bike.

"That Grace is *that* pretty plus smart as hell. She totally cheated rolling stats." Darci stared at her bike without getting on.

Harper glanced over at her. "Did you just make a D&D joke? We haven't touched that game since eighth grade."

"Yeah, well... Once a nerd, always a nerd."

"Actually, maybe I did play D&D yesterday. Guy ran at me waving a sword and I shot him with an arrow."

Darci chuckled. "Well, Cliff *is* a ranger."

Harper smirked. "Not the same kind of ranger. Umm... Is something wrong with your bike? Why are you just standing there?"

"Those guys are still watching us. They're going to see under my skirt when I get on. I'm trying to decide if they're specifically hoping for a peek or are watching us because they don't trust the cops."

"You should wear jeans."

"Screw that. Pants are a tool of patriarchal control."

Harper sighed. "Okay, super hippie. You could move around to this side and give Henry a heart attack instead."

Darci laughed, then looked at the house. "He's not watching us." She stepped around the bike and kicked her right leg over it so no one at the garden got an up-skirt peek.

"Sometimes, the answer to a problem is really as easy as attacking it from the other side." Harper wagged her eyebrows.

15

ABNORMAL WORLD

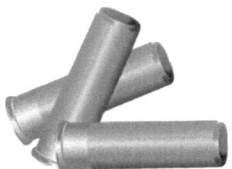

O n the ride north, Harper reluctantly participated in a debate with Darci over the inappropriateness of various clothing. Primarily, why did people think seeing a girl's underpants was risqué and embarrassing but a bikini bottom—which covered less skin—didn't elicit the same reaction? And did wearing a bikini bottom *like* underwear make it subject to being embarrassing?

Harper had no good answer beyond 'because they're underpants' even though she thought nothing of going outside in public wearing a bikini but would be mortified at getting caught outside in panties. To bail out of that conversation, she randomly mentioned Logan not wearing underpants.

"Remember those baggy greenish-grey pants I used to wear in school?" asked Darci.

"The ones that kinda looked like Army fatigues, just all grey? With the big ass pockets on the legs?"

"Yep." Darci grinned. "Every time I had them on, I went commando."

"Lies." Harper shook her head. "You're just trying to mess with me."

"Seriously. Those things were sheer and thin and felt wonderful on my bare ass."

Harper cackled. "Stop. You're too much."

"So, candles? Think so?"

"Maybe. If they can't get the windmills working."

"Where do candles come from, other than Bed, Bath, and Beyond?" asked Darci.

"Uhh, factories. But you're really asking me if we can make them. Paraffin wax is made from petroleum, so, no. That's gone. When the candles we have are done, we're gonna need to go old school."

"Which is what? Oil lamps? There's going to be so much fire." Darci made a creepy face and spoke in a raspy whisper. "*Soooo much fire.*"

"Nah."

"Epic amounts of fire." Darci whistled. "They better reinvent water pumps before they start giving idiots oil lamps."

Harper chuckled. "That didn't really happen that much back then."

"Sure it did. Remember that story about a cow burning down a whole city?"

"Umm, wasn't that entire city made out of wood or something? Like, even the roads?" Harper scrunched her nose. "I kinda remember that from history class."

"Wow, you were awake in that class?"

"Yeah. Unlike some people, I cared about getting good grades so I could get into a good college."

"How is that working out for you?" Darci stuck out her tongue.

Harper sighed.

"Sorry, just teasing."

"I know. Can't tell if I'm more upset that it's all gone or that I busted my ass for nothing."

"Lies." Darci laughed. "You're totally upset it's all gone."

"Yeah."

"Hey. School doesn't matter. Career doesn't matter. Fancy stuff doesn't matter. The world forgot that. Maybe that's why someone hit the reset button. The only thing we should care about is our families and friends." Darci smiled. "And weed."

Harper laughed.

"Tallow."

"Huh?" Harper looked over at her, trying not to swerve into a collision.

"I think that's what they used to make candles out of like way back in the day."

"What the hell is tallow?"

Darci waved a hand around in thought. "Umm. I read about it during my occult phase. This witch from England said that the tallow candles had a more natural energy and worked better for focusing magic. It's oils or something... maybe animal fat. Real old school. Stuff we don't need technology to do. Just need to figure it out."

"Oh, well, at least we'll always have candles." Harper daydreamed about wandering the halls of a medieval castle while carrying a giant candle holder. "Hopefully, fashion doesn't revert, too. Those dresses looked uncomfortable as hell."

"No kidding. And people gasped if a girl showed her bare ankles in public."

"Right? Do you think society's going to go backward? Force us to wear dresses?"

"Probably not. Everyone who's still alive remembers the modern world. We might get a weird cult or two with messed up dress codes, but we had that before the war."

Harper laughed. "What like Amish and Mormons?"

"Among others. People are weird."

A short distance ahead, a slim black woman in her later thirties walked out onto the highway, waving her arms to get attention.

"Oh, shit. Hope this is something that doesn't involve death."

"Cake or death?" asked Darci.

"What?"

"Forget it. I'll explain later."

Harper and Darci slowed their bikes to a stop in front of the woman.

"Afternoon," said the woman. "Couldn't help but notice that giant gun you're carrying. You militia?"

"Yes. I'm Harper." She squeezed the handlebars. "What's up?"

"Name's Trisha. I's just wonderin' if you all got that killer yet. Heard they found a dead man on the big farm."

Harper exhaled. *Whew. Not an emergency.* "We're still investigating. Haven't made any definite conclusions yet. Roy's in charge of the investigation. He was a real cop before the war, so he knows what he's doing."

"That's good. We're all on edge 'round here. Someone else gonna die soon. Hopefully, it's the killer." Trisha patted a handgun on her belt. "They come down this way lookin' for trouble, they gonna find it."

"I, umm…" A nervous smile formed on Harper's lips. "Don't really think this killer is looking for random victims. It's not official, but it kinda looks like the victim was killed for personal reasons."

"Huh." Trisha nodded, her expression contemplative. "Any idea what?"

"Not yet. If we understood that, we'd know who did it. They really don't want me talking about it until we have things figured out."

"Right on." Trisha stepped out of her way. "Thank ya for takin' the time. You sure it ain't no serial killer?"

"That's my thinking. But, I'm basically just a kid who's watched a lot of cop shows."

Trisha laughed. "Well, that's somethin' at least. Better than some deer hunter with a rifle that jumped on the militia to keep their gun. Least you tryin'."

"Yeah. I'm definitely trying." Harper smiled, waved, and resumed riding.

A few minutes passed in silence broken only by the noise from the mountain bikes' gears.

"Darce, what's the difference between vigilantes and what we're doing?"

"Vigilantes operate outside the law of society. You guys *are* the law of this society. Crap fell to pieces and you're trying to keep it together."

"Wow. Sometimes you actually sound smart."

"Consume a phallus," said Darci.

Harper coughed. "What?"

"Eat a dick sounds too crass for a girl to say." Darci examined her fingernails.

"Oh. Hah." Harper blushed but laughed. "Why'd you sleep through class if you're really smart?"

"Bored, and I knew all that crap they tried to make us learn was just pointless nonsense to keep us under control. Feed everyone the same template of information no matter what their interests or aptitudes are. People aren't factory-produced goods. Education ought to be based on the student, not what's best for an industrialized society."

"You should talk to Violet Olsen. I think you would make an awesome teacher."

"Right, whatever."

Harper tried to pat her on the shoulder and nearly dumped the bike again. "Gah!" She fought the wobbling handlebars, stabilizing herself in a few seconds. "I'm serious. You'd be the cool art teacher everyone wanted to get because you'd be so baked you'd let them get away with anything."

"Fo' sho'." Darci cackled. "You seriously think I'd be good as a teacher?"

"Well, you might produce an army of anti-establishment radicals, but the establishment is dead. So, yeah. I mean, if the town isn't cool with your 'job' just being growing weed. No reason you can't do both. Not like pot plants are high maintenance."

"I'll think about it." Darci let go of the handlebars and stretched, easily balancing herself.

"Bite me."

Darci leaned over and bit her on the shoulder.

"Not funny."

"I phink imf himariouf." Darci released her toothy grip on Harper's shirt and righted herself.

Harper swallowed a sudden explosion of wanting to cry. She'd missed her goofy-ass stoner friend *so* much. Finding her in that Army camp had been a one in a million long shot. She forced herself to smile through the grief of what almost happened. *Embrace the positive. Stop dwelling on the bullshit.*

"You okay? Now what?"

Harper cleared her throat. "Think I swallowed a fly."

"Lies."

Harper laughed.

"Aww, I wub joo, too." Darci winked.

They chatted about random funny things that happened at school, like the time Darci got detention for smoking weed senior year, then got busted smoking weed *in* the detention room. That got her sent to counseling.

"The counselor and I smoked together outside the psych place," said Darci.

"No way."

"Serious as a heart attack. I swear. He thought the principal was a stuffed shirt."

"That's... Wow." Harper whistled.

"Right?" Darci grinned. "We are the weed nation. Our numbers are legion."

A spot of bright beige caught Harper's eye on the left.

She slowed, staring into the trees along the side of the road. A little boy no older than five or so wandered naked on a side street, covered in some manner of orange sauce, probably from canned ravioli. He bounced a tennis ball off the pavement, occasionally darting after it if he missed the catch.

"Lorelei's got a kindred spirit. They're both forest nymphs." Darci chuckled. "At least it's warm out."

"Umm. Should I check that out?"

"He doesn't look alarmed."

Harper walked her bike a little closer. "He looks pissed."

"That's focus. He's trying not to miss the ball."

"He's naked."

"He's like five." Darci shrugged. "That randomly happens at that age."

"Why is he smeared with sauce?"

"Kids cover themselves in stuff all the time. Remember Renee and the peanut butter?"

Harper bit her lip to stop from laughing. The girl's mother had photos of two-year-old Renee after she'd gotten into a giant Costco jar of Jif. "Okay, true. But... that also means someone left him unsupervised. Cops in the normal world would definitely check on a little kid running around with no clothes on."

"The world isn't exactly normal."

"Yeah, but..." Harper hopped off her bike, leaned it against a tree, and walked toward the kid in earnest. "Neither is this. Something's bothering me."

16

A GOOD PLACE

The tennis ball bounced on the pavement, again and again, the soft *pop* it made echoing into the nearby trees. Harper approached the child at a nonthreatening pace, waiting for him to look up and make eye contact. He didn't. Long, wild light brown hair framed a cute, narrow face with large hazel eyes. If he'd been wearing anything, she wouldn't have known him a boy. He didn't appear *too* skinny, but everyone now more or less had the same sort of build due to rationed diet of mostly vegetables plus fresh chicken or venison and no overly sugared junk. Also, rationing kept people from overeating.

Maybe in a generation or two, people would have to worry about getting fat again. Maybe.

She watched the boy bounce the ball a few more times, trying to put a name to him. Untamed hair concealed most of his face, but an obliging breeze gave her a decent look at him. Still, she didn't recognize him. Then again, this far south, he probably didn't go to school. Anne-Marie Kirby, the town manager, tried to get everyone with school-age kids to go north. Granted, this boy looked a bit young to start school yet, so maybe his parents hadn't bothered relocating.

"Hi. I'm with the Evergreen Militia. My name's Harper. What's your name?"

"I'm Elijah."

She smiled. "Is everything okay?"

He caught the ball and looked up. "I dunno."

"You don't know?" She crouched to eye level and poked one finger into the hair over half his face, pushing it aside. "Why don't you know if you're okay?"

Elijah looked past her at Darci, then back to her. "I made a mess. I'm gonna get in troubles when Daddy wakes up."

"Is that why you don't have any clothes?"

He bounced the ball once, wobbling his head in an exaggerated nod. "I took shirt off afore open the can so's it don't get all sauced. But I messed up wif a can open machine, an' puhsketti-Os went *splat* onna floor."

Harper's worry increased. "You opened the can? While your Daddy was asleep?"

"Yeah. He won't wake up."

Darci sucked in a breath.

Harper grasped Elijah's shoulders, staring into his eyes. "How long has he been asleep and not waking up?"

Elijah jammed a finger up his nose. "I dunno."

"Couple hours?"

"Longer."

"A day?"

Elijah pulled his finger out of his nostril and looked at the snot. "Yeah. I sleeped two times."

"Crap," whispered Darci.

Harper guided the boy over to her. "Keep an eye on him?"

"Sure."

"You gonna wake Daddy up?" He peered up at her.

"That's what I'm hoping," replied Harper in a brittle voice. "Where's Mommy?"

Elijah pointed up. "Inna sky. Mommy went away when the sky lit on fire. Daddy says she inna good place now."

I hate this stupid world. Why does it have to be like this? A lump formed in Harper's throat. "Be right back."

She stood.

Elijah resumed bouncing his tennis ball. "Okay."

Harper walked from the road to the tree-shrouded driveway marked by child-sized footprints in cheap tomato sauce. A length of sidewalk connected to the front porch of a house nearly three times the size of her new one with a double garage on the left. The front door had been left wide open. Not too surprising given the heat. Also, few people in Evergreen locked their doors. People knew each other; no one really owned anything worth stealing, and almost everyone had at least a handgun if outsiders barged in.

Even though she didn't expect dangerous trouble, she still kept a hand on her .45 as she stepped inside. The instant she crossed the threshold, the stink of death hit her. Fortunately, it hadn't become overwhelming. She coughed, pulled her T-shirt up to cover her mouth and nose, then headed for the stairs to the second floor, assuming the bedrooms would be on the upper level in a two-story.

The stink worsened in the hallway at the top of the stairs, but fell short of making her spontaneously vomit. Various toys, mostly action figures or spaceships, littered the hallway. Crayon markings covered a patch of wall near a bathroom. She kept going to the end and peeked into the master bedroom.

Sure enough, the bed contained the body of a man, covered to the waist by a thin sheet. She couldn't tell his age due to swelling of his face and the complete loss of hair, including eyebrows. The rest of him also had a high degree of swelling as well as purplish red patches and bleeding sores. Spaghetti-O sauce smeared the sheets near the head, and a child-sized handprint in orange marked the pillow. As soon as she processed that all his hair had fallen out, she flashed back to the instant she'd put the irradiated man out of his misery.

Oh, shit!

Harper backed away and ran down the hall, down the steps, and out the front door, coughing on the clean air outside. She hurried over to Elijah and Darci, scooped the boy up into her arms, and hurried to her bike.

"Hey, where are you going?" called Darci. "Shouldn't we get him a shirt or something?"

"Don't go in there. Don't take anything out of that place." She climbed onto the bike and set Elijah in her lap facing her. "Hold on tight, okay? I need to get more help."

"Okay. Did Daddy wake up?"

Harper bowed her head and squeezed the tiny person clinging to her. "I'm sorry, Elijah. He didn't."

She remembered passing the old Sheriff's office barely a minute before spotting the boy, a building next door to the giant library. Harper steered to the right, heading south again. Darci trailed after her, keeping quiet though she had to have a hundred questions brewing. It didn't take long at all to reach the entrance to the library area, a short but wide five-lane access road leading straight ahead to the library and left to the sheriff's department.

Three useless police cars and one pickup truck with sheriff's markings parked in front of the beige one-story building that served as the official headquarters of the Evergreen Militia. Harper had no idea why Walter ran the show from the secondary HQ at the north end of town. Probably because the majority of the residents collected up there and he wanted to be closer, leaving Janice to look over the building that had an armory and jail cells, even if they had little intention to ever put anyone in the holding cells.

She rode up onto the sidewalk, leapt off the bike, and carried Elijah inside like he was on fire.

17

ROLE MODEL

H arper rushed up to the front desk, behind which sat a late-twenties woman in an actual sheriff's department uniform. The woman looked up, her gaze bouncing back and forth from the Mossberg over Harper's shoulder to the quite naked Elijah in her arms.

"Oh… you must be Harper," said the woman, relaxing. "Not used to seeing random people running in here carrying semi-auto shotguns. What's up with the kid?"

"Umm. Found him wandering like this. I, umm…" She handed the boy to Darci. "Mind looking after him for a bit?"

"Yeah, sure." Darci collected him. "Oof, you're a bit big to carry around."

"My Daddy won't wake up," said Elijah.

"Aww, shit," muttered Celeste.

"Yeah. It's that." Harper approached the reinforced door to the left of the counter and whispered, "Don't wanna talk in front of him."

Celeste let her in. "C'mon back. Might as well keep Janice in the loop."

"Great. Yeah. My thoughts, too."

The woman led her down the hall and around a corner to the office once used by the actual elected sheriff, now occupied by Janice Holt, the second in charge of the Evergreen Militia and the person responsible for managing the south portion of town. She had a former-cop air about her, hair back in a bun and a no-nonsense stare, but also gave off a sense of friendliness. The sort of friendliness that could turn on a dime to fire if someone stepped too far out of line.

A tall Hispanic man sporting the neatest hair Harper had ever seen on anyone since the bombs fell sat in one of the chairs facing the desk, evidently in conversation with the boss—before they barged in.

"Janice," said Celeste. "We have a situation. Something happened to Aaron North. Harper here just brought Elijah in bare as the day he's born. Kid said his father won't wake up."

"Aww, damn," muttered the guy.

"What happened?" Janice looked at Harper.

"Walt sent me down to deliver pills to this guy Henry Rogers. Did that. On the way back, I spotted the boy wandering around alone. Something about him bugged me. He just didn't seem to be acting right, so I decided to check on him. His father's dead in bed upstairs. From what the boy told me, it's been two days. He's been feeding himself, but... yeah."

"Crap." Janice sighed. "Poor kid. Any idea what killed him?"

"Yeah. Radiation poisoning."

Everyone stared at her.

"Say what?" asked the guy.

Harper glanced at him. "All his hair had fallen out and his face was puffy. I mean eyebrows, arm hair, chest hair, all of it. He had purple blotches on his skin. I saw a guy a while ago who'd been irradiated. Basically turned him into a zombie. Guy could only moan and flail around. The man in the bed kinda looked like that, but not quite as bad."

"Where the hell did North go to get exposed to radiation?" asked the guy.

"Harper, this is Calvin Velasquez." Janice gestured at him.

"Oh, hi." He shook hands with Harper. "Must be weird not being a celebrity anymore."

"Umm. I never was a celebrity." She fidgeted, then glanced at Janice. "I got the boy out of there as fast as I could. No idea if he's been exposed. He didn't look burned."

"That why he's naked?" asked Celeste. "Worried about contamination?"

"YouTube videos?" Calvin smiled. "Shotgun prodigy."

"Not famous." Harper faced Celeste. "No, found him like that. He didn't want to get sauce on his shirt. But, yeah... contamination is why I didn't bother grabbing anything to put on him. I have no idea how hot that house is. Do we have any way to find out what in there is radioactive? This could be dangerous for the whole town."

Janice stood. "Aaron North went on frequent scavenging trips. It's possible he ran into something radioactive out there. I hate to say this, but if the radiation was around here, the boy would be in the same shape as his father."

Harper and Celeste cringed.

"Pretty sure Roy Ellis has a Geiger counter. He used to be a doomsday prepper survivalist type before the morons in DC proved him right." Janice frowned. "Assuming we started it. Hell, even if we didn't, only morons would fire back."

"That's not terribly patriotic, boss," said Calvin.

"I'm all for retaliation, but nukes are just stupid. Kill mostly civilians, ruin the entire world for everyone. Makes no damned sense to me at all for anyone to use a weapon like that." Janice walked around the desk and patted Harper on the arm. "Would you mind running north and seeing if Roy'd be willing to head down here with that counter, or at least let you use it?"

"Sure. On it." Harper hurried back to the lobby.

Darci, seated in the small waiting area beside Elijah, looked up. "What's going on?"

"Wait here a bit? I gotta run and get Roy real quick. Watch him. I'll be back in a few minutes." She ran out to her bike, not waiting for an answer.

Harper pedaled hard, leaning forward like some kind of

motorcycle racer. Normally, Roy worked with Cliff patrolling around the western part of town, south of the militia HQ all the way down to the Safeway. The residential areas there held mostly childless single adults. Today, they wouldn't be on their late rotation, so they ought to be in that area. However, since Roy worked the investigation into Weldon's murder, he could be almost anywhere.

Dammit. We need personal radios!

The most frustrating part about not having radios was that the town *did* have a whole bunch of walkie talkies… but they'd all been killed by EMP. No amount of wishing would resurrect the dead technology. Even if they could find some working radios, the way the new power grid kept going up and down would make them unreliable. Rechargeable batteries didn't work so well without somewhere to plug them in to actually recharge.

As fast as she could make the bike move, she rode to the north part of Evergreen. Eventually, she headed left on Stagecoach Road past the Big R store, steering for the residential area where Roy and Cliff would most likely be. Having no other way to communicate, she swallowed her introversion and shouted, "Roy!" every five to ten seconds as she cruised along. Making noise, drawing attention to herself in public, had been the thing that scared her the most during high school. But a little social embarrassment seemed insignificant in light of a possibly irradiated child.

Fortunately, a world without electricity, working cars, or aircraft tended to be quiet.

The sixth time she yelled, a quick air horn pip sounded from her left and a little behind. She slammed on the brakes, yanked the bike around in a 180, and headed right on Quarter Horse Road.

"Roy?" shouted Harper.

"Yeah," called Roy, a fair ways in.

She stopped at a Y-shaped fork in the road a hundred or so feet in from the turn. "Where are you?"

"What's wrong?" shouted Cliff to the left.

Harper rode that way, nearly crashing into the two men while taking a hard left turn. She ended up hitting a street sign marked

'Silverleaf Oak,' but not hard enough to damage the sign—or the bike.

Cliff jogged over and pulled her back onto the road. "What's got your butt lit on fire?"

Winded from the fast ride and lightheaded from the shouting, she took a moment to simply breathe. "There's... need... Roy."

"Here I am." Roy smiled, arms out to either side.

She looked up at him, never happier to see a cop. Even if she technically was one herself, he still *looked* like one. "Do you have a Geiger counter?"

"Yeah. And crap. That's never a good question to ask. What happened?"

"Who got into what mess?" Cliff's grip on her arm tightened a little from nervousness.

Harper shook her head. "This guy past the lake, Aaron North. Walter sent me down there to deliver some medicine. On the way back, I saw this little boy wandering around in his birthday suit looking lost. Checked on him... found his father dead in bed. Looked like radiation poisoning. All his hair fell out. Swollen. Been there a couple days. Janice sent me up here to ask for the Geiger counter."

"You know how to use it?"

"Not a clue."

Roy nodded. "All right. Guess I'll take the ride then. You handle it okay up here?"

"You know it." Cliff rubbed Roy's bald head. "Careful with the radiation. We'd never notice if you got poisoned."

"You're a funny man, Burton." Roy made a 'come here' gesture at Harper. "Let me use the bike to go grab the counter and a second bike."

Harper dismounted. "All right. Guess I'll head back out onto 74 and wait for you there?"

"That works." Roy swung the bike around, got on, and rode away.

"Exciting day." Cliff folded his arms. "You see anything hot?"

"Nothing obvious. Just a house with kids' toys littered all over the place. Not like he had a warhead taken apart on the coffee table."

Cliff chuckled.

"Does radioactive stuff really glow or is that just movie BS?"

"Yes and no."

"That helps." Harper followed the road east, cutting across the residential area to avoid going around in a circle.

"Depends. Like the stuff they put in nuclear weapons doesn't glow. Just looks like metal. Radiation *can* glow, but the only time I've heard of it doing so is in the water of some nuclear reactors. Something about photons interacting with the water making blue light. There's a Russian-sounding name for the effect I can't remember." He waved a hand around. "Chekov Radiation or Chelensky… something like that."

"Wow. You're really smart for a mall security guard."

"Hey. I resemble that remark."

She chuckled.

"*Cherenkov* Radiation." Cliff snapped his fingers. "I think that's it."

"That'll come in really handy to know."

He gave her a flat look. "You asked."

"I wanted to know if we needed to keep an eye out for anything making light. The name of a scientific phenomenon isn't going to help us."

"Whatever, Miss Too Cool for School."

"Hah."

"Learning is important. Just because the world blew up doesn't mean you should stop doing your homework. People need to learn so we don't slide back into being cavemen."

"I'm not in school. I don't have homework."

He held a hand up at her. "Technicalities."

"And cave*men*? Isn't that sexist?"

Cliff gave her major side eye.

She laughed.

Upon reaching Route 74, Harper sat to rest. She explained in detail what she'd seen inside the house, the body, the smell, and the boy's appearance.

"I'm inclined to agree with Janice. Doesn't sound like the boy suffered the same exposure to the source. If this North guy was a scavenger, he probably walked back and forth through an irradiated zone multiple times. Radiation damage doesn't show up right away. If he went into a nasty enough spot, he could've picked up a fatal dose in only a few minutes."

"Didn't you say the radioactivity from a nuclear weapon strike falls off pretty rapidly? Like, nowhere near what the movies show where places are uninhabitable for decades and decades."

"That's true. The contamination from a nuke strike falls off relatively fast. A nuclear power plant melting down is a different story. That can create a dead zone that'll last a good few centuries. Much more radioactive material involved, and it isn't mostly consumed in an instant critical reaction like with a weapon."

Harper shivered. "You think this guy might have gone into an old power plant?"

"Well, if the staff died before they could shut down, or panicked and left... the reactors might have run away. Those things, as far as I know, are supposed to shut themselves down if they're abandoned. But, it's not like anyone ever tested what happens by abandoning a real plant. Almost a year after the blast, who the hell knows what's happened inside those places?"

"Great. Now I'm going to be scared of radiation."

"That's a good thing to be scared of." Cliff rubbed a hand back and forth across her back. "Don't freak out too bad. Roy runs around with that counter every so often. Hasn't found anything really scary in town."

"Whew."

A few minutes later, Roy Ellis came riding down the highway while towing a second mountain bike at his side. She gave Cliff a quick hug, hopped on the extra bike, and started heading south again.

"Be home before ten, and if any boys try to give you radiation, say no," called Cliff.

"Okay, Dad!" shouted Harper.

Riding fast made it somewhat difficult to attempt a conversation, so as much as she felt tempted to ask Roy about the Weldon investigation, she figured Elijah needed attention more urgently than a man who'd already died. It didn't take them too long to cover the slightly more than a mile ride south to the sheriff's department. Bikes definitely made the town feel smaller compared to walking everywhere.

Harper skidded to a stop in front of the sheriff's office and blinked in shock at Darci sitting on the curb next to Elijah… inhaling from a joint her friend held to the boy's lips. He appeared to have been given a bath as well as an adult-sized T-shirt to wear like a dress.

"Darce!" shouted Harper.

Her friend looked up. "Oh, hey. Welcome back."

"What the hell?" Roy stared at the boy. "You better tell me I'm seeing things here."

"What he said." Harper jumped off the bike and stormed over to her. "Are you seriously giving a four-year-old weed?"

"I'm five," said Elijah, his words written on the air in smoke. He barely even coughed. "Not four."

"Oh, five." Roy rolled his eyes. "Well, it's totally okay then. *Four-*year-olds are a bit too young."

"It's all natural," said Darci, right before taking a pull on the joint herself.

"So is arsenic." Roy unstrapped a yellow metal box from the side of his bike and fiddled with some knobs. "I'm gonna pretend I didn't see that kid tokin' up. Better not happen again until he's fifteen."

"Must you?" Harper sighed at Darci. "Really? He's just a little kid. People have to be at least fifteen for beer. Weed's gonna be the same."

"He needed it." Darci looked down. "He knows what's going on."

"Still… He's too small." Harper crouched and examined the boy's face. Eyes, slightly bloodshot. "He's high."

Darci made a 'duh' face at her. "Yeah. That's the whole point. Besides, he only took three hits. It'll wear off fast."

"Would Daddy be this sick if we still had ambulances?" asked Elijah in a dazed voice.

"Umm. If we still had ambulances, he wouldn't have gotten sick from this." Harper wanted to pick him up like a lost kitten, but resisted.

Roy approached and waved a metal wand over the child. The box in his other hand emitted a series of ticking noises.

Elijah looked down. "We're all gonna die, aren't we?"

"Nah. We'll be okay." Harper ruffled his hair. "Yeah, things are different and a little scary, but people existed before technology. We can do it again."

"You can stay with me." Darci put an arm around the boy. "I'd like a kid brother."

"You gave him weed. Not sure that qualifies you as a good role model to raise a kid." Harper folded her arms.

Darci laughed. "In this world, I think the most important thing any of us can do is just take whatever happens in stride. There's no point getting worked up over anything. Stuff's gonna happen that we used to be able to stop, but can't anymore. Like diseases. Getting sad or pissed off won't change a damn thing." She took a long drag, held it for a moment, then exhaled. "All we can do is have fun while we can and deal with the bullshit."

Elijah leaned up, trying to get his mouth on the joint.

Darci patted him on the head. "You've had enough for now, little man."

"He's clean of radiation," said Roy, turning the counter off. "If he had any contaminated dust on him, looks like they washed it off already."

"Yeah, we gave him a bath in a sink. Janice said he might have particles on him." Darci brushed a hand over the boy's hair.

Harper nodded. "Let's go talk to her. Darce, can we trust you not to turn him into a pothead by age six?"

"Okay, okay. I promise I won't give him any more until he's old enough. Little man's Dad went to the Good Place. Cut him some slack." Darci glanced at the joint. "Call it a one-off for severe circumstances. Medicinal, not recreational."

Harper sighed, shook her head, and went inside with Roy.

18

GLOWING

F ollowing a brief conference in Janice Holt's office, Harper accompanied a small group back to the house where she'd found Elijah. She didn't need to lead them, since Janice knew where Aaron North lived. On the way, she explained to Roy that the man had been a scavenger, heading out on his own again and again. Sometimes, he brought back useful things—ammo, weapons, clothing, medicine, canned food. Most of the time, he came back with 'curiosities.'

Harper and Roy exchanged a look at that.

"If he didn't get irradiated from being at a ground zero location, he might have found a piece of a radiotherapy machine." Roy shook his head. "Maybe he found a capsule of cesium chloride. There was a bad accident involving that stuff in Brazil, around '87 I think. If he found that shit, we are in deep, deep trouble. Could wipe us all out."

A sensation came on like fleas crawling all over Harper's body under her clothes. "Am I contaminated? I was in the house."

The group stopped walking long enough for Roy to check her over with the Geiger counter. It made some scary noises, but his expression remained calm.

"Nope. You're clear."

"It's squawking."

"Background radiation. It's unusual if these things are completely silent. That usually only happens in a shielded environment where nothing can get in."

"Wow. You know a lot about radiation for a cop."

"Hazmat training." He bowed his head and shut the machine off. "Used to get some trains coming through transporting spent nuclear fuel, so we had to learn this stuff. Never imagined I'd need it for the end of the world."

"Yeah…"

They continued without conversation, walking the relatively short distance down the road from the sheriff's building to the street leading to Aaron North's house. Roy turned the counter on again a good distance from the front door, then advanced on the property at a slow, cautious pace.

Harper stared at the needle. The squawking and ticking increased in volume and frequency as they neared the house. She almost asked how bad it was, but the noise lessened after they went inside. Still, it appeared the living room had more radiation than outside away from the house.

Janice and Calvin Velasquez accompanied them as they went upstairs and down the hall to the master bedroom. The Geiger counter increased in noise the whole way down the hall, going almost crazy when they entered the bedroom.

"Aww damn." Calvin covered his mouth and nose under one hand. "Stinks."

"Poor son of a bitch," muttered Janice, seemingly unfazed by the odor.

Roy's face scrunched up at the stink, but he didn't hesitate entering the room and going over it with the sensor. The counter squealed louder near the floor and when he held it near the body.

"The guy's hot, for sure. Definitely radiation sickness." Roy took a step back. "Don't think it's *too* bad. Shouldn't be dangerous exposure for the team carrying him out to a grave somewhere. Definitely suggest the hole be dug first to minimize time near the body."

"All right. Let's back away for now," said Janice.

"Where's it coming from?" Harper kicked a plastic fighter jet out of her way. "If there's something radioactive in the house, shouldn't we get rid of it so no one else gets sick?"

"Yeah. Mind looking for it, Roy?" Janice raised an eyebrow.

"No problem."

Harper followed in curious silence as Roy went room to room upstairs. Elijah's bedroom at the opposite end of the house from his father's room didn't have any more radiation than background. The steps registered a mild increase, likely from dust he tracked around. Roy followed the 'glowing' trail into the living room to the sofa, then another trail down the hall to the bathroom.

"Hey…" Harper pointed straight. "The guy's bedroom is right over the garage and the counter went nuts when you held it near the floor."

Roy backed out of the bathroom. "Makes sense. He'd put those curiosities in the garage."

Calvin hung back, seeming worried. Roy led the way to the garage. Janice pulled Harper back by one shoulder.

She blinked. "What?"

"You're too young to get radiation sickness. Hang back." Janice stepped past her. "My ovaries are retired."

"You're not that old." Harper nudged her.

Janice laughed. "Age has nothing to do with that retirement decision."

Roy opened the door at the end of the hall and the Geiger counter went nuts. "Whoa. Cheese and rice, that's hot."

"What'cha got?" Janice stopped short and blocked Harper from moving forward.

Calvin retreated to the living room.

"It's not 'melt your face off,' but it's significant. Being in here for a minute is probably about the same as getting a few x-rays." Roy entered the garage. "Mostly machine parts. Washers, dryers, generators. Road signs, traffic lights for some stupid reason. I don't see anything that looks like it came from a hospital. Must be all this metal that's giving off radiation."

"What the hell?" asked Janice. "Radioactive laundry machines?"

Roy walked out of sight from the door. "Yeah, all this junk is glowing. Doesn't look like any singular high source of radioactivity, but a collective dose... If he's been around this stuff, working on it, for weeks. Kid's been in the house. Probably climbed around in here watching his old man tinker. We need to get him to the clinic. No idea how much of a dose he got." Roy retreated from the garage and shoved the door closed, pointing the Geiger wand back over his shoulder. "We're going to need to get all this crap away from town. Best to bury it, but that's a shitload of work. At least we need to get it out of here. My guess is that most of this stuff had been close enough to a ground zero to become irradiated but not vaporized."

Janice faced Harper. "Will you run Elijah up to the med center?"

"Yeah. Sure. No problem." She didn't necessarily mind getting away from radioactive junk, especially to rush a potentially at-risk child to the doctor. "On it."

Janice patted her on the arm. "Nice job, kiddo."

"Thanks."

Harper ran out the door and hurried back to collect her bike, one slightly irradiated child, and her friend Darci.

19

DANGEROUS STUFF

R iding a mountain bike while carrying a five-year-old tested Harper's sense of balance.

Her mother's voice needled at the back of her mind for doing something dangerous, but no one had bothered installing kid seats on the militia bikes or even cargo racks. So, she did the best she could, balancing him in her lap with one arm around him. Darci, having no reason to stay in the south part of Evergreen, jumped on her bike and rode alongside.

Elijah didn't seem to mind or even fidget much. Neither Janice nor anyone else at the sheriff's office said one way or the other if the boy had been told his father died, but she had a feeling he knew. Darci giving him a few hits of pot likely explained his mellowness. Or, maybe he did know what happened and his relative calm came from sorrow.

The little orb of light brown hair under her chin smelled of scented soap, though she couldn't place the brand.

Any radioactive contamination probably went down the drain already, but he might've gotten it inside. Kids eat and lick everything.

"Hang on, okay? We'll be there soon," said Harper.

"Where are we going?" Elijah peered up at her.

"To see the doctor and make sure everything's okay."

Elijah squirmed. "Is I gonna have'ta get needles? I don't like needles."

"I hate needles, too" Darci made a sour face. "Usually make me cry."

"But you're big!" The boy flailed. "You's not s'posed ta be scared o' nothin'."

Harper pictured her friend saying something typically Darci like 'when you get big, you see all the *really* scary stuff they keep hidden from little kids—like jobs.'

"I'm scared of spiders, too." Darci shivered. "Are you?"

"Nope." Elijah grinned. "Spiders are good. They eat all the bad bugs."

Harper chuckled. "Don't worry. I don't think this doctor is going to give you any needles."

He dramatically wiped a hand across his forehead. "Whew. That's good."

"You know all the junk your daddy put in the garage of your house?"

"That wasn't our house." The boy looked down. "Our house is far away. It's busted so we can't stay there. We hadda walk for a long time."

Harper squeezed him a little tighter as the road curved. They didn't go too fast, but a fall on pavement would still hurt him. "Sorry. I mean, the house where I found you. He had stuff in the garage."

"Lots of stuff." Elijah held his arms out to the sides. "Big stuff."

"Did you play in there a lot?"

He shook his head in a wobbly, exaggerated manner. "No. Daddy liked to find stuff that goes"—the boy made an explosion sound —"an' 'cause that, he didn't let me go in the g'rage."

Harper smiled a conspiratorial little smile. "So, that means you used to sneak in."

"Umm." He fidgeted. "Maybe."

"It's okay, Elijah. I'm not that old yet. Still basically a kid, too. I promise you won't get in trouble if you tell me the truth."

"You're not a kid 'cause you got boobies." Elijah poked his finger into her left breast.

"Ow. Hey! Brat." Harper tickled his side, distracting his errant hand to defense.

Darci cackled.

He thrust his left arm out, pointing at Evergreen Lake going by. "That's where fishes live!"

"Yes. That's where they live… until we catch 'em."

"Wow, I'd like totally kill someone for some decent sushi." Darci smacked her lips. "Wait, I probably shouldn't say crap like that now. Someone might think I'm being literal."

Harper cringed.

"I don't like eating fishes." Elijah flexed his biceps. "But I gotta or I won't get big."

An uphill grade forced her to pedal harder, causing the bike to wobble since she only had one hand to steer with. "My little sister doesn't like eating animals at all, but she'll do it now if it's all we have."

"Yeah." Elijah rubbed his belly. "I like French fries. But the bad guys blew up France so there's no more."

Darci laughed. "Well, we'll have to make Evergreen fries then."

"Cool!" cheered the boy. "What are those?"

"Kinda the same thing but made here instead." Darci held up a finger. "Just gotta find some oil."

"Oh, boy. Please don't try cooking. There isn't a fire department anymore." Harper winked.

Darci stuck out her tongue.

She kept quiet for a little while, letting the boy stare out at the lake until Route 74 curved away from the water, still going uphill. "So, just between kids, how many times did you sneak into the garage?"

"Couple times." He held up four fingers. "It wasn't fun, so I didn't stay long."

Hopefully, he didn't get too much exposure.

They talked about random things like trees, fish, what if

vegetables could eat people instead, and so on for the remainder of the ride. As soon as she stopped outside the medical center, Elijah wriggled loose, slid to the ground, and ran to the edge of the parking lot—where he proceeded to hike up the T-shirt and water the grass.

Darci got off her bike. "Yeah, total kindred spirit to Lorelei."

"She's not an outdoor pee-er. Just 'forgets' to put clothes on. Must be a boy thing." Harper folded her arms, waiting. *He's used to being left alone. No rules. If Darce does get the okay to take him in, she's going to have her hands full.*

Once finished, Elijah ran back over. Harper took his hand and they went inside.

"Good afternoon, Harper," said Ruby from behind the reception desk. "Find another stray?"

"I'm not Stray. I'm Elijah."

Harper approached Ruby's desk. "He was living in the south part with his dad. Need to ask Dr. Khan or Tegan to check him out. There's a bit of a possible situation."

"Oh?" Ruby partially stood out of her chair to look at him. "What happened?"

"He might have been exposed to radiation," said Darci.

Harper cringed, unsure how much detail to talk about in front of a five-year-old, but he probably wouldn't understand it, anyway. "Yeah. We're not sure how much of a dose he got, but the house had a bunch of glowing junk in the garage." She silently mouthed, "His father died."

"Oh, my. Go right on back. Dr. Hale is free. Dr. Khan is with someone." Ruby gestured at the hall. "Room 3."

"Thanks." Harper led Elijah into the hall, Darci following, and walked up to the door marked '3.' "Hello?" She peeked in.

Dr. Tegan Hale sat in a blue padded chair by the window, reading. "Come in." She bookmarked her place, set the novel aside, and got up.

Harper walked in, scooped the boy up, and set him seated on the exam table. "Elijah, this is Dr. Hale."

"Hiii." He waved energetically.

"Why hello there, big guy." Tegan smiled at the boy, then looked at Harper, eyebrows up. "What brings you in today?"

"Darce," muttered Harper. She nodded at the door and stepped outside.

Darci proceeded to keep Elijah's attention.

Tegan walked into the hall. "Bad?"

"Elijah's father spent some months scavenging things from blast zones. He collected a bunch of radioactive junk… and we found him deceased. Made Roy's Geiger counter squeal."

"Oh, no." Tegan put a hand over her heart. "That poor child. Does he know?"

"Not sure. He told me his father 'wouldn't wake up.' Best I can figure, the man died a day or two ago. I kinda think Elijah has an idea what happened. As far as contamination goes, he'd been left alone long enough that he decided not to wear clothes. So, he wouldn't have had any fabric keeping radioactive dust close to him. Darci gave him a thorough bath at the sheriff's office. He's clean on the outside, but we were worried about him suffering exposure. He told me he went into the garage a couple times but didn't stay long. Roy said the junk pile was about as hot as an x-ray."

Tegan glanced left down the hall. "Hmm. We're not really equipped to deal with contamination. No DTPA or Prussian blue. We do have some potassium iodide though. I'll give him that as a preventative."

"Okay."

"Be right back." Tegan hurried into the storeroom at the end of the hall, returning to the exam room a moment later with a pill bottle.

"Hiii!" Elijah waved.

Harper and Darci stood off to the side while Tegan performed a basic physical exam on the boy, including weighing him and listening to him breathe via stethoscope. She appeared concerned by the reflex test and when she examined his eyes.

"Is something wrong?" asked Harper.

"Has this child been given marijuana?" Tegan shot a pointed stare at Darci.

"Just a tiny bit. Little man had a bad day." Darci tried to stuff her hands in her pockets, but miniskirts didn't have them, so she tried to be smooth and pretended to adjust it.

Tegan frowned. "I'd strongly advise against repeating that."

"Okay." Darci looked down, kicking at the floor.

Harper couldn't help but smile.

"What's funny about this?" Tegan shifted her displeased glance to Harper.

"Nothing. I mean it's just… Roy already chewed her out for it but, she didn't look anywhere near as ashamed of herself as when you did."

"She's a doctor," said Darci in a 'well duh' voice. "Cops always lie about stuff like that."

"So, you believe her?" Harper held her hands up in exasperation. "What about me?"

"You're technically a cop now." Darci wagged her eyebrows.

Harper sighed.

"All right, kiddo. Need you to be really brave. This isn't going to taste good." Tegan cut an iodide pill in half and gave one piece to him with some water.

Elijah made a face after swallowing it. "Eww."

"Good! You did really well." Tegan patted him on the head. "Taking a little eww like a warrior."

He puffed out his chest.

"Well?" whispered Harper.

Tegan brushed a hand over the boy's wild hair, trying to set it to some kind of order. "He's not showing any outward signs, so I'm thinking he should be okay. However, I'd like to keep an eye on him in case something happens down the road. If he received enough of a dose to be problematic, any symptoms would develop over the next few days."

"Are we gonna need that DTPA stuff? If it's that important, maybe we should hit the hospital in Denver again." Harper narrowed her eyes, thinking of Lawless. She wouldn't necessarily mind trimming their numbers, but asking for a fight felt like teasing fate too much.

"DTPA?" asked Darci.

"Diethylenetriamine pentaacetic acid," said Tegan. "It reacts with some radioactive metals to help purge them from the body."

"Oh. Sounds expensive." Harper bit her lip. "I mean... before."

Tegan chuckled. "If nothing else, the war broke the strangle hold the pharma companies and big insurance had on medical care." She grimaced. "Of course, it also broke medical care in general... so we're not exactly better off. But hey, I no longer spend eighteen hours a week filling out forms."

"Yeah. So, he's okay?" Harper forced a big smile. Maybe excessive hope would help.

"As far as I can tell right now, probably. We don't have any of the stuff I'd need to evaluate his level of radiation exposure more thoroughly."

"Thanks." Harper exhaled, relieved. "Okay. He'll be staying around here up north to be closer to the school. Whenever you want to check on him again, just let me know... or did you mean you wanted to keep him at the clinic for a few days?"

Tegan shook her head. "I don't see any reason to keep him cooped up since he isn't showing any outward symptoms. Why don't you have him back here in three days, or sooner if you notice any vomiting, rashes, unusual changes in behavior, mood, eating habits, hair loss, and so on."

"Don't cut my hair." Elijah grabbed his head in both hands. "I like it."

Darci scooped him up into a hug. "No one's gonna cut your hair. C'mon, I'll show you where you're gonna stay now."

"Okay."

"Umm." Harper offered a weak smile. "We should really go see Anne-Marie so she can assign him to a family."

"I'm serious." Darci pivoted the child away defensively. "I wanna take him in."

"Since when did you have baby fever? You never talked about wanting kids."

Darci smiled. "Because I didn't want to have to deal with a guy."

Harper blinked. "Wait, you're saying the girl who did you know what you know where with you know who at sixteen isn't into boys?"

Tegan whistled innocently.

"Boyfriends are one thing. Having a kid with a dude is totally different. Keeping a guy around long term is way more work than it's worth." Darci laughed. "And, your face. I am totally teasing you."

Harper sighed out her nose, her eyebrows flat. "Not funny."

"Nah, I never really thought about it, yanno." Darci looked at Elijah, almost nose-to-nose. "Something clicked in my head when I saw him."

"He's not a stray puppy," said Harper. "Having a kid to look after is a big responsibility."

Elijah looked back and forth between them. "Why can't I stay with Daddy?"

A ten-ton anvil of guilt fell out of the sky and flattened Harper. Or at least crushed her heart. Darci rocked him, patting his back.

"Elijah…" Harper gently took his hand. "The stuff in the garage is bad. It made your daddy very sick. He, umm, went to be with your mother."

The boy stared at her, his huge hazel eyes growing even larger. Realization set in after a few seconds and he looked down. "Oh."

Harper squeezed his hand. "He didn't want to leave you. It just happened. The kind of sick he got from that stuff happened slow. Your father didn't even know it was making him sick."

Elijah nodded, continuing to gaze at the floor for a while before sighing. "Okay. Are he and Mommy happy now?"

"Pretty sure." Darci looked around. "I bet their ghosts are right here with you now making sure you're okay."

Elijah gasped in awe.

Ugh. Harper fidgeted. She'd never believed in ghosts, an afterlife, or anything spiritual. *He's five. What's wrong with a little Santa Claus if it makes him feel better?* She smiled. "Yes. I'm sure they're together now. They were worried about you, but now that you're safe, they can be happy."

He grinned, waving randomly at the room. "Bye, Daddy. When you get to the good place, tell Mommy I miss her."

Tegan choked up. Harper closed her eyes, trying not to cry.

"Aww, man." Darci sniffled. "Whoever hit the button needs to get ball cancer and die painfully over the course of six weeks."

Harper barked out the bastard offspring of a sob and a laugh. "Yeah. Seriously." She stared at her friend and the kid for a long moment. "I really should have you talk to Anne-Marie. If you tell her you're interested in looking after him, she'll probably be okay with it. You're eighteen, after all. But—please don't give him pot again. At least not until he's fifteen."

"Swear." Darci grinned at him. "No more kind bud for little man."

Elijah blinked in confusion.

Tegan walked them out to the front, past Room 2 where Dr. Khan and Grace worked to stitch up a nasty slice in a man's shin. Harper shivered at the poor guy clutching the sides of the exam table and trying not to scream.

"Thank you." Harper smiled at Tegan when they reached the waiting area. "I'll make sure he's back here in a few days."

"Sounds good. You girls be careful out there."

Darci followed her outside. "Okay. Let's go talk to Anne-Marie."

"Cool. Thanks."

Harper headed across the street to the militia HQ building. Her perpetually high friend didn't strike her as the ideal candidate for being the guardian of a child, but maybe having the boy to look after would do her some good, too. Harper could keep an eye on them, and if she worried too much about Elijah's safety, she could always intervene. She wondered if Aaron North understood the junk might have been radioactive, and that's why he'd told the boy to stay out of the garage. Perhaps he simply underestimated the strength of it. If not, there might be other dangerous things in there. Either way, cleaning up that garage would be a giant mess.

Fortunately, she wouldn't have to deal with it. That thought made her feel a little guilty, but not enough to stop her from being relieved.

"Am I gonna see Mommy and Daddy again when I go to the good place?" asked Elijah as they approached the HQ building.

"Yep." Darci opened the door for Harper. "But you're not allowed to go to the good place yet. You're way too little. Gotta be an old fart to get in there."

The boy laughed—and made a fart noise.

20

SMART

The aroma of fire-roasted vegetables, chicken, and bread hung in the air over the table.

Harper teased her fork at a hockey-puck-sized disc of potato crisscrossed by grill burn lines. She ate in no great hurry, due mostly to being lost in thought but also to savor it. Having a large gathering for dinner time no longer felt like a special occasion or a holiday. It made sense to pool resources and share. Less firewood, no wasted leftovers, people to talk to and appreciate being alive with.

In addition to her family, which she now considered to include Carrie and Renee, Grace and Darci (who brought Elijah over) had come by to eat. Despite the large group, they had enough food even if most of it consisted of potatoes, squash, and carrots. One whole chicken went pretty quick given all the mouths clamoring for some. Madison happily offered to trade her portion of meat for extra veggies, but Harper insisted she eat it for the protein.

The arrival of Elijah naturally precipitated an explanation of how he'd come to be there.

Cliff got that look in his eye like he wanted to have a 'teaching moment' the instant Harper mentioned the junk being radioactive, but waited for her to finish telling them how Anne-Marie agreed to let Darci look after the boy provisionally. If she thought things worked out, they'd consider it a permanent family placement.

"Does Anne-Marie know Darce pretty much has a continuous ten percent level of THC in her blood?" asked Grace.

Darci raspberried her. "It's not that high, and yeah. I told her I smoke often. Agreed to cut back a bit. But you know, I never get totally wasted."

Harper and Renee exchanged 'yeah okay' glances, which made Darci sigh dramatically.

"Suppose it needs saying." Cliff wiped his mouth, then wiped his hand on his leg. "Everyone should be careful about metal objects that came from places damaged by a strike. They become radioactive. Way back when they were first making nukes, they had an accident with a plutonium core. It didn't explode, but it let off a nasty burst of radiation that killed the lead scientist. All the men in the room had to drop their watches, rings, belt buckles… anything metal."

Darci whistled.

"Neutron activation." Grace held up her hand while she finished chewing. "Exposure to strong sources of neutron radiation can irradiate various metals. Something like that demon core experiment you mentioned or the detonation of a nuclear weapon releases a ton of high energy neutrons which can bombard metals they come into contact with, changing them into inherently radioactive isotopes of their former material. Some substances are harder to activate since they take double or even triple neutron captures in the nucleus in order to change it into the radioisotope. Like water. I'm pretty sure hydrogen needs a double capture to become unstable tritium, and oxygen needs a triple capture. That's why water makes such a great coolant for reactors."

Cliff gawked. "She's an alien."

Laughter went around the table.

"Alien?" asked Harper.

"Look at her. Captain of the cheer squad with the brain of the kind of nerd that goes to college at twelve." Cliff grinned and stabbed his fork into a hunk of squash. "Damn smart. Ought to go to college. Oh, wait."

Grace blushed, chuckling hesitantly. The kids looked around, unsure how to react. Darci laughed, which made Elijah laugh. Renee sighed. Harper pushed food around her plate.

Carrie playfully swatted at Cliff. "That wasn't nice."

"Sorry. Too soon." Cliff took a gulp of water from his glass.

"It's okay." Grace shrugged. "It's almost been a year. We can't stay gloomy forever. Besides, the world needs smart people now more than ever. We have to figure out how to re-create all the stuff that's lost. And, dark humor is a good way to manage impossible situations."

"You okay," whispered Renee.

Harper looked up. "Yeah. Mostly worried." She looked across the table at Elijah. "Life's become so brittle."

"Not as brittle as you think." Cliff smiled and indicated Lorelei with a glance. "Sometimes the most delicate looking little critters just refuse to quit." He grinned in a 'that goes for you, too' way.

"Heh. Just trying to do what I can." Harper kept pushing food around her plate, wondering how she could be simultaneously embarrassed at being called a 'delicate critter' and grateful to have a dad.

Madison faced Lorelei. "Two out of three?"

Lorelei nodded.

The girls started doing rock-paper-scissors.

"What are you two deciding?" asked Cliff.

Madison paused. "Harp's sad, so one of us is going to pull teddy bear duty tonight."

"No need to decide that way." Harper flashed a mischievous smile. "I'm going to need both of you."

Lorelei and Madison laughed, and their laughter spread around the whole table.

21

PRECIOUS

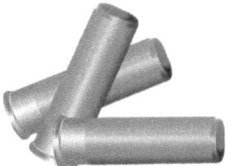

Despite it not being Saturday night, Harper found herself stuffed into the back end of the bathtub, washing Madison's hair. Her little sister sat in front of her, washing Lorelei who sat in front of her attempting to sing *Let it Go*. Not having seen the movie — or any video — in ten months, the little one completely mangled the words except for the main chorus. But at least she had the melody right.

The reason Harper had decided to invoke bath night, a normally once-a-week ritual, early was due to the power being stable all day long. That meant the water heater had a chance to produce hot water, which made for a highly normal feeling bath. Normal, except for the three of them sharing the tub.

When they first started taking baths together to save firewood, they'd both been numb from the shock of losing their parents, home, and entire world. Too numb to care about trivialities like privacy or embarrassment. Every single time Harper sat in the tub with Madison, she remembered the first time in that house by the mall when her sister leaned against her, asking her to 'become Mom.' She'd come to think of bath night as a symbol of it being the two of them against the world. Now, them plus Lorelei.

Madison would turn eleven in three months on October ninth. Hopefully, by then, Harper would be able to decide if she wanted to make a big deal out of it to make up for the complete nonevent of her tenth birthday not quite a month after the nukes went off. No one had time to care about birthdays amid that chaos. Calling extra attention to it might make Madison think of their parents' deaths or the war itself. She'd been mostly back to her old self lately, and Harper didn't want to upset that delicate balance.

She still looked too thin, as did Lorelei. Then again, Harper considered herself underweight, too. None of them appeared unhealthy or close to starvation, but they all had the sort of physiques that would get the health counselor at school asking if everything was okay at home.

Underfed isn't abnormal when everyone looks like this.

While cleaning her sister's hair, she thought about people back in Pioneer times, wondering if anyone in those days cared about counting calories or getting fat. *Probably not. If someone handed me two Big Macs right now, I'd scarf them both down and not even feel like a whale.*

Harper caught herself salivating at the thought of fast food. She'd never been all that big a fan, thinking it woefully unhealthy, but couldn't argue it tasted yummy. Now? She'd eat whatever landed in front of her.

Except maybe escargot. But, the odds of that happening roughly matched the odds of the Universe hitting rewind and undoing the war. No, they'd permanently gone into a frontier world where families shared bathtubs and didn't think it strange to have fifteen people gathered around a dinner table every night, not just on Thanksgiving and Christmas. She knew the names of mostly everyone who lived in her patrol area, but couldn't think of the names of her old neighbors back in Lakewood even two houses over.

"Okay, stand up," said Madison.

Lorelei obliged.

Madison proceeded to wash the girl's legs and feet.

Having cleaned her sister's back and hair, Harper washed her own hair, then the rest of herself.

Once she'd finished bathing Lorelei, Madison stood to clean her lower half. "Harp? Do I have a big black mark on my butt?"

Harper looked. A noticeable bruise darkened the left side of her kid sister's rear end, but it hardly counted as a 'big black mark.' "Little bruise." She poked it. "What happened?"

"Fell and landed on a rock at the farm. Hurt like a bitch."

Lorelei gasped. "That's a bad word."

"Not that bad," muttered Madison. "Not like I said F—" She stopped herself and glanced over her shoulder flashing an impish smile, like she never intended to actually say it, merely tease Harper.

"Ha. Ha." Harper tickled her sides.

Madison squealed and whirled to face her.

This, naturally, caused Lorelei to tickle her from behind. Madison again squealed and shouted, "Stop!"

A brief tickle battle ended after water started splashing out of the tub and Harper called a 'cease fire.' Eventually, bathing finished and they all got out to dry off.

"Harp?" asked Madison while toweling off her hair.

"Yeah?"

"How long are we gonna have to keep sharing baths?"

Harper pulled her towel down off her face, unusually saddened by the thought. Of course, she expected her sister would eventually outgrow it. "As long as you want to. But, if you'd rather have privacy again, we should at least take turns in the same water, especially when we're on firewood. Everything's precious now, even water."

Madison shrugged and shifted the towel around to dry her body. "Whatever. I'm just thinking we're gonna run out of room in there when I grow up. It doesn't bother me anymore. I used to be a brat."

"Nah." Harper play-punched her sister's shoulder. "It's not bratty to want privacy. That's normal."

"Nothing is normal anymore." Madison's expression became fearful, as though she'd just awakened from a nightmare. "I'm still scared of being alone. I'm okay sharing the tub, the bed… I don't want you to go."

Harper wrapped herself in a towel dress, then hugged her. "Relax, Termite. I'm not going anywhere."

"Cool. Guess it's childish to be afraid of being alone."

"It's not. We've been through some crap."

"Eww," said Lorelei.

Harper smiled. "Not actual crap. Just bad stuff."

"Oh." Lorelei bent forward, letting her hair hang down to the floor while shaking her head side to side and making a whirring noise.

"What the heck are you doing?" asked Madison.

"Post mapoc-a-lips bow dry," said Lorelei.

Madison giggled.

Harper chuckled and 'captured' Lorelei in a towel, drying her off. "You are a nut."

"I know." Lorelei laughed.

"Umm…" Madison bit her lip. "Is Logan gonna move in here if you guys like decide to stay together?"

"Haven't really thought about that. I dunno. If that happens, probably not before you're a teenager. You and Lore would end up sharing a bed then, since I'd probably room with him."

Madison stared pleadingly at her.

"But, I'm not ready to outgrow my two favorite stuffed animals." Harper clamped Madison and Lorelei together in a hug, making them laugh.

Madison appeared to relax and traded the towel for her nightgown. The instant Harper released her towel grip on Lorelei, the child zoomed out the door. Not wanting to streak after her, Harper merely sighed and finished drying herself off. Madison got another case of the giggles.

A moment later, happy squealing approached the door.

Carrie walked in, holding Lorelei. "Got an escapee."

Harper laughed, tossing the girl's nightgown to Carrie. "Thanks for the assist."

"No problem." Carrie set the child on her feet and dressed her. "Glad you're okay with me being around."

"Oh, stop." Harper pulled her nightgown on and collected the towels. "It's fine. Feels good having a mom again."

Lorelei hugged Harper, but smiled up at Carrie. She still reacted to Harper more like a mother than big sister, but she also still loved everyone, having zero fear or apprehension around strangers. Everyone—including Harper—expected Darci to have a kid before high school ended, but the girl had gotten way lucky. However, Harper never expected to be a mother before eighteen, much less before she'd ever had sex.

"Yeah." Madison smiled, then hugged Carrie. "It's cool. Harper needs the help. I like having you here, too."

Whoa. Harper blinked at Madison. A happy tear hung at the corner of her eye. All the dread that had been haunting her about medicine, that everyone she loved would die within five or ten years from lame stuff that wouldn't have been a worry in the modern world, evaporated. Seeing her little sister accept Carrie into their family gave her hope.

And Harper's world needed all of that she could find.

22

JUDGEMENT

July plus no air conditioning made for uncomfortable sleeping, especially with her two little sisters sharing the bed. Being high up altitude wise resulted in some nights having a pleasant, even cool, temperature, but tonight decided to be stuffy. Somehow, the tiny one didn't care and passed right out. Madison joked in a half-awake, delirious voice about going to sleep outside. It probably would be cooler if for no other reason than a breeze.

Harper drifted in and out of sleep. Eventually, the need to pee forced her out of bed. She crept across the hall to the bathroom. On autopilot, she flicked the light switch, nearly yelping in shock when it worked. Squinting at the glare, Harper fumbled around to close the door and took a seat, holding her head in both hands while unloading her bladder.

Once finished, she shut the light off—blinding herself—and felt her way out into the hall. Faint light from the front of the house pulled her down the hall out of curiosity. Cliff, in olive drab boxer briefs, sat at the table swishing something around in a mug.

"Hey," rasped Harper. "You okay?"

"Hmm?" He looked over, then away. "Aww, geez. Put something on."

"I am wearing something. A nightgown."

"Can see right through that thing. Put on something we grabbed from your old place."

She chuckled, looking down at the faintly pink fabric. Somewhat more opaque patches covered the sensitive areas, but the garment had an amount of transparency that would have mortified pre-war Harper. "It's hot. I'm channeling the spirit of Lorelei. What's up?"

"Just thinking. I don't really sleep like normal people anymore." He sipped from the mug.

"Well, no kidding if you're drinking coffee at two in the morning, or whatever time it is."

"Tea, not coffee. Had some chamomile left. Want a cup? This stuff's supposed to help ya sleep."

"Thanks, but it's too hot for tea." She sat in the chair. "Ugh. Even the chairs are warm. Isn't it supposed to be cool up here in the mountains?"

"This *is* cool. You've just gotten used to it. Now, if you want to talk about hot, Iraq. 117 in the shade some days."

"Eww. I'd melt."

He chuckled.

"So what about your sleep isn't normal?"

"Four hour blocks. No matter how tired I aim, I can only stay out for four hours. Basically, I'm permanently on fire watch." He winked. "I've gotten used to it."

"Right." She yawned. "I just can't sleep because it's warm."

"Go stand in the yard for five minutes, that'll cure it. It's much cooler out there."

She smiled. "Good idea. Oh, it's probably too late now, but..."

"If you're pregnant, I'm going to—"

"No." She folded her arms on the table and bonked her head a few times. "No, *gawd*, please no."

"It worries me that you are worried."

Harper lifted her head, a thick curtain of red blocking her face. "Dr. Hale gave me some BC pills. And Logan pulled out."

"'I'll pull out' is the greatest lie ever told right after 'no new taxes.'"

"Logan's not like that. Look, can we maybe change the subject?"

Cliff smiled into his tea. "You brought it up."

"I did not. I'm talking about tracks." She sat up, pulling her fluffy hair out of her face to drape down her back. "The guy I found dead on the farm. Weldon. I followed a trail from the body like you taught me. It went straight off the farm to the west, but I lost it. He wasn't killed where we found him. I'm pretty sure whoever killed the guy knew him and killed him for a specific reason."

"Roy's been saying that, too. But, he hasn't said anything about tracks."

She resisted the sleep tugging at her eyelids. "Will you take a look in the morning? Maybe you can figure out where that trail went."

"After this long, it's doubtful much of a track will be there, but I'll check it out. Exactly where did you find what so far?"

"We found his body in the third row of tomatoes from the left. Go north to the end of the row, then left. Basically straight west from there, all the way out of the farm into the hills."

"All right. I'll check on it once the sun's up." He drained the last of the chamomile in his mug. "Might as well give that sleep thing another chance for now."

"Yeah, me too."

They stood at roughly the same time.

"Hey…" She grasped his hand. "You make a really good dad."

He shrugged. "Just doing what anyone would in my position. Except putting a gun to your forehead." He cracked a wry smile.

"Hah. That scared the shit out of me. But… thinking back. *Now?* I'd probably do the exact same thing if I saw someone running after Jonathan with a rifle. Guess I changed. Or grew up."

"We've all changed. I used to be a mall cop who didn't really give a god damn if I saw tomorrow. Lost too many damn friends, most of them *after* the war. Just couldn't fit back into a civilian world. One day, I'm an elite Ranger commanding respect, the next, I'm chasing fat kids out of Cinnabon for shoplifting and getting laughed at."

"Sorry." She hugged him. "You're definitely elite and worthy of respect. And, just in case you didn't notice, we all really like Carrie. So if anything happens between you guys, we're totally cool with it."

Cliff coughed, glanced off to the side, and set his hands on his hips. "I… umm… Logan seems like a good kid. I trust your judgement."

She snickered. "I'm not sure *I* trust my judgement, but thanks."

"Heh. Well, if I'm Dad, then… go the F to sleep."

"Night, Dad."

He smiled, gestured for her to go first, and followed her into the hall. "Night, Harp."

"Oops," whispered Harper, upon reaching her bedroom door.

"What?" Cliff, paused in the midst of stepping around her.

She looked down at herself. "I've spent the past like twenty minutes not having a gun near me. Feels like I'm naked."

"In that thing, you basically are." Cliff averted his gaze and shuffled to his bedroom.

"It's not *that* thin."

"Maybe to Logan, it's fine. Not to your old man."

Grinning, Harper slipped into her room and tried to get in bed without waking either of the girls. No sooner did her head hit the pillow than Lorelei rolled over and clung. Fortunately, trying to stay awake to talk to Cliff made her tired enough to drift off despite the warmth of a tiny human clinging to her.

Never too old for stuffed animals.

23

IMPORTANT

The next few days brought a welcome dose of calm, and even happiness.

After her patrol shifts, Harper took the kids to the former country club by the golf course so they could swim in the pool. Quite a few people wanted to escape the heat, resulting in a fairly packed crowd that would have felt normal if not for the hazy sky and numerous improvised—or omitted—swimsuits. Fortunately, no adults opted for skinny dipping, though several women went topless. Oddly enough, exposed breasts and a handful of small streakers—which naturally included Lorelei—made her more uncomfortable than Marcie, Fred, Dennis, and Sanchez standing watch over the swimmers with rifles in case outsiders decided to attack Evergreen.

Being the proud owner of a real bathing suit, Harper decided to take advantage of the water while she could. Given the food situation in this world, she didn't expect to put on weight by her thirties and lose the ability to fit into the suit. However, it would probably fall apart by that point, anyway. Not to mention the pool itself had a good chance of turning into a stagnant mess once the chlorine ran out in a few years.

Aside from swimming for a little while most days, Harper made some time to sneak off with Logan. In a rare feat of telling Follows Rules Girl to go to hell, she brought him to one of the fancier houses at the edge of the old golf course that hadn't been assigned out to any resident. At a huge black lacquer table, they had a romantic dinner of sandwiches she'd assembled ahead of time, then made love in a queen-sized bed. Much to her surprise, he'd found condoms somewhere and used one. Of all the things people would scavenge, those seemed fairly low on the list compared to food, clothes, and medicine—but maybe someone had left them in the house he called home.

When they finished, she lay in his arms staring up at the ceiling, wondering who used to live in the house they'd helped themselves to. Had to be someone who used to have a ton of money. What would the former owner say about a couple of eighteen-year-olds barging in and doing it on their bed? It probably didn't matter, anyway. No more so than her opinion of anything someone did in her old house in Lakewood.

She brushed thoughts of the past out of her head and let herself revel in the strange feeling of getting away with something naughty —even though no one would really care they borrowed the house for a few hours.

CLIFF MENTIONED THAT HE'D FOUND SIGNS OF A TRAIL LEADING about 200 yards west from the farm and off to the south. Significant disturbance to the dirt at the point where the tracks changed course suggested the killing most likely happened there, but other than trees and forest detritus, he didn't find anything useful to explain who killed Weldon.

Harper still found herself dealing with random people approaching her to express their fears over a killer on the loose. People she spoke to appeared to tentatively accept her opinion that the killing hadn't been the work of a psycho, but a specific grudge against the victim.

Three days after finding Elijah wandering alone, Harper left the house in the morning, walking Madison, Jonathan, and Lorelei to the farm. Thus far, Madison hadn't complained about farm work on what basically amounted to summer break from school. It still technically felt like a vacation since they could leave the farm about two hours or so earlier than class let out. Given the complete lack of television, movies, the mall, dance classes, or anything of that nature, having something to do ended up being a welcome thing—even if it was work.

Harper hadn't told them much about the conditions she found on the farm in Kittredge. She couldn't say for sure how those men would have treated them. Based on what Rain and Kelsey said, it might be that the convicts treated the kids reasonably well for being held against their will. It baffled her how they could have thought nothing of forcing themselves on the two women they held captive but didn't mistreat the children, even giving them extra food. Cliff mentioned something about criminals having a weird code of ethics, the same reason kid-touchers often died in prison. Still, the day Madison, Mila, and Lorelei ceased being 'children,' they would have been in serious trouble.

"How come Carrie doesn't do a job?" asked Jonathan at random while they walked down Hilltop Drive toward Route 74.

"She does a work," chimed Lorelei. "Just at her house."

Harper patted her head. "It's not 'does a work.' She does work, or she has a job."

"Oh." Lorelei. "I said it bad?"

"It's okay. You're learning." Harper smiled.

Lorelei beamed.

"What's she do?" asked Jonathan.

"She and Renee are learning how to make fabric and clothes and stuff. Kind of like how people used to do it way back before they had factories. By the time you guys all grow up, you'll be wearing clothes we made here in town."

"Neat," said Madison. "Hope they don't make ugly stuff like in those old movies."

"Or like primitive tribes. Guess they're not gonna make jeans, huh?" Jonathan picked at his pants. "When these are too small on me, someone else can have them."

"That's nice of you." Harper ruffled his hair.

"It's stupid to just keep them and not wear them." He shrugged.

Madison sucked in a sharp breath and grabbed onto Harper.

Without conscious thought, Harper yanked the Mossberg off her shoulder and followed Madison's fearful stare to a young man walking down Route 74 toward them. His dark blond hair had grown out, half covering his face, but she recognized Zach right away. The look in his eyes reminded her of Tyler after he'd fallen off his anti-psychotic meds. Worse, Zach carried a handgun, though didn't point it at them.

Shit. He looks like he's on the way to murder someone specific.

Harper glanced to her right at a beige building, formerly Evergreen Fine Art. A wall behind a deer statue enclosed a mini porch, offering a decent amount of protection from stray bullets. "Take cover in there. Go on." She nodded toward it.

Madison continued clinging to her for a few seconds before finding the nerve to let go. As the kids scurried out of sight, Harper steeled herself to confront the former spoiled varsity jock who tried to impress her by joining the militia—and failing disastrously. He'd shot Renee, mistaking her for a threat. Granted, Renee *had* been with a group of Lawless, though she didn't do anything remotely aggressive. After he'd shot her best friend, Harper's feelings toward him changed from simple disdain to active dislike.

Months ago when that happened, he'd had this 'rich kid out of his element' air about him, like his parents could just throw money at any problem he created to make it go away. Now, he seemed intent on causing damage and didn't care what happened. Harper didn't quite aim the shotgun at him, but held it in the same ready posture she used at the range while waiting for a target to pop up. If his gun hand so much as twitched upward...

"Zach, something wrong?"

He continued walking in the same slow, deliberate stride of a horror movie killer, turning his head toward her. It didn't look like he'd been too concerned with personal hygiene as of late. His hair and beard went where they pleased, his clothes filthy. He shifted his attention from her eyes to the shotgun, then appeared to give her a 'go ahead and do it' stare.

"Where ya going with that gun, Zach?"

"Not against the rules to have a gun, is it?" He stopped about eight paces away, easy range for shotgun or pistols.

Harper tightened her grip, keeping her eyes on the 9mm Glock in his right hand. Cliff's voice in the back of her mind whispered to watch the hands. She'd made that mistake once, when they'd found Summer Vasquez. Fortunately, Cliff had been there to shoot the guy going for a gun that she'd totally not seen coming. Presently, Harper had only herself to rely on.

"No. It isn't. But, it's a little concerning the way you're carrying it. Like you're planning to use it."

He gave a disaffected laugh. "Probably will need to, but not before I'm out of town."

"You're leaving?" Harper stole a quick peek at his facial expression—defeated.

"Yeah. Hell with this place. I'm tired of learning how to be a goddamned plumber. It's lame. I'm going home, even if I gotta walk."

Okay, this might not end in gunfire. "Home? Like, you're talking about where you used to live?"

"Yeah."

She shook her head. "Zach, come on… there's nothing there. Colorado Springs is gone. Like *totally* gone. It's flat ground. And it's probably radioactive as hell."

"Don't care. I wanna go home. I want to sleep in *my* bedroom again. Wanna live in *my* house."

"Do you hear what you're saying, Zach? Your house is even more gone than my old home. That place is full of mold because it had a giant hole in the ceiling. It's gotta be collapsing already. Everything in Springs got vaporized. There's nothing there."

"Don't care." Zach started walking again.

"Hey." Harper pivoted to keep facing him. "Wait. Are you going out there to die?"

"Not trying to, but so what if I do?"

She walked after him, still watching his gun hand. "There's no reason for you to be foolish. Look, I get it. You're used to being important. Had money. Parents were important. Probably had your own car already. But—"

"Yeah. Brand new. Only had it a month." He looked down. "I miss my Mustang."

Oh, there's a shock. A kid like him had a Mustang. "Zach, that world is gone. There are no varsity jocks or rich kids anymore. We're all just trying to survive now. You miss being popular and important."

He sneered at her.

Ugh, this guy. "You can still be important, but not because your family's got money or kids at school think you're movie star handsome. Anyone who can preserve a slice of civilization is important. Working pipes, running water, working toilets... all of that is gold now."

He laughed. "So what, I'm that guy from *Mad Max* running around in leather overalls, covered in shit, building the mess of leaky water pipes?"

"We're not gonna devolve that much. People who know how to do things are going to keep us from losing too much. C'mon. You're learning plumbing. That's important. My only real skill is shooting stuff. You figure out plumbing, and you're vital. Don't be stupid and wander off to die. Seriously. You don't even have any provisions or water."

Zach stood there in silence, staring off down the highway.

"Even if you survive the radiation and whatever bad guys might be out there, you're going to drop dead from dehydration in three days. C'mon. Don't be stupid. The old social order is gone, but it's not the end of the world—oh wait." She offered a cheesy smile.

He looked over at her. "Pff. You wanted nothing to do with me. Now you're saying I'm important? No girl's ever said 'no' to me, especially not for a Mexican."

She clenched her jaw, trying not to let anger show too much on her face. "Look, even without the nukes, I never would have wanted to date the prom king. That's totally not me. And, that whole 'I'm better than the brown people' thing is total bullshit. There aren't enough people left alive in the country to give a crap how dark someone's suntan is. I don't know you enough to say if you're like that because it's who you are or because it's what you saw from your parents and friends. But, in case you haven't been aware of stuff lately, we're clinging to life by a hair. We have to help each other no matter what the other guy looks like."

Zach raised his right hand.

Harper swung the Mossberg up at his face.

He froze. "Whoa. Take it easy. Just putting it away."

She stared over the gunsight at his eyes. "Guys like you have a habit of shooting girls who say no. Just being careful."

"Heh. No one's ever said no to me before." Zach gingerly put the Glock in a holster. "There. Gun's away. Maybe stop pointing that cannon at me?"

"You really need to drop that ego thing. Girls aren't going to care about that in a world like this. Now, someone who can keep things working is sexier than perfect gelled hair and an expensive car. When no one is sure they'll have food a week from now, perfectly white teeth don't mean a damn thing."

He turned away, again gazing off down the road. "I've never had a girl point a gun at me before. That's a first, too."

"You shot my best friend. Be glad I'm only pointing it at you."

"So it's about revenge, is it?"

"No. I don't want revenge. You panicked. Renee *was* wearing a Lawless sash. But she also had her hands up and no weapons. If you want my honest opinion, mixing you with a firearm is a really bad idea. You've never had to live in a situation where your actions had any consequences or you didn't immediately get what you wanted before. And roaming off into the desert like a dumbass isn't going to change what happened. So what if you think being a plumber is 'beneath you.' There is no more Ivy League. No more high powered careers or fancy lifestyles. If we're ever going to have anything like that again, it's going to take a lot of people working their asses off for a really long time. You want to matter? Fix pipes. Learn how to do electrical stuff. Or hell, even work on the farm. That's important. But there aren't as many people who can make pipes work. You want to be important? Do something that matters to people."

"If you hate me so much, why are you trying to talk me out of going away?"

"Harp saves bugs from the bathroom," shouted Madison from the distance. "She can't help it."

Zach chuckled. "Did your sister just call me a bug?"

"Not intentionally. She just means I try to help everything and everyone—except those Lawless bastards." She scowled off to the side, and finally lowered the shotgun back to a ready posture.

"No, that was intentional," yelled Madison.

Harper forced herself not to smile or chuckle. "Whatever you think you're going to find in Colorado Springs, you won't. Trust me. It's taken me nine months to stop wanting to run home to Lakewood."

"Heh. Okay. I guess you might have a point."

"That all you intended to do with that Glock? Self-defense on a long walk?"

He wiped both hands down his face, and groaned. "Yeah. No, I'm not gonna shoot anyone. Just had a bit of a meltdown. One day, I'm captain of the hockey team trying to decide between Cornell, Dartmouth, or Brown... now I'm standing up to my shins in someone else's shit beating on a pipe with a wrench. It just... I dunno. Guess I snapped. Just had this moment of feeling like I didn't care about anything anymore."

"You wanted to go home, but not just your old house. You wanted things to be the way they were before. Like just walking out of Evergreen would somehow transport you back in time." Since the freakiness had faded from his eyes, Harper let the Mossberg hang from her right hand, and put her other hand on his shoulder. "I totally get it. I've wanted to 'go home' so bad it hurts, but we can't. We have to survive using what's left. I haven't known you all that long and what you've shown me so far hasn't made me like you much at all, but I'd still risk my life to stop some shitheads like the Lawless from killing you."

He finger-combed his hair and attempted a suave smile. "Am I really that bad?"

"You act like the entitled jerk bad guy from every teen drama ever made, plus a dash of racism."

"It's just shit we all said. I don't really hate anyone. Just used to be cool to make fun of them."

"I guess your old friends and people around you thought so, but making fun of minorities is not cool. Maybe if you stopped trying to play the part of homecoming king and just be Zach, it'd work out for you. Give it some time and I'm sure some girl will be interested in you."

He half smiled at her. "If you could get the world back the way it used to be like the war didn't happen, but to do that, you had to sleep with me, would you?"

She looked away and down. "That's exactly the opposite from not being a pig, Zach."

"I'm not trying to get in your pants. Just trying to gauge where I stand in general."

"You're making me feel cheap and selfish. How am I supposed to answer that? If I say yes, I'm a whore. If I say no, I'm being selfish. How can you even ask me to weigh the lives of millions of people on having sex with a guy I'm totally not into?" She scowled at him. "That's a really shitty thing to ask."

Hands on his hips, he sighed at the road. "Damn. I didn't even think about it that way. You're right. Sorry. Forget I asked. Guess I'll go stand in shit again." He walked off up the road.

"Zach," said Harper a few seconds later.

He stopped. "Yo?"

"We're all up to our knees in poop right now, but it's not going to stay that deep. Especially if you get the pipes working."

"Yeah. I guess. Anyway, thanks for stopping me from being a dumbass." He waved, bowed his head, and trudged off.

The kids emerged from their hiding place and gathered around her.

"Is he crazy?" asked Jonathan.

"I don't like that guy." Madison glared at him.

"I forgot my underpants," said Lorelei.

Harper pinched the bridge of her nose and laughed.

"No you didn't." Madison poked her. "You tried to forget, but I reminded you."

"I know," chimed Lorelei. "I just said it so Harp would smile."

She sighed at the clouds, not knowing if Zach had really been suicidal, murderous, or simply having a brat attack. Either way, she'd probably prevented *something* bad. "Thanks. I needed to smile."

"Can we go swimming after the farm again?" Madison grinned up at her.

As long as nothing goes wrong today... "Sounds like a good idea. It's going to be warm again."

The kids cheered, and followed her down the highway to the farm.

24

STRANDED

Erie silence saturated the residential area, so oppressive Harper began to question if some other apocalypse happened in the past hour that left her the last person left alive in the world.

Cars sat in driveways where they'd been at the moment of the nuclear strike. Some houses' doors hung open as though the residents had fled in a panic only minutes ago. Here and there, a tricycle or toy car lay in the grass or on the sidewalk. Those, at least, usually moved from day to day. One house had an above-ground pool in the backyard, but the water had already turned green and nasty.

In the months since society disintegrated, Harper had become slowly accustomed to the oppressive quiet that came from a complete lack of cars, aircraft, radio, and television. At least in summer, birds made *some* sound. The absence of 'modern' noise more or less felt normal now, except for mornings like this where it struck her as unusually empty. She'd even started to ponder what Darci said about the world being better off returning to a natural way of life. Cars and other machinery probably still existed in any country not targeted by nukes, but given the sheer amount of destruction likely to have occurred to the world as a whole, it didn't seem likely anyone would have fuel. Cliff was pretty sure all of the petroleum-exporting countries in the Middle East had been flattened purely out of spite.

She wandered her usual patrol area, as comfortable there as she would have been walking around the block back in Lakewood. Thoughts of high school, home, past holidays, hanging out with her friends, and a thousand random moments she considered trivial and meaningless at the time replayed in her mind. They no longer brought on an overwhelming sense of maudlin sorrow, but a wistful smile. Happy moments to remember, but nothing more. She felt grateful for the time she had with her parents, friends, and First World life, but also cautiously optimistic that whatever the future held for her, it might bring more happy moments after all.

Like the afternoon she and Logan spent in that house. Or watching Madison be normal. Even Lorelei, as frustrating as she could sometimes be, always warmed her heart.

Harper walked counterclockwise today for a change of pace. She followed Interlocken Drive around the eastern perimeter of her patrol area, heading for South Hiwan Drive to go past the Evergreen Middle school. As she approached the corner, she spotted someone moving in the trees close to the road ahead on the left. The person didn't appear to be running away or trying to hide as much as hadn't noticed her. They also appeared to have made some attempt to conceal themselves, which struck her as odd.

Cautious, she approached, shotgun ready, and called, "Hello?"

A startled gasp came from the trees, the pitch that of a child. Rustling stopped for a second, then shifted direction, coming straight at her.

She felt awkward pointing a gun in the general direction of a kid, but Mila had killed two men—proof that children could still be dangerous. Harper neither aimed directly at the figure in the trees nor lowered it.

A weary-looking tween boy, rail thin and dirt-smeared, wandered out of the cluster of pines, staring at her the way someone stuck in the desert for months might stare at water. Fine blond hair hung past the shoulders of a lightly torn black T-shirt. Large holes in the legs of his jeans revealed scratches on his thighs and shins. His battered sneakers looked one long walk away from completely disintegrating. He didn't carry any obvious weapons, merely an apparently empty blue backpack that probably once held school books, decorated with little superhero pins.

Oh, crap. Did this kid get hit by a bus? "Hey… you okay?"

The boy raised his hands. "Please don't shoot. We need help."

Harper looked around, but didn't see anyone else in the area. "We?"

"I'm alone. I mean where I live. I came to get help."

She slung the Mossberg over her shoulder on its strap.

He slouched with relief.

Harper didn't get a bad vibe from the kid, so she hurried over to him. "Are you hurt? Hungry? Thirsty?"

"Not hurt. Tired. And I haven't had any food or water like all day." He slouched, breathing hard. "Can I have some water, please?"

"Of course. C'mon." She waved for him to follow, continuing straight west past the corner in the road. Faster to bee-line to Route 74 on the other side of the trees and follow it straight down than weave among the residential streets. "I'm Harper."

"Daxton Oliver," said the boy. "Are you alone here?"

"No. We're a pretty big town. Where'd you come from?"

He pointed generally north. "I live with my mom and some other people up at Kriley Pond. There's like fifteen people left, and we're not doin' good. Don't have a lot of food and these crazy people keep attacking us. There's a shootout like every day. I don't know who they are 'cause my mom makes me stay down and not look outside."

"She let you run off on your own to get help?"

Daxton whistled innocently and kicked a rock. "Umm, she's probably gonna be mad at me. I didn't really ask if I could go."

"Oh, boy." Harper exhaled. "Wow. She's probably going crazy with worry."

"I had to do something!" Daxton flailed his arms. "The bad guys never attack at night, so I left in the dark. Mr. Cortez said he heard there's people in Evergreen and it's safe there, but no one wants to ask for help. Mr. Henderson thinks we'll be okay, but I'm scared."

"Who's Mr. Henderson?"

"He's like in charge. Tells everyone what to do."

Harper raised both eyebrows. "What do you think of him?"

Daxton shrugged. "He's okay. Keeps telling everyone we'll be fine, but I don't think he believes that. He knows we're in trouble, but he says it'll be worse if we try to go somewhere else, since we got the pond and can fish. My mom's had to shoot people, and it's givin' her bad dreams. She said that Mr. Henderson just tells us it's going to be okay so no one is scared."

"Sounds about right." She shook her head, sighing.

"You ever shoot anyone?" Daxton peered up at her.

"I have. Yeah. But only bad people who tried to hurt me."

He nodded. "Cool. I mean, that you beat the bad guys, not that you gotta kill and stuff."

This kid needs food. She walked faster, leading him down Route 74 to the medical center.

He followed her in, looking around. "Whoa. This looks like a doctor's place."

"It is." She smiled, heading over to the desk. "Hi, Ruby. Are Tegan or Dr. Khan available?"

"Who've you got this time?" Ruby smiled at the boy. "Aww, poor thing. He get hit by a truck?"

Daxton glanced down at himself, half chuckling. "Fell down a hill."

"Ouch." Ruby sucked air in through her teeth. "That looks like it hurt."

"Nah. Not really." He looked at Harper. "They have food at the doctor's place?"

"I'm gonna go get you some food while the doc checks you out."

"Okay." Daxton stuffed his hands in his pockets.

"Go on back, hon." Ruby smiled at her.

Harper led the boy down the hall, peeking into each room until she found Tegan in Room 3, still reading her novel. "Doc?"

"Good morning… and that's not Elijah. Unless he soaked up a lot more radiation than we thought." Tegan chuckled, set her book down, and walked over.

"Dammit." Harper scowled at the ceiling. "Darci didn't bring him in?"

"Oh, she did. Yesterday. Hello, young man. I'm Dr. Hale, but you can call me Tegan if you like."

"Hi. My name's Daxton, but my mom usually just calls me Dax. Umm, does she have to be here for you to do doctor stuff to me?"

"Once upon a time. Looks like you've got a few cuts and scrapes that could use cleaning up." Tegan guided him over to the exam table.

He shrugged and hopped up to sit on it.

"I'll be right back with food." Harper waved and hurried out.

She ran across the street to the quartermaster's building and had a brief chat with Liz Trujillo to explain why she wanted to grab a meal from the communal cooking area that prepared food for residents of Evergreen who had no families. Mass cooking ended up being more efficient for power or firewood, since allocating food to single people resulted in all of them needing to cook separately. People like Harper who belonged to a 'family unit' eligible for a food ration each week usually got frowned at for hoarding food if they tried to use the 'buffet.'

After collecting a venison burger and some potato salad—or at least someone's best attempt at it in a world that lacked mayo—on a plate, she fast-walked back to the medical center. She stepped into Room 3 and nearly choked on the smell of rubbing alcohol in the air. Daxton lay stretched out on the table in his underpants, his expression somewhere between bored and grimacing each time Tegan dabbed gauze at several nasty scratches on his left side. Scratches on his legs appeared already cleaned, and he had a few on his arms and chest as well. Though his expression remained mostly stoic, tears rolled from his eyes. Tegan coaxed him through it with soft spoken words of encouragement.

"It stings," rasped Daxton.

"I know. I'm sorry. You got some dirt in these scratches. Gotta clean them out so you don't get sick."

Harper stood there holding the plate for a few minutes while the doctor worked on cleaning out all the scrapes.

"There. All done," said Tegan.

Daxton shoved himself upright to sit and reached for the plate.

Harper handed it to him, then went out to ask Ruby for a cup of water, which she brought back. The boy devoured the food like he hadn't eaten anything in several days, a distinct possibility given his prominent ribs and bony physique. He didn't look as dangerously thin as Lorelei had been when she first arrived in Evergreen, but she worried he'd end up that way if she didn't help.

"Here, take this, too." Tegan handed him a reddish pill.

"Wmm?" asked Daxton over a mouthful of food.

"Just a vitamin."

He shrugged, accepted the pill, and downed it, chugging water.

"Daxton's borderline malnourished. It's not merely from a couple days not eating during a journey." Tegan ran a fine metal comb through the boy's hair, then studied it. "No fleas or lice at least."

"Yeah. We don't have a lot of food. Fish don't like to bite. That's why I knew we needed help." Daxton turned his attention to the potato salad, picking it off the plate in his bare hand.

"Oops. Forgot a fork." Harper bit her lip.

He gave her an 'I don't care' look, and kept eating.

While he finished off the meal, Tegan applied a small gauze bandage to his back. After he'd licked every trace of food from the plate, the boy hurriedly put his shirt, jeans, and sneakers back on.

"Give me a sec and I'll give you his slip to take to Anne-Marie." Tegan walked over to the counter and opened a drawer.

"Okay. He might not be staying here. Apparently, he's got a mother at another settlement. And a bunch of other people," said Harper. "I gotta go talk to Walter."

"Either way, let me do the slip. It won't take long." Tegan grabbed a pad from the drawer and scribbled a few lines on it before tearing a page off and handing it to her. "There. By the way, Elijah seems fine. I don't think he suffered a significant dose of radiation."

"Whoa, there's rads here?" asked Daxton, his dark blue eyes widening.

"Not here... someone collected some bad junk they shouldn't

have touched. It's been cleaned up. And, it's at least a mile south from here."

"Oh. Whew." He slapped himself on the forehead. "Radiation sucks. So, umm. Can you guys help us?"

She waved for him to follow. "That's why we need to talk to Walter and Anne-Marie. They're basically our leaders."

"Okay."

Harper led him across the street and down a bit to the militia HQ. Since they didn't have a 'desk clerk,' she walked right up to Walter's office and knocked on the doorjamb.

"Come in," said Walter.

"Mr. Holman?" Harper peeked in. "Got a minute?"

"Of course." He looked up, spotted the boy, and stood. "Aha. New arrival?"

"Yes and no. This is Daxton. I found him up by the school. Apparently, he's been walking for a while trying to find help for another settlement."

"Oh?" Walter raised both eyebrows. "Another settlement? Whereabouts?"

"Kriley Pond. My mom's there, and like fifteen others. We're almost out of food and these crazies keep trying to attack us and steal our stuff. This guy, Mr. Cortez, said that he heard someone talking about Evergreen and how a lot of people went there. I thought you'd have an army or something and you could get rid of the bad guys. Maybe send food even."

"Hmm." Walter rubbed his chin. "Kriley Pond is a ways northwest of here. Too far away for us to commit to any sort of long-term protection. We could probably spare a little food. Problem is, all our vehicles are down. No gas left, and Rafael hasn't gotten any biodiesel to run longer than a couple minutes. If you ask me, it's a problem with the fuel more than his machinery, but I'm no mechanic."

"Umm... so you can't help?" Daxton looked up at Harper, his expression wide-eyed and heartbroken.

"It's not logistically possible for us to transport a sufficient quantity of food that distance to make a difference. This long after the war, I doubt there are any usable stores of gasoline left anywhere in the country, barring the strategic petroleum reserve. But that's not gasoline, and it's no good without a working refinery." Walter rubbed his forehead. "About the best solution I can think of would be for your people to pick up and join us here in Evergreen. You say it's only about fifteen?"

Daxton nodded. "Yeah. Maybe less if anyone got shot after I left to get help."

Walter looked at Harper. "Are you up for leading a team out to the place to escort them back here?"

Her heart sank. How would Madison react to her leaving town, even temporarily? She'd been *so* thrilled when the militia officially stopped doing scavenger missions and Harper no longer needed to go anywhere. However, the scrawny, desperate boy staring up at her and his giant, pleading eyes proved utterly impossible to resist. Only a heartless bitch could say no to that face.

This is where I get killed, isn't it? Finally starting to think life might not be so bad. Dammit. Oh, hell. That could've happened when we raided Kittredge. An attack mission has to be karmically worse than trying to rescue a bunch of people, right?

"Okay." She patted his shoulder. "How far away is this place?"

Walter approached the giant map on the wall of his office, hunted around for a moment, then poked a finger at a spot. "About twenty-five miles, give or take. Roughly a ten to thirteen hour walk depending on how fast you go."

It's not quite noon yet. It'd be dark before we got there.

"Wow. Okay. Guess we better get moving. Give me a bit to get ready." Harper patted Daxton on the shoulder and pointed at a chair. "Wait here."

"I gotta show you how to get there." He grabbed her arm.

"I'm just running to get some supplies together before we go." She smiled. "Not going to make you wait here while your mother's out there."

"Oh. Okay." He smiled sheepishly and sat in the indicated chair.

Harper jogged out, heading toward home. *I am such a sucker.*

25

PERMISSION

Obligation dragged her up Route 74 instead of across to Hilltop Drive and the house.

Before she did anything else, she had to confront the Madison situation head on. Not only had she promised never to 'trick' her sister again, she also owed it to her to be up front and honest. If her sister begged her not to go, she'd most likely try talking Cliff into leading the trip instead. Of course, Walter would probably complain about the town's only Army Ranger being elsewhere — but that hadn't stopped him from being sent on scavenging trips. Harper felt reasonably sure she could use either logic or guilt to convince him to let Cliff go.

Walter did have a point in saying that Daxton, an unarmed eleven-year-old, had made the trip alone. But, skinny tweens could hide in places even Harper couldn't fit. He hadn't said anything about being chased or attacked on the way here, only that he'd fallen down a hill. Whether or not he'd slipped or been running for his life, she had no idea.

It took Harper a few minutes after reaching the farm to find Madison among the squash plants, dragging a big basket along while picking any ripe ones. She had a look of grim determination, clearly not having fun, but dealing with it because she didn't like starving. Plus, she figured if they had tons of veggies, she wouldn't be pressured to eat meat.

"Maddie?" asked Harper. *Please don't freak out.*

"Hey. Look at this one?" Madison peered up from a squash she'd been examining. "Is it ready to pick? I can't tell for sure. It's a little small."

Harper shrugged. "Umm. No idea. If you're in doubt, might as well leave it to grow longer. Hey, I gotta tell you something."

"Uh oh." Madison whistled. "You're not preggo, are you?"

Instant blush. "No. Maybe worse."

"You're sick?" Madison's already pale face went whiter.

"Nope." Harper hugged her. "I need to go on a mission away from Evergreen. Might be gone for two days."

Madison tensed, clinging tighter. "Why? You're not gonna go kill the blue gang are you?"

"Nah. Some people need help. We'd be going away from Denver. Shouldn't be any Lawless out there." Harper explained meeting Daxton, the fifteen or so people barely surviving at Kriley Pond, and her plan to help them relocate back here. "If it bothers you, I'll nag Walter until he lets Cliff go instead."

"It's okay." Madison leaned back from the hug and smiled up at her. "You're turning back into old Harper who wants to help everyone all the time. It's fine if you want to go, but please be *super* careful."

"I will. Hey, the boy walked here all alone and he was fine. We're not going anywhere near Denver."

"Can I come with you?"

She debated the idea. While her sister would worry much less if they stayed together, having her out there would make *Harper* worry constantly. And if anything happened to her... "I'd really rather you stayed here safe. If you go, then Jonathan's going to ask to come along. Then Lorelei, and Mila, and Becca and Eva and... the point here is to bring those people *to* Evergreen, not move Evergreen there."

"Yeah. Figured you'd say that." Madison laughed, but it trailed off to a sad sigh. "I'm going to be scared until you come back, but I missed how you used to be."

"How did I used to be? Other than shy and quiet?" Harper chuckled, bowing her head against her sister's.

"You've started smiling again. And you always wanted to help people when they needed help. You're not as quiet as before, but you used to be *too* quiet. Now, you're brave."

"Or foolish."

"Nah." Madison leaned back, grinning. "Foolish would be going back to Lakewood and getting shot at by the blue bastards just to get some clothes from your bedroom. You're going to help people. That's not foolish. That's brave."

Oh dammit. I better not screw this up. She's going to shatter into a billion pieces if I don't come back. Daxton got here okay. I'm not going alone. Right. We can do this. "Thanks. You're brave too, willing to trust me not to mess up. Let me get going. Faster I start, faster I'm back."

"Okay."

After one more hug for good measure, Harper hurried down Route 74 and went to the house. Renee and Carrie laughed and chatted next door, but she didn't go over there. That conversation would take too long. She already expected to run out of daylight as it was. Maybe she could make up time by walking faster. Average walking speed for people was something like two miles an hour. It shouldn't be *too* hard to go a little faster than that.

In her bedroom, she crawled into the closet and rummaged her stash of shotgun shells. Between bundles of fifty and loose, she counted 220 left—an amount she could blow through easily in a weekend practicing for a competition. Like much else in the world she once took for granted, she never paid much attention to how many she used when a simple drive to the store could easily get more. Never in her life did she imagine 12-gauge buckshot would become a critical commodity that had to be nursed carefully. Some practice sessions, she could go through hundreds of shells in a few hours. That didn't matter when a simple trip to the store could replace them.

I should really practice harder with the bow... especially at longer ranges.

These are going to be gone before I know it. But... better to overdo it than not have enough. Maybe we'll get lucky and I won't need to fire a shot. Daxton didn't even have a gun. She counted out forty shells and dumped them into a hip bag, which she clipped around her waist. Expecting to be gone at least overnight, she raided the stash of MREs that they found in the cabin, packing two in a small backpack as well as some water bottles.

That done, she rushed back to the militia HQ and returned to Walter's office, finding only him and the boy there. No other militia. Daxton paused gnawing on a hunk of bread and peered up at her.

"Okay. I'm set." Harper exhaled from all the running back and forth. "Who else are you sending with me?"

"Daxton got here in one piece alone and unarmed." Walter smiled. "I was half hoping you'd be able to manage this one without us needing to divert too many resources from our defense."

"He got lucky," said Harper, arms folded. "Are you seriously expecting me to go alone?"

"Sending too large a force could leave us vulnerable—"

She leaned forward. "Are you going to explain to Madison why I didn't come back?"

"It's not that dangerous," whispered Daxton. "I only got shot at once. It's why I fell down the hill. Had to jump off a bridge to not get shot."

Harper thrust her left arm out at him, eyebrows flared.

"No, no... you're completely right. It would be stupid to send you out alone. We have to defend each other as much as the town." Walter shifted his jaw side to side. "At best, you'll be gone two days since there's no way you're walking twenty hours nonstop."

"Bikes?" asked Harper.

Walter pursed his lips. "You're going to bring fifteen or so people back here on a couple of bikes?"

She cringed. "Oh. Good point.

"Hmm." Walter raised an eyebrow. "Could send Zach along."

Harper furrowed her brow. "Pass. Besides, he resigned. He's not on the militia anymore. And he's maybe cracked."

"I meant that as a joke." Walter started to laugh, but stopped, his expression concerned. "What do you mean cracked?"

She explained her encounter with Zach earlier. "Talked him down, but he might decide to flip out again if something doesn't work out the way he wants it to."

"Hmm. I'll ask Dr. Hale to speak to him then."

"I'll go," said Logan as he walked in.

Harper whirled. "What?" She blinked. "What are you doing here?"

He walked up, grasped her arms at the elbows and gave her a quick kiss. "Maddie told me you were about to go on a mission or something. I was right next door at the QM's, still working there for now."

"Yeah." She poked him in the stomach. "Because you're recovering from a gunshot and they don't want you doing stressful stuff. Going on a mission is stressful stuff."

"It's not lifting and carrying heavy crap." Logan rubbed his side where the drain tube had been. "I feel fine. Spot's not even tender."

"You're not militia."

He grinned. "Exactly why Mr. Holman won't mind me going. I wouldn't be reducing the town's defenses."

Madison walked in wearing a — for her — giant backpack.

Harper stared. "What the f — udge are you doing here?"

"I changed my mind. Gonna go with you, too. I can carry the food and water and stuff so you don't have to."

"Absolutely not!" Harper grabbed Madison by the backpack straps and shook her. "I can't risk you getting hurt."

Madison sighed. "No one's gonna shoot a kid. Worst they'll do is kidnap me. And if you're gonna risk getting shot, I'm gonna risk being kidnapped."

"No way. You're only ten!"

"So's he!" Madison pointed at Daxton.

"I'm twelve," said the boy.

"Wow." Madison blinked at him. "You're kinda small for twelve."

He shrugged.

Harper held a finger up. "Twelve year olds can't order off the kids' menu. He's old enough to go. You're not."

"That's lame!" yelled Madison.

"Lame is me going crazy trying to make sure you're okay the whole time we're out there." Harper clamp-hugged her.

"You did it before. When we had to leave the old house. I'm not scared."

Harper looked at Walter. "Please tell her this is a horrible idea."

"Sorry, kiddo. I have to agree with your big sister here. It's not really a good idea for a little girl to go on an armed rescue mission."

Madison hung her head. "If I'm with her, I won't be scared she's not gonna come back. You might have to get into a fight, and carrying stuff is gonna slow you down. Let me carry the food and water."

"We're not marching for weeks, Termite." Harper ruffled her hair. "It's only like twenty-five miles."

"Sit tight here for a bit." Walter walked around his desk. "Going to see what kind of team I can round up for you." He crouched eye level to Madison. "Your big sis will be back in a day. Please don't make her worry about you, okay?"

"Fine." Madison sighed at the floor. "You said a kid walked alone, so I figured it would be safe."

"I got shot at, but they missed." Daxton ate the last of his bread in one big bite.

Madison gawked at him. "Why would anyone shoot at a kid?"

His smile had way too much innocence in it. "I maybe stole some food from them when they weren't looking."

"Still! Only buttheads would shoot at kids." Madison banged her head against Harper's chest repeatedly while saying, "Please be careful" over and over.

"And you…" Harper stared at Logan. "I need you to stay safe. I don't know what I'd do if you got hurt."

Logan took her hand and stared into her eyes. "What if *you* get hurt? I don't want to let that happen."

Oh, gawd. He really would risk his life for me. She swallowed hard, her hands shaking from emotion at the thought he'd rather die than lose her. "Okay. If you're sure."

"I am. Hopefully, Walter will let me borrow a gun or something." Logan chuckled.

"You ever shoot before, son?" asked Walter.

Logan nodded. "Yeah. Not a ton, but my brother and father were both military. Took me to the range a couple times. I know my way around an AR-15 or M1 Garand if you have one of those. Or a shotgun."

"Sounds good." Walter patted him on the shoulder. "Let me check on that team real quick. Daylight's fading." He rushed out the door.

"Sorry for making you guys argue," said Daxton. "But I'm really happy you're gonna help."

Madison shrugged, wiping tears. "She's like that. Loves helping people."

"If you really don't want me to go, I'll ask Cliff to do it." Harper fussed at her sister's hair.

"Those morons from the airplane crash tried to attack us a couple days ago." Madison grimaced. "I think Cliff should stay here. That way *you* don't have to kill anyone if we get attacked while you're gone."

"You're sure, Termite? We don't know how bad it is out there."

"Yeah. If you see bad guys out there, you could hide or run away. Here, if we get attacked, you'd *have* to fight. Just… please come back okay?" Madison looked down. "If you die, I'm gonna make Mila look like Lorelei-level cheerfulness."

Logan cringed.

"Right. No pressure at all then." Harper exhaled.

26

MS. TILLER

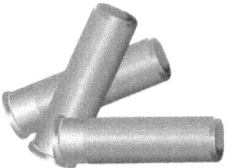

For the twenty or so minutes it took Walter to return, Madison held on to Harper.

It didn't feel like the same kind of desperate clinginess as before, rather like her little sister wanted to spend every possible second at her side until she had to go. Logan gave off an air of mild nervousness, but far less so than she'd seen from boys who'd approached to ask her out on a date.

That doesn't mean much. Some boys can handle being shot at better than saying three words to a girl.

She figured Madison's sudden change to wanting to go along probably came from Logan's insistence to go along. He, at least, was eighteen and could handle a rifle. Not that she wanted her boyfriend to cross that threshold of having taken someone's life, but better him than her little sister. Going out there beyond the relative safety of Evergreen meant all sorts of possible dangers. The post-apocalyptic movie running in her mind had legions of face-painted crazies carting her off for horrible purposes like something out of *Mad Max*. That didn't seem at all realistic. Far more likely a worst-case scenario would be a garden variety pervert, sociopath, or a group who'd kill her for her stuff. Maybe even cannibals.

Harper closed her eyes and wished really hard that no one had become *that* desperate or depraved that they'd resorted to eating people.

The 'bad movie' part of her brain also teased her with the idea that Daxton might be bait, sent into Evergreen to lure out a small group for ambush or abduction. He didn't seem fidgety like a kid who tried to lie, nor apprehensive about getting underway. The Lawless used captives—like Renee—as decoys, throwing them into the line of fire. But this kid looked every bit as skinny as would fit his story of a starving settlement. Looking into his eyes also didn't set off any red flags. He seemed genuinely worried about his mother.

She studied the map on the wall, plotting out the best way to get to Kriley Pond. They'd go up Route 74 to Route 65, and take that to US-40 or I-70, which basically ran next to each other. From there, Route 6 looked like the only way over to 119, which would bring them up to Golden Gate Canyon Road. Seemed reasonably simple, but she still wrote down the turns on a scrap of paper just in case.

Walter came back carrying an AR-15, which he handed to Logan along with two magazines. The weapon didn't appear to be loaded. Logan pulled back the charging handle and peered into the chamber as soon as he took the rifle.

Walter appeared to relax a little at seeing him check for a round in the chamber.

Crap. Harper eyed Walter. *He's giving him permission to go.*

"Don't I get a gun?" asked Madison with a cheesy smile.

"Heh. Not yet, hon." Walter patted her on the head, then looked at Harper. "Ready?"

"Yeah."

Walter led them outside to meet Deacon and Lennie Horne who waited a few steps from the door. That he'd only assigned *two* more people disappointed her somewhat, but it definitely beat going alone, or having only Logan along for help.

With a cowboy hat, long grey hair and a big mustache, Lennie somewhat resembled a wiry cartoon gunslinger a bit past his prime. He'd been a fairly recent addition, having ended up on the militia due to wanting to keep his M4 carbine. The bolo tie and revolvers on his hips matched the Wild West aesthetic of his hat; his light bulletproof vest in Army green plus a belt full of pouches and a small pack, not so much.

Deacon carried an AK-47 instead of his usual pump shotgun as well as a metal baseball bat in a back sheath, like some kind of budget Conan the Barbarian. He grinned at the sight of Harper, but quirked an eyebrow at Madison exiting the building wearing a backpack.

"Please tell me she ain't goin' out there," said Deacon.

"No. She wanted to but"—Harper brushed a hand over her sister's head—"I asked her to stay safe. It's going to be scary enough trying to keep an eye on Daxton."

The boy shrugged. "I can run pretty fast."

"I see that look." Walter chuckled. "Don't be too disappointed. Deacon's basically a small army on his own. Anyone who'd give you trouble would probably think twice as soon as they saw him."

Mila's imaginary voice said *or shoot him first* in the back of Harper's mind.

"We're ready to go." Lennie nodded once. "Already got water and some grub, figurin' on a two day affair."

"Yeah. It's about twenty-five miles, so the rest of today out there, tomorrow back." Harper exhaled. "Hope they don't decide to be dumb and refuse to relocate."

"I'd hate to waste a trip." Deacon smiled.

Daxton shook his head. "You won't. Even if Mr. Henderson decides to be a butthead, my mom and I will come back with you."

"All right." Harper looked around, taking stock.

She had forty shells in her hip bag plus nine in the tube. Deacon's AK appeared to have a thirty-round mag, two more on his belt. Walter gave Logan two twenty-round mags for the AR. Lennie also had a twenty-round mag in the M4, but she couldn't tell how many spares he had in the various pouches on his belt. She also didn't see any loose bullets for his revolvers. They had to at least be loaded or he wouldn't bother carrying them. That Deacon had swapped the pump shotgun he usually carried for an AK made her worry a bit, though it did increase their effectiveness at longer ranges.

Ugh. Yeah, the world is totally broken. The girl who collects faerie stuff is thinking tactically.

In a complete moment of self-conscious embarrassment, Harper realized that she'd been on the militia longer than either man. No one had ever said anything about ranks or seniority or who would be in charge. Lennie *looked* like he had experience as a soldier, but equipment didn't prove anything. Guys loved to go to the Army Navy surplus and buy stuff to be a weekend warrior. Looking the part had nothing at all to do with being capable under fire.

Also, Deacon was basically twice her age. Lennie had to be past forty-five. She felt awkward giving orders to guys old enough to have fathered her. Still, Walter had been talking about this the whole time as though she ran the mission. It took her a moment to find the nerve to speak like she did so.

"Okay. Everyone ready?"

Deacon and Logan both nodded. Lennie tipped his hat.

"Can I walk with you guys at least to the buses?" asked Madison.

"Okay, Termite. But you really gotta promise me you're not going to sneak after us." Harper poked her in the nose.

"I promise." Madison squirmed out of the backpack and set it on the ground by the door to the militia HQ; canned goods inside rattled. "I'll leave this here as proof."

Harper smiled. "I believed you when you promised, because I know you know how sad I'd be if anything happened to you."

"Back at'cha," said Madison, folding her arms.

They walked up Route 74, heading north. At the point where the militia had a barricade made of two city buses—the sniper's guard station—Madison hugged Harper again rather fiercely, then as promised, stopped following them. She climbed up onto one of the buses to watch them walk off. Harper figured she'd probably be there for at least the next hour, and might need to be physically carried home when it got dark.

However, her kid sister didn't cry, melt down, or even try to guilt her out of going—all things Harper considered progress. Even before the war, Madison had been moody at the idea of her going out of state to college. She wouldn't have admitted it out loud, but she'd always been close and a little clingy.

"Best keep yer finger off the trigger while you're carryin' that," said Lennie. "Rest it along the top of the trigger housing like this."

Harper glanced back at the 'old cowboy' holding his M4 out so Logan could see his grip.

"Okay." Logan mimicked the hand position.

"Got that thing on safe?" asked Lennie.

Logan looked at the AR-15, tilting it over to check the switch. "Yeah."

"Good. Don't forget that if ya need ta shoot anything." Lennie grinned.

"Okay, dumb ass question." Deacon held up his AK. "Never fired one of these before. Where's the safety?"

Harper bit her lip. *Good question. Where* is *the safety on one of those?*

"Right side near the back. That giant flat lever." Lennie tapped it. "Up is safe, down is hot."

Deacon fussed at the AK, which clicked once, then again. "Ahh. Got it."

"Normally, I'd warn someone who's never shot an AK before that it's gonna kick more than you're probably expecting." Lennie looked up at him. "But I don't think you're gonna notice."

Deacon's deep baritone laugh echoed into the woods.

Eager to be there and back again as fast as they could move, plus wanting to spend as little time as possible walking at night, Harper hustled along, not quite jogging. Daxton kept up without too much effort, and didn't appear exhausted or overly tired. She suspected he'd been sleeping in the trees where she'd found him. No way could he have enough energy to go all the way back to Kriley Pond after spending all night on the road. Then again, to help any of her siblings, she'd find a way to march for two days straight. The boy could probably do the same for his mother.

The sun had gone slightly past its apex, bright enough to cause blinding flashes wherever the windows of various abandoned cars caught it. Most of the vehicles had rolled partially off the highway, many having crashed into trees, each other, or signs. Harper imagined people driving along in the wee hours on their way to work or wherever when the EMP flash killed the cars. Not really understanding how nukes worked, her mind created two imaginary scenarios: one in which the electromagnetic pulse left everyone confused while struggling to control their dead cars, and another in which they all saw the flash and panicked.

They had to have seen the flash. Couldn't be a pulse without a detonation, and the detonation would've been bright. None of this is melted here, so far off. She frowned at a mangled Jeep Cherokee that had veered into the oncoming lane and hit a Lexus sedan head on. *People could've been blinded if they looked right at it.*

It didn't take them long to reach the intersection of Route 74 and Route 65. Brown metal bus stop shelters on the corner to her right showed signs of having been temporarily used as residences, stuffed full of sleeping bags, empty cans littering the area outside. She, Madison, Cliff, and Jonathan had walked around this corner—coming in from the right—when they first arrived at Evergreen. She didn't remember anyone being here then. Of course, she'd been so freaked out at the time, someone probably could have driven a car covered in flashing lights past her and she'd have missed it.

They veered left onto Route 65. Ahead, hilly fields covered in trees stretched off toward distant mountain peaks. Power line poles along the right side of the road had burned like giant charred matchsticks.

She eyed a 'speed limit 35' sign. *Yeah, no danger of anyone going that fast anymore.*

Daxton kicked at the occasional rock or fragment of damaged car. Deacon and Lennie walked behind Harper and Logan, the two men mostly watching their surroundings. Harper found herself staring at the oncoming road, momentarily annoyed that the world decided to blow up so soon after she finally got her license. Even the working truck she and Cliff had found only lasted a few weeks before the gas ran out.

A huge field surrounded by fencing went by on the left, empty of anything alive or visibly useful. She gazed around at pine trees, grass, rocks, dirt, and the twisted remains of power poles. A few minutes later, they passed another field on the left, surrounded by a strange zig-zagging fence made of stacked logs. She couldn't imagine what it had been intended to contain as the fence looked pretty easy to climb.

Just ahead of a rightward curve, a spaghetti tangle of power lines crisscrossed the road. A small box truck had gone off the side and flipped, taking out a tree and one utility pole. No one hesitated at stepping among the wires, as any power generation had long since ceased.

They followed Route 65 for a while, eventually passing a large house that had a private tennis court on the right at the bottom of a short, steep hill studded in slender pine trees. It seemed an altogether random thing to find out in the middle of nowhere. If she'd been wandering with no specific destination or place to return to, she'd probably have checked out the house. Someone wealthy enough to have their own tennis court probably had a bunch of cool stuff. Then again, they might also have a bunch of guns and still be there.

She didn't have the best view of the house from the street, but didn't see anyone threatening—or even nonthreatening—watching them, so she kept going. They had to reach Kriley Pond as fast as possible to avoid getting caught out in open country after dark. That didn't leave any time for exploration.

Before long, they walked past a tall ridge on the left that formed a veritable wall of green trees she would have found pretty and scenic if not for the constant fear of attack.

Not everyone's going to try to kill us. What are we going to do if we meet someone nice? Ask them to follow us? Just say hi and go our separate ways? Walter might not be happy if she went out to collect fifteen people and came back leading a group of forty. Her need to help others fought with her need to keep the people of Evergreen safe. They couldn't absorb too many residents too fast or the farm would be unable to keep up. Some people in town still avoided eating fish for fear of nuclear contamination.

Does it matter? We were all exposed to whatever radiation came from the blasts. Does having a house on top of us really help that much? For a little while, worry of random cancer overpowered her worry of someone trying to kill them in a more direct way. The terrain had plenty of trees and hiding places, but few spots looked appealing for long-term living. She eyed a row of mailboxes between two stonework pillars under a little roof on the left. It stood near the end of an offshoot street leading off to the left that ended at a metal gate, like some kind of private community. No one hid there to ambush them either.

"Where was it the people shot at you?" asked Harper.

"Umm, by the highway bridge." Daxton pointed ahead. "We're gonna be there soon."

"Highway bridge?" Deacon scratched his bald head. "Don't remember any bridges around here."

"It's a bridge over a highway. Duh. Overpass." The boy punted a hunk of headlight off the road. "These people had a camp at the corner with a bunch of trailers."

Harper scanned the area ahead. *Keep an eye out for trailers.* "What did they look like?"

"Umm. Three guys. One kinda fat, the other two skinny. Jeans and stuff. They didn't look mean or nothin' 'til I grabbed a hunk of meat and ran."

Lennie chuckled. "That'd probably get me at least chasin' ya."

"Did you try asking them for food first?" Harper nudged him.

"Yeah. They told me to piss off." Daxton veered to the right so he could kick a rock off the road. "So I pretended to go away, then snuck back and grabbed the bird."

"Might be trouble when they see him." Deacon checked his AK as if trying to remember where to find the safety lever. "Hope they think twice before pulling a gun on all of us."

"Yeah." Logan cracked his neck side to side. "If they tried to kill a kid over a pigeon, who knows what they might do."

"Maybe a warning shot trying to scare him?" asked Lennie.

Daxton shook his head rapidly. "I don't think so. It hit the road right next to me and"—he indicated a bullet bouncing with his hand—"went like *pzing!* That's when I jumped over the guardrail and fell down the hill."

"Not going to let them hurt you. But, maybe keep your head

down so we can get past without them recognizing you," said Harper.

"'Kay."

A little over an hour later, they reached the intersection where Route 65 met Route 70. Harper's directions called for going left here, but I-70 ran along on a lower grade at the bottom of a relatively steep hill. Not wanting to risk a fall and sprain, she continued ahead onto the overpass that spanned it. They could just as easily walk along Route 40, which followed I-70. *Actually, I think we want 40.*

"There," whispered Daxton, pointing at the far side.

Left of where Route 65 met Route 40 at a T-junction, a cluster of RVs and trailers sat in a former parking lot, positioned nose-to-end such that they formed a wall. Harper held her Mossberg in a ready position, watching the RV that formed the eastern wall of the compound. Signs of motion in the windows put her on edge, but no one moved close enough to see clearly. Better still, no one pointed a weapon at them.

"It freakin' sucks out here," said a man on the other side of the RV. "How the hell long are we gonna get stuck wandering this damn road?"

"As long as we need ta be," replied another man with a slightly deeper voice and mild Russian accent. "We don't gotta wander now we found this place."

Harper crept to where Route 65 met Route 40. From there, it became apparent that the RVs and trailers had been arranged in a C-shape around an interior 'courtyard.' Four men surrounded a fire pit-slash-grill made from scorched car parts and rims. A pair of birds roasted on spits, possibly chickens, though they seemed a little small.

The two guys facing her on the far side of the fire pit made eye contact. One had long, stringy black hair, a denim vest, and a bolt-action rifle. The other, slightly pudgier guy, wore an absolutely filthy white polo shirt bearing an Amazon logo as well as khaki pants. An Mp5 submachine gun hung on his chest, suspended from a strap.

Both wore blue fabric sashes around their necks.

Lawless! What the hell are they doing so far west?

The instant her brain processed that, the men's expressions

changed from 'someone's here' to 'she's old enough—and damn cute.' Amazon Polo pointed at her, grinning. The two guys with their backs turned spun around to stare at them. Flannel shirts and jeans made them resemble a pair of ranch hands who'd spent the past three hours making snow angels in dirt. Both of them carried handguns in belt holsters.

"These aren't the same guys who tried to shoot me," said Daxton.

"That'd be them three." Lennie pointed to the far side of I-40 where three corpses lay at the base of a rocky ridge behind a green sign marked 'Beaver Brook Drive Floyd Hill' above a leftward pointing arrow.

Daxton gasped.

"Well, hey there, Red," said the stringy-haired guy, hefting a hunting rifle. "You folks just joined the Lawless."

"Not happening." Harper raised the Mossberg. "You bastards shot my parents. I *will* die to send all four of you straight to hell before I let you touch me."

"I suggest you four stand the fuck down," said Deacon. "Less you wanna become hamburger."

Their overwhelming confidence faltered at the sight of him.

This is going to turn into a gunfight. I should just blow them away.

Logan looked around and whispered, "Backtrack, jump the guardrail, we can take cover behind the hill."

"Good plan." Lennie nodded. "Didn't take you for a soldier."

"I'm not. Played a crapton of paintball though." Logan smiled.

"This ain't paintball." Lennie spat to the side.

The stringy-haired guy chuckled. "That's a big attack dog you brought along for protection, but you've got a little math problem, sweetie. There ain't just four of us."

Doors on the RVs and trailers opened. At least six more people started to emerge.

Harper, her face stony, snapped her aim point up and fired, shredding the stringy-haired man's face. Like the rapid-target range exercise she'd been running since age fourteen, she pivoted and shot the Mp5 guy, before running to her left, shooting at the other two one after the next, four shots in about six seconds.

Three died on their feet, throwing their handguns into the air as they tried to draw them on her. The fourth man grabbed his bloodied neck and collapsed to the parking lot, howling in pain.

Daxton's scream of "ohhhh craaaaaap!" went by like a passing train whistle. Harper sprinted for cover behind the RV at the left end of the compound, vaguely aware of the others jumping the guardrail at the spot where the overpass met the hill. Gunfire erupted from the Lawless, a few bullets whistling behind her or zinging off the pavement. Daxton let out another yell as Deacon tossed him out of sight behind the hill. Harper dashed around the front end of the RV and huddled low by the tire, her shotgun ready for anyone who tried to follow her.

Lennie hit the dirt on his chest beside a streetlamp at the inner corner, firing twice under the guardrail at someone coming toward Harper's position. One shot ricocheted off the pavement, the other made a wet *thump* as it hit a body. Another man shrieked in pain.

"Go!" shouted Logan. "We're covering."

"Don't shoot into the trailers!" yelled Harper. "They might have kidnapped someone."

Logan aimed to the right and fired, but didn't hit anything.

Crap! Okay, that was stupid. But less stupid than just standing there and being abducted. She squeezed the pistol grip of her shotgun, prepared to blow the face—or balls—off the next person to walk around the RV.

Someone started shooting at the guys from a window in the RV. Both Logan and Deacon returned fire, despite a spark flashing by Logan's face where a bullet struck the guardrail.

Harper screamed at him to get down.

Screw this. I can't sit here. Get behind them. They won't expect it. She shifted to face the other way and scurried to the back end of the RV, swinging around the corner—the tip of her Mossberg's barrel less than two inches from the nose of a woman who'd been trying to sneak up on her.

They froze, staring at each other while intermittent gunfire zinged back and forth between the guys and the Lawless inside, on top of, and in front of the RV.

If the woman's huge brown eyes meant anything, she needed clean pants from having a shotgun close enough to her face that she could probably see the red front of the shell ready to fire. She carried an Uzi, but held it sideways in front of a *Star Trek* shirt showing Spock's unamused face above the words 'Negative, Captain. There is no intelligent life on this planet.' Her pale dirt-smudged face and dirty-blonde hair looked so damn familiar.

"Harper Cody?" squeaked the woman.

"I know you...?" Harper glanced down past the side of her shotgun at the Uzi. She didn't need to use iron sights to hit a target an inch away.

"You were in my physics class junior year."

Harper blinked. "Holy crap! Mrs. Tiller?"

They both flinched at a deep *boom* from inside the compound. Lennie's M4 fired so rapidly it sounded like full auto. A man on the other side of the trailers yowled.

"Yeah," said Mrs. Tiller. "Guess it's 'miz' now, since Robert's gone."

"Crap. I've got my physics teacher at gunpoint."

"You do. But I haven't been teaching physics lately."

Harper scowled. "You joined the fu—freakin' Lawless? I know teachers get paid so little they sometimes work different jobs, but 'murderous thug' is a bit extreme."

"They made me a 'killer' offer. I literally couldn't say no." She reached her left hand up, grabbed the blue sash around her neck, and pulled it off. "You gotta believe me I've just been playing along, waiting for a chance to disappear."

"Lawless killed my parents," said Harper, her voice toneless.

Ms. Tiller's jaw tightened like she expected to die any second.

Harper sighed. "But they also kidnapped Renee and forced her to join them."

"I only stayed with them because I didn't want to die."

Even after everything that happened, pointing a gun at one of her teachers felt like a seriously wrong thing to do. Ms. Tiller had been one of the teachers she liked quite a bit, having a geeky sense of humor and being obsessed with *Star Trek*. The students made a joke about calling that period the 'Tiller Wormhole' because of time compression. It always felt like her class passed in mere seconds. Harper stared into the woman's eyes, trying to gauge if she could trust her. She pictured her former teacher laughing after dropping a painful *Star Trek* pun or making a reference to *Big Bang Theory*.

Deacon fired his AK twice rapidly. A body thudded to the roof of the RV.

Still having a Mossberg in her face, Ms. Tiller about fainted at the unexpectedly loud gunshots.

"Okay." Harper lowered her weapon. "You were one of my favorite teachers. This war has changed people. I hope I'm not being a gullible idiot."

"You're not." Ms. Tiller put a hand to her chest, evidently trying to remember how to breathe again. "C'mon. They won't think I'm a threat at first." She spun around in a 180 and hurried along the trailer to a gap where it nearly touched another RV.

Harper swiveled to look at Logan and Deacon, making a hand sign she hoped they'd interpret as 'don't shoot into the camp.' Their rifles would penetrate anything the campers had been made from like paper. Logan fired at someone near the front of the RV, his bullet emitting a loud *clank* as it glanced off hard metal, then gave her a thumbs-up.

Ms. Tiller squeezed through the space between the trailer and the second RV, entering the compound from behind at the middle. Harper gingerly stepped over the hitch and peered past the corner. Ms. Tiller hurried over to two guys taking cover at the front of the RV, still trading bullets with Lennie, Deacon, and Logan. Another two figures inside the RV huddled down out of sight, no doubt waiting for the right moment to pop up and fire at the guys.

Ms. Tiller approached the two at the front of the RV, who didn't appear alarmed by her presence. When she got within about fifteen feet, she raised her Uzi and fired a few short bursts of automatic fire. One man fell to the left, wounded. However, the instant he hit the ground, his head jutted out past the bumper. A shot from—probably Lennie—exploded his skull all over the parking lot.

Harper rushed to the RV that served as a wall between the camp interior and where her friends hid behind the guardrail. She stopped shy of the door for fear that the guys would shoot her if they saw motion inside. At a lull in the firing, she spun into the doorway, leveling the shotgun off at the people she'd seen hunkered down — but both women she thought had been waiting in ambush were, in fact, already dead. They'd taken multiple hits from bullets the RV wall couldn't stop. Blue sashes identified them as Lawless, both still gripped handguns, and neither appeared to be captives, so she didn't feel *too* upset that they'd died. Of course, they could have been forced to join like Ms. Tiller. No way to know, now. Then again, her former teacher hadn't been shooting at them like these two.

"Check your fire. I'm in the camp!" shouted Harper at the window.

She swung around, aiming at the other two trailers and one RV. Nothing moved other than the flames lapping at the two roasting chickens. "Ms. Tiller, is there anyone else here?"

"Harper, just call me Sherri. It's all gone. Who cares? I'm not your teacher anymore." The woman sighed. "And no, that's all of them."

A ROUGH WORLD

Harper stared at her once physics teacher for a while. For some reason, seeing that woman mow down lawless with an Uzi shocked her more than Mila killing two guys. That made no sense. A child having to kill *should* be jaw dropping.

"It's not *all* gone. Just, changed. Feels weird using your first name, but if you want me to…" Harper approached the front of the RV, but didn't lean out into view. "Clear. C'mon over. Little, umm… bloody over here. Someone make sure Daxton doesn't see this."

"Aww, man," yelled the boy.

"One friendly. Please don't shoot Ms. Til — I mean Sherri."

Lennie came around the RV first, M4 raised. Upon seeing Harper and Ms. Tiller standing there, he relaxed, frowning at the guy with a blown-open head. "Hoo-eey, what a mess."

Logan arrived next at a jog. He hurried up to Harper, looked her over, and exhaled in relief. "You really do have weird ideas of what to do on a date."

She started to frown but noticed blood on his arm. "Ack! You're hit!"

He twisted to look. A small hole a few inches above his left elbow oozed blood. "Oh, wow. I didn't even feel that."

Deacon entered the camp, carrying Daxton who had his eyes closed. The boy folded his arms, his lips curled in a grumpy smirk. The big guy bled from his right ear and left shoulder. Harper ran over, on the verge of freaking out.

"You're hit, too!" She looked around for a first aid kit, as if one would appear out of thin air.

"Nah, it's little. Ain't nothin' to worry about." Deacon made a 'pff' sound. "Just a nine mil."

"That is a hole." Harper pointed at his shoulder. "You have a bullet inside you."

"Figured that might happen. Brought some alcohol." Lennie ambled over.

Harper blinked at him. "You're limping. Did you get hit, too?"

"Just once. Vest took it, but it knocked the wind out of me. Don't think a rib broke, but that's gonna be a bruise." Lennie gestured at Logan. "You two check them trailers for anything interesting. I'll take care of the big guy."

"Logan's hit, too."

"'Tis but a scratch," said Logan in a lame British accent, which he dropped before adding, "probably a fragment of guardrail, not a bullet."

Reluctantly, Harper forced herself not to insist he get bandaged right away and headed around the other RV and all three trailers, Logan and Ms. Tiller following to help. Other than bedding and a modest stash of ammunition (mostly 9mm handgun rounds as well as a scattering of .30-06) she found no sign of any kidnap victims or useful supplies beyond water jugs. Every thirty seconds or so, Daxton asked if he could look yet. Deacon kept replying 'not yet.'

By the time they gathered the ammo and cleared the rest of the camp, Lennie had finished bandaging Deacon, who sat there examining a bloody 9mm bullet between his thumb and index finger.

Logan walked up to him. "Might want to clean this out before Harper yells at me."

"Damn right," she said, her voice a mix of playfulness and worry.

Lennie held up a small plastic squeeze bottle containing clear liquid. "This is gonna sting a wee bit."

"Won't be as bad as last time." Logan offered the man his arm.

Ms. Tiller went into the third trailer and came back with a small piece of luggage, a nylon carry-on bag. As far as Harper knew, the woman had been married but didn't have any kids. She vaguely remembered stories of a younger brother doing something science-related, possibly working for the USGS, but forgot the details.

"Oh, that does sting a bit," said Logan. His face remained calm, but a few blood vessels in his forehead swelled into view.

"Heh." Lennie dribbled alcohol into the relatively small wound, then bandaged it.

"Can I look yet?" asked Daxton.

"Almost. We're about to get going again." Harper looked around. "Anything here worth taking?"

"That chicken?" Logan pointed at the fire.

Daxton stared at the birds, drooling.

Having finished bandaging Logan's arm, Lennie put his supplies away, then ran around collecting all the guns from the Lawless. "Heh. This sumbitch had a Desert Eagle. That explains the damn thunder."

"Okay well... let's grab the chickens and get away from the dead people. We can eat it somewhere else." Harper looked at Ms. Tiller. "So, umm... do you want to stay with us?"

"Just the four of you and a boy roaming around? I suppose. Better than those idiots." She smiled at Deacon. "Guess you're pretty safe."

"We're not roaming. Actually, we've got a nice little town going in Evergreen. You should come back with us. Teachers are in demand."

Ms. Tiller chuckled. "What's the pay like?"

"Food and a place to live. Clothes. And you won't need to shoot anyone."

"Sign me up. That sounds like more than my last job."

Harper laughed. "Wow. Was it really that bad?"

"Unfortunately... yes. If I hadn't been married, I wouldn't have been able to make rent unless I got a roommate." Ms. Tiller shook her head. "This is what happens. Keep skimping on education, you end up with nuclear war and gangs of murderous creeps."

Harper blinked. "I'm not sure if I should laugh at that or cry."

"Both are appropriate," said Ms. Tiller.

Logan put an arm around her from behind. "It's going to be dark fairly soon. Don't think you want to sleep near dead guys."

"Nope. I do not." Harper fished four shells out of her hip bag and stuffed them into the Mossberg. "Okay. Let's get going."

They continued following Route 40, eating chicken while trying to hustle.

Between mouthfuls, Harper filled Ms. Tiller in on their present mission and a little bit about Evergreen. From there, they compared stories of what happened after the nuclear strike. Her former teacher spoke in a somewhat detached, emotionless tone as if relaying the tale of something that happened to someone else. She'd been gathering canned goods from a King Sooper when a pack of Lawless found her. Terrified, she'd pretended to be tough, channeling the Klingon character she occasionally cosplayed at conventions, always intending to slip away from them at the first chance.

Within hours of 'joining' that group, they ended up at the house where she and her husband had been hiding out. Another group of Lawless had already killed him.

"Oh, man," said Deacon. "That just ain't right."

"Hardest thing I ever had to do in my life was to pretend I didn't recognize my husband. Don't think I did it too well. Bet a few of them knew." Ms. Tiller took a deep breath. "Guess they showed me that as a warning what would happen if I didn't do what they wanted."

Harper blushed.

"No. Not that. Couple of them asked. Figured sooner or later, someone would take it if I kept saying no, but I guess they have this weird code of honor. I acted like a tough bitch, faking being a little nuts and a lot violent. They didn't even grab my ass."

"Wow." Harper whistled. "They had my friend Renee for a while. She had to pretend she was fourteen to keep them from forcing her to have sex with them."

Logan scowled. "We're not hunting them down why?"

"Because they didn't actually touch her and it's not worth getting killed for revenge." Harper spat a nugget of gristle off to the side. "But... if we find any."

"That was some *damn* fine shooting there, kiddo." Lennie smiled. "Would've liked a bit more warning, but I ain't never seen four headshots in four seconds like that."

Harper bit off another piece of chicken. "It was more like six seconds. Heads are bigger than clay pigeons, so it's easier shooting. Sorry about the lack of warning. Figured we were about to get overrun."

"Oh, I wasn't yellin' at you about the warning. That was directed at them bastards." Lennie emitted a wheezy chuckle.

"It's kinda freaking me out you're so casual about killing people." Ms. Tiller looked over at her. "But, I guess after what happened with your father, and everything else, it's understandable."

"I don't like killing people. But shooting Lawless in the face doesn't bother me... much."

"They killed the guys who tried to shoot me," said Daxton. "Think those guys tried to shoot at them, too?"

"Probably. But them Lawless dudes usually shoot first." Deacon bit off a huge hunk of meat.

"Hungry?" asked Logan, smiling.

"No fridge. Whatever we don't eat, we're gonna have to toss." Lennie broke off a smaller piece of chicken and handed it to Daxton. "Eat as much as you can. Better not to waste it."

"Those three guys were staying at that trailer village when we found the place," said Ms. Tiller. "They, umm. Didn't want to join. No, I didn't kill any of them. Missed on purpose."

"Guess we're lucky you decided to change sides when we showed up." Lennie wagged his eyebrows at her.

"Nah. You guys are the first time it felt like someone had a chance at surviving. I was trying to sneak away since I figured you'd just shoot at me, too. But ran into Harper. She didn't blow my head off."

"Yeah. She's sweet like that." Logan grinned.

Harper didn't know whether to blush or raspberry him.

After a long period of silent walking and eating, Harper looked over at Ms. Tiller. "Is it true that the sports arena has gone full *Mad Max*, like the Lawless have a king and stuff? Make people run these long obstacle courses while trying to dodge snipers in some kind of twisted game show?"

"Sorta. I've never been there, but a few of them said they have a camp in a football stadium. Most of what you've heard are probably wild stories to make people scared of them so anyone they run into will just surrender right away or join."

"So they don't make people run murder gauntlets?" Harper raised both eyebrows.

"Uhh, they do, but it's not *that* involved. It's only done for people who joined and then either tried to steal stuff and leave, killed another member of the group, or did something they consider bad— like turn traitor." She whistled nervously. "Good thing we didn't leave any witnesses."

"It's kinda freaking me out that you're so casual about shooting people," said Harper, faintly smiling.

Her geek-culture-obsessed former physics teacher looked down at her Uzi. "Yeah. It's a rough world out there. This thing doesn't really have a stun setting."

"Heh." Harper picked at the shotgun's pistol grip. "That would be awesome. Stun settings, I mean."

"Right?" asked Logan.

Harper looked at Ms. Tiller. "I heard they made random people run that gauntlet thing for amusement, and no one ever survived."

"It's not as involved as I'm sure the stories make it out to be. Basically, they send the prisoner running down a street that's been blocked off on the sides, creating a track with only one way out at the end, an arch they call 'Heaven's Gate.' Someone makes it to that thing alive, that's freedom."

"Do they actually let them leave if they make it there?"

Ms. Tiller shrugged. "Not sure. No one's made it yet. At least not that I've seen or heard about."

"It's beyond messed up to hear you talking about this in the same tone you used to teach physics," said Harper.

"I agree. I've probably disassociated to a point. Feels more like I'm no longer in the real world and just stuck playing a character."

Harper peered over at her. "Can you stitch your brain back together?"

"Yeah. Hopefully. If Evergreen's as calm as you're saying it is, I'll probably start to feel safe there sooner or later. Then it will finally hit me that Robert's dead. Couldn't process that around those guys. So, I'll most likely be a complete mess for a little while, then gradually level off into something approaching normal."

"I used to think normal was boring." Harper sighed. "Now, I miss it."

"Yeah." Ms. Tiller stared at her portion of chicken like she couldn't bear to eat any more, but still took another bite.

"I hear that," said Deacon.

"Normal *is* boring." Lennie smiled. "Don't mistake normality for civilization."

Deacon whipped a cleaned bone into the trees. "Lawless are real far outside Denver."

Harper frowned. "I was thinking that, too."

"Route 70 goes right to the city. They sent us out here as a 'remote scouting team,' looking to ambush-recruit anyone going by. I didn't mind it so much since we didn't see anyone out here in months except for those three men at the trailer lot and you guys. I'd much rather sit around doing nothing except hunting for food than messing with people who are only trying to survive."

"Dunno if Walter is going to ask you to 'donate' that Uzi to the militia or not since it's basically a pistol, but you won't *have* to use it back home. Except for the constant worry about being raided, it's pretty close to civilized." Harper smiled.

Ms. Tiller laughed. "We do extreme things when we have to. I wouldn't mind going back to carrying textbooks. If I never fired a gun again in my life, I'd be happy. If your Walter wants this thing, he's welcome to it."

Eventually, little remained of the chickens but bones and cartilage that ended up scattered across the roadside, each piece dropped when it held no more edible meat. Despite a break or two for bathroom needs, the group reached the intersection to Route 6 about an hour and a half after leaving the Lawless camp. For a little over two miles, they followed a picturesque elevated highway flanked by mountainous hills. A whitewater creek running along the side started on the right, then passed under the road to the left. Maybe fifteen minutes later, they arrived at a tunnel in a sheer rock face. A little white sign at the top read 'Tunnel 6.'

Predictably, none of the lights on the ceiling worked.

No abandoned cars had been left in the tunnel, perhaps indicating that the rock had shielded those vehicles from EMP at the moment of the blast. Then again, there hadn't been all that many cars out here to begin with. The ones they did see had likely run out of gas rather than been wiped by electromagnetic waves.

The tunnel only lasted for about five hundred feet or so, not long enough to become pitch dark. Not far from that tunnel, they reached 'Tunnel 5,' an even shorter one. Harper wished she could have come out here before the war to enjoy nature without having to worry about being killed at any minute or starving to death. She wanted to take a kayak or raft down the creek, or maybe bike the trail beside the water. Alas, it would be a while before anyone did that sort of thing for fun anymore.

So weird. We used to do stuff for fun that people way *back had to do in order to survive. Well, okay, sorta. Lewis & Clark didn't have bikes to ride on trails. But rafting and hiking used to be life for people, not recreation.*

Eventually, after covering a little over two miles, they reached 119. Based on her ruler jockeying the wall map in Walter's office, she'd guessed they'd need to go about five miles more before reaching Golden Gate Canyon Road. Tall hills carpeted in pine trees stretched up from both sides of the road. Tree cover in some places, plus bushes, had grown so thick that the Lawless—or some other dangerous thugs—could be hiding four feet away from the pavement and she'd never notice them. Every so often, mostly whenever the road curved with the valley, she caught a glimpse of more distant green-covered hills. Scraps of scorched power lines occasionally hung from utility poles that hadn't burned to charcoal. Except for that and the road itself, the place appeared mostly untouched by humanity, and so quiet that every scuff of a shoe on the blacktop seemed to echo all the way back to Evergreen.

Harper kept her attention on the densest spots in the foliage, on guard for attack. If not people, perhaps a mountain lion or bear. Given the remoteness of the area and the unlikelihood that anyone would travel this road often at all, it didn't make sense for anyone to set a trap here. Heck, Ms. Tiller said that Lawless had been wandering back and forth out here for a long time without seeing anyone until they went farther out and bumped into those three guys Daxton grabbed food from—and they stuck to a major highway leading to Denver. Their leader decided to take over that camp as a permanent base from which to extend the Lawless' reach. Ms. Tiller figured the guy she called Randall merely got tired of walking around.

All things considered, they made reasonable time, but the sun went down before they made it to the next turn in her route.

"Think we should stop somewhere?" asked Logan.

"Nah, we're kinda close now." Daxton pointed ahead. "It won't take us that long to get there and it *just* got dark. It's not time to sleep yet. We got a few hours."

Harper looked to her left where the road widened into a tiny parking lot. Beyond it, a glint of moonlight shimmered on the surface of a smallish lake. A couple park service signs stood at the edge of the parking lot near the start of a dirt path, but she couldn't make out what they said in the dark.

"That's not Kriley Pond is it?" asked Harper.

"No. That's... I dunno." Daxton shrugged. "Way little."

"Okay. Might as well keep going if everyone's up for it. Better to spend the night at a settlement than out here in the open."

Lennie and Deacon nodded, murmuring agreement.

"If we had to, we could go up the hill a bit and take cover in the trees." Logan pointed left at the less steep side. "Wouldn't mind a pee break."

Before Harper could even say anything, all the guys plus Daxton appeared to get on the same mental wavelength. The instant he said the word 'pee,' they scrambled to form a firing line at the right side of the road.

To her absolute horror, Ms. Tiller went to the other side, casual as anything, and proceeded to water the grass. More than the realization that a former teacher was actually a human being who had working biological processes, the woman's complete lack of hesitation unnerved her. *She's been among the Lawless for a while.* Still, Harper couldn't argue the need to go. Short of an annoying hike up a steep hill into trees, this area had zero cover.

At least it's super dark. They can't see my butt or *me blushing.*

She did her best to empty her bladder and not give anyone too much of a show.

Conversing amongst themselves about their expectations for what awaited them in Kriley Pond, the men kept their backs turned until Harper and Ms. Tiller stepped back onto the road.

A few minutes into their resumed walk, Ms. Tiller shook her head. "I never imagined I'd see one of my students walking down the highway with a shotgun, wary of an ambush."

Harper let her arms—and shotgun—hang low, tired of carrying the damn thing all day. "Yeah, but like you said… it's a rough world for a girl."

Ms. Tiller chuckled. "Guess a can of pepper spray doesn't quite do the trick anymore."

"I don't need pepper spray. I have a Deacon."

"Religious?" asked Ms. Tiller.

"Not really," said Deacon.

Harper pointed a thumb over her shoulder. "He's Deacon."

"Oh." She looked back. "Yes. I can see how he'd be a deterrent to violence."

Deacon laughed.

Logan fake pouted at her.

"Aww." Harper leaned against him. "*I* know how far you'd go to keep me safe, but you're not seven feet tall and four hundred pounds."

"Hey, now. I'm 335," muttered Deacon. "Or at least, I was the last time I had a working scale nearby."

The hill on the right curved away from the road, creating a modest flat area covered by sparse grass and a few picnic tables near a paved loop that branched off from the highway. A tiny sign by the entrance had white lettering that read, 'Kriley Pond, fishing, picnic sites, self-serve pay station.'

"I think we found it," said Harper.

Daxton looked up from the ground, spotted the loop, and cheered—for two seconds. He fell quiet and stared up, at her, mortal dread in his eyes.

"What's wrong?" Harper glanced at him briefly before surveying the D-shaped parking lot for threats, worried she might have missed something.

"My mother's gonna kill me. I mean, I wanna see her bad, but she's gonna freak out at me for running off."

Logan patted the boy on the back. "She should. That means she cares. And you are a bit young to go off alone just because you heard a story."

"Who else but a young boy would have that much faith or hope in a story." Lennie chuckled. "Old men tend to sit where they are and die."

A short distance past the parking loop, an oddly rectangular lake, much larger than the last one, came almost up to the road. It looked about as long as a football field, maybe three times as wide.

"So where is everyone?" asked Deacon.

"Keep going." Daxton pointed. "It's just up ahead on the left. Kriley Ranch."

Not long after they passed the end of the lake, Harper spotted a weird building on the right that looked like a giant Monopoly house with three garage doors in the middle, a dark roof, and grey siding. Probably some type of Park Service garage or some such thing. More or less across the street from it on the left, a few paces farther, a picket fence surrounded a large property containing several individual buildings, two houses and a number of cabins. A dirt trail led from the road to a gate, under a wooden arch that bore a sign reading 'Kriley Ranch.'"

A man holding a rifle stood a short distance inside from the gate, clearly on guard duty. At their approach, he raised his weapon toward them. "Who is there?" he asked, his voice thick with an Indian accent. "Please identify yourself."

Harper, Logan, Deacon, Lennie, and Ms. Tiller all pointed their weapons at him.

"Oh, heavens," muttered the man.

"Vijay!" yelled Daxton as he ran up to the gate. "It's me. I found help. It's okay. They're friends."

The man stepped closer, lowering his weapon. He looked to be in his middle thirties, wearing a long camo raincoat and bucket hat. "Daxton? Where the heck have you been? We'd thought the raiders got you." Vijay ruffled the boy's hair, patted him on the shoulder, and looked at Deacon—the man tended to draw attention. "Who are your friends?"

"Mind if we come in so I don't have to explain twice?" Harper smiled and slung the Mossberg over her shoulder, grateful to spare her arms the weight of it.

"Oh, by gosh. You're a kid, too." Vijay whistled. "What are you, Army?"

"I'm not *that* young." Harper smiled. "And no. We're Evergreen militia. Dax here said you needed some help."

Vijay's eyes widened. He opened the gate—a relatively flimsy bit of steel fencing. "Evergreen? So it's true? Quickly, please come in."

KRILEY POND

D axton sprinted up the dirt road inside the ranch compound, going past a light grey house at the front corner to a larger brown one behind it. Harper followed Vijay past two enormous soup pots apparently used to boil-sterilize water from the lake. A woman inside the house shouted Daxton's name, then a mostly unintelligible string of yelling at him for scaring the hell out of her.

"Should we do anything if she starts hitting him?" asked Harper.

"I would," said Logan.

"Nah. Jen wouldn't raise a hand to him." Vijay smiled. "'Course, she doesn't have to. Buried a hatchet—literally—in the head of one of the raiders. Ain't much that woman's afraid of, except losing her boy."

They made their way into the living room and the overpowering smell of cooked fish and wood smoke. Daxton embraced a fortyish woman with slightly darker blonde hair than him. He appeared to be crying harder than his mother, but grinned broadly. A handful of other people, all adults, occupied the sofa, recliners, and a few folding chairs. They appeared significantly underfed. Except for

Daxton's mother, they all had plates in their laps containing partially eaten fish.

Apparently, Harper and her group had interrupted their meager dinner.

"What the hell were you thinking?" Daxton's mother peeled him out of the hug and shook him by the shoulders. "We've been searching all over for you." She picked her plate off the chair she'd been seated in and offered it to him. "Here. Eat."

"No, Mom." He pushed her arm back toward her. "Go ahead. I already ate tonight. I'm stuffed. We found chickens on the way here."

"Seems we didn't go far enough afield in our search," said a man in his early forties. His black hair still somehow looked neat and perfect despite the beard stubble on his cheeks. He reminded her of her junior year English teacher who used so much hair gel that all the students joked it could deflect bullets.

Daxton spun around, leaning back into his mother while gesturing at that man. "Mr. Henderson, I found help. What that lady said about Evergreen is true!"

"Looks like your boy snuck off, Jen." Mr. Henderson looked at the kid, his expression part annoyed, part impressed. "Spent a lot of hours looking around for a body. You have any idea what you did to your mother?"

Daxton bowed his head. "I'm sorry. But we're not gonna make it much longer. I had to do something. We barely have food. The raiders won't stop."

His mother squeezed his shoulders, staring at Harper and her team. Her expression said 'thank you for keeping him safe.'

Some murmurs went around the other locals, grumbling at spending two days searching for him while fearful that he'd been taken by a wild animal or fallen into a hole, drowned in the lake, or so on. Despite the near universal scolding, Daxton maintained the most endearingly defiant expression Harper had ever seen. He didn't appear to feel guilty for risking himself to get help, or ashamed of making those people waste time hunting for him, though she got the feeling it bothered him that he'd worried his mother.

"So, who are you?" Mr. Henderson approached Deacon. "Carl Henderson. I'm basically in charge here since no one else wanted to be."

"Deacon Owens. Daxton tells us you're in a bad way up here. This is"—he indicated everyone while introducing them—"Harper, Lennie, Logan, and Shari. Harper"—he gestured at her—"got this thing about helpin' people. So, here we are."

"Sherri," said Ms. Tiller.

"My bad." Deacon smiled. "Sherri."

"You're well-armed, I'll give ya that." Carl looked them over. "But it's going to take more than the five of you to deal with the raiders. Real squirrely bunch they are."

Harper stepped up to him. "We didn't come here to be assassins or mercenaries. As I'm sure you've figured out by now, there isn't any gasoline left."

"The hell do we need gasoline for?" snapped a fiftyish woman with long, black hair and a grey sweatshirt.

"Easy, Margaret." Carl raised a placating hand. "Let the girl talk."

"Mrs. Olson's mean to everyone. It's not your fault," whispered Daxton.

Jen sighed, staring an apology at Margaret. "Be nice."

"The boy ain't wrong." A thirtyish man sitting in the recliner wagged his half-eaten fish at Daxton before taking a bite.

"Mason, she'll stab you in your sleep," said an older man on the way into the room from a hallway. "Trust me. I know."

Margaret rolled her eyes in exasperation at the older guy, but leaned against him when he sat beside her.

"That's Mr. Olson," whispered Daxton. "They're married. He's the only one she isn't mean to."

"So, where were you going with the gasoline thing?" asked Mr. Henderson.

Harper exhaled. "Dax said you're having problems feeding your people and the attacks aren't making things any easier. We've got a fairly established farm and a good-sized militia for defense. Since we don't have gasoline, it's not really possible for us to send a meaningful amount of food up here. We can't carry it and don't have any wagons."

"I'm guessing you didn't walk all the way out here to tell us you can't help." Mr. Henderson looked over their group again. "And if you're not here to help us fight the raiders, what's your plan?"

"We're here to offer an escort back to Evergreen." Harper smiled.

Everyone got quiet, exchanging glances.

"I'm gonna go back with them no matter what. They have food there. Even a school. And doctors." Daxton held one leg up to show off gauze bandages through the giant hole in his jeans. "Mom, you gotta come, too."

Mr. Henderson raised both hands in a 'hold on a moment' gesture. "Now, let's not get to panicking right away. I appreciate your concern, miss. But, there's no reason for us to uproot ourselves and relocate. We have plenty of fish in the pond to sustain things."

Daxton lifted his shirt to show off his ribs. "The fish are tiny, and they don't catch many. Doctor Hale said I'm malnourished."

"Mr. Henderson, with all due respect..." Harper looked from person to person around the room. "You and your people are clearly not eating enough. I mean, everyone's lean nowadays, but seriously. Look at yourselves. The boy's right. You're not really hanging on here."

"Did you own this land before the war? What's important about staying here over your lives?" asked Logan.

Carl bowed his head. "Nah. Over a couple months after everything hit the fan, we all kinda ran into each other and decided to stay together for protection. Found this place right before winter set in. Sure we've got our issues. Fish ain't biting like they used to, and them jackasses show up every couple of days to test our defenses. But, we'll be okay."

"I dunno, Carl." Jen kept her arms around Daxton, pinning him against her chest as if afraid he'd run away again the instant she let go. "It's been rough here past couple weeks. That girl's right. Look at us. We're walking skeletons. If that place has decent food, we should consider going."

Margaret slapped the remains of her fish onto her plate. "I'm so damn sick of fish. Maybe we ought'a listen to them."

"Whatever she wants," said Mr. Olson.

"Clive, do you ever have an original thought or just do what your wife wants?" asked Mason.

The locals all laughed.

Mr. Olson pointed upward. "I always get what I want, because what I want is Margaret to be happy."

"Umm," said Daxton. "She's ne—"

Jen covered her son's mouth.

The boy shifted his eyes up at her, his expression saying 'really, Mom?'

"All right." Carl looked around. "It's too dark to think right now. In the morning, we'll get everyone together and have a vote. I'm not attached to this place *that* much, but it's got everything we need and travel is dangerous."

"The boy made it on his own," said Logan.

"Only got shot at once." Deacon chuckled.

"What!?" shouted Jen. "Someone shot him?"

"No." Harper shook her head rapidly, her hair swooshing back and forth. "They shot *at* him. Missed. And... they're dead now."

Carl pointed at Deacon and Logan's bandages. "Doesn't really look like you had a safe trip."

"Nothing we couldn't handle." Lennie smiled. "Bunch of Lawless."

"The hell's a lawless?" asked Margaret.

"Gang." Harper frowned. "Short version, they're a group of convicts who got out of prison after the nuclear strike and decided to take over Denver. Not really sure how many of them there are, but they're basically shoot-on-sight. Wear blue sashes around their necks as a sign of membership."

"Probably so they don't kill each other in the middle of a raid." Deacon grinned.

"Doesn't always help." Ms. Tiller shivered. "Some of those idiots get so riled up when they see blood, if they accidentally hit another Lawless, they'll laugh at it."

Carl walked up on Harper. "How much of a problem are these guys? Do they raid Evergreen? What's the point of us going there if it's just going to be the same thing all over again?"

"Whoa, slow down." She leaned back, uncomfortable at his proximity. "They mostly stay around center city Denver. We haven't seen them anywhere else until we made the trip up here. They followed Route 70 west to set up an ambush point. So far, they haven't come near Evergreen. Even if they do, our militia has about fifty people split between north and south, and we're carrying decent weapons. Like a third of the militia are ex cops or soldiers."

"What kind of raids are you having here?" asked Logan.

"Bunch of idiots come at us from the northeast. They usually fire at us from far away, not too accurately." Carl pointed at a bullet hole in the wall, high up. "Couple times, they tried rushing the gate and things got rough. We used to be twenty-six. Now, it's about fifteen."

"Crazy as hell." Mason leaned forward, setting his empty plate on the coffee table. "They don't even take anything. Just attack, kill what they can, and run away whooping like freakin' coyotes."

"That's messed up," said Harper. "Psycho. Yeah, you guys should really come back with us. Evergreen is about as close as it gets to civilization at the moment."

Carl headed for the door, waving Harper to follow. "We'll discuss it with everyone in the morning. You all can sleep across the way. The room looks lived in but everyone who used to sleep there's been killed."

"Damn. This place isn't safe for you," said Logan.

Grumbling, Carl walked across the dirt outside the house to a small, rectangular cabin. He stopped a few paces from the door and gestured for them to go on in. "Place is all yours for the night. None of the toilets in the houses work since the water's dead. We built a latrine over by the firewood pile down the back end of the yard. Just head toward the gate, turn right and go all the way back."

"All right. Thank you." Harper shook Carl's hand and approached the door.

The one-room cabin contained three cots and five sleeping bags arranged around a few stacked crates serving as tables. She couldn't see much as a pair of skylights only let in a tiny amount of moonlight. Logan, Deacon, Lennie, and Ms. Tiller walked in behind her, feeling their way around.

"You go on and take a cot." Deacon patted her on the head. "I'm too big for them, anyway."

"What do you think?" asked Logan. "Safe here?"

"From the locals or from the raiders?" Lennie chuckled.

Harper sat on the nearest cot, looking up at the shadowy figures of her friends. The people here didn't concern her *too* much. However, she couldn't help but worry that falling asleep with her guard totally down would result in all of them being robbed of everything useful and either killed or sent at gunpoint naked into the wasteland.

"I don't think these people are a threat." Harper rested the shotgun sideways across her lap. "But whoever is attacking them could show up in the night. And... I also don't want to be stupid. We should keep watch."

"Agreed," said Lennie.

Harper, not feeling at all tired, suggested she take first watch, then Deacon, Logan, and Lennie last.

"I could take a watch, too. Or do you guys not fully trust me yet?" asked Ms. Tiller.

"It's not that. We have five people. Hmm. I guess we could take shorter shifts and get more sleep?" Harper looked at the shadow that spoke in Lennie's voice.

"That works." Lennie felt around for a sleeping bag. "I'll wake her for last watch then."

"You take the last cot." Logan nudged Lennie toward it. "I can crash on a sleeping bag."

"I ain't an old man just yet."

"Too late." Logan stretched out on the floor.

Lennie sighed, then sat on the cot grumbling about 'young whipper-snappers' in an overacted 'old man' voice.

Harper sat on her cot watching and listening. Distant voices suggested the residents of Kriley Pond had already started their debate about relocating. With no way to really tell time, she figured she'd take her best guess at an hour and a half.

Hope they don't stay up all night arguing.

BEST INTEREST

H arper woke groggily to Ms. Tiller shaking her by the shoulder. Sunlight flooded the cabin, filtering down from two large plastic skylights covered in a scattering of dirt and small debris bits. It hadn't yet become too terribly warm, but she had a feeling this cabin would turn stifling soon enough.

"Morning," muttered Harper.

Everyone dragged themselves upright and trudged out the door as a group in search of the latrine. The dirt road leading from the middle of the compound to the highway branched off to the right not far from the gate, heading toward a huge pile of firewood beside a fenced-in garden. Several flowerpots of varying sizes hung from a wooden frame, though it didn't look like the gardener had any luck getting vegetables to grow. Or maybe they didn't have any seeds.

After using the latrine, Harper and the others returned to the cabin, but sat outside on the ground to eat. Logan plopped down next to her and rummaged a pack of Fig Newtons out of his bag. She took an MRE from her backpack and opened it. Logan, Deacon, and Lennie all ate directly from cans they'd brought along. Deacon tossed Ms. Tiller a can of peach halves plus an opener.

"Fig cookies?" asked Harper. "Breakfast of champions."

"Breakfast of what I had." He chuckled and tossed a Newton whole into his mouth.

"Boys will eat anything." She grinned. "Didn't your mother tell you, cookies aren't breakfast?"

"Maybe not, but they're easy to carry, last forever, and are yummy." He wagged his eyebrows.

While sucking 'chicken stew' out of a pouch, Harper watched people emerging from the other two houses, heading to the bathroom, then back to gather in the dirt lot. A relatively young Hispanic couple with a little girl smiled in their direction. Both the mother and daughter wore simple dresses, the man in sweat pants and a tank top. None of them had shoes. The child appeared heartbreakingly skinny, but smiled in their direction as if she'd spotted angels come to whisk her to safety.

If Carl decides everyone's going to stay here, I'm tempted to grab that kid. She needs food.

Mason crossed the lot on his way to the latrine, waving at her. The Olsen's followed soon after. A skinny guy with a narrow, angular face emerged from the smaller grey house, glanced over at the Evergreen crew, and paused on his way to the latrine. Behind him, a mid-thirties Chinese man exited the house and also stopped to check them out before continuing to the bathroom.

Eventually, a group of thirteen adults plus Daxton and the small girl gathered in the middle of the property around Carl. Harper stuffed the empty plastic pouches from her MRE into the outer pouch, and put the trash in her pack. Despite the war, it felt wrong to throw it wherever. Perhaps *because* of the war, littering made her feel even worse. Civilization had taken a step back, yielding to nature. Granted, some areas would have gone quite far the other way, full of poison, radiation, or other contamination as a result of the bombs.

Washington DC is probably as flat as Salt Lake for miles.

She looked up from stuffing the pouches in the backpack to find the little girl standing right in front of her. Harper jumped, which made the child giggle. Up close, she looked even skinnier and about seven or eight years old. Long, straight black hair framed a face so innocent that Harper had to fight the urge to pick her up and squeeze her like a plushie.

"Hi there." Harper smiled.

"Hey, kiddo." Logan offered her a cookie.

"Hi." The girl snagged the Fig Newton and stuffed it into her mouth as if worried someone might take it away from her before she could eat it. "Thank you!"

Logan offered her a few more.

She grabbed them happily. "You're nice, and her hair is pretty."

"Thank you." Harper offered her a water bottle that still had a Pepsi label. "So is yours. Straight hair is so much easier to live with."

The girl chugged half the water before coming up for air. "What's your name? I'm Alma Cortez."

"Harper Cody, and this is Logan Ruiz."

"Thank you for the cookies." Alma bit her lip. "There's not much food here."

Her heart melted into a puddle. "I didn't bring too much, but here…" Harper took the second MRE from her backpack, tore open the outer package, and handed it to her. "There is food inside these pouches. This is a whole meal."

"Thank you!" Alma hugged her, then darted over to her parents, pointing at Harper while holding the MRE up to show them.

Her mother and father waved and mouthed thanks. Mr. Cortez helped Alma open the meal pouch. The girl attempted to give food to her parents, but they insisted she eat the main entrée, snacking on the crackers and cookies instead.

"It's really bad here," said Logan. "We should press them to pick up and follow us. That kid's gonna starve."

"Yeah. Another few days here and she'll look like Lorelei did when Tyler found her." Harper zipped her backpack. "This is the part I hate the most."

"Walking?"

"No, dork." She laughed. "Speaking in front of people. I've always been painfully shy. Up until fifth grade, everyone thought I could only speak in whispers at school."

"A shy redhead? Seriously?" Lennie laughed.

Harper sighed. "I know... I know."

"You can't be that bad." Logan tossed a Newton into his mouth whole. "Never pegged you for being shy."

She smirked. "You didn't know me before things went crazy. And I kinda grew out of it. In fourth grade, I almost got suspended for refusing to stand up in front of class and read a report out loud. I was so damn terrified I threw up all over my desk."

"Damn. Why would they suspend you for having a panic attack?"

"Wasn't a real panic attack, just social anxiety. Teacher was a bitch. Accused me of being defiant."

"So what happened?"

"The principal gave me a choice between reading the paper or getting an F for that assignment. I said 'I'll take the F' without hesitation. Guess that convinced him I wasn't just being a brat or something. Got away with a C, didn't have to read it aloud... and they made me see a psychologist."

"How did that end up?" Logan put an arm around her. "You seem normal."

"Apparently, I was mortally terrified that someone might not like me, so I tried to stay as unnoticed as possible. Or something like that. Would you believe me if I told you I hate conflict? Like even arguing over lame stuff. When Maddie and Mom would start shouting at each other about cleaning up her room, I'd have to go outside because it stressed me out so much to even hear them fight."

Logan stared at her for a long moment. "You blasted the faces off four dudes like a Navy freakin' SEAL. I can't even picture you losing it because of an argument between your mother and little sister."

"Yeah, well. I'm not the same person I used to be." Harper stood. "None of us are."

He leapt to his feet and took her hand. "That's not always a bad thing. To change."

She half smiled at him. "Didn't say it was." *C'mon Harp. You can do this. Just talking to people.* "Here goes."

"You got this." He rubbed her shoulder.

"Hah. Yeah…"

Harper approached the crowd, heading for Carl Henderson who stood at the center fielding a barrage of questions. Most of what she could pick out of the raised voices sounded like people demanding 'good reasons' to stay here. A few asked about the risks of a long trip, while a younger Hispanic guy worried aloud that Evergreen was a trap and they'd all wind up prisoners or dead.

"Excuse me," said Harper, raising her voice enough that her hands shook a little from drawing so much attention to herself.

Everyone more or less shut up at once, and looked at her.

"A gang that wanted to kidnap you or force you to join them would have already started shooting people as a show of dominance and intimidation. We didn't come here to *make* you do anything." She paused, measuring the group's reaction. All but three regarded her with warm expressions. Carl appeared flustered. *He said he didn't want to be in charge, but he looks scared of losing control.* "Even a boy Daxton's age can tell the situation here is unsustainable."

"Girl's got the big words," whispered the twenty-something who worried about Evergreen being a trap.

"Not her fault you dropped out of school in fourth grade, Leo," said a pale boy about eighteen or nineteen. Black hair and clothes made him look goth.

Leo gave him the finger and muttered something in Spanish that caused Mrs. Cortez to cover Alma's ears and Logan to fight laughter.

The goth boy chuckled.

"Look." Harper exhaled. "It's pretty obvious just by looking at you that there isn't enough food here. None of us are getting fat, but we're definitely not starving. Maybe you can start finding fish or resurrect that little garden back there, but you can *definitely* do better in Evergreen."

"There's too many unanswered questions." Carl frowned off to the side. "What happens to us there? Put to work? Take our weapons away? What?"

"Everyone who has skills is asked to use them. People who aren't like plumbers or electricians or whatever usually end up on the farm. I guess you could call it a job. But you're not working for a boss.

We're working for everyone. Surviving is everyone's responsibility. Those who have skills do whatever they're good at. Certain weapons, Mayor Ned asks be given to the militia to help protect everyone. Mostly, combat rifles and such. Or, you could join the militia if you want to keep them. That's how I ended up here. Didn't want to give up my dad's shotgun. No one's going to ask for handguns or anything else. Only military style weapons."

"You're welcome to keep carrying a combat rifle if you're willing to stand up to defend the town." Deacon stepped forward. "Ain't no money. They allocate out food as needed, clothes, and such. Isn't like we got a king gettin' rich off our backs. We're all just a bunch of survivors tryin' ta do right by each other."

Harper's anxiety lessened with him standing next to her.

"Sounds too good to be true." Carl folded his arms.

Margaret narrowed her eyes. "Yeah, it kinda does."

"I'm not saying it's perfect. We're trying to get electricity back, but it's down more than it's up. Sometimes, people try to attack the farm and steal food. Which is really stupid because if they just walked in and asked to live there, we'd feed them. Nowhere is perfect anymore, just less crappy than other places."

"It isn't perfect here, but we're managing." Carl shifted his jaw side to side.

"Are you though? Your people are starving." Harper gestured around. "Considering what you had to work with in this place, the lake, the land, that tiny garden... you've managed to keep these people alive because you didn't know about a larger, safer settlement. Now that you know, a good leader will decide to act in his people's best interest."

The people started talking back and forth among each other. The Olsons wanted to go. A woman named Kelli about her mother's age also voiced her desire to trust Harper. Natalia and Miguel Cortez practically demanded they pick up and get out of here as fast as possible. The goth teen, Luke, had no strong opinion either way, figuring they had 'just as much chance to die here as there.'

Guess he is *a goth. He and Darce should get along.*

Daxton and his mother Jen pushed hard to relocate. Vijay

clutched his rifle, a long-barrel variant of an AR-15, close, but also agreed with the idea of moving.

He's going to join the militia. Harper smiled at him, then fell somber, wondering if that rifle belonged to someone he loved... like her Mossberg.

James Wong, a mid-thirties guy dressed like an office worker, spent most of the discussion time bemoaning that they're not going to need digital artists or computer programmers, so he and Vijay would be stuck doing some 'bullshit work.'

"Is doin' BS work worse than getting shot or starving?" asked Logan.

James sucked in a breath to respond, paused, then sighed. "Nah. I'm just suffering tech withdrawal. Haven't touched a working computer since the blast."

"You're an artist?" asked Harper.

"Yeah."

"People always need art. Maybe it won't be on a computer, but you can still like draw or paint, right?"

"Been a while, but yeah."

The group's discussion shifted strongly toward leaving. No one appeared to have any sentimentality for Kriley Ranch, since they'd come from various places and merely holed up here to survive the winter. Plus, this place had many bad memories due to them being so critically low on food plus watching more than half their original number die to the raider attacks.

Harper closed her eyes, worrying about that. If psychos harassed this town, they might be watching it and could follow them all the way back to Evergreen. Some people only resisted giving in to their depraved urges due to fear of punishment. Without any organized law enforcement, those individuals would do whatever they wanted to whomever they cared to harass.

"All right. Pretty obvious a consensus here." Carl bowed his head. "No point delaying if there really is food waiting for us. Might as well gather our stuff and get going as soon as possible. Tell me again how exactly this is going to work?"

"It's about ten to twelve hours walking," said Harper. "When we get there, you'll all need to be checked out by the doctors, then talk to Anne-Marie — she's the town manager — and Mayor Ned. Anne-Marie will assign you a house and figure out what, umm, 'job' you'll do. Then you hit the quartermaster's place, grab food, and go to your new home."

The people mostly nodded their approval.

Harper smiled at Alma. "There's even a bunch of other kids you can play with."

"All right. Any objections to following these people to Evergreen?" asked Carl.

No one said anything.

"Okay." Carl shrugged in a 'well, that's that' sort of way. "Everyone, grab your stuff and let's go."

Miguel Cortez, Mason Pruitt, and Clive Olson hurried off to the houses. Everyone else stood there. Jen Oliver and Daxton already had backpacks over their shoulders as if they'd expected the vote to go in favor of leaving.

"That's it? Only three people?" asked Carl.

"We ain't got nothin' worth carrying." Leo Ruiz laughed.

Miguel, Mason, and Clive returned in a few minutes carrying bags or backpacks. Miguel added a red sweatshirt over his tank top and handed his wife a pair of sneakers. Among the residents of Kriley Pond, only Vijay had a rifle. Carl, and Kelli both carried handguns. Jen Oliver wore a pair of hatchets on her belt and the goth kid, Luke, sported a ninja sword on his belt.

"Miguel, Mason, Abe, and Leo," said Carl, "You guys feel like lugging water?"

"Sure thing boss," said Miguel.

He and the other men went over to the two giant boil pots and filled gallon milk bottles, each of them carrying two. Harper and Lennie worked out an escort formation, putting her and Deacon up front — since she had the directions. Lennie and Logan would follow behind the group in case of attack from the rear. Ms. Tiller, she asked to cover the middle along with Vijay.

Harper looked around at everyone watching her expectantly. Before the war, having a group even as small as fifteen people all looking at her as the boss would've sent her scurrying out of the room. She still had a little anxiety goblin pulling its hair out deep inside her stomach, but it didn't scare her that much anymore. Not after having been shot at.

"Okay, looks like we're set. Let's get going." She exhaled, eager to get home, and walked for the gate.

"Man, screw this place," muttered Leo.

30

FIRE AND BRIMSTONE

The group headed southeast along Golden Gate Canyon Road, past Kriley Pond.

Going downhill made the trip a little easier, though with more people, some in their fifties, they didn't go quite as fast. Since she didn't have shoes, Alma ended up being carried in rotation between her mother, James Wong, and Kelli Randolph. Ms. Tiller asked what happened to the girl's shoes. Apparently, the family hadn't been awake during the strike. A concussion wave from a blast near their apartment building literally knocked them out of bed. They'd run out the door in their pajamas. Everything they had now, they'd found or scavenged later.

Harper thought back to when she'd fled her old house. Madison would've ended up being stuck barefoot, too, if not for her flip-flops being in the front yard. If not for Harper's toes getting cold in the basement, she wouldn't have had shoes at all—at least until they found their way to Evergreen. Thanks to numerous Walmart runs, the quartermaster had a fairly decent stock. No one bothered collecting impractical shoes like high heels. The thought that all these people would get out of the rags they'd been stuck in for months, have food, and be safe, made her smile.

The people assembled in a fairly orderly line. Harper kept her eyes on the thick bushes and trees that lined the road. Roughly a half-hour after they left Kriley Ranch, they approached a rightward curve.

Something moved in the weeds.

Harper reflexively aimed toward that spot.

Nine people—seven men and two women—rushed out of the foliage at them. All but one wore 'skirts' made of torn, brown fabric wrapped around their bodies and smears of some dark substance on their bare chests and faces. The one man who wasn't half naked wore a ripped black trenchcoat over a dingy grey shirt and pants that appeared handmade from a grey plastic tarp. Bushy brown hair and beard hung down to his waist, as wild as the glint in his eyes. He'd painted the upper half of his face black with the same substance smeared all over the others.

Since none of them had guns, Harper held her fire, though she aimed at the bearded guy. The mostly naked people all brandished knives, machetes, or carpenter hammers.

The survivors from Kriley Pond backed away from the 'wild' ones, edging to the right side of the road up against a fairly steep rocky hill. Harper and the other militia, plus Ms. Tiller and Vijay, pointed their weapons at the strange group.

"The hell are you supposed to be?" asked Deacon.

"Other than crazy?" whispered Logan. "Look at their eyes."

"Sinners!" shouted the trenchcoat guy. "You have rejected His will."

"Go away," yelled Harper. "You're clearly insane. We don't want to hurt you."

He pointed at her. "God has judged humanity and found it failing. He has rained down upon us great holy fire as a purge of the unworthy. *He* commands death. All who live are sinners as they defy his will!"

"Then you should stop sinning first," said Logan.

Lennie leaned closer to him. "I think that's their plan. You ever hear of suicide by cop?"

"The guy's nuts. Just back away slowly." Harper started to creep down the road, waving for the people she escorted to keep going. "If they twitch—"

"Heed his command!" shouted the bearded guy. He yanked his left hand out of his trenchcoat pocket, a small, dark object in his hand.

Harper blasted him in the face, but not before he lobbed a hand grenade in the general direction of the group. Her rapid shot turned his throw into a limp-armed toss. The grenade hit the street with a metallic *clack*, rolling toward the Cortez family, Mason, and the Olsons.

Screaming in rage, the other eight people charged at them.

"Shit!" shouted Mason. He ran forward and kicked the grenade back toward the lunatics—but it exploded a half second after his foot touched it.

Shrieks of pain came from everywhere. Mason bore the brunt of the blast, both of his legs shredded below the thighs. He hit the ground, riddled with shrapnel, dead in an instant. Everyone carrying a gun opened fire on the charging nut-jobs. Harper pivoted toward a woman rushing her, leaning out of the way of a giant Rambo knife while shooting the crazy bitch point-blank in the chest. The woman crumpled to the street, the momentum of her run causing her to tumble past Harper, who pivoted left looking for another target. Deacon had already killed the leftmost man, who'd gone after him wielding a huge kitchen knife.

She spun the other way.

Three attackers lay dead on the road, having been mowed down before they got close enough to attack anyone. The other woman among the crazies somehow made it past the firing line into the group of survivors. She'd pounced on Jen Oliver, the two women grappling for control of a knife that came perilously close to Jen's throat. Daxton hung from the insane woman's back, trying to drag her away from his mother.

Harper aimed, but couldn't get a clear shot at the woman, so she rushed toward them.

Miguel and Natalia Cortez lay on the road, bleeding from all over. Alma sat on the pavement closer to James Wong, who rolled side to side clutching his left leg and howling in pain. The little girl stared into space like she had no idea where she was.

Luke yowled in agony.

"Gah!" Harper spun to aim in that direction.

The loon who stabbed Luke already paid for it by taking a ninja sword across the throat. Despite a knife sticking out of his left shoulder, Luke lunged again and rammed the straight sword into the man's chest.

Alma screamed, "No!"

Harper whirled back the other way.

A machete-wielding crazy man stood over the little girl. He seemed torn between 'following God's command' to kill all human life and feeling sorry for a child. Before he made up his mind, Harper —as well as Lennie, Deacon, Logan, and Ms. Tiller—all shot him.

"Get your tits out of my face!" shouted Jen.

Harper swiveled to aim in that direction. The bare-chested crazy woman staggered backward, reeling from a hard right hook to the nose, Daxton still hanging on her like a human cape. She grabbed the boy's arms and swung him around in front of her, raising a huge knife. Before the woman could stab him, Jen hammered a hatchet into the side of the nut-job's head.

The zealot collapsed limp in an instant, falling to the road and convulsing. Jen grabbed Daxton and dragged him back, turning him so he couldn't see the twitching body. Carl, lying on the road not far from there, finished the convulsing woman off with a shot from a handgun.

Silence fell over the group except for the moans of the injured.

"Lennie!" yelled Harper. "Still got that first aid kit?"

"I have one too," said Jen. "Used to be an RN."

"Used to be?" asked Logan.

Jen laughed. "Yeah. Patient stuck his hand in my pants, so I broke his nose with a bedpan."

"You lost your license for that?" asked Deacon.

"Bedpan was full at the time," muttered Jen.

Harper cringed.

"Didn't lose my license. Just got fired." Jen opened her satchel and pulled out a white box. "Unfortunately, some idiot decided to hit *the button* before I could find another job."

"Mom really beat the shit out of that guy," said Daxton.

"Technically, I beat him *with* crap. And watch your mouth." Jen rushed over to Mrs. Cortez.

The boy gave her a stare that said 'we just killed people and you're worried about bad words?'

Harper stood guard, all she could really do, while Lennie and Jen went around dealing with the injured. Alma's parents had both been hit by shrapnel from the grenade. Mr. Cortez hadn't been hurt as badly as his wife. The woman had evidently jumped on top of Alma, who she'd been carrying at the time, to shield her. James Wong took a fragment to the shin. Mason, unfortunately, died instantly, having been like two feet away from the grenade when it detonated. However, he absorbed most of the shrapnel, stopping it from spreading over more people.

Luke suffered the only wound not caused by the grenade, as only two of the crazies made it close enough to attack anyone using their small weapons. Apparently, that guy tried going for Margaret and Clive, but Luke intercepted him.

"Gotta work on defense," said Lennie while removing the knife and doing a bad Kung Fu movie accent.

"Gah." Luke winced as Lennie tended to the wound in his shoulder. "I have no idea what I'm doing. Just found this sword. Looked cool, so I kept it."

"Mommy!" shouted Alma, running over to her mother, who lay on the road.

"I'm here," said Natalia in a weary voice.

Harper approached, watching Jen apply bandages. "How bad is she hurt?"

"It doesn't look like she got hit in any vital areas, but she has a lot of holes. Biggest danger is blood loss—and possible infection. You guys have any antibiotics in Evergreen?" Jen finished one bandage and moved on to extracting a piece of shrapnel from the next hole.

"I think so, yeah." Harper cringed at the dead bodies. "What the heck was wrong with those idiots?"

"No idea. You'll drive yourself nuts trying to understand what makes some people do the things they do."

Abe Cohen and Leo Ruiz had a few minor hits from shrapnel as well, though nothing bad enough to require gauze. A rock tossed by the grenade blast nailed Carl, ripping a tear in his forehead and knocking him somewhat senseless and off balance. Fortunately, his skull hadn't cracked.

Crazy people. Harper sighed. *Wonder if these are the 'raiders' who have been attacking them? Who else would want to just kill people without stealing their stuff?* She decided not to suggest that out loud in case Carl tried to use it as a reason on top of people being hurt to claim Kriley Pond would be totally safe now. Even if no one attacked them, they would still most likely starve.

She stared at the clear blue sky overhead. *I'd kill for a car right about now.*

31

A NEW FRECKLE

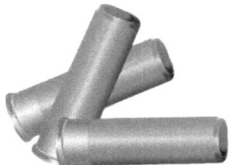

Eventually, their 'medics' got all the leaks patched enough that the journey could resume.

They left the people who attacked them where they fell. Mason, they dragged off the road and had a cursory funeral for. Margaret seemed the most upset at his death, remarking that she'd miss him teasing her about being the 'mean old woman' of their group. Natalia could barely walk. Miguel tried to pick her up, but his injuries made him too weak to lift her. Deacon ended up carrying her.

Conversation among the residents of Kriley Pond confirmed Harper's suspicion that those had been the 'raiders' who'd been harassing them. However, they hadn't seen the trenchcoat guy with the giant beard before, only the nuts with bed sheets for pants and war paint. Since none of this group had a firearm, Harper guessed they'd run out of ammunition at some point.

"Bet that guy didn't believe *he* deserved to die," said Deacon. "Dudes like that love the control, makin' other people kill and die."

"I dunno." Harper sighed at the Mossberg. "Unless he was blind, he had to see all of us pointing guns at them. Did he really think he'd chuck a freakin' grenade at us and *not* end up dead? Like, we'd just kill off his minions and let him walk away?"

"Final showdown," said Carl.

Everyone fell quiet.

"They've been after us for weeks. Must have had a scout that saw us leave, and he figured this would be his only chance to wipe us out." Carl pressed a hand to his head bandage. "Probably wasn't expecting us to have you folks escorting us. Guess he really was as crazy as he sounded if he *still* attacked us after he saw your weapons."

"Yeah, sick bastard." Lennie spat to the side.

Harper's mind roamed through the subsequent silence, wondering who those people had been prior to the war. How could someone have gone from a delivery truck driver, office worker, professional, or whatever they'd been to a knife-wielding savage so out of their mind they'd charge at people holding rifles while they only had knives and hammers? Even the two women among them had appeared consumed by bloodlust. The only possible explanation she could come up with was that they'd all been broken mentally. Maybe the Lawless got a hold of them and abused them into insanity. Or the sheer mental shock of civilization being gone proved more than they could handle. Likely, they'd watched people they cared about die.

Guess that's the final stage of 'oh, F-it all.'

The grim thought that if Madison hadn't survived their attempt to get to Evergreen, on top of the deaths of their parents, Harper might have been the same... not caring if she lived or died. She couldn't picture herself ever gleefully murdering someone purely for the hell of it, but she also never imagined she'd be capable of killing anyone at all, even in self-defense. She'd clung to her sense of self, her sanity, because of her need to protect Madison. And now, she had a whole family to survive for—not to mention Logan.

A wry smile curled her lip. *They say love kills. One swimmer sneaks in and I could end up dead.* She squirmed, trying not to think about how much natural childbirth could hurt. *Getting shot doesn't sound like a bad alternative.*

To distract herself from the somber thoughts of what could have driven those people to madness, she wondered how she'd react if Logan got her pregnant. Hopefully, spending nine months petrified of dying in childbirth wouldn't hurt a developing infant. No one made formula anymore, so she'd pretty much *have* to breastfeed. Taking care of an infant would be a full time job. Did that mean they'd boot her off the militia and take the Mossberg? Or would they let her be like a 'reservist' until the baby grew old enough to stay with a sitter during her duty times?

Best I avoid getting knocked up. I'm looking after enough children already.

At a small line of post mailboxes beside a narrow dirt road, she headed to the right, not remembering the name of the road. It didn't even have paving, being dirt. However, they'd come in that way. It connected to 119 in about five miles, a bit over an hour of walking… perhaps longer since a bunch of people with grenade shrapnel in their legs slowed them down.

That road ran along the bottom of a narrow valley, the hills on both sides treacherously steep. More trees carpeted the left than the right for whatever reason. Every so often, a footpath made its way up the hill to who-knows-where. Little private cabins, hermit houses, or maybe secret government research stations.

Ugh. I'm losing my grip. She chuckled at the idea of finding little grey aliens sneaking around out here.

Following a mostly uninterrupted hour and a half (or so), Harper set foot on a tiny spur of paving at the end of the dirt road where it met State Route 119. A street sign called the path they'd been on Smith Hill Road, though she thought someone had a lot of nerve referring to a strip of dirt not wide enough for two cars to pass each other in opposite directions easily as a 'road.'

She veered left on 119, walking past a tall, rocky cliff on the left and lush pine-covered hills on the right. Colorado had nothing if not beautiful scenery. Even though she'd never been all that much of an outdoorsy type person, she felt happy the nukes hadn't ruined it too much out here. Only the haze in the sky offered any clue that something drastic had happened to the planet.

Another hour or so later along 119, they passed several buildings on the right that included a huge concrete pit crisscrossed by walkways and two round structures with silvery domed roofs that looked like someone buried grain silos so deep only one story stuck up above the ground. A nasty, outhouse-like smell saturated the area, causing most of the group to cough, clear their throats, or pull shirts up to cover their faces. Past two more large squarish buildings that resembled offices, she spotted a white sign by the entry road identifying it as the Black Hawk County city sanitation bureau wastewater treatment facility.

Eww. Harper walked a little faster. *That crap has been sitting for a long time. I don't even want to know what kind of germs are breeding in there.*

Not far down the road from the plant, they passed a Shell station with a Z Stop convenience store. They'd bypassed it on the way up due to their haste of reaching Kriley Pond before nightfall. Given the remoteness of the area, she had some hope that there might be something useful in there.

No sooner did she start into the gas station, than two men inside the convenience store pointed rifles at her out the smashed windows. Both wore mostly camo gear and hadn't seen the business end of a razor or hair trimmer in over a year.

"What'chu want?" yelled one.

Harper stopped. "Umm… looking for supplies, but I didn't realize anyone was here already. No trouble. We'll just keep going."

"You do that," shouted the other guy.

"Calm down. We're going." Harper walked sideways back to the road, keeping her eye on the men.

They lowered their rifles once she reached 119, continuing to watch them as they proceeded down the highway.

"Geez. Touchy," said Logan.

"Defending what they got. They didn't shoot us, so figure they ain't too bad." Deacon shrugged.

Soon after they crossed the large three-way intersection where 119 met Route 6, a pack of wild dogs started tailing them, a group of several pet breeds left to run loose. Alma appeared happy to see the dogs, but Harper did *not* like the vibe the animals gave off. These didn't exactly appear to be man's best friend anymore. They looked... hungry. Though she loathed the thought of shooting dogs, better that than they hurt any people. Only the golden retriever had the slightest trace of friendliness about him. A chihuahua growled as if ready to kill them all by itself.

Fortunately, the pack only tailed the group for about ten minutes before losing interest. Whether they decided against eating humans, sensed the threat of multiple firearms, or the goldie talked the others out of it, she couldn't tell, nor did she care. Not having to kill dogs counted as a big win.

They spent a few hours walking along Route 6, taking the occasional break to rest, drink water, and unload overfull bladders. Alma complained of a stomach ache, which Jen blamed on her eating the MRE. Her system wasn't used to processing a normal quantity of food. She didn't appear to be in too much pain, so they merely worked on distracting her from it.

In the middle of the day, the successive tunnels along Route 6 offered a welcome reprieve from the heavy sun rather than worrisome murky darkness. The day turned out to be unusually warm for the elevation. So much so that they'd already gone through half the water jugs, but no one said anything about slowing down on the drinking. She told everyone that they'd be in Evergreen probably a little before dark. At a point where the road traversed a bridge above a creek, Daxton couldn't resist the urge to spit off the side.

Late in the afternoon while walking down Route 40, they neared the intersection to Route 65 where they'd run into the Lawless yesterday. Harper turned, walking backward while facing the group.

"We had a little trouble up ahead here at the bridge. There's gonna be some bodies on the ground by those campers. Anyone who doesn't want to look at that, should not look over there."

"Don't let Alma see," said Natalia, still draped in Deacon's arms.

"I won't look, Mama. Don't wanna see dead guys."

Harper faced forward again, giving the campsite the evil eye— until she saw motion. She dropped into a ready stance, raising one hand in a signal for everyone behind her to stop, get down, and be quiet.

Two men stood by the bodies that fell near the front end of the RV closest to Route 65, the easternmost 'wall' of the camp. Both had nearly shaved heads, plain white T-shirts, and jeans. They also had blue sashes around their necks, one of which appeared to be a plastic shopping bag.

She stopped short and faced the group, speaking low enough that the thugs hopefully wouldn't hear her. "We have a problem. Two Lawless ahead."

Ms. Tiller crouched, pulling her *Star Trek* shirt up to cover most of her face like a bandit mask.

"Easy enough to fix that." Lennie sighted over his M4. "Simple shot from here."

"Wait," rasped Harper. "Doesn't feel right to just ambush them. *We* aren't murderous savages."

"You know they're going to attack us." Deacon gingerly set Natalia down, supporting her weight until she sat on the road.

Harper nodded. "Yeah. Probably. But that still makes the difference between defending myself and not being a murderer. Deac, Lennie, c'mon."

She approached the Lawless, Mossberg aimed. Logan went along despite not being asked to. Harper sighed in her mind, but didn't say anything. Her desire for him to stay safe crashed into feeling so loved he refused to let her risk her life alone.

The two thugs appeared so engrossed in the sight of the one guy's brain splattered on the dirt that they didn't notice Harper and the others approach. One had a camo-green AR-15 across his back, the other a pump shotgun. They also carried a handgun each in belt holsters as well as multiple knives.

She stopped about fifteen feet behind them. "Drop your weapons."

Both Lawless turned to look at her—and chuckled.

"What's a little girl like you doing with a big toy like that?" asked the one on the left.

"Protecting myself from creeps like you."

"Aww, don't be like that, sweetie." Staring at her chest, a 'come to papa' look in his eye, the man carrying the AR-15 took a step closer.

Harper shot him in the face and shifted her aim to the second guy before he had his handgun all the way out of his holster. "Still think I don't have it in me? I get a new freckle for every soul I take. Don't have too many, since I've been shooting Lawless."

The guy froze, neither letting the gun slide back into the holster or pulling it out more.

"You're not as fast as you think you are." Harper narrowed her eyes. "Drop the damn guns and get out —"

Bang.

A tiny hole appeared in the man's forehead, gore spraying out the back of his skull.

He teetered on his feet, eyes crossed, then fell over backward, arms splayed out to either side.

"Nice shot," said Logan.

"Thanks." Lennie clicked the safety of his M4 on. "Wastin' time jaw jackin' with the likes of that."

Harper sighed. *At least I didn't kill that guy. He might have surrendered. Yeah, right. And my parents are going to come back from the dead.* A little guilt gnawed at her, but she didn't have too much trouble setting it aside. Like everyone else, those Lawless had been normal people ten months ago. Maybe. True, they might've been incarcerated felons. Still, wherever they'd come from, they'd made a choice to be thugs. A choice she and everyone else in Evergreen refused to make.

The Wild West had outlaws. This isn't that strange. Just proves we've gone back in time. Harper looked back at the group of people and waved for them to follow.

"Think we'll live to see law and order again?" whispered Harper.

Logan chuckled. "That show's always a rerun."

She sighed. "No, dork. I meant actual law."

"I know." He put an arm around her. "But I love the way you smile."

Slightly blushing, she flicked the Mossberg's safety on. *If we are the law and order, the world's kinda in trouble.* "Oh, hey... shells." She searched the guy who had the pump action and found eleven 12-gauge buckshot shells in his various pockets, which she transferred to her hip bag.

Carl took the camo AR-15 for the time being while Abe grabbed the pump shotgun. The handguns went to Miguel and Jen.

Harper stared down at the two dead guys. *What's one more freckle?*

32

GROWING UP

Roughly eleven hours after leaving Kriley Pond, Harper reached Route 74.

The promise of being home in time to have dinner with her family reinvigorated her. She sped up, walking a little too fast for the injured to keep up, so forced herself to resume the pace she'd been keeping all day. It didn't take long at all for the bus barrier to come into view up ahead.

Harper slung the shotgun over her shoulder and waved both hands, then took her air horn from its holder and sounded two short pips, a non-emergency request for help. Hopefully, whoever happened to be on sentry duty at the moment would interpret that more as a 'here we come' than an alarm.

One short pip came back, an acknowledgement.

"The hell is that noise?" asked Carl.

"We don't have radios, so we use signal codes from these things." She waved the horn at him and put it away. "Now, the people pointing sniper rifles down the road know we're friendly."

Carl gave a nervous chuckle.

"Okay…" Harper spun to walk backward again. "Everyone, please follow me. We're going to the medical center first. Obviously, anyone who is hurt will get looked at first. Like I explained this morning, the doctors only need to check people over for contagious diseases and stuff like fleas or lice before they give the okay to join the town."

Some people murmured, but no one voiced any complaints.

Walter and Anne-Marie arrived at the bus alongside Cliff, Roy, and Darnell about the same time as Harper did. Cliff strode right up to her with a 'nice job' expression, but his hug nearly squeezed all the air out of her lungs. The other militia escorted the new arrivals to the med center.

He was worried… "Sorry, Dad."

"You did good. Gave me a scare, but ya did good." He chuckled.

"How's Maddie?"

Cliff tilted his hand in a so-so gesture. "Didn't eat much last night. Didn't sleep much either. Been groggy all day. She didn't freak out either, so… not too far away from normal."

"Ugh." Harper looked down. "I feel bad for doing that to her."

"She knows why you did it. Looks like those people really needed a hand, too. Gah!" Cliff eyed Lennie. "Get that man a hamburger, stat."

"He's not one of the—oh…" Harper chuckled.

Lennie flipped him off, laughing.

Logan handed the AR-15 to Walter and held up his bandaged arm. "Thanks for the loan. Need to hit the med center." He kissed Harper. "Be right back."

"Ahem." Cliff coughed, but he sounded more like he made fun of the stereotypical overprotective dad than genuinely objected.

"I can't wait until we can get a little time together." Logan stared into her eyes.

"You and me both." She kissed him again, then gave him a little shove. "Go get that boo boo checked out."

"Yes, ma'am." He saluted her, winked, and jogged off toward the medical center.

"It seems you had some difficulties," said Walter. "What happened out there?"

Anne-Marie surveyed the people trailing by to see the doctors. "Fourteen. That shouldn't be a problem."

Harper explained the events of the trip. In the midst of her describing their initial run-in with Lawless, Madison's distant shout of, "*Haaaaaaaaarp!*" caused her to trail off and stare down the road. Her little sister sprinted up Route 74, followed by a much slower Jonathan and Lorelei. Becca, Eva, Mila, and Christopher dashed along behind them.

"Brace for impact," said Cliff.

Madison crashed into a hug, neither crying, nor screaming, nor able to speak. She merely clung with all her strength. Jonathan and Lorelei both hugged her like normal people, letting go after a moment. For the remainder of the time Harper relayed the details of the trip, Madison held on for dear life. Having the kids in earshot, she downplayed the dangerous parts, referring to them in terms like 'encountered some crazy people and it involved gunfire.'

"And," said Harper. "Jen Oliver is a nurse. She's the mother of the boy who came here looking for help."

"Nice." Anne-Marie smiled. "Always wonderful to have more medical people around. Just wish we had more actual medicine, but…"

"You can fill us in on the minutiae tomorrow." Walter waved in a 'go on home' sort of way. "Looks like you need some rest after all that walking."

Harper exhaled. "Yeah. Thinking I might even take a bath even though it's only been a couple days since the last one. Feeling a bit funky."

"Hey…" Logan jogged over. "New bandage. Some cream, and a few pills. Good as new."

"That was fast." Harper whistled. "Some of those people had a lot of shrapnel wounds."

"Ruby took care of me since I didn't need much. Just a bandage." Logan shrugged. "Told you it's not a big deal. Scratch really."

Madison finally released her hold. Her eyes had gone red, but she didn't cry. "Can I be a little bit mad at you for scaring me?"

"Sure, Termite. But only if I can be a little bit guilty for scaring you."

"Deal." Madison slouched, exhaling hard. "It's good you helped people, but don't forget I need help, too. At least for a little while more."

Harper pulled her into another hug. "Sorry."

"It's okay. You don't have to say sorry. I'm being needy."

"Heh." Harper chuckled. "If after everything we went through, 'needy' is your worst issue, that's awesome."

"Can we go to the pool tomorrow?" asked Madison.

"Sure. Might as well enjoy it while we can."

The kids all gasped in horror.

"Is it gonna dry up?" Lorelei bit her lip.

"Not exactly. There's only so many chemicals in the garage there. Eventually, they won't be able to keep the water clean and it could turn into stagnant muck."

"Eww." Madison stuck her tongue out, then gave a sad sigh. "Why does everything have to die? Even pools."

Harper walked toward home, Cliff and the kids surrounding her. "I dunno. Just the way things are. We have to enjoy stuff before we lose it."

"Life, death, rebirth, all just a big, weird circle no one understands." Cliff swept a hand across in front of him.

"Enjoy stuff?" Madison looked up at her. "Is that why you and Logan had sex?"

Harper sputtered, unable to come up with words.

"Uhh." Logan coughed.

"Who said we did anything like that?" stammered Harper.

"Lies." Madison shook her head.

Harper indicated Logan with both hands like a game show hostess revealing a prize. "Usually, Termite, girl talk happens when the guy being talked about isn't *right* next to us."

"Mm-hmm." Madison leaned around her to look at Logan. "Pretty sure you guys did, but if you didn't, she definitely wants to."

"Gah!" Harper grabbed and tickled her.

Madison squealed into laughter. "Stop!"

"Gotta enjoy having a little sister before she grows up." Cackling, Harper tickled Madison until she squirmed away and ran down Hilltop Drive.

She handed the Mossberg to Cliff... then chased her. "This isn't over yet, Termite!"

33

LITTLE NIGHTMARE

Afer dinner, Harper took a bath.

Despite her nightgown being awkwardly close to transparent, she adored the lightness of wearing it after two whole days stuck out in the sun in the same clothes. The jeans, shirt, and underpants from that trip, she tossed right in the 'must be washed' pile after briefly considering starting a 'must be burned' pile. Madison, after her initial mega-hug, surprised her by not turning into an unstable ball of emotional energy. She did hover close, and they stayed up a bit late playing a board game since the electricity happened to be in a good mood and the lights worked.

The next morning, Harper dragged herself out of bed and changed out of her nightgown. Today, she opted for jean shorts. Lorelei went straight out the bedroom door in her nightie while Madison put on a plain white dress.

Jonathan knelt on one of the kitchen chairs, still in the shorts he slept in, munching on cereal. Cliff, fully dressed and outfitted for patrol, munched on toast and jam. Carrie set a bowl of cereal down for Lorelei, then looked at Harper while shifting her eyes back and forth between the toaster and the box of Cheerios.

Apparently, they had milk again. Of course, it had come from live

cows. As far as she knew, someone did their best to pasteurize it…
but drinking it still felt weird with the actual cows so close.

"Toast, please." Harper slid into a chair.

Madison sat in her spot. "Cereal, please."

A mild debate ignited between Madison and Jonathan about a
vegetarian having no problem with milk. Madison argued that the
animal didn't die or even suffer pain to generate the milk, so it didn't
bother her.

In the midst of breakfast, the back door opened. Mila walked in,
her loose black top and capris pants covered in dirt. More dirt
covered her face, hair, hands, and bare feet—to the point she left
tracks on the kitchen floor.

"What the heck?" Harper chuckled at her. "Did you dig a tunnel
down here from your house?"

Mila paused by the corner of the table between Cliff and Harper.
"You guys gotta see this. Serious stuff."

"Serious?" asked Cliff.

"Yep. Consider me a kid telling the cops they saw a crime."

Cliff shot Harper an 'uh oh' look. "Okay. Let's see what you got."

"Sec. Need shoes." Harper ran to the bedroom to grab her
sneakers and the shotgun.

"I got things here." Carrie smiled. "What the heck day is it? Do
the kids need to go to the farm?"

"No, it's Saturday," said Jonathan, munching on cereal.

"Nice. Everyone gets to relax today." Carrie sighed at the fridge.
"I really do miss orange juice."

"Lead on, kiddo." Cliff gestured at Mila.

She headed out the front door, crossed the yard to Hilltop Drive,
and went up Route 74 to the farm. A few workers there gave Mila
odd looks. Some told her she didn't need to be there on a Saturday.
She smiled at them and kept going out past the western edge of the
farm into the hills.

"Looks like she's heading for the spot where I think a fight
happened," said Cliff.

"Maybe." Mila kept walking.

"How did you get so dirty?"

"Hiding in the dirt." She pointed. "It's right over here."

"Yeah, this is the same spot." Cliff raised an eyebrow. "Did you dig that?"

Harper, not being as tall as him, had to take a few steps closer before she noticed a rectangular hole in the ground. "That's too small for a body."

"No. I didn't dig this." Mila stopped at the edge. "I saw some guy sneaking around last night, so I followed him. He came here and met another man. The two of them dug a green box out of the ground."

Cliff crouched by the hole. "It's about the size of a footlocker."

"Where did they go after that?" asked Harper.

"They carried the box to a house. I followed them there, too."

"Seriously?" Cliff stood. "They didn't see you?"

Mila grinned. "I'm sneaky."

"Did they say anything?" Cliff wandered in a circle, studying the ground.

"Yeah. They didn't want anyone finding the box or what's in it. One man said it's worth a fortune, but the other man said money doesn't matter. Then they argued the rest of the way to the house about fortune not meaning literal money." Mila rolled her eyes. "Lorelei could have followed them and they wouldn't have noticed her."

"Heh." Cliff chuckled. "She's not exactly big and clumsy."

"No, but the girl does not stop talking." Mila shook her head.

"Let's check this out. Which house did they go to?" asked Cliff.

Mila headed south. "I'll show you."

They followed her, cutting across the southwest corner of the farm. She went over a soccer field behind the Rocky Mountain Academy and south along the outer edge of the residential area where many of the single farm workers lived. After passing six houses, she headed left into the development and approached the seventh house more or less in that row. The place looked large and expensive, the sort of home that would have been awesome for a family with four or five kids.

"In there." Mila pointed.

Cliff approached the door. "This is the house where Weldon used to live. The other people he came in with are still here." He knocked.

A moment later, a youngish woman around nineteen or so answered the door. Her eyes seemed a little bit too large for her face, her nose like that of a baby doll. Slender, long black hair, and skin as pale as Harper made her look like a grown up Wednesday Addams given a Japanese anime makeover. A men's large T-shirt hung off her bony frame, exposing one shoulder. If she had any pants on, they'd be shorts too tiny to see past the hem of the giant shirt.

"Yeah?" asked the woman.

"Hayley, right?" Cliff smiled.

"Uh huh. Oh, you're that militia guy. Where's the bald dude?"

"Roy's probably still eating."

"Guess you wanna look around about Weldon again, huh?"

"Yep."

Hayley shrugged and walked inside, leaving the door open. "Knock yourself out."

Cliff proceeded into the house. Harper followed him into a giant living room painted a bluish-grey. The television looked as big as her mattress. Harper gawked at it. She'd never seen a set that big before. Pity it didn't work. Or, if it had somehow survived the EMP, no stations remained on air to use it with.

Mila entered behind them, calm as could be.

Two men in their middle twenties sat on the couch, sipping Earl's homemade beer from mason jars. Both wore clean white tank tops and boxer briefs, but their hands appeared dirty, the same shade of brown as the dust covering Mila. Another guy draped himself sideways over the recliner, wearing only sweat shorts. Harper recognized him as the 'yellow hat guy' from the Fourth of July party. Steve.

"Okay, let me just make sure I remember. Howie, right?" asked Cliff.

The more distant man with shaggy brown hair nodded. "Yeah."

"Curtis." Cliff gestured at the other man on the sofa, who also nodded. "And Steve on the... why would you sit on a recliner sideways? What are you, a cat?"

Steve laughed. "It's good for the back."

"So who here knows anything about a box that used to be buried out near the farm?" Cliff looked back and forth among the guys. "Was found right about the same spot we think your friend Weldon was killed."

"Whoa." Steve shifted to sit normally. "You figure out who did it?"

Both men on the couch tensed.

Howie picked at the sofa cushion. "No idea, man."

"Mmm." Cliff nodded, then stared Curtis down. "What about you? Any idea what might be in a box someone had to bury?"

"That's kinda messed up." Haley flopped in the other recliner.

"Yeah, it is. No idea." Curtis scratched at his head. "Bury a box? Heh. That's kinda funny."

Howie managed a weak smile. "Who knows? Might have been something Weldon found after we got here."

"So you guys still have no idea who might want to hurt your buddy?" Cliff set his hands on his hips.

"No, man. Like we said." Howie shrugged. "No idea."

"We don't know anyone here. No one followed us across Colorado and waited 'til we found this place to off the dude." Curtis raked a hand over his head. "Has to be a sicko random killer or something."

Mila stepped around Harper and pointed at Howie. "He's the guy. I saw him stab Weldon. Snuck up behind him, covered his mouth, and jammed the knife into his heart."

"Heh. You're funny, kid." Howie smirked at her.

Mila stood there glaring at him.

"What's wrong with her?" asked Curtis.

"Check his left hand for teeth marks. I think the dead guy bit him." Mila gestured at Curtis. "That guy helped carry the body to the farm where you found it. They didn't even see me following them, like they didn't see me follow them when they carried the big green box to this house last night."

"What?" blurted Haley. "*You* guys killed Wellie?"

"I thought he killed himself because you kept calling him 'Wellie'," muttered Steve.

Haley gasped. "That's not funny!"

Cliff lowered his left hand toward the air horn on his belt.

"Son of a bitch!" shouted Curtis at Howie. "You said no one saw us."

Howie screamed unintelligible gibberish and leapt from the couch, throwing his half-finished beer at Cliff's face before running left toward the dining room.

"Now that's a waste of fine beer." Cliff shook his head, dripping.

Curtis vaulted the arm of the sofa, heading for the hallway to the kitchen. Harper grabbed at him, but he palmed her face and shoved her off her feet. She landed on her shoulders, butt in the air, staring between her legs at the guy running to the kitchen.

Cliff rushed after Howie, yelling, "Mila, stay put."

After scrambling back to her feet, Harper chased Curtis out the back door, over a deck, and down to the yard, shouting, "Don't run. All they're gonna do is exile you."

He glanced back at her, but kept going, curving around the house to the left toward the street. Maybe a hundred feet ahead of them on the road, Howie lunged at Cliff with a knife—and ended up eating pavement, his arm twisted up behind his back into the shape of an octopus tentacle. Howie screamed like he burned alive.

Growling, Harper poured on speed and threw herself into a leap, shoving Curtis forward hard enough that he tripped. He rolled around and kicked her feet out from under her. Harper landed on her left side, barely managing to avoid coming down on her elbow and breaking it. He scrambled upright and tried to run, but she jumped into his legs, clamping her arms around his knees and dragging him to the ground.

Curtis let out a bark like a kicked goose as he landed flat on his back.

Harper crawled up on top of him, pulled her .45, and pointed it at his face. "Stop."

"Don't shoot!" He raised his hands, gasping for breath.

Not far behind them, Howie continued screaming, intermittently cursing at Cliff for 'breaking his arm.'

"What the heck did you guys kill Weldon for?" asked Harper.

Curtis stared up at her.

"Seriously. We don't put people in jail, and yeah, they might execute psycho killers, but if you guys just murdered him for a specific grudge and aren't a threat to other people, they're most likely only going to kick you out of town. Walter hates executions."

"Dammit," rasped Curtis. "I'd rather sit in jail."

"Jail is stupid. You take up food and don't add anything back to the town."

"Whatever. Look, I didn't kill anyone. All I did was help him carry a body around, okay? They don't have to kick me out for that."

"What's in the box worth killing over?"

"Just bullshit. Drugs. Booze. Some assault rifles and ammo we kept for ourselves. Nothing super important."

Harper pushed herself up to stand, still keeping the gun on him. "If it's not a big deal, why did Weldon die for it?"

"Because he was gonna steal it and take off."

"Didn't you just say you'd rather sit in jail than leave?" She tilted her head. "If you guys are so scared of being out there, where the heck did he expect to go?"

Curtis pointed. "Denver. Said he knew some people with a big army or something. Lawless."

Harper snarled. "Are you sure he said that exact word?"

"Pretty sure. Ask Hayley or Steve. They heard him say that… but they didn't know Howie's the one who killed him."

"If he really was going to run off and join the Lawless, you guys might not even get in trouble for the killing."

Curtis blinked. "Seriously?"

"It's a good chance. Lawless are total shitbags." She gestured the .45 toward the road. "C'mon. get up."

Roy Ellis had apparently heard the commotion and come running. He and Cliff hauled Howie to his feet.

Harper walked Curtis over to them at gunpoint. "Hey, new twist."

They looked at her.

"This guy says the box is full of stuff like drugs, booze, and guns. Weldon was going to steal it from them and, get this—run off to join the Lawless."

"Son of a," muttered Cliff.

"Dude!" shouted Howie at Curtis. "Shut your face."

"Will you calm down?" She stared at him. "If Weldon was going to join the Lawless, killing him might not even matter. You basically protected Evergreen."

Howie gawked at her. "What? You're saying… this goddamned caveman broke my freakin' arm and it doesn't matter? Why the hell were you up our ass for weeks over it then?"

"Because no one said Weldon intended to join the Lawless." She put her .45 away and folded her arms. "Is that true?"

"Yeah," said Howie.

"Of course, he's going to say that now that he knows he might not get in trouble." Roy frowned.

"Go ask Steve or Haley." Howie nodded toward the house. "They won't know it means you won't be pissed at him being dead."

Roy looked at Harper. "How do you figure they *protected* Evergreen killing that guy?"

"Because. Weldon worked on the farm for a couple months. He knew the layout of the town. He knew enough about us to talk the Lawless into attacking and help them hit us where it hurts." She locked stares with Howie. "You could have just reported his plan to us and *we'd* probably have shot him. Why didn't you do that?"

Howie offered a sheepish shrug. "Footlocker full of contraband."

"Not sure anyone even cares about that stuff anymore." Cliff shrugged. "Probably be more upset over the rifles and ammo than the drugs, really."

"Shit, my arm." Howie whined.

"It ain't broken. Stop crying." Cliff clapped him on the shoulder, making him moan. "Let's go sort this out with Walter. Where's the box? We should at least have a look."

"Back room," said Curtis.

They returned to the house.

Hayley and Steve stared at Howie in shock.

"Quick question for you two." Cliff walked up to them. "Did either of you ever hear Weldon talking about going somewhere else or meeting up with some other group?"

They both nodded.

"Did he talk about it at all? Maybe refer to them by a particular name?" asked Harper.

"Umm, yeah I think he said Lawless or something like that." Haley scrunched up her nose. "Said they had a lot of power and he wouldn't have to slave away on a farm there."

"Sounds right." Steve scratched his butt. "I heard some bad shit about those dudes. Tried to talk him out of going. He said he'd think about it, might not go. But... got the feeling he just blew me off."

"Well crap." Roy exhaled. "So it looks like you killed Weldon because he planned to steal your crap and run off, but you ended up doing Evergreen a favor by it."

Howie cringed, rolling his right shoulder around. "Technically, I did kill him because he was stealing from us. Caught him digging the box up in the middle of the night."

"Wait, Wellie was gonna bail on us and join those Lawless creeps?" Hayley fumed. "Ooh!"

Harper cringed. *Whoops. Guess she ended up liking the wrong guy.*

"Mila?" asked Harper.

"Hmm?" The girl looked up at her.

"Why didn't you say anything about witnessing the killing weeks ago?"

"Oh." Mila smiled. "Because I didn't actually see it. I made that up."

Howie and Curtis stared at her.

Cliff burst out laughing.

"Crap, kid." Roy shook his head. "You really, really can't say stuff like that unless it's true."

Mila pivoted to look up at Roy. "It's true that he killed that man, but not that I saw it. When Mr. Barton and Harper were talking about it, those two guys got really nervous. Howie started sweating and he kept twitching his right eye. A repetitive tic like that is usually a sign of lying or being scared. I said that to see how he'd react. Curtis gave him away. Otherwise, I would've admitted making it up."

"Damn." Roy whistled. "That kid is scary."

Mila smiled a little smile to herself.

"You have no idea." Harper sighed, then patted Mila on the shoulder. "You okay?"

"Yeah." Mila shrugged. "Only had a little nightmare."

Harper patted her on the head. "Cool. I'm here if you ever need to talk."

"You patted me on the head. I am too old for such cuteness."

Roy snickered.

"But you are cute." Harper patted her on the head again.

Mila folded her arms. "I'm scary."

"That kid can put a leaf knife in a one-inch target spot at twenty feet." Cliff gave a thumbs-up. "That counts as scary."

"See?" Mila pointed at him.

"Right…" Harper booped her on the nose. "Your mix of cute and scary is adorable."

"She's not wrong," said Cliff.

"Nope." Roy smiled.

Mila narrowed her eyes and fake fumed, but ended up laughing.

"C'mon. Let's go talk to Walter." Cliff ushered Howie and Curtis down the street.

Harper walked behind the men, beside Mila. "You're a little young to go looking for dangerous situations."

"So are you, technically." Mila swatted at her top, trying to knock dirt away. "Besides, I have knives. And they didn't see me."

"You can't *always* have a knife on you."

Mila gave her the best 'bitch please' look a ten-year-old could muster.

"Bathtub?" Harper raised both eyebrows.

"Yeah. Well, it's not *on* me, but close enough to grab." Mila tilted her head. "Does that make me weird?"

Harper exhaled. "If that makes you weird, I'm weird too. Have a gun in arm's reach even when I'm in the tub."

"Okay. Good. I'm not a freak."

"That's just the world we've been thrown into." Harper looked down.

"It's not *that* bad. An' you guys are trying to make it better." Mila poked her in the side. "You know stuff's messed up when the gloom faerie is telling you to have hope."

"Hah." Harper ruffled her hair. "Good point."

"You touched my hair again."

"Yep."

"If you call me cute again, I will cut you"—Mila narrowed her eyes—"with biting sarcasm."

Harper laughed the rest of the way to the militia HQ.

34

SCHRODINGER'S NORMAL

Per Madison's request, the next afternoon, Harper cheated off her patrol shift a little early and went with the kids to the pool. In a strictly technical sense, she still had the Mossberg and remained inside the area of her patrol responsibility. A lime green bikini didn't make for the best militia uniform, but it worked perfectly at the pool.

She cooled off at a point where the water only came up to her chest, near the edge so she could jump out and grab the shotgun if needed. Naturally, Renee and Grace made the obligatory jokes about Harper being so pale she blinded them from sun glare, and hung out with her in the water. None of them minded standing immersed near the edge since the middle of the pool contained a ton of frenetic children and a handful of adults who didn't presently need to be elsewhere.

Darci and Elijah showed up maybe an hour after they got into the water. After guiding the boy over to the former hot tub connected to the main pool, now serving as a kiddie swim area, she stopped by the lounge chairs to remove her T-shirt and miniskirt, approaching the water in only bikini bottoms.

Renee blushed, despite there being two other women swimming

topless. "Darce, you're seriously taking the hedonism a bit far. Society hasn't broken down *that* much yet. Put on a top."

"Girls only need tops when they're old enough to have something to put in them," said Mila as she swam by.

Harper clamped a hand over her mouth to stop herself from laughing.

"Ooh, need some aloe for that burn." Grace made a hissing noise.

Darci waved a middle finger at Mila, not that the girl saw it. She lowered herself to sit on the edge of the pool and slid in. "You guys just don't get it. Boys can go topless and no one cares. It's just the patriarchy controlling us."

Renee and Harper exchanged 'here we go again' looks.

Ordinary conversation bounced back and forth among them for a while, initially about Darci 'adopting' Elijah. Other than Anne-Marie sending Summer Vasquez to check on them every couple days to make sure she wasn't screwing up the big-sister-slash-mom thing too badly, it seemed to be going well. Harper thought it worked out for both of them, since looking after the boy had the effect of Darci toning down how much weed she smoked. Impressively, Darci even kept an eye on the boy in case he climbed over the wall into the deeper pool.

Renee rambled about making clothes while Grace caught them off guard by saying their new reality didn't bother her as much as she expected it to since learning to sorta be a doctor ended up as way more rewarding than attending a super expensive school picked by her parents to study a major picked by her parents and get a job picked by her parents.

Harper chatted, observed the kids playing a bizarre version of water polo that had no rules or net, and kept an eye on their surroundings. Except for the background worry that someone might show up and start trouble, the scene around her could have been any other summer in her life at the community pool.

"Wow, this feels so bizarre," said Harper.

"What, trying not to look at Darce's boobs?" asked Renee.

Darci thrust one fist into the air. "Overthrow the patriarchy!"

"Heh. No, I mean, how abnormal and normal it feels right now to be in a pool." Harper sighed. "I could close my eyes and pretend the war didn't even happen."

Grace put an arm around her. "You say that every time we come here."

"I know. It just feels that way every time we're here. Gotta find normal when I can."

"Heard you got the killer. So we're all safe now." Renee patted her on the shoulder. "Nice work."

"Wasn't me really. Mila found him... and get this—Weldon, the victim, was going to leave Evergreen and join the Lawless."

Renee shivered. "Holy crap..."

"Wow." Darci blinked. "So, like what did they do there? Murderer, but the vic was a piece of crap."

Grace opened her mouth to say something, but a volleyball bounced off her face emitting a hollow, rubbery *thud* and knocking her underwater.

"Sorry!" shouted Noah Bowden. The boy turned fourteen a couple months ago. "Didn't mean to send it over there."

"Not a problem." Darci grabbed the floating ball and chucked it to him.

Grace resurfaced. "Ouch."

"Yeah, you should have seen the look on Walter's face when we told him. So, they don't really like putting people in jail because then they just take up food and don't do anything for the community. Howie killed a guy who could have helped the Lawless plan a raid on Evergreen. They ended up giving him an 'official warning,' whatever that means. Said he should have reported the intent to join the Lawless to the militia."

"So..." Darci blinked. "Dude kills a dude and gets off with a warning?"

Harper shrugged. "Yeah. Basically."

"The dead guy was stealing from him, too. Walter sorta hand-waved it off as 'self-defense.'" Harper shook her head. "That's kinda bogus because Howie ambushed Weldon from behind. No defense involved."

"Except for the roundabout defense of the whole town." Grace held up one finger.

"Guess this Walter guy doesn't think the killer's a threat to anyone else," asked Darci.

Harper held her hands up in a 'what can ya do' gesture. "Basically. They confiscated some kind of drug, heroin I think, let him keep the weed and other minor stuff, and took the military style rifles. The killing happened over that stuff, so it's unlikely Howie would randomly kill anyone else."

"Cool. I hated thinking there might be a psycho murderer around." Renee overacted a sigh of relief.

"So…" Renee smiled. "Summer at the pool again. So weird not thinking about school or college at all."

"Yeah," said Harper. "No doubt."

Grace pointed. "It's even weirder that Lorelei still has her swimsuit on."

Harper laughed. "Give her an hour."

"She's a true nature child." Darci smiled. "Wish I could get away with that."

"You don't have the nerve." Renee gasped.

"Don't I?"

Harper grabbed Darci's arms before she could take her bottoms off. "We believe you. And it's not so much that she's a 'nature child.' She's still underweight. Those bottoms are going to fall off her and she just doesn't care. Keeps on going like it's no big deal to run around bare ass naked."

"Depending on where you are, it isn't." Grace shrugged. "Certain tribes in the Amazon region do that all the time… assuming the war didn't kill them off."

"That's the only way we're going to survive this new world." Darci smiled like an old wise woman.

"What, going naked?" Harper blinked.

Darci laughed. "No, dumbass. I mean not caring. What happens, happens. Jump in the pool and your pants come off, just keep on keepin' on. World blows up to nuclear fire, just keep on going. Stress is pointless. It does nothing but damage you on a cellular level."

"I swear, if she starts singing *Let it Go*," mumbled Renee.

Harper sighed. "Sure. 'Don't stress.' Easier said than done."

"Got plenty of green stuff to help you let the bad things roll off your back." Darci grabbed her in a playful headlock. "You game?"

"Nah," said Harper.

Renee lightly splashed her. "You always were a good girl. No drugs, never stayed out too late…"

"Pot. Kettle." Harper raspberried her.

"How messed up is that?" asked Darci. "You won't touch pot, but you've shot people."

"Yeah. So?" Harper twisted to watch Madison, Lorelei, and Jonathan playing pool Frisbee. "The world's a strange place. It was pretty weird even before it caught fire. Now, it's even stranger."

"Right?" Renee whistled.

"But…" Harper smiled. "I think we're gonna be okay."

fin

ACKNOWLEDGMENTS

Thank you for reading *Nuclear Summer!*

Harper's story will continue in book 5.

Additional thanks to Lee Sheridan for editing and Alexandria Thompson for the cover and interior artwork.

ABOUT THE AUTHOR

Originally from South Amboy NJ, Matthew has been creating science fiction and fantasy worlds for most of his reasoning life. Since 1996, he has developed the "Divergent Fates" world, in which *Division Zero, Virtual Immortality, The Awakened Series, The Harmony Paradox, and the Daughter of Mars series* take place. Along with being an editor at Curiosity Quills press, he has worked in IT and technical support.

Matthew is an avid gamer, a recovered WoW addict, Gamemaster for two custom RPG systems, and a fan of anime, British humour, and intellectual science fiction that questions the nature of reality, life, and what happens after it.

He is also fond of cats.

Visit me online at:
  Facebook: https://www.facebook.com/MatthewSCoxAuthor
  Amazon: https://www.amazon.com/author/mscox
  Pinterest: https://www.pinterest.com/matthewcox10420/
  Goodreads: https://www.goodreads.com/author/show/7712730.Matthew_S_Cox
  Email: mcox2112@gmail.com

OTHER BOOKS BY MATTHEW S. COX

- Prophet's Journey

Divergent Fates Anthology

(Fiction Novels - Adult)

The Roadhouse Chronicles Series

- One More Run
- The Redeemed
- Dead Man's Number

Faded Skies series

- Heir Ascendant
- Ascendant Unrest
- Ascendant Revolution

Temporal Armistice Series

- Nascent Shadow
- The Shadow Collector
- The Gate to Oblivion
- The Queen of Discord

Vampire Innocent series

- A Nighttime of Forever
- A Beginner's Guide to Fangs
- The Artist of Ruin
- The Last Family Road Trip
- The Phantom Oracle
- How Not to Summon Demons
- Ordinary Problems of a College Vampire
- A Vampire's Guide to Surviving Holidays

- An Introduction to Paranormal Diplomacy
- A Vampire's Guide to Adulting
- Six Easy Steps to Prevent a Vampire War

Standalones

- Wayfarer: AV494
- Axillon99
- Chiaroscuro: The Mouse and the Candle
- The Spirits of Six Minstrel Run
- Sophie's Light
- The Far Side of Promise anthology
- Operation: Chimera (with Tony Healey)
- The Dysfunctional Conspiracy (with Christopher Veltmann)
- Of Myth and Shadow
- The Girl Who Found the Sun

Winter Solstice series (with J.R. Rain)

- Convergence
- Containment
- Catalyst
- Catacombs

Alexis Silver series (with J.R. Rain)

- Silver Light
- Deep Silver
- Silver Quarrel
- Silver Crucible

Samantha Moon Origins series (with J.R. Rain)

- New Moon Rising
- Moon Mourning

- Haunted Moon

Vampire For Hire series (with J.R. Rain)

- Moon Master
- Dead Moon
- Lost Moon
- Vampire Destiny
- Infinite Moon
- Vampire Empress

Maddy Wimsey series (with J.R. Rain)

- The Devil's Eye
- The Drifting Gloom
- Dark Mercy

Samantha Moon Case Files series (with J.R. Rain)

- Blood Moon

Immortal Operative (with J.R. Rain)

- Broken Ice

Four Elements series (with J.R. Rain)

- The Elementalist
- The Black Rose
- The Wakefield Curse

⁓ ⁓

Young Adult Novels

The Eldritch Heart Series

- The Eldritch Heart
- The Cursed Crown
- The Sapphire Soul

Evergreen Series

- Evergreen
- The World That Remains
- The Lucky Ones
- Nuclear Summer
- The Nuclear Frontier

Standalones

- Caller 107
- The Summer the World Ended
- Nine Candles of Deepest Black
- The Forest Beyond the Earth
- Out of Sight

Middle Grade Novels

The Adventures of Ubergirl series

- My Dad is a Mad Scientist
- Aliens Ate My Homework
- The End of all Halloweens

Tales of Widowswood series

- Emma and the Banderwigh
- Emma and the Silk Thieves
- Emma and the Silverbell Faeries
- Emma and the Elixir of Madness
- Emma and the Weeping Spirit

Standalones

- Citadel: The Concordant Sequence
- The Cursed Codex
- The Menagerie of Jenkins Bailey

www.ingramcontent.com/pod-product-compliance
Lightning Source LLC
Chambersburg PA
CBHW032157190626
46814CB00005BA/2006